FOLLO\

MW00852749

"Which is the more beautifu ... adventure: stalking a cheetah across the plains of the Serengeti at night or following one's own defiant heart and leaping into a forbidden love that will alter everything one knows about the world? Penny Haw might say both, and her readers will say it's even better when the two are interwoven, as is the case with *Follow Me to Africa*. In her latest work of high-stakes biographical historical fiction, Haw transports readers from the East African bush to the lecture halls of academic London and back again. Haw has gifted readers with a textured and atmospheric ode to a bold woman who dared to blaze a new path for herself and the countless others who may now look to her story."

—Allison Pataki, *New York Times* bestselling
author of *Finding Margaret Fuller*

"An engaging dual-timeline story of Dr. Mary Leakey as she immerses herself in discovery of the origins of man in the vast African panorama, and her later life mentorship of a teenage girl, encouraging her to embrace her own future career in the wild. Haw's love and respect of her subject imbue every page. A thoroughly captivating read."

—Shelley Noble, *New York Times* bestselling author
of *The Tiffany Girls* and *The Colony Club*

"*Follow Me to Africa* is a fascinating adventure and a page-turning look into the life of Mary Leakey, renowned paleoanthropologist. Combining intrepid women, wild animals, and the raw beauty of the Olduvai Gorge, Penny Haw has crafted a unique and spellbinding tale. Makes me want to book a trip to the Serengeti!"

—Sara Ackerman, *USA Today* bestselling author
of *The Uncharted Flight of Olivia West*

"Fans of *Circling the Sun* by Paula McLain will revel in returning to Africa, this time following the story of renowned archaeologist Mary Leakey, whose ambition, curiosity, and desire to disregard norms cement her as one of the great trailblazers of her time. Atmospheric and engrossing, this novel will delight historical fiction fans and all who love a good tale about a woman determined to carry her own dirt."

—Jenni L. Walsh, *USA Today* bestselling author
of *Unsinkable* and *Ace, Marvel, Spy*

"A warm tale of identity and growth, as a youthful heroine breaking free of her own troubled past proves the perfect foil to the amazing life of archaeologist Mary Leakey. A story as layered as the real ancient humanity inspiring its core."

—Elizabeth Wein, #1 *New York Times* bestselling author of *Code Name Verity*

"Captivating and deftly woven. I loved this exploration of complex relationships, set against the backdrop of Africa's wild beauty in the cradle of humankind. I'm sure Mary Leakey would approve of Penny Haw's meticulous research, which brings the world-famous archaeologist's work to life in this skillfully crafted dual-timeline novel."

—Fiona Valpy, bestselling author of *The Dressmaker's Gift*

Praise for
THE WOMAN AT THE WHEEL

"From the author of *The Invincible Miss Cust* comes another powerful novel about a woman bringing change, this time to the world of the internal combustion engine. *The Woman at the Wheel* by Penny Haw is the story of Bertha Benz, wife of the automobile pioneer Carl Benz. In 1872, Bertha and Carl marry, and she alone believes in his dream of creating a horseless carriage. Supporting him with her love, encouragement, visionary ideas, and even her dowry, Bertha's behind-the-scenes contributions assist Carl in producing the first two-stroke engine, which led to the creation of the first automobile. Once again, Penny Haw has created a commanding tale of a woman who follows her heart and succeeds in accomplishing her dreams. Readers will be thrilled to get to know this inspirational woman."

—Julia Bryan Thomas, author of *For Those Who Are Lost* and *The Radcliffe Ladies' Reading Club*

"Penny Haw makes us care for Bertha from the first page: she's a smart, gutsy, determined heroine, whose love for her inventor husband pervades this glorious novel. The nuances of their marriage are explored in a way that feels fresh and realistic. I enjoyed learning about the technical challenges of building the first-ever motorwagen and yearned for it to be a success. This is fine historical writing, transporting us back to another era while telling a compelling adventure story about characters we feel we know. A triumph!"

—Gill Paul, *USA Today* bestselling author of *The Secret Wife* and *The Manhattan Girls*

Praise for

THE INVINCIBLE MISS CUST

"A girl with unusual spunk and an innate love for animals becomes a woman determined to forge her own destiny in Penny Haw's beautifully written novel. In a world where women are relegated to needlepoint and parlor chairs, Aleen sets her sights on barns and veterinary surgery. Her journey to become the impossible is inspiring, heartwarming, and ultimately triumphant."

—Lisa Wingate, #1 *New York Times* bestselling author of *The Book of Lost Friends*

"I loved *The Invincible Miss Cust*. The book is an important reminder of how hard women have had to fight for the right to work and study. From Ireland to France, I enjoyed every moment of Aleen Cust's unpredictable journey. What a remarkable woman—and what an enthralling story!"

—Janet Skeslien Charles, *New York Times* bestselling author of *The Paris Library*

"*The Invincible Miss Cust* is an absolute delight, an exceptional, immersive work of historical fiction set amid the beautifully detailed landscapes of Ireland and England. Readers are sure to adore and admire Aleen Cust for her compassion for animals as well as her courage as they follow the unpredictable twists and turns of her enthralling story."

—Jennifer Chiaverini, *New York Times* bestselling author of *Switchboard Soldiers*

"I loved this gripping and inspirational book! Aleen Cust's story is one of a heroine for all ages, defying family censure and social barriers to fulfill her ambition. Her courage and independence of spirit shine through on every beautifully written page as she faces life's triumphs and tragedies. I cheered her on every step of the way."

—Fiona Valpy, bestselling author of *The Dressmaker's Gift*

"A skillfully told story of an extraordinary woman's grit, determination, and devotion to her dream of becoming Great Britain's first female veterinary surgeon. Haw brings Aleen Cust to vivid life, from her aristocratic but stifled childhood to her difficult days at school, to her eventual acceptance as a highly skilled vet—all the while fighting a patriarchal system designed to thwart her every step. Detailed and evocative, *The Invincible Miss Cust* is an engrossing read."

—Shana Abé, *New York Times* bestselling author of *The Second Mrs. Astor*

"A vivid, compelling story of a daring and determined woman. Emotionally rich and bringing light to an incredible life and legacy, you won't want to miss this inspiring novel of England's first female veterinary surgeon."

—Audrey Blake, *USA Today* bestselling author of *The Girl in His Shadow*

"An amazing story! *The Invincible Miss Cust* introduces readers to Aleen Cust, Britain and Ireland's first female veterinary surgeon, and we are better for the acquaintance. Haw's descriptive prose and deft characterizations lead us through Cust's remarkable life, setbacks, and triumphs, and leaves us in awe of her perseverance, determination, and loyalty."

—Katherine Reay, bestselling author of *The London House* and *The Printed Letter Bookshop*

"A gripping story of one woman's unrelenting quest to treat and care for our four-legged friends. Readers will be rooting for Aleen as she comes up against and triumphs over a mountain of obstacles. A must-read for all animal lovers."

—Renée Rosen, *USA Today* bestselling author of *The Social Graces*

"A fascinating true story of a woman determined to become a veterinarian in the late 1800s. Aleen Cust is everything I love in a heroine: fiery, determined, confident, and smart. No matter what life threw at her, Aleen continued to pursue her passion. We could all learn a thing or two from Aleen Cust."

—Martha Conway, award-winning author of *The Physician's Daughter*

"*The Invincible Miss Cust* is the gripping true story of a young woman who dreams of becoming a veterinary surgeon. Aleen Cust is a determined free spirit whose love for animals surpasses the challenges and hardships faced by a woman pursuing a profession in the 1890s, a time when women were rarely allowed to dream of an education or a career. Readers of James Herriot will find this a delightful, inspiring read."

—Julia Bryan Thomas, author of *For Those Who Are Lost*

"This work of historical fiction is a powerful portrait of an inspiring woman whose stubborn determination and passion for her calling drove her to defy her family's wishes, stand up to the sexist norms of society, and take the reins of her own life no matter the cost. Bravo!"

—Samantha Greene Woodruff, author of *The Lobotomist's Wife*

"Penny Haw takes us deep into the heart and choices of Aleen Cust, who defied convention to become Britain's first woman veterinary surgeon. A vivid, beautifully written, and compelling novel."

—Louisa Treger, author of *Madwoman* and *The Dragon Lady*

ALSO BY PENNY HAW

The Invincible Miss Cust
The Woman at the Wheel

FOLLOW ME TO

AFRICA

a novel

PENNY HAW

sourcebooks
landmark

Copyright © 2025 by Penny Haw
Cover and internal design © 2025 by Sourcebooks
Cover design by Zoe Norvell
Cover images © Look and Learn / Zaeper, Max (b.1872) / Bridgeman Images

Sourcebooks and the colophon are registered trademarks of Sourcebooks.

Published by Sourcebooks Landmark, an imprint Sourcebooks
P.O. Box 4410, Naperville, Illinois 60567-4410
(630) 961-3900
sourcebooks.com

Cataloging-in-Publication Data is on file with the Library of Congress.

Printed and bound in the United States of America.
VP 10 9 8 7 6 5 4 3 2 1

For Sally and Colin,
who made it all possible

GLOSSARY

ACHEULEAN: An early Stone Age culture characterized by large, almond-shaped tools called hand axes.

ANTHROPOLOGIST: An expert in or student of the study of mankind (anthropology).

ASANTE: The Swahili word for "thank you."

AUSTRALOPITHECUS: A genus of extinct hominids who existed in Africa.

BEDS I, II, III, AND IV: The stratigraphic formations at Olduvai Gorge were distinguished as follows: Bed I (1,700,000 to 2,100,000 years old), Bed II (1,150,000 to 1,700,000 years old), Bed III (800,000 to 1,150,000 years old), and Bed IV (600,000 to 800,000 years old).

BOMA: A word used in areas influenced by the Swahili language to describe an entangled fence built from thorny branches to protect camps and domestic animals from wild animals.

CLACTONIAN: The archaeological name of the industry of European flake tool manufacture.

DIPLOE: The spongy, mesh-like bone that separates the inner and outer layers of the cortical bone of the skull.

FLAKE TOOLS: Stone Age hand tools, often made of flint, shaped by flaking off small particles or by breaking off a large flake to be used as a tool.

HOMINID: A member of the family Hominidae, which includes Homo and Australopithecus. Although the definition has been broadened in recent years, during the time span of this novel and according to Mary Leakey, it excluded the apes.

HOMO: The generic name for the hominid group containing fossilized and modern man.

HOMO HABILIS: Species of man from Olduvai Gorge from about five million to one million years ago named by Louis Leakey.

KNAPPER: Someone who shapes (knaps) stone into flake tools.

KORONGO: Swahili for "gully."

LIVING FLOOR: A horizontal layer of an archaeological site, which was once the surface occupied by a prehistoric group.

MAASAI: A nomadic and pastoralist Nilotic ethnic group who inhabits northern, central, and southern Kenya; and northern Tanzania.

MIOCENE: A geological period that extended approximately from 23,000,000 to 5,300,000 years ago.

NEANDERTHAL: An extinct species or subspecies of archaic humans who lived in Eurasia until about forty thousand years ago.

NEOLITHIC: Also known as the New Stone Age, during which agriculture, pastoralism, and pottery were developed.

OLDOWAN: The archaeological name of an early Stone Age industry that was first recorded at Olduvai Gorge. It was followed by a later industry called the Developed Oldowan.

PALEOLITHIC: The Old Stone Age, characterized by the use of basic stone tools.

PALEONTOLOGY: The study of extinct animals and plants.

PLASTER OF PARIS: Quick-setting gypsum plaster comprising a fine white powder (mined extensively from Montmartre in Paris many years ago), which hardens when moistened and allowed to dry.

PLEISTOCENE: The geological period spanning five million to two million years ago.

PRECAMBRIAN: A period extending from about 4,600,000,000 years ago (the point at which Earth began to form) to 541,000,000 years ago.

PROCONSUL: An extinct genus of primates that existed from 21,000,000 to 17,000,000 years ago during the Miocene.

RHODESIA: The name by which Zimbabwe—an African country bordering Botswana, Mozambique, South Africa, and Zambia—was known until 1980.

TANGANYIKA: A colonial territory in East Africa, which merged with Zanzibar in 1964 to form the United Republic of Tanganyika and Zanzibar and was later renamed the United Republic of Tanzania.

ZINJANTHROPUS BOISEI (**ZINJ**): The generic name originally given to *Australopithecus boisei*, and meaning "the man of East Africa." *Boisei* referred to Louis and Mary Leakey's benefactor Charles Boise.

CHAPTER 1

1983

Olduvai Gorge, United Republic of Tanzania, East Africa

THE ONLY THING WORSE THAN BEING SOMEWHERE YOU DON'T WANT TO BE IS discovering no one else wants you there either, thought Grace as she followed the narrow, sandy path out of the camp.

"We can't have a teenager just hanging around. This is a dig, not a discotheque. She'll have to do something."

Grace had overheard the words on her way to breakfast, recognizing the sharp-edged, plummy voice of Dr. Mary Leakey. She wasn't surprised. Dr. Leakey had eyed her over the rim of her whiskey tumbler with overt displeasure when they were introduced the previous evening. Still, it stung, being unwelcome.

George—an upshot of recent years was that Grace thought of her father as "George" rather than "Dad"—had told her not to wander into the bush alone. It was dangerous, he'd said. But that was when they'd arrived in the dark yesterday. Now, the next morning, though it was apparently winter and not yet eight o'clock, the sun was in full bloom in an immense, cloudless sky. Even the shadows seemed cowed by the intensity of the light. That, and the scrubby, squat vegetation, made it unlikely that she'd trip over a lion or rear-end an elephant.

She scrambled up a sandy mound and scanned the view. It was nothing like the African savanna she'd imagined when the plane left Heathrow and she'd yielded to the fact that she couldn't avoid the trip. Where were the swaying grasslands crowded with herds of wildebeests, zebras, gazelles, and giraffes? Where were the branches decorated with the dangling tails and limbs of leopards and the rocky lairs from which lions might contemplate their culinary desires? Why couldn't she see the vast spans of water she'd admired on wildlife documentaries, the promised lakes strewn with flocks of big-billed pelicans and pink flamingos?

Olduvai Gorge wasn't a savanna at all, she thought. It was as bleak as a desert, weathered and dry, with smatterings of stiff, spiky bushes and trees. The earth was crusty and bleached. It was a wonder anything grew there at all. To Grace's right, a monolith with a messy green flattop rose like the remnant turret of a giant sandcastle. Or it might've been a craggy mound of ice cream. Vanilla at the bottom, followed by a layer of chocolate with fuzzy green peppermint on top. Except ice cream was smooth and cold. Here, everything was dehydrated, scorched, and ragged.

Her father had tried to warn her how barren the place might seem to her, particularly since it was the dry season. Much had happened since the lake and its fertile shoreline and all the creatures that existed there two million years ago had disappeared. Tier upon tier of sand, soil, stones, volcanic rocks, and other deposits—each separated by hundreds of thousands of years—had accumulated over the ages, shifting when volcanoes erupted and the earth fractured, and were eroded by water and wind. Nowadays, the gorge was rich with fossils, some as old as two million years, he'd enthused. Fossils. Ancient bones. Stone tools. Leftovers. Archaic litter. The remains of the dead and extinct. Not people he'd known who'd died recently, but creatures who'd been alive thousands upon thousands of years previously. Like they mattered more. Indeed, they did to some. *That*, her father had told her, was why Dr. Leakey called Olduvai Gorge home. That's why he was there. Why he'd insisted Grace accompany him was still unclear to her.

Grace felt the familiar sense of something knotting in her stomach. The grief was back, binding itself into a ball too big to contain. It hadn't stayed in England. Perhaps if she screamed loudly enough, she could expel it across the gorge and into the endless African expanse.

She looked at the sandy track etched into the earth across the ravine. It wound up and over the sandy valley like a faded ribbon, disappearing into a huddle of low, dense trees before reemerging on the crest of the hill on the other side. Was that the road they'd driven to the camp after the interminably long journey from Nairobi the day before? She turned to look around. It had to be. There were no other tracks to be seen. The hills behind were higher. Those in the distance, rugged and blue, could've been mountains. It's possible, she thought, that a savanna lay between her and the farthest range. She couldn't be sure from her vantage point. Maybe that's where the animals were. Would they hear her scream?

"Here you are!"

George struggled toward her, his narrow face pink and shiny beneath a wide-brimmed khaki hat. Grace wondered if she loathed him more now that he'd forced his way back into her life than she did when she'd accepted years previously that her mother was right: he had discarded them.

"You shouldn't go off on your own," he said, puffing as he approached. "It really isn't safe."

She shrugged, looking around pointedly.

He took off his hat, pulled a handkerchief from his pocket, and wiped his face. "Just because you don't see anything doesn't mean there aren't any animals around. Please, my girl, you *have* to stay in the camp."

Grace was silent.

Her father cleared his throat. "Dr. Leakey wants to see you."

"What for?" she asked. "To explain that we're on a dig, not at a disco?"

He stared at her, opening his mouth as if to speak. When he couldn't find the words, he looked at his feet and sighed instead. Somewhere in the distance, a raven gave several short, deep croaks.

"She wants you to help her sort some of her things," said George eventually. "Do a bit of labeling, filing, and packing. I told you she's leaving the camp for good in a few months. She can do with the help."

"Of course," she said, still not looking at him.

"It's only ten days, Grace. It means a lot to me. To be here. It's the only chance I'll have. Please be reasonable." He raised his arms. "Look at this place. Isn't it magnificent?"

She sniffed.

He went on, "It's nothing like Cambridge. Or Tewkesbury. Nothing like anything you've seen before."

"Thank God," she muttered, stepping past him to descend the hill.

Grace led the way until the camp came into view, when she moved aside to allow her father to go ahead. She followed at a distance, watching as he carefully picked his way around the spiny bushes that lined the path. George Clark was a cautious, meticulous man—except when it came to her and her mother Eleanor, thought Grace. He'd trained as an archaeologist because he was curious, but also, he said, because he liked the idea of searching for clues and then painstakingly filling in the blanks. He enjoyed the slow pace and thoughtfulness required to examine, unravel, and reconstruct the past.

He stopped, turned to her, and gestured at a cluster of tall, pointed plants growing alongside the path. "Sisal," said George. "Originally from Mexico but grows wild here now. Olduvai means 'place of the sisal' in Maasai. Actually, it's a misspelling. It should be 'Oldupai,' with a p, not a v."

Grace gave a tiny, dismissive shrug. As he walked away, she stepped closer to the plants and touched the sharp, rigid tip of one of the lance-shaped leaves. She stifled a cry when the spike impaled her finger, and as she watched a tiny drop of blood balloon, Grace thought how George might've warned her to beware of the sisal rather than the animals.

With almost everyone else having gone to the dig for the morning, the camp was quiet but for the crunching of their footsteps as father and daughter made their way between the huts, tents, mishmash of other small buildings, windmills, water tanks, and trucks. Earlier, Grace had sniffed dust lightly infused with smoke from the kitchen. Now she breathed in dust that was lightly scented with mint.

Dr. Leakey's whereabouts were marked by the presence of her dogs, who lay outside her large workroom. The space was enclosed on three sides with stone walls and covered by a thatch roof. An open front looked south across the gorge toward the imposing extinct volcano, which, said the man who'd driven George and Grace to the camp the previous day, was called Lemagrut.

The self-assured-looking young dalmatian—Grace had heard someone call him Matt earlier—gave them an indifferent glance from his sandy station in the sun. However, the scrawny mongrel—he with the throwaway name, Brown Dog—stood and ambled to them, his skinny torso and long tail whipping left and right in feverish greeting. Grace paused to pat him.

"Come," said George, tipping his head toward the room.

Brown Dog followed, but when he drew close, Matt gave a deep growl. The mongrel slumped and, head and tail low, slunk back to his spot in the sand.

Alone in the workroom, Dr. Leakey leaned over a large table, strewn with rocks, bones, books, and papers. She raised her head, flicked a gray lock from where it lay above the right lens of her spectacles, and considered Grace briefly before looking down once more. George gave Grace a tight smile and clasped his hands together like an anxious schoolboy. Grace looked away. He was embarrassing.

A lifeless, half-smoked cigar rested on a pile of papers as if it had been gently extinguished and ceremoniously laid there for future revival. Grace took the opportunity to examine Dr. Leakey, taking in her small, lean frame, dusty tennis shoes, too-short khaki trousers, and pale-blue cap-sleeved blouse. She imagined her mother's response.

"Women of a certain age shouldn't wear short sleeves and, my God, when did that head last darken the basin of a salon?"

Grace felt warm, as if her mother's imagined words resonated around the room.

Certainly, Dr. Leakey's arms were freckled and a little wrinkly, but they were also strong and tanned. The imprint of her sun hat encircled her bare head in a sweaty ring. The top half of her hair was pressed flat against her skull, while below the indent left by the hat, it billowed as if eager to escape. Before she fell ill, Grace's mother wouldn't have made her way to the bathroom first thing in the morning half as disheveled. Grooming and style were clearly not priorities at Olduvai Gorge—though Grace suspected they might *never* be important to Mary Leakey.

"So, Grace, is it?" said Dr. Leakey, slowly straightening her back and lifting her eyes to look at Grace.

"Yes," she replied, so startled by the intense blue of Dr. Leakey's eyes that she almost clutched her hands together the way her father had.

The woman nodded. "Hmm. We haven't had anyone your age in camp since my sons were teens," said Dr. Leakey, transferring her gaze to George, who gave a short, inane chortle.

"What can you do?" she asked, addressing Grace once more.

"'Do'? Um, well, um, what do you mean?" she replied, adjusting the band fastening her long light-brown hair in a ponytail.

"What are your strengths, girl? Are you good with numbers? Words? Detail?"

Grace's stomach roiled. She wasn't good with numbers, words, or anything else. When her mother fell ill more than four years ago, Grace had taken care of her. She'd run errands, fed and bathed Eleanor, and kept her company, making sure she was as comfortable as possible. Grace had only followed the doctor's orders. She had no other skills.

"She's very organized. Responsible," said George.

Grace looked at her feet. She was struck by how desperate her father sounded. Organized? Responsible? How would he know? What did that even mean? She glanced up. Dr. Leakey was staring at her.

"Good, good," said the older woman, her tone suddenly pensive. It was as if she'd lost interest in them and was thinking about something important.

After a moment, she looked at Grace's father—who shifted awkwardly from foot to foot—and said snappily, "That'll do. Thanks, George. You can go. We'll see you at lunchtime."

George looked at Grace, blinking nervously, the way a small boy might look at his mother at the gates on his first day of school. Grace gazed outside to where Brown Dog lay. He, too, was watching her.

"See you later, George," said Dr. Leakey firmly.

He mumbled goodbye, turned, and left. Grace didn't move. Dr. Leakey picked up the half-smoked cigar.

"Come," she said, gesturing outside. "Let's take the dogs for a short stroll before it gets too hot."

Matt and Brown Dog scrambled to their feet to greet their mistress when she stepped outside. Grace followed as Dr. Leakey made her way past the buildings and tents, which, George had explained the night before, served as offices, laboratories, accommodations, storage for excavated material, and other work areas. At the kitchen, where a fire smoldered beneath a large black kettle, Dr. Leakey carefully extracted a long, thin piece of firewood, relit her cigar, and replaced the kindle.

They walked for several minutes without speaking. The dogs trotted up the dusty tracks in front of them, and Dr. Leakey smoked. Eventually, after she'd discharged a sizable cloud of curling white smoke, the older woman spoke.

"What is it you're afraid of?" she asked.

"Afraid of?" echoed Grace.

"When I asked about your strengths, you looked terrified. I don't expect you to edit my book or make deliberations on artifacts. Good grief, no! It's not that kind of work. Is that what you're worried about?"

"No," said Grace.

"Well then?"

"It's just...well..."

Dr. Leakey stopped and turned to Grace. Brown Dog and Matt stood still too. Three pairs of eyes were locked on hers.

"Go on," said Dr. Leakey.

Grace stared at her. She felt angry but wasn't sure why. It was bad enough that she had to come to Africa with her father. Now she was being forced to explain herself to a strange old woman who seemed determined to humiliate her.

She held her gaze. "I'm not afraid. It's just that I haven't done a lot since my mother became ill."

"Your mother's ill?"

"Dead," said Grace.

Dr. Leakey glanced at her cigar—now a mere stub between her fingers—let it fall, and ground it into the sand beneath her canvas shoe.

"I see," she said, sounding as annoyed as Grace felt.

The girl looked down to where the remnants of the charred tobacco had been pulverized. She recalled Father Donald's words at the funeral: "We commit this body to the ground, earth to earth, ashes to ashes, dust to dust."

"How old are you?" asked Dr. Leakey.

"Seventeen," said Grace.

CHAPTER 2

─────◦─────

1930
54 Fulham Road, Kensington, London

MARY GRIMACED AT THE SIGHT OF HER MOTHER'S COAT HANGING IN THE HALLway as she ushered Fussy and Bungey into the flat. She'd hoped to have dried the dogs before her mother saw them. As if privy to Mary's thoughts, the black cocker spaniel stretched her neck and tilted her head, indicating a shake-off was imminent. It began with the spinning of her long, sodden ears; traveled tailward in a vigorous, loose-skinned body roll; and ended with a final flourish as she flicked her wet, stringy tail left, right, and left again.

"Thank you, Fussy," said Mary, scowling at the bespattered floor and walls as she wiped the droplets from her coat. "That's just what we needed."

Fussy wagged her tail again, pleased with the praise, impervious to the sarcasm. Mary gave the other dog a pat on his head. "There's a lot to be said for your short coat and thin tail, Bungey."

"It's your own fault for taking them out in the rain," came a voice.

Mary looked up to see her mother in the doorway. Slight and pristine in a white blouse with a high collar and a black pencil skirt, Cecilia Nicol could've been posing for *Weldon's Ladies' Journal*.

"Here," she called, tossing a large brown towel toward her daughter.

Mary stumbled, almost falling over Fussy as she lurched to catch it.

"I thought we'd manage a quick trot around the gardens before the weather turned," she said, spreading the towel over the spaniel before rubbing her dry.

"But you took them out this morning," said Cecilia, as if her seventeen-year-old daughter might've forgotten. "You were gone before I left."

Mary whipped the towel off Fussy, draped it over the dalmatian's head, and gently dried his ears. "We've discussed this, Mother. Fussy is accustomed to having a garden at her disposal, and Bungey is a youthful ball of energy. When you moved us here, you knew they'd have to be walked regularly."

"We're here because it suits *you*," said her mother. "Don't forget that. Wipe the wall and floor when you're done with the dogs."

Mary looked up to see Cecilia—shoulders back, head held high, and stride decisive—disappear into the sitting room. She was right. They'd moved from Wimbledon to Kensington several months earlier for Mary's convenience. Once the girl had made it clear that she'd pursue a career in archaeology and her mother acknowledged her earnestness, Cecilia Nicol had sold their house in Wimbledon with its garden, packed their sturdy furniture—only recently out of storage since her husband's death four years previously—and rented a flat above a dry cleaner's shop on Fulham Road.

Uncomfortable with being the reason for the move, Mary had tried to convince herself that her mother had relocated because the flat was within walking distance of Lincoln Street, where Cecilia's mother and sisters lived. However, she knew that that was simply a happy coincidence for the women. The decision to move was all about securing a future for Mary. Her mother was determined to find her an appropriate occupation, one that would place her within a refined, respectable circle where she'd meet suitably sophisticated, intelligent people, including—perhaps, most importantly—a decent well-to-do man.

That Mary was intrigued by archaeology and serious about studying it placed mother and daughter in an unusual situation; for once, they were on common ground. Mary was finally passionate about something Cecilia approved of and saw merit in pursuing. A career in archaeology promised her daughter the kind of prestigious direction Cecilia hoped for her. The Kensington flat might've been noisy and without a garden for the dogs, but it was spacious, comfortable, and, indeed, closer to Cecilia's family. Crucially, it provided easy access to Central London, where Mary could attend public talks in archaeology, geology, and the like whenever possible; meet the right kind of people; and do the right kind of things.

With the dogs dry and the floor and walls wiped, Mary removed her coat and went to the sitting room. Fussy and Bungey followed as far as the door but went on to the kitchen, presumably to wait for their supper.

"Fresh pot of tea?" Mary asked, glancing at the teapot and cups on the trolley.

Her mother looked up from where she sat across the room. "Don't you want to know where I went today?"

"I'd rather have tea."

Cecilia pouted. "Sit down."

Mary recognized the tone. Her mother was frustrated. Things weren't moving fast enough for her. Although Mary had insisted that she'd attend as many relevant talks as possible at the London Museum in Lancaster House and University College, the approach wasn't structured or proper enough for Cecilia: she wanted more. Mary perched on the edge of the chair nearest the door.

"I took the train to Oxford," said her mother.

Mary was surprised. "Oxford?"

"Yes, to the university," said Cecilia, po-faced.

"Why would you go there?"

Her mother leaned back and laced her fingers together on her lap. "I wrote and requested an interview with William Sollas. He agreed to see me." She paused for effect. Mary knew her mother was needling her. When the girl didn't move or speak, Cecilia continued. "Professor Sollas. He's the professor of geology, with a particular interest in paleolithic archaeology."

Mary gave her head a tiny shake. "Why?"

"Why not? I told him about you, your interests. How you've been fascinated by archaeology ever since you and your father visited the excavations in Les Eyzies. Your joy of collecting and sorting. I said how excited you were when Uncle Percy took us to Stonehenge and how Miss Liddell so kindly described her work to you at the excavations at Windmill Hill at Avebury. He seemed impressed that we know her and said if anyone understands the science and standards required in archaeology, it's Dorothy Liddell."

"We hardly 'know her,' Mother. We met her and she showed us around," said Mary, though, in reality, Dorothy Liddell had made a lasting impression on her, demonstrating for one thing that a career in archaeology was possible for women.

Cecilia ignored her. "I also told him how you've inherited your father's talent for drawing. How suited you are to the field. I explained how dedicated you'd be to your studies if they accepted you."

"Accepted me? Why would you say such a thing?" asked Mary, running her fingers through her short hair. It wasn't only the futility and humiliation of her mother demanding a meeting with a professor on her behalf that unsettled her, but also the mention of her father. He'd understand if he was here.

"If you don't ask, you don't receive."

"So, you asked. Did you receive?" said Mary.

Her mother sighed.

Mary stood. "Why would you do that, Mother? Embarrass yourself and an Oxford professor. We had an agreement. You know my plans."

Cecilia held her gaze. "It was worth a try. Archaeology at Oxford. Imagine the prestige. Not to mention the caliber of people you'd meet there."

Mary snorted, reached for the teapot, and left the room.

Fussy and Bungey greeted Mary in the kitchen, tails wagging and eyes dinnertime bright. She patted them absent-mindedly, filled the kettle, and lit the stove. As she prepared the dogs' supper, her mother's words rang clear: "Ever since you and your father visited the excavations in Les Eyzies."

Finally, the sharp stab of shock and its dizzying aftermath that had accompanied thoughts of her father for years following his death were gone. The rage and disbelief had diminished. What was left was numbness and regular twinges of panic that she was forgetting him, that she could no longer picture the six-foot frame of Erskine Edward Nicol Junior, with his serious eyes, abundant gray hair, and equally ample and silvery beard and mustache. He'd only been gone four years. How could the likeness of the most important person in her life fade so quickly? Mary wouldn't let it happen, and resolved to imagine him every night before she slept. She reasoned that if, when she closed her eyes, she could conjure his face, her father wouldn't entirely vanish from her life—and that was crucial. She'd never been happier than when she was with him. They were kindred spirits. She couldn't let him go.

Her mother was right about her interest in excavating and examining the artifacts of historical sites having taken root when she, not yet a teenager, was with her father in France. He'd explained what archaeology was, showed her his world, and taught her to read. While Mary's mother had argued that *Alice in Wonderland* and *Robinson Crusoe* were unsuitable books to start off a child's reading, Erskine had ignored her, and Mary quickly proved her father right. Lewis Carroll and Daniel Defoe were, it seemed, perfectly appropriate for a beginner reader who was determined to reward her father's expectations.

His greatest hope was that Mary would become an artist like he was.

"She's a natural," she'd heard him say to her mother after he'd set her up with a new clutch of pencils and a sketch pad and instructed Mary to illustrate a bunch of grapes on a plate. "I don't recall learning so quickly. She must keep it up. She'll be an exceptional artist."

"You're a good teacher," her mother had replied.

Mary had silently agreed. She'd learn anything he taught her. In fact, Mary believed that everything she knew, she'd learned from her father. That included her inclination to spend her life doing something *really* interesting that wasn't too regulated and allowed plenty of travel and adventure.

Now, in the flat on Fulham Road, with Fussy's and Bungey's eager panting warmly polluting the kitchen, Mary wondered what it was about the way her father had lived that appealed to her.

Like his father, Erskine Nicol was a painter. He sought inspiration in France, Italy, and Switzerland in winter and early spring, trekking to scenic spots in the countryside and small villages with his family in tow. In summer, they'd returned to London, where Erskine held exhibitions and sold his paintings. When his stock was sold, Erskine and his family sailed back across the Channel and the cycle began again.

Their time on the Continent was an unstructured, nomadic existence that seemed to little Mary an endless series of adventures with freedom she took for granted. She formed transitory friendships with local children and learned their languages. Where they lingered long enough, she adopted stray animals, shedding tears for them when it was time to move on. Occasional sad goodbyes notwithstanding, Mary was happy. There were always new places to discover, people and animals to meet, and explorations to undertake. The life suited her independent, carefree character. It also afforded her ample time with her father.

While Erskine painted alone in the mornings, he spent the afternoons and evenings with her. They explored the countryside, often taking such long walks, as they grew distracted by the plants, animals, and sites along the way, that they'd have to beg rides home in farm carts. Mary was in awe of her father's intelligence and was quite sure that he knew everything about everything. He and she were alike, she thought. Unlike her mother, her father didn't worry about appearances. Regardless of whether he was at his easel or not, Erskine dressed in shabby, old clothes. What interested him were animals, plants, topography, history, and places. To Mary, there was no place more fascinating than alongside her father—and never had she been more fascinated than when he took her to visit the Cap Blanc rock shelter near Les Eyzies in Dordogne, France.

Her father explained what he knew about Cap Blanc as they slogged up the steep, wooded hillside to the shelter. It had been discovered by workmen about twenty years previously and was believed to have been occupied by ancient hunters more than fifteen thousand years before that. Mary understood the number to be large but couldn't imagine what might make such an old cave interesting. It didn't take long to find out.

As they emerged from the trees and walked across a wide strip of short grass, Mary looked up at the sheer sandy-colored cliff in front of her. Drawing closer, her father took her hand and led her to where the limestone seemed to hang above them like a giant lip. Mary pushed her hand deeper into her father's. For a moment, she imagined the ancient hunters' eyes on her. Then she saw the animals.

As Mary's eyes adjusted to the light, a line of horses—each large, well rounded, and looking to the right as if for a way out of the cave—grew out of the shadows. The sculptures had been carved into walls.

"Horses," said Erskine, his voice thin.

Mary pulled her hand from his and walked closer to the carvings. She was entranced. In places, the artists—for these hunters were most certainly also artists—had used the natural contours of the limestone to shape heads, necks, bellies, and rumps. The effect was curiously organic and otherworldly.

She turned to her father. "Why?" she asked. "Why did they make these?"

Wide-eyed, he shook his head. "Perhaps it was their way of recording what they'd seen. What lived here all those years ago. They hadn't yet devised a form of writing. That's why the era is called 'prehistoric.' They had no way of writing their history. So they recorded it like this," he said, gesturing to the wall.

"Or perhaps they just liked making art—like you do, Father," suggested Mary.

"Yes. Perhaps they liked sculpting horses," he said.

"Not only horses," she replied. "This is a bull. A big one."

He looked at her, frowning. Mary pointed to the front of one of the horses, where, at first glance, it seemed there were some natural bulges and lines in the stone. Mary's father leaned forward, peering through his spectacles. It took him a while to make out what his daughter had recognized so quickly.

"My goodness, Mary," he said. "You're right. It's a bison. How clever of you to spot it! You have a very sharp eye."

She felt herself grow warm. There were few things more satisfying than hearing his praise. Mary silently repeated his words so that they were forever imprinted in her mind.

I am clever and have a very sharp eye.

Even now, as she stood in the kitchen in London four years later, with the dalmatian's cool, wet nose nudging her hand to draw her attention back to the preparation of his supper, Mary heard the words in her head. She didn't always trust them, but if her father believed them, they must be true. How she wished that he were alive to assure her that she was clever and observant just once more.

Shortly after they'd visited Cap Blanc, Mary's father took her to the museum in Les Eyzies. Father and daughter had barely stepped onto the pavement outside their small hotel to make their way there when Cecilia rushed out, having decided at the last minute to accompany them. Mary clamped her teeth. Outings with Father were never as enjoyable when her mother was there.

As it was, Cecilia proved useful. She was the linguist in the family, providing a smooth introduction to the French prehistorian Monsieur Élie Peyrony, who was taking care of the museum and happened to be there when the Nicol family arrived. Charmed by Cecilia and pleased with Erskine's and Mary's interest in his work, Monsieur Peyrony spent an entire afternoon showing off a collection of finely shaped flint tools and wonderfully decorated bone points and harpoons found in the rock shelters in the region. Mary's intrigue multiplied as she examined the objects. She saw how, as her father had explained, what they'd left behind offered a glimpse into the lives of people who'd existed thousands of years previously. Mary was fascinated by the items themselves, about why and how they might've been crafted and the way many were decorated with etchings. Just as her father treasured his easel, paints, and brushes, ancient people had treasured their tools. However, their lives must've been different in every other way.

It was dark outside when Monsieur Peyrony finally escorted the Nicol family to the museum door. The afternoon had gone too fast, and Mary wasn't the least bit tired. She resolved to ask her father if they could come back the next day. However, before bidding them farewell, Monsieur Peyrony invited the trio to visit another nearby rock shelter. Called Laugerie Haute, the site was being excavated by Monsieur Peyrony and his father, fellow prehistorian Denis Peyrony. When her father agreed they'd do so in a few days, Mary's heart raced. She skipped back to the hotel ahead of her parents, wondering if she'd ever been as excited.

Days later, after he'd escorted the family around Laugerie Haute for an hour or so, Monsieur Peyrony took out his pocket watch, glanced at it, and apologized, saying he'd have to leave them to attend to something else. Mary's disappointment showed; she didn't have a knack for duplicity or diplomacy. He hesitated, turned to her mother, and spoke quietly, pointing to a pile of rocks and sand some distance away. Erskine looked inquiringly at Cecilia as Monsieur Peyrony walked away.

Her mother was impassive. "He said Mary is welcome to sift through that heap of soil for any spoils he and his men might've overlooked," she said.

Mary turned to the pile as a man tipped a wheelbarrow of rubble onto it. She looked at her father. "May I?"

He nodded, glancing at Cecilia. "We'll be a while," he said, before leading the way to the earthy mound.

It was like hunting for treasure, thought Mary as they rummaged through the soil. With every interestingly shaped stone and unidentifiable object located, they'd stop to examine and discuss it. Should Mary place it on the "keep," "reexamine," or "discard" pile? Was it so interesting that it should be left for Monsieur Peyrony's attention? Yes, it was like treasure hunting, but better because her father enjoyed it too.

"We should make our way back," said her mother eventually from her spot on a large rock in the shade.

"Just a little longer," chimed Erskine and Mary in unison.

As they continued to hunt through the sand and rocks, Mary realized that it wasn't only the excitement of looking for treasure that thrilled her but also the realization that beautiful things that might tell intriguing stories could be discovered in the ground. She was increasingly careful with every object she found, gently brushing and blowing the dirt from it and adding ever more classifications to her sorting. Could this sharp-ended stone have been used for hunting, preparing food, or creating art? Was this ax head–shaped rock older than the other similarly shaped one? Was this arrowhead-like object an even older version of the one that Father had found earlier?

Eventually, though, her father, too, was ready to return to the hotel. Mary bundled their treasure into her cardigan, which she'd taken off earlier. Cecilia grumbled as the girl struggled to lift it, stretching the garment in all directions. Her father crouched, tucked his hands and arms around the jagged parcel, and carried it for her. That evening at supper, his body was sore and his appetite poor. He'd overdone it, he said, rising to go to bed before Mary had finished eating.

The next day, while the girl sat beneath a large tree in the hotel gardens, reexamining and re-sorting the artifacts, her mother stood alongside the village doctor as he examined her husband. Erskine's discomfort had nothing to do with heavy lifting or too many hours on his knees, sifting through the spoils of an excavation, said the doctor. His symptoms indicated something far more worrying.

When, a week later, Mary's father was too ill to want her at his bedside, and she realized he wasn't getting better, she laid her cardigan on the ground, placed the collection back in it, dragged it down the street, and left it outside the museum. She couldn't bear to look at the artifacts any longer, knowing that she and her father would never examine them together again. But certainly, the items were valuable, and she couldn't simply throw them away.

Just as Cecilia's linguistic skills had been helpful when they met Monsieur Peyrony, her commitment to Catholicism rewarded the family. The village priest, who'd worked as a medical orderly during the First World War and seen Mary and her mother in his church, made daily visits to administer morphine to ease Erskine's pain. The priest and Mary's mother sat at his bedside while Mary took long walks alone. She taught herself stealth and silence in the countryside, listening for signs and facing the breeze to prevent wild animals picking up her scent. Every day, she tested her aptitude to track and observe wildlife. It helped take her mind off her father and, as one week turned into two and he ate less and less and slept more and more, Mary left the hotel earlier each morning, averting her eyes from the crockery sticky with congealed food and drink, discarded medicine bottles, and soiled cloths outside his door. She ran down the empty street and between the avenue of trees that led to the farmlands. She'd found a dark, quiet forest hidden from the road and farming activities. It was there Mary snuck up on wild boars and rabbits.

One morning, as she made her way through the dewy meadow that led to the trees, she came across a skulk of foxes. She crept forward and crouched behind a knoll of tall grass. A kit followed two adults into the open. Then another emerged and pounced on the first. They tumbled about, and suddenly two more kits joined them. The four raced across the field, leaping and wrestling one another to the ground while the adults sniffed around. Mary's knees were stiff and stained green by the time the kits scampered into the trees behind the larger animals.

"They had *no* idea I was here," said Mary, rising to her feet.

As she made her way down the shady lane back to the village, Mary wondered if her father might be alert enough to be interested in her account of the foxes. How he would've enjoyed watching them with her. When she arrived at the hotel, her mother was at the entrance. Mary knew the moment their eyes met across the street: her father was dead. She turned and fled back the way she'd come. She was barely thirteen, and she'd forever lost the best person in the world.

"Were you planning to make another pot of tea or simply allowing the kettle to boil dry?" said her mother, startling Mary as she glided into the kitchen at Fulham Road and switched off the gas. The dogs, having resigned themselves to waiting for their supper, lay on either side of the girl.

"I was just feeding these two," she said, placing their bowls on the floor. Fussy and Bungey skidded over and plunged their muzzles into the containers.

"You were daydreaming," said Cecilia. "You've got to stop it. If you're going to make anything of your life, you need to get serious. You're seventeen, Mary. It's time."

CHAPTER 3

1983
Olduvai Gorge, Tanzania

THEY WALKED WITHOUT SPEAKING FOR SO LONG THAT GRACE WONDERED whether Mary Leakey had forgotten she was there. She glanced at the older woman, whose lengthy strides seemed to Grace brisker than those of any other women she knew, irrespective of age. The pair kept pace but, separated by the low, stubbly knoll between the sandy tracks, were more than an arm's length apart. Even so, Dr. Leakey seemed to sense Grace's look.

"Yes," she said. "We should go back."

As if on cue, Matt and Brown Dog, who'd been trotting sedately ahead until then, took off in a blast of scrabbling claws and dust.

"Oh, damn," said Dr. Leakey. "It's a cat."

Grace stared at her. She pointed to the left of the track beyond a clump of short bushes to where Matt—his dark-spotted white coat distinct against the dull brown earth and dry grass—raced up a small hill ahead of Brown Dog. The girl narrowed her eyes against the glare, straining to see what they were chasing. A cat? She expected to spot something small streaking through the vegetation or hopping over the rocks but saw only sand, mounds of earth, bush, and dry grass, static and iridescent in the sunlight.

"Way ahead of them," said Dr. Leakey, wagging her pointed finger higher now. "It's a cheetah."

"Cheetah? But that isn't a cat, is it?" said Grace, scanning the hills urgently.

"Of course it's a cat."

Grace recognized the sneer in her voice, but before the discomfort fully registered, she saw a flash of movement near the top of a hill about two hundred yards in front of the dogs. It was the cheetah. The animal sailed up the highest point and stopped to look back. For an instant, its profile—slender body, long legs and tail, small head, and round ears—created a tawny imprint against the sky.

"There! They'll never catch it!" she shouted, breathless and unaware, until that moment, how excited she was.

The cat slid out of sight.

Grace spun around to face Dr. Leakey. Their eyes met and held. It was as if they were seeing each other for the first time. Dr. Leakey adjusted her spectacles and gave in to a small smile. Grace felt herself blush.

"Anyone would think you'd won a race," said Dr. Leakey.

Grace snorted and looked away to where she'd seen the cheetah. She couldn't remember when last she'd experienced such a thrill. "Will the dogs come back?" she asked.

"Yes. We have Brown Dog to thank for that. *He* gives up when he can no longer see what they're chasing. Dalmatians are inclined to run forever. However, Matt eventually stops when he realizes he's hunting alone."

"But they'd never catch a cheetah?"

"No, but that doesn't stop them from trying, particularly when there's a pack of them. Oh, those were the days!"

"You've had packs of dogs? Dalmatians?" asked Grace.

"I've had at least one dalmatian at my side since I was your age. No—younger, even. Out here, I usually had two or three at a time. For a while, there were four. Nowadays, one's enough," said Dr. Leakey.

She was silent for a moment and then pointed to the extinct volcano. It was a dominant feature of the landscape wherever they were.

"Old Lemagrut," said Dr. Leakey. "Now it's hazy in the distance, but you watch—later it'll be sharp and clear. Its hues change with the passage of the day. It's always there but always different."

Her arm fell to her side, and she exhaled loudly. There was something sad about the moment. As if she was saying goodbye.

"Ah, there's Brown Dog. Matt won't be far behind," she said.

Panting hard and with his head low, Brown Dog trotted along the track toward them. Dr. Leakey turned and began walking the way they'd come.

"What makes you think a cheetah isn't a cat?" she asked when Grace drew alongside her.

"I read they have claws like dogs, not cats."

Dr. Leakey nodded. "Well, their claws are semi-retractable. They use them for traction as they run. It's one of the reasons they're so fast. But they still belong to the feline species. Just one look and you can't mistake it. In fact, they're the only ones in the big cat family that purr, like domestic cats. They don't roar like lions or leopards. Cheetahs also make chirping, meowing sounds. Do you have pets at home?"

"Not anymore," said Grace. "We had a dog before my...when I was younger."

They walked without talking for a while. Grace didn't want to think about Cambridge, or about how she'd sobbed when they'd had to find a new home for her corgi, Watson. Neither did she want to think about how, for a short while before her mother was bedridden, she'd volunteered at Tranquility Animal Rescue on the outskirts of town. There, she'd worked in the cattery, kennels, and stables, feeding and cleaning up after the animals, and fantasizing at every session about who among the dogs, cats, rabbits, ponies, donkeys, and cows she'd take home. She didn't want to think about how she'd failed them all. Instead, she gazed across the vast plains. How different the place seemed since she'd annoyed her father by leaving the camp to look around earlier that morning. It was almost beautiful. Still, there were no herds of animals or flocks of birds to be seen.

"Have you seen many? Cheetahs, I mean," she asked.

"Yes. More than I can recall. Though it's unusual to see them around here at this time of year. It's too dry. They typically follow the migration and have gone farther north by now."

"Is that why there are no animals? Because of the migration?" said Grace.

"No animals? Oh, there are animals here. Nothing like after the rains, of course. When I arrived here the first time—April 1935, it was—there were animals of all sorts everywhere. It was animal Eden, an extraordinary introduction to Africa for me. But even now, just because you don't see them doesn't mean they aren't here. You need to learn how to spot them. Didn't you see any on your way yesterday?"

"A few warthogs and giraffes in the distance," replied Grace, regretting how she'd slept or pretended to sleep for most of the drive to avoid talking to George.

"You'll see more. Not all the animals migrate. Many are like me. They'd stay here permanently if they could," said Dr. Leakey.

She emitted a short, self-deprecating laugh and then, as if to shift Grace's attention, glanced behind her. "Ah, Matt, you're back. Nice run?"

Grace turned to see the dalmatian slow to a walk as he caught up with them. He was panting even harder than Brown Dog had been after the chase.

"Do they go after all kinds of wildlife?" she asked.

When she didn't receive a reply, she looked at Dr. Leakey. She was staring at something beyond her, her expression stern. Grace followed her gaze to see three vehicles navigating the bumpy main road to the camp.

Dr. Leakey glowered. "Who now?"

Grace winced, recalling how unwelcome she'd made her feel the night before and earlier that morning. It was naive of her to think that anything had changed because they'd taken a short walk together and seen a cheetah. She held back as Dr. Leakey increased her pace, Matt trotting alongside her now.

They'd almost reached the kitchen where Dr. Leakey had relit her cigar earlier before she stopped and waited for Grace and Brown Dog to catch up.

"What's wrong? You're surely not tired from such little exercise?" she asked.

"No. Nothing's wrong," said Grace.

The anger she'd experienced earlier was back.

Dr. Leakey sighed. "Look, Grace, if you're going to make anything out of being here, you've got to stop hoping that other people are going to instinctively know what it is that'll make you happy, what interests you, and what will make you feel as if you have something to contribute," she said.

"I don't need to feel as if I have something to contribute," said Grace, before she could stop herself.

"Everyone wants to contribute," replied Dr. Leakey, her eyes narrow. "We all want to be worth something, do our bit, matter somehow. Work it out, girl, for yourself—before someone else does it for you and you find yourself stuck in a life you don't want."

CHAPTER 4

1930
Hembury Fort, Devon, England

MARY HAD CRINGED AT HER MOTHER'S IMPLYING TO PROFESSOR SOLLAS THAT they were more than acquainted with Dorothy Liddell. However, a few days later, and without mentioning it to Cecilia, Mary had mustered the courage to write to Miss Liddell, applying to be her assistant at the Hembury Fort excavations in Devon. It was one of several similar applications she posted, but the one for which she held out the most hope. A letter of acceptance followed within a fortnight, which was how Mary came to work alongside Miss Liddell at Hembury for three summers beginning in 1930.

The year was a busy one for British archaeologists. It was the last of V. Gordon Childe's three-year excavation of Skara Brae at Mainland in Scotland's Orkney archipelago. His work revealed a Neolithic village believed to have been built in 500 B.C. It was also the year John Garstang began a major excavation of Jericho, starting at the settlement mound at Tell es-Sultan. At the same time, excavations began at Tell el-Ajjul south of Gaza under the direction of Sir Flinders Petrie. At Kharga Oasis in Egypt, excavations were directed by the archaeology–geology partnership of Gertrude Caton-Thompson and Elinor Wight Gardner.

While Mary couldn't ignore the tiny jabs of envy and impatience she experienced when she read and heard about excavations in far-flung places, she knew she was fortunate to be at Hembury, which had been occupied during the Neolithic, Iron Age, and Roman periods. As director of digging, an expert in Neolithic studies, and a patient teacher, Dorothy Liddell couldn't have been a finer mentor. At her side, Mary learned the intricacies of working on a dig. There was a great deal more to it than searching for material remains by digging, scraping, picking, and brushing the earth. Miss Liddell taught her how to scrutinize her surroundings, the kinds of questions she should pose to others and herself, how to plan her days, and the importance of meticulously recording everything. Mary's eyes were also opened to the magnitude of the demands of directing an excavation. She watched and learned as Miss Liddell organized and oversaw logistics on- and off-site; and led the process by meeting site managers every day, making decisions, and ceaselessly urging and guiding everyone to achieve the research aims. Poring over a large ledger every evening, she also managed the budget and, several times a month, organized teaching and tours of the site.

While the men lodged at the local pub, Miss Liddell and Mary stayed at a homely boardinghouse in the nearby market town of Honiton, driving to and from the site in the director's two-seater Morris. She was up much later than Mary and awake much earlier. It was tiring, just watching. However, Miss Liddell was unflappable. She was precise and measured in her approach, energetic and unafraid of spending long hours doubled over a trowel or kneeling with her nose to the earth. She managed the role calmly, and Mary never saw her flustered or irritated. Indeed, while she was unstintingly polite and modest, Dorothy Liddell made it clear to anyone who might doubt it that women could rise to the top in archaeology.

Although Mary was the director's assistant, Miss Liddell encouraged her to work alongside and learn from other archaeologists wherever possible. As such, Mary one day found herself working with the site foreman, William Young.

"You're spending your university holiday getting some experience, then, are you, Miss Nicol?" he asked.

It wasn't an unexpected question, but the implication that only university students might work on a dig peeved Mary.

"No, I'm hoping to learn as I work," she replied.

William looked at her. "Ah! Is that so? I hope you'll find it as effective as I have."

"How so?"

"Well, I'm the son of a blacksmith who didn't see a future in beating metal when I returned from the war. I took a job at a dig because there wasn't anything else going. It turned out to be the best thing. All my training has happened in the field, and you know what?"

Mary shrugged.

William lowered his voice. "It doesn't seem that I've missed anything—though I wouldn't tell our more scholarly colleagues that."

Work at Hembury was fascinating, with moments of great excitement, including the time Mary was excavating the framed entrance to the hill fort and discovered a cobble causeway. Stimulating work notwithstanding, she missed Fussy and Bungey, and planned to return to them in London every second weekend.

Although Cecilia never said as much to her daughter, Mary knew that her mother was proud of her for having secured work on Dorothy Liddell's dig. She couldn't contain a smug smile as she told others that Mary "was on-site in Devon in her role as the assistant to esteemed archaeologist Miss Dorothy Liddell, sister-in-law of Mr. Alexander Keiller of Windmill Hill fame." Cecilia was hopeful that her daughter was on her way to establishing a favorable career in a field in which she might encounter a decent man.

"So, tell me all about it. How are things in Devon?" asked her mother as they ate supper after Mary's first fortnight at Hembury.

While she knew Cecilia had no real interest in her work and wanted to know about the people—that is, the men—on-site, Mary embarked on an exaggeratedly detailed account of the excavations. She spoke about the place and its history, and explained where they were digging, how deep, what they'd found and the importance thereof, and what they'd do next.

Cecilia allowed her to talk without interruption, nodding and blinking as if intrigued.

"You and Miss Liddell stay at separate quarters from the men—as you should, of course—but do you ever have meals or a drink with the other archaeologists? The, er, men?" she asked when her daughter fell quiet.

"I sometimes sit with the diggers while I eat my sandwiches," said Mary, despite the fact that the designation "digger" was not used on-site since most of the field-workers were highly experienced and trained. In truth, Mary almost always sat with Miss Liddell and the other archaeologists.

Her mother sighed. She was accustomed to Mary's goading. "It's just as well, then, that I agreed with Margaret Harris that you would accompany her son to a dance in Chelsea tomorrow night," she said.

Mary stopped eating and stared at Cecilia. "Good grief, no! I'm not going anywhere tomorrow night and certainly not with Edward Harris," she said. "What on earth made you think I would?"

"His younger sister—you must remember Louise—will accompany you. Margaret says they're meeting others there. It'll be fun. The Harris family are very old friends of your grandmother. If you're not going to mix with suitable young people in Devon, then at least do so when you're here for the weekend. Anyway, Edward is quite the young man now. You probably won't recognize him."

"I won't recognize him because I won't see him," said Mary, pushing back her chair and standing up. "I came home to rest and walk the dogs. I don't want to go dancing."

"Rest? My girl, you're in bed by eight o'clock every night. You said so yourself. You don't need rest; you need to socialize. To meet people your own age."

Mary began clearing the table. "Thank you, Mother. I appreciate your concern about my social life, but I'm perfectly happy with things the way they are. I don't understand why you aren't pleased. You wanted me to find something worthwhile to do and take it seriously, which I'm doing. Now you're upset that I'm not out every night drinking punch and dancing."

"I didn't say anything about punch," said her mother, tossing her napkin on the table. "Is it wrong for a mother to want her daughter to be happy?"

"But I *am* happy. That's what I keep telling you. I don't need a beau. I'm busy. I'm learning. I'm doing well. Why do I need a man to add to a picture that is already perfect?"

"I didn't say you needed a man."

Mary stared at her mother. "Really? Isn't that what tomorrow is all about? Finding me a suitable man?"

She went to bed that night determined not to go to the dance. However, her mother persuaded her otherwise, insisting that Margaret Harris would be tremendously offended, which in turn would upset Mary's grandmother.

Neither the dance nor Edward surprised her. If anything, the event and her escort were worse than she'd feared. The crowded dance floor was suffocating, and Edward was the same awkward youth she remembered, with little to say for himself and a high-pitched laugh, which he emitted unpredictably and frequently. She allowed him to lead her onto the dance floor, but Mary had no sense of how to move to the loud, unfamiliar music. She felt foolish as she and Edward collided several times when he pulled her toward him. Was she meant to go left or right or spin around on the spot? When Edward cackled loudly for the third time, Mary snatched her hand from his, shook her head, and left the dance floor. For a while, she watched but was disconcerted by how childish everyone seemed, with their inane movements and excessive smiling. The people she worked with at Hembury were poised, intelligent, and interesting. They did and spoke about important things. Mary felt silly, and when Edward went to get them drinks, she told his sister that she felt ill and left. She was home by nine thirty, shushed the dogs as they greeted her, and went to bed before her mother noted her return.

When she left for Hembury the next afternoon, she silently apologized to Fussy and Bungey. She'd decided she'd only come back to London at the end of summer, when the excavations closed for the season.

One of the things Mary enjoyed about being at Hembury Fort was working outside. She couldn't imagine a better place, particularly early in the morning, when the sunlight seemed to set alight the dewdrops on the grass and wildflowers. The surrounding hills, dense woodlands, and patchwork fields and birdsong reminded her of being in the French countryside with her father.

There were moments, particularly when she thought about her father, that Mary wondered if a career in archaeology was right for her. He'd hoped she'd become an artist. Would he have been disappointed? Surely not. After all, he'd introduced her to archaeology. He'd want her to do what most interested her. To make the most of being clever and having a sharp eye. Wasn't she on her way to proving her worth at Hembury?

One morning, with her father on her mind, Mary took a pencil to her notebook and absent-mindedly sketched one of the umbrella-like clusters of frothy white cow parsley flowers growing on a nearby bank.

"You're very good," said Miss Liddell, glancing at the drawing as she handed Mary tape, a clutch of surveying arrows, and a ranging pole. "Perhaps you could draw some of our finds. It would be useful, especially between field seasons. We're always on the lookout for illustrators for publications."

So it was that Mary worked alongside Dorothy Liddell and others at Hembury Fort during the summers of 1930, 1931, and 1932, and illustrated flints and other stone tools for publication. Whenever possible, she also attended the geology and archaeology lectures occasionally made available to the public by University College and the London Museum.

"I wish I could draw. It's such a useful talent for an archaeologist," reiterated Miss Liddell in an uncharacteristically wistful tone as she paged through an early set of Mary's illustrations one evening during the 1932 season. "Combined with your other skills, it'll take you far. Well done, Miss Nicol."

It reminded Mary of how proud she'd been to hear her father's praise when she'd pointed out the bison. It was understandable; she was very young then. She felt a little foolish now by how pleased she was by Miss Liddell's approval. Even so, Mary wished she could tell her father how she was combining two things he'd taught her to love and apparently, doing it well.

Pleasure notwithstanding, Mary was intimidated when, sometime later, Dorothy Liddell told her she'd recommended Mary to Gertrude Caton-Thompson to illustrate Gertrude's new book.

"You know about her work in Egypt, of course," said Miss Liddell.

Mary nodded. She also knew that little over a decade earlier, looking for evidence to support a theory that Malta and Africa were once connected by land, Dr. Caton-Thompson had searched for Neanderthal skulls near the temple of Borg in-Nadur. Then she'd blown several pith helmets askew when, having led an all-women expedition to the Great Zimbabwe ruins in Southern

Rhodesia, Dr. Caton-Thompson had declared the ruins the work of Africans and not, as other archaeologists had asserted previously, of some other civilization. However, she was best known for her work in Egypt, where, among other things, she'd uncovered one of the earliest farming civilizations, dated around 4,000 B.C.

Miss Liddell continued. "The book is about her work in northern Fayum in Egypt with Elinor Wight Gardner."

Mary felt a tug of self-doubt. What did she know about illustrating beyond what her father had taught her? Miss Liddell was pleased with her drawings and wouldn't have recommended her if she doubted her talent. But what if Mary had simply been lucky up until now? Why would a scientist of Dr. Caton-Thompson's stature want someone with so little experience to work on her book? While Mary had worked as an assistant about one hundred and fifty miles from London, Dr. Caton-Thompson had excavated sites in remote deserts and wildest Africa.

"Surely she'd prefer to work with a more experienced illustrator," said Mary.

"You're a talented artist, Miss Nicol, with an excellent eye for detail. She's in London and will contact you when you get home. I've given her your number," said Miss Liddell.

So it was, some weeks later, that Mary took the tram from Fulham Road to Mayfair. The rain had stopped for the first time in days, but the air was cool enough for everyone to have looped scarves around their necks, buttoned their coats, and pulled their hats low.

We're bundles of flesh and bone, thought Mary, glancing at the middle-aged woman to her left and the lanky boy on her other side in the packed carriage. Both stared straight ahead. She wondered what they were thinking about and whether anyone's thoughts resembled hers. Did they contemplate their ancient ancestors? Did they wonder what it was like living here thousands of years ago, when grassland and forests grew far and wide on either side of the Thames and humans were few?

The boy jostled Mary as he rummaged in his pocket. He extracted an apple and bit into it with a loud crunch and began chewing noisily. The woman glared at him before turning her eyes to Mary and rolling them theatrically.

No, thought Mary, *they don't share my thoughts.*

A while later, Mary glanced at herself in a mirror in the lobby of Brown's Hotel. With her short dark hair clipped in waves away from her eyes, and wearing a pale-blue cashmere top beneath her best gray coat, Mary was satisfied with how adult she appeared. She made her way to the tearoom, where, barely through the door, she recognized Dr. Caton-Thompson immediately. It wasn't that she was the only middle-aged woman alone in the room, but that she was reading *The Archaeological Journal*. At forty-five, Dr. Caton-Thompson was slightly older than Miss Liddell. However, there was little evidence of sun or wind damage in her pale, smooth face. Mary was still staring when Dr. Caton-Thompson looked up, caught her eye, smiled, and stood to shake her hand.

"Pleased to meet you, Dr. Caton-Thompson," said Mary.

"Dorothy's spoken so highly of your talent, I feared you might not have time for me," she said as Mary sat down. "And please, 'Dr. Caton-Thompson' is such a mouthful. I'm Gertrude."

Mary was surprised. Even after working alongside her for so long, Miss Liddell had never suggested they address each other informally.

"Tell me all about your season at Hembury. I haven't visited for a while," said Gertrude.

They talked over two pots of tea and a plate of scones, and by the time Gertrude outlined her plans for her book, *The Desert Fayum*, Mary's concerns had vanished. This, she saw, wasn't an interview. Gertrude wasn't testing her knowledge or skills. She wasn't even trying to establish whether she liked the girl or not. It didn't matter. She'd seen enough in Mary's drawings to know that she wanted her to illustrate her book.

Their conversation was nothing like those Mary had with Dorothy Liddell, who, while unwaveringly courteous and reasonable, was always Mary's boss. Gertrude was different. They were colleagues. It didn't matter that Mary was so young, wasn't formally trained, and hadn't traveled beyond Europe. She had something Gertrude wanted. Her talent and skills were required. Mary was needed. It was an extraordinary feeling. For a moment, as she contemplated the silver teapot with its ornate lid that sat between them, Mary wished there was a way she could contain how she felt in that moment. She wanted to put a lid on her feelings so she could take them home to open and inhale should she doubt her self-worth in the future.

Of course she'd work on the book, said Mary.

As usual, having heard Mary's footsteps on the stairs, Bungey and Fussy were on the other side of the door when she opened it on her return from Mayfair. Her mother stood between them.

"You were out without the dogs," said Cecilia, as if her daughter might've left them unintentionally.

"Yes, I met someone for tea. I'll take them out now."

Her mother's eyes widened. "You met someone? Someone I know?"

Mary reached past her to take the dogs' leads from where they hung on the coatrack. It was likely that Cecilia would recognize Gertrude's name if she mentioned it. She might even know how important the archaeologist's work was and share Mary's excitement over the illustrations for her book. However, Mary wanted to keep the news to herself a little longer. Her mother had a way of almost immediately taking the shine off things. She'd cast doubt on the advantages of taking on the work. She might even question whether Mary was up to it. She'd ask about Gertrude, how the work would be undertaken, and when Mary would be paid. On the occasions Mary had complained about her pessimism in the past, Cecilia had argued that it was simply because she had a practical approach to matters and liked to encourage people to see both the disadvantages and advantages. Mary couldn't see any drawbacks to working with Gertrude but was certain her mother would.

"No, you don't know her. She's an archaeologist who wants me to do some illustrations for her," she said, trying to sound dispassionate.

Cecilia sighed. "Oh, another woman archaeologist," she said, as if there were many women in the field. "Much older than you, is she?"

"Yes. They all are," said Mary.

"Perhaps they have children your age. Though how you'll ever meet them if you never go out, I don't know."

"I was just out, Mother, and I'm going out again now," said Mary as she leashed the dogs and opened the door.

On the street, Fussy and Bungey walked eagerly ahead of her, tugging at their leads. They knew the way to the gardens. Mary increased her pace and smiled, thinking again how independent and liberated she'd felt talking to Gertrude. Perhaps working with her would lead to work elsewhere in the world, somewhere far away from London and her mother's incessant concern about her social life.

It wasn't that Mary wasn't amicable. She enjoyed meeting people and believed herself to be friendly and easy to talk to. Look how easily she and Gertrude had communicated. It was just that she wasn't interested in socializing for the sake of meeting others. It seemed so desperate, as if one was only worth anything when one was surrounded by other people—regardless of whether one liked them or not. Mary wanted to meet interesting people, men and women who'd been places and done and seen things. She was like her father. Erskine Nicol had worked alone and enjoyed it. He hadn't needed the constant attention of people to validate his worth. Mary's mother wanted her to spend time with people her own age. She wanted Mary to attract the attention of young men who came with the promise of a decent, reliable future. What Cecilia couldn't understand was that Mary was impatient. She didn't want the promise of what might evolve; she wanted to be with people who knew what they wanted because they'd already at least partially experienced it.

Fussy and Bungey veered off the pavement and into Kensington Gardens. Mary followed onto the grass, pulled them to a standstill, and uncoupled their leads. As the dogs galloped away, Mary exhaled, as if she, too, had been unleashed. Her meeting with Gertrude was a turning point, she thought. Finally, she recognized her place in the world and saw that she had something worthwhile to offer. This, she hoped, was her ticket to freedom.

CHAPTER 5

1983
Olduvai Gorge, Tanzania

WHEN GRACE EMERGED FROM HER HUT—ESSENTIALLY A TINY ROOM CONTAIN-
ing a camping stretcher with a sleeping bag supplied by George and a gas
lantern on a rickety three-legged stool—she found Brown Dog waiting on the
path. He greeted her, head low and tail wagging. She rubbed his ears, which
accelerated the wagging. It occurred to her that Dr. Leakey might've sent him
to fetch her. However, when she gazed into Brown Dog's eyes, she decided
he'd come because he liked her. She liked him too. She'd seen how he played
second fiddle to Matt. Perhaps they connected because they were outsiders,
uncertain of their place at Olduvai. That was a good enough reason to be
friends, wasn't it?

Once they'd returned to the workroom the previous day, after Dr. Leakey
had castigated Grace for not knowing what she "wanted to contribute," their
few exchanges had been snappish. They were like a pair of ill-tempered weasels
forced to share a den, thought Grace.

The vehicles they'd seen earlier had brought several government repre-
sentatives to camp. It annoyed Dr. Leakey that they'd come to see if she was
on track to leave on the appointed day. Once they were gone, she'd issued

terse instructions to Grace on how to sort and document the array of labeled artifacts, books, and files spread across the large table. The items were miscellaneous, mostly minor fossils, bone fragments, teeth, stone implements, and various other hard-to-identify bits and pieces. Dr. Leakey was uncertain of their exact future now but wanted them sorted so that when she left the camp, she could quickly decide their fate based on how they were categorized. She was pressed for time, she said, having to also work on her memoir.

Grace had tried to ignore the resentment she felt as she worked, but it gnawed at her. What made Dr. Leakey think she might've worked out what to do with her life? She knew nothing about what Grace had endured and how ill-prepared she was for any kind of future. And anyway, had Dr. Leakey known what *she* wanted to do when she was seventeen? Perhaps she'd forgotten what it was like to be young.

Dr. Leakey and her father were alike. They didn't understand or care to try. Grace was in the African wilderness, with its big sky and endless plains. However, she felt as trapped as she'd been in Tewkesbury, where the sky was low and the walls of the flat crushingly close. She'd never thought of running away in England; her mother had needed her. Everything was different now, but if she fled, where would she go? Even if she knew what she wanted to do, she couldn't do it without her father's support. She had no more self-rule than the artifacts she was sorting; to be placed wherever her father ordered, first with her mother and now in Africa, where a strange woman insisted she "work out" what she wanted from life.

Now, with Brown Dog at her side, Grace made her way to the dining room for breakfast. Although the sun was already in full bloom, its rays were diffused by dust particles suspended in a quiet dance. A light breeze brought with it the herby scent she'd noticed yesterday. Grace inhaled, thinking how familiar Olduvai seemed, though she'd only spent two nights there. The dust no longer made her sneeze. She'd slept soundly, oblivious to the indistinct scuttling in the roof and distant calls and cries of unknown creatures, which, the first night, had kept her awake, rigid, while her heart thundered as if trying to escape her chest.

Yesterday, the paths and tracks that strung the buildings and tents together were all the same, but today she knew the shortest route to the dining room.

Left at the big tree with the broken branch, left again at the fifth hut, straight beyond the circle of stones around the empty firepit, and then follow the smell of cooking. The sky was as large as it was the previous day, when it had cowed her, reminding her of her insignificance. Today, it was an immense azure umbrella. Grace looked at Lemagrut, its outline a gentle blue in the distance. Sure enough, as Dr. Leakey had said it would, the volcano looked different in the early light; it was a warm, agreeable sight.

The dining room was part of a large area with a thatch roof, which included a living room and additional places to work and hold meetings. As Grace drew closer, she heard raised voices. Words tumbled over one another in high excitement. She wondered if they'd found something extraordinary while excavating.

Grace peered into the room. Her father was among the men sitting at the long tables. He looked up, caught her eye, and gestured to her to take a seat alongside him.

"There was a cheetah in the camp this morning," he said as Grace sat. "It was possibly here all night."

She stared at him. "Did you see it?"

George shook his head. "Just its prints. Dr. Leakey came across it before sunrise when her dogs gave chase."

"The dogs chased it. Here? This morning?" asked Grace.

"Yes."

"Are you sure?"

"Yes. Why do you doubt me? I told you there were wild animals around. That's why you're not to wander about on your own," said George.

Grace looked around. "Where is Dr. Leakey?"

Her father shrugged. "She's already eaten. She's apparently up well before anyone else in the camp."

Grace stood.

"Where are you going?" he asked.

"To work," she said.

"But you haven't had breakfast."

She ignored him and made her way to Dr. Leakey's workroom, where Matt growled at Brown Dog as they approached. She tapped on a wooden pole before entering. Dr. Leakey looked up from the other side of the high table, pushed her spectacles into place, and acknowledged the girl with an upward bob of her eyebrows.

"My father told me there was a cheetah in the camp this morning. Was it the one we saw yesterday?"

"Probably," said Dr. Leakey, her eyes on a wad of notes in front of her. "I got a better look at her today. Before Matt chased her off."

"Oh?"

"She's scrawny. People think cheetahs are always thin, but they're naturally muscular. Lean but muscly. That's why they're so fast. But this one is in poor condition and covered in lion-flies. She's in a bad way. Seems hungry and desperately thirsty. She was drinking from the dogs' water bowl."

Grace raised a hand to her mouth. "That's why she's here. Poor thing."

Dr. Leakey lifted her eyes again and looked at the girl. Her spectacles had slipped once more. "That's not all. She's wearing a large radio collar."

"Radio collar? What's that?" asked Grace, noticing how, while Dr. Leakey's eyes were always obviously blue, they seemed to change hue with her moods. Or was it the light? Like Lemagrut.

"It's a collar that emits a radio signal to allow people to track her. She must've been captured or perhaps raised by someone. Now they've released her but want to know where she goes. It's bloody ridiculous since she won't survive." Dr. Leakey scratched her head and picked up a dead half-smoked cigar. She looked at it, grimaced, and put it down. "The collar is massive, heavy. She depends on her speed to hunt and survive. It's like putting a weight belt on a sprinter and expecting him to win the race. She's handicapped."

Grace stared at her. "What can we do?"

Dr. Leakey rubbed her head again and shrugged.

"We have to do something," said the girl, approaching the table. "We—I mean, you—can't just let her die."

They looked at each other, silent for a moment. It was the first time their eyes had met since the previous day after the dogs had chased the cheetah. This time, though, Grace felt no awkwardness. This was something she was sure about. They *had* to save the cheetah. They needed to feed and water her. Find a way of removing the collar so that she could run, hunt, and survive.

"We'll have to confine Matt and Brown Dog," said Grace. "Tie them up.

Lock them away. Then we'll get water to her. Feed her somehow. I don't need to eat meat. She can have mine."

Dr. Leakey blinked and shook her head. Grace felt an unpleasant jolt. She was going to object to the idea of locking up the dogs. She was going to tell Grace she was being ridiculous. Cheetahs needed a great deal more meat than Grace would be offered in camp. What did Grace know about wild animals? How could they save her? Grace steeled herself to argue. She wasn't going to let this go. She was going to fight for the cheetah. But Dr. Leakey didn't argue. Instead, she smiled, and then, to Grace's amazement, she laughed.

"I see you've discovered what matters to you," she said.

Grace took a deep breath.

"Good," said Dr. Leakey, still chuckling. "But slow down. I've radioed several people in the region already. Put out the word about the cat. Let's find out where she comes from and who put the collar on her. It's possible they care about her. Perhaps the radio has failed and they've lost track of her. Hopefully, they'll come for her."

"But what if they're too late? She wouldn't have risked coming into the camp if she wasn't desperate. You said yourself she's thirsty and starving. Surely we can do something now," said Grace.

Dr. Leakey nodded. "Give it time. Things need time out here. She drank this morning. Cheetahs only need to drink every few days." She glanced at her watch. "You're early. Did you already have breakfast?"

Grace shook her head.

"Go, then. Eat. Drink. You're no good to me or the cheetah if you're hungry and thirsty. Have breakfast and come back. We've got lots to get through this morning. And if anyone knows anything about the cheetah, they'll radio it in," said Dr. Leakey.

The girl hesitated.

"Go!" said Dr. Leakey, as if admonishing her dogs.

The others had left, but Grace's father was still at the table when she returned to the dining room. He was a slow eater. Grace sat across from him and, as if by magic, a mug of tea and plate of porridge appeared before her.

"Thank you, Mr. Jackson," she called to the khakied back of the man who'd brought her breakfast as he returned to the kitchen.

George pushed the sugar bowl toward her. "Changed your mind, then?" he said.

Grace nodded, ignored the sugar, and took a sip of tea. It was spicier, tastier than what she was accustomed to. She wondered if it was a different kind of tea to what she typically drank in England or whether drinking tea in Africa made it seem better.

Her father folded his arms and leaned forward. "So, how are you finding it?" he asked.

"What?" she said, stirring her porridge without looking at him.

"The work. With Dr. Leakey," said George.

"Fine."

They were silent for several minutes while Grace ate and drank. She felt a cold, wet nudge on her bare calf. It was Brown Dog. She hadn't noticed that he'd followed her back to the dining room. She stroked his head.

"I'm glad you're working indoors," said George. "The sun is relentless. Even when you're not moving about much, it saps your energy. It's remarkable how she—Dr. Leakey, I mean—has withstood it all these years. She might be working inside now, but most of her work has been outside, hunting fossils, exploring, mapping out the excavations, digging."

"Why are we here if you hate the sun?" said Grace between mouthfuls.

"I don't hate it. I was simply saying it's fortunate that *you* don't have to work outside," he replied.

Grace put down her spoon and glared at him. "Because I don't like being outdoors? Is that what you think? Is that why you left me to take care of Mum? Because you thought I'd *like* to be cooped up in a tiny, airless flat that smelled of medicine and death all the time? Is that why you did it? Should I thank you?"

George swallowed. His face was pink and shiny. "It wasn't what I wanted. It wasn't my decision to leave. What do I have to do for you to believe me? To listen?" His voice was ragged, as if he was running rather than sitting at a table, drinking tea. "Your mother—"

But Grace wouldn't listen. "You can say what you like. I know what I saw. Mum's not around to disprove your lies," she said, standing.

"Why would I lie to you? All I want is for you to talk to me. To treat me as…like a father, your father," he argued.

"I'm here with you. At this precious place you *had* to see. That's what you wanted. Don't ask for more," said Grace, before turning and walking away.

Brown Dog trotted ahead, leading the way back to Dr. Leakey's workroom. The unexpected calm Grace had experienced when she'd left her hut—and found the dog and the sights, smells, and sounds of the camp welcoming—had disappeared with the cool of the early morning. She was angry again. Her father's clumsy attempt at small talk had riled her. She wished he'd leave her alone. There was nothing between them to rescue. She'd submitted to his imploring and come to Africa with him. However, she'd agreed to nothing more. All she wanted to do was to get the ten-day trip behind her, go back to England, and try to live a normal life without him.

Neither Dr. Leakey nor Matt was in the workroom when Grace arrived. She watched as Brown Dog lay down in the shade opposite the entrance. Even without Matt around to remind him, he understood his place. Grace oriented herself by glancing briefly at the table before she began sorting notebooks and papers, as instructed the previous evening. Some of the notes had been typed but most were handwritten. Grace read only what was necessary to enable her to allocate the documents onto the right piles. She'd initially wondered why Dr. Leakey hadn't insisted on a neater, more practical system while she and her colleagues had worked over the years. However, Grace soon saw that there *was* a system, a good one that suited the nature of the work. Dr. Leakey was much more organized than one might imagine when first seeing the multitude of boxes, trays, and piles of papers and books on the table and floor of the workroom.

There was a scuffle outside. It was Matt, who, tail high and shoulders rocking, was greeting Brown Dog. He had the swagger of a playground bully who never let his friends or enemies forget he was top dog. Brown Dog lowered his head and slapped his tail in the dust. Dr. Leakey walked in, pulling off her hat.

"Right! The cheetah," she said. "Her name is Lisa. She was hand reared."

"She's tame?" asked Grace, wondering why she was surprised; the animal was wearing a collar.

"Her mother was apparently killed by poachers, and she was raised by a couple who run a safari lodge in the western Serengeti. The authorities wouldn't let them keep her and said she must be released," said Dr. Leakey as she ran her fingers through her damp hair.

"But the collar," said Grace.

"She wasn't ready, so one of the men at a research farm studying cheetahs said he'd take her in and fit her with a collar so that he could keep track of her. The idea, I guess, was that he could make sure she was okay."

Grace snorted. "That clearly hasn't worked!"

"No. It sounds as if he's having problems with his tracking equipment, but even that's uncertain. His wife has just had a baby, and they're in Nairobi for a month or two. I suspect he was feeding Lisa or at least supplementing her meals."

"So you were unable to speak to the man. Did someone else tell you this?"

Dr. Leakey nodded. "His colleague assured me he'd pass on the message, but it's unlikely anything will happen for several weeks."

"We'll have to feed her," said Grace.

"I've asked Jackson to buy extra legs of beef when he goes for supplies tomorrow, but I'm not sure how we're going to make it work. There's no way the dogs will allow her in camp, and I have no doubt the dislike is mutual," mused Dr. Leakey.

"I'll take meat and water to her in the bush. Do you know which way she ran?" said Grace.

Dr. Leakey scowled. "Don't be ridiculous, girl. You can't drag a large hunk of meat into the wild, calling, 'Kitty, kitty,' in the hope of being helpful to anyone—not even the cheetah. Have you forgotten where you are?"

Grace felt herself redden. "Then we have to lock up the dogs."

"It's not ideal. Particularly since we have no idea when or, indeed, if she'll return. I don't want the dogs locked up all the time. That's not fair on any of us," said Dr. Leakey, her eyes on Matt.

"What if we place some water not too far from the camp and I keep watch? From somewhere safe. If I see Lisa approach, I'll run back and put the dogs away. So that she can at least drink. Then, when we have meat, perhaps we can do the same," said Grace, not bothering to disguise that she was breathless with excitement.

Dr. Leakey looked at her, nodding. "It's possible we might be able to get them used to one another gradually if we monitor them closely. I've seen stranger friendships develop between animals."

Grace smiled.

"Are you sure you're up to this?" asked Dr. Leakey. "Being on Lisa watch?"

The girl nodded. "I want to do it. I mean, I'll come back here and work as soon as we know she's had something to drink and eat."

"All right, but let's go and do a bit of scouting. We need to decide where she's most likely to come from and where you can safely keep watch."

She pulled her hat on and walked out of the office. Matt scrambled to his feet, and he and Grace followed. Brown Dog took his place at Grace's side. They'd only taken a few steps when Dr. Leakey stopped and turned around to face the girl.

"You have to assure me you will *not* wander off into the bush at any time. We'll agree where we'll leave the water and the place from which you can keep watch. You will not venture anywhere beyond that point. Is that clear?" she said.

"Yes, of course, Dr. Leakey," replied Grace.

The older woman didn't move. Her eyes searched Grace's. "I believe you mean that now, but I suspect you're stubborn, and at some point, you will quite possibly decide that you know better than I do, and you'll do something silly."

Grace tried to protest. "No, I—"

Dr. Leakey went on. "I know what it's like, thinking that people don't understand you, that they don't know what you want or what's best for you. Being young can be frustrating, and sometimes the frustration is blinding. It distorts your senses, and you do things impulsively. Sometimes you make choices simply because they're things others don't want you to do."

"I won't. I want to do this," said Grace, her hand resting on Brown Dog's head. "I've never wanted to do anything so badly."

Dr. Leakey sighed. "That's the problem."

CHAPTER 6

1932
54 Fulham Road, Kensington, London

THERE WAS NOTHING MARY WANTED MORE THAN TO EXPERIENCE AN EXCAVA-
tion in a foreign land. It wasn't just that she'd inherited her father's wanderlust;
she also wanted to work elsewhere. After two seasons at Hembury Fort and
continually hearing and reading about new excavations underway in places like
Greece, Greenland, New Mexico, Syria, and Turkey, the musty earth of Devon
seemed tame and familiar. Work had begun at the Roman city of Antioch,
where a team hoped to unearth Constantine's Great Octagonal Church and
perhaps even the imperial palace. In Troy, American Carl Blegen and his colleagues from the University of Cincinnati explored no less than forty-six levels
of building. Around the same time, excavations in Clovis, New Mexico, sought
clues to the prehistoric people believed to be responsible for amassing huge
piles of mammoth bones.

Mary accepted that, at nineteen, she still had much to learn from Miss
Liddell and others at Hembury Fort, but that didn't stop her from yearning
to appease her curiosity and to seek the earth's treasures in other places. She
was restless, wanted adventure, and longed to loosen her mother's reins on
her life. With every month, Cecilia's concern about her daughter's apparent

indifference to socializing with people of her own age and the absence of suitors deepened.

"If only you were a little more interested in your own life and not entirely preoccupied by the lives of prehistoric others, you might see how you're allowing your youth to fritter away. I admire how seriously you approach your career, and indeed, you clearly have the aptitude for it, but must you be so single-minded? It's not normal," she said one morning when Mary turned down another proposition regarding an outing with a "suitable young man."

"I already have plans with Gertrude," said Mary.

"Another talk, I suppose," said Cecilia. "But surely that won't take you into the evening. You could come home, change, and be ready to go out again. I know you'll hit it off with this young man."

"The lecture will be followed by dinner. I'll be out all evening."

Working with Gertrude Caton-Thompson hadn't resulted in a trip to Egypt, as Mary had fantasized it might. However, she couldn't deny the many other advantages of their association, which, despite the twenty-five-year age difference, had quickly evolved into a friendship. So pleased was Gertrude with the drawings Mary produced for *The Desert Fayum* and so taken was she by the girl's interest in and grasp of archaeology that she took it upon herself to help further Mary's career in every way she could. She invited her to events; lent her books, papers, and journals; and introduced her to others in the field.

Gertrude was a member of the Royal Anthropological Institute, which, on this occasion, had invited Kenyan-born Dr. Louis Leakey to address its members about the Paleolithic material and stone tools he'd discovered in East Africa. The son of British missionaries, thirty-year-old Dr. Leakey was educated at the University of Cambridge, to which he'd recently returned, having received a postgraduate research fellowship at St. John's College. His plans to look for early man in Africa were considered entirely misguided by most academics, who believed Europe to be a more likely location for the origins of humans. However, Dr. Leakey had begun his research in East Africa, the results of which he was to include in his book, *Adam's Ancestors,* for which, said Gertrude, he needed illustrations.

"Come to his lecture with me," she proposed. "There's a dinner at the restaurant next door afterward. I could arrange for you to sit next to him."

Mary wrinkled her nose. "Really? Why? Surely he should sit alongside someone senior?"

"Nonsense. He's looking for an illustrator. You're the perfect person for the job. It'll be a good way to get acquainted and talk about the work," said Gertrude.

So it was that Mary sat in the second row alongside her friend when Louis Leakey strode onto the stage and took his place behind the lectern at the Royal Anthropological Institute in Bedford Square. He was tall and lean, with a tanned, angular face; a small rectangular mustache; and a glossy, dark head of hair, which—because he frequently ran his fingers through it—pointed upward as if growing toward the light. Mary's initial impression was that, despite his origins, leathery skin, and disorderly hair, he was as tame as any Englishman. Although she had no idea what she might've expected, his accent carried nothing of Africa in it, and the poise with which he launched into his speech gave no sense of him belonging anywhere but in London.

It wasn't long, though, as Dr. Leakey entertained the audience with tales of his childhood in Kenya and knowledge of the Kikuyu people, that Mary felt drawn to him. He was barely a teenager, he said, when he built and lived in his own Kikuyu-style hut, which he filled with natural objects like animal bones, birds' feathers and eggs, and curiously shaped stones found in the bush. It wasn't just that Mary pictured him assessing his treasures the way she and her father had at Laugerie Haute, but also how enthusiastic he was about Africa and his life there that appealed to her. He described the fossil hunting he'd undertaken in East Africa, traversing the wilderness where no roads or railways existed and camping in remote, dangerous places. It was all worth it, he said, because the archaeological promise was unprecedented. He told of the expedition he'd led the year before to Olduvai Gorge in the Great Rift Valley, between the Ngorongoro Crater and the Serengeti. Formed about thirty thousand years ago after aggressive geological activity and storms, the gorge, he insisted, was littered with fossils and tools. It was here in 1913 that German geologist Professor Hans Reck had found a human skeleton, which Reck believed dated back to the Lower Pleistocene period.

Dr. Leakey spoke of how elephants, giraffes, leopards, lions, wildebeests, and other types of wild animals Mary hadn't heard of wandered through their camps. He described the intensity of the sun and how the local people appeared so silently and suddenly, it was as if they'd traveled on the breeze. Dr. Leakey was fluent in Kikuyu, which he demonstrated by rattling off an account of the flamingos that fed on Lake Elmenteita in the Great Rift Valley, where he'd excavated a site called Gamble's Cave. Mary forgot about Egypt, Greece, New Mexico, and Troy. Instead, she pictured a bushy-maned lion sauntering into the shallows of the lake to drink as a flock of flamingos took flight in a pink cloud. She'd never wanted to be anywhere else so badly.

Without thinking, she leaned forward, placed her elbows on her knees, and rested her chin on the palms of her hands. The movement caught Dr. Leakey's attention, and he glanced at her. Their eyes met briefly. His mouth twitched in a tiny smile, but he continued speaking, his voice smooth and low. Mary grew warm, and as she straightened and leaned back, she felt Gertrude's eyes on her.

A while later, after Dr. Leakey had accepted the audience's applause with a wide smile and several theatrical bows, Gertrude drew alongside Mary as they made their way to the restaurant. "We can swap seats if you'd like," she said.

Mary looked straight ahead. "No, it's all right. I'd like to ask him about his book."

Gertrude was silent as they entered the restaurant and took their places—Mary alongside Dr. Leakey and her friend several places to her right, on the other side of the table.

It *was* all right. Mary wasn't the only one who'd found Dr. Leakey intriguing. There were questions and comments from everyone seated within earshot of him that evening. He answered eloquently and with good humor. He was generous with his attention, but Mary couldn't help noticing that whenever possible, he directed his conversation to her. However, there was nothing coy about it. Instead, like Gertrude had from the moment they met, Dr. Leakey spoke to Mary as a colleague and an equal. She felt foolish for having imagined he'd singled her out in the audience earlier and might've found her attractive. Even so, she avoided looking down the table, for fear of catching Gertrude's eye.

Later, after coffee was served, people began leaving. With the chair on the other side of him empty, Dr. Leakey turned to give Mary his full attention. "It's been a pleasure to meet you, Miss Nicol. Do you mind, since we're alone now, if we dispense of the formalities? I'm Louis. Can I call you Mary?"

She nodded. He took her hand from where it rested on the table and made a show of shaking it, holding it a moment longer than what might be appropriately playful. He gazed into her eyes. Mary looked away and pulled her hand from his. She felt lightheaded.

Louis cleared his throat as if he, too, was unsettled. Perhaps she hadn't been mistaken after all.

"Before you disappear back onto the streets of London, I have something to ask you. I believe you're an accomplished artist," he said.

Mary looked at him. It had seemed impossible to raise the subject without sounding as if she was soliciting work earlier.

"Yes, I've done some drawings," she said.

He gave a short laugh. "Some drawings? You've illustrated for Dorothy Liddell and worked on Dr. Caton-Thompson's book. From all accounts, you're highly accomplished." She didn't respond. "I'm looking for someone to illustrate my book. Can I tell you about it?"

Without waiting for her reply, Louis described *Adam's Ancestors* and the drawings it required. Mary gave no indication that she already knew about the book. Would she take on the job, he asked?

"Don't you want to see samples of my work?" she said.

He shrugged, looking relieved, as if she might've turned him down. "If they're good enough for Miss Liddell and Dr. Caton-Thompson, I have no doubt they're good enough for me. I'll be going back to Cambridge on Friday and could arrange to get some specimens to you within the next week."

They'd agreed that Louis would have a package delivered to the institute, where Mary would collect it, when Gertrude appeared on the other side of the table. "Mr. Wyatt has offered us a lift home in his motorcar," she said, giving Mary a tight smile.

Mary and Louis stood. He held out his hand as if to shake hers once more. Mary fiddled with the shawl around her shoulders, pretending not to have noticed his gesture.

"Goodbye, Dr. Leakey. I'll let you know how things are going when I have the specimens," she said.

He tilted his head to the side, as if amused. "Goodbye Miss Nicol, Dr. Caton-Thompson."

As they made their way out, Gertrude touched Mary's elbow and leaned toward her.

"He's married and has a child," she said in a low voice.

Mary tugged her shawl once more. "Should I not illustrate his book because he has a wife and family?" she asked.

Gertrude sighed. "That's not what I'm saying."

For the first time, Mary recognized something of her mother in her friend.

CHAPTER 7

———◉———

1983
Olduvai Gorge, Tanzania

GRACE ASSUMED THAT ONCE SHE AND DR. LEAKEY HAD AGREED ON WHERE they'd leave the water and where Grace would sit to keep watch for the cheetah, Dr. Leakey would return to her workroom. However, as she half filled a dented steel bucket with water, Grace heard her ask Mr. Jackson to keep Matt and Brown Dog in the kitchen. Perhaps she wanted to ensure that Grace placed the water just so and was safely lodged at the lookout before she left, thought Grace. But, having helped the girl lug the bucket up the sandy knoll over which she'd seen Lisa disappear earlier, Dr. Leakey led the way to the lookout spot they'd identified.

"Yes, this is perfect," she said, stepping into the dappled shade of a small acacia tree about sixty yards from the bucket. "We won't miss her, regardless of where she comes from."

The view was like the one from Dr. Leakey's workroom, looking south across the gorge toward Lemagrut. Dr. Leakey's hut also faced the old volcano. Unlike the other small cabins, which were constructed of stone, her accommodation was a large rectangular structure made of prefabricated material and located a few yards from her workroom. Its glazed windows and wide veranda were protected by a thatch roof angled away from the rest of the camp and looking toward the volcano. Lemagrut was something of an idol to Dr. Leakey, an effigy of sorts, thought Grace.

The metal bucket, though dull with age, was distinctly out of place on the bald hillside. They'd agreed that they'd lure the cat with water and then, depending on how she behaved, decide where to feed her.

Grace sat, her back resting against the rough bark of the tree. The day had grown warm, and with the sun higher and the canopy of the tree small, the shade was skimpy.

"I'll let you know the moment I spot her," she said.

Dr. Leakey adjusted her hat but, instead of returning to camp, lowered herself to sit alongside Grace, shifting her buttocks in the sand so that she could also lean against the tree. Their shoulders were almost touching. Grace inhaled, trying to make herself smaller. She itched to edge away.

"Did I tell you why she's called Lisa?" said Dr. Leakey.

"No."

"Her rescuer is apparently an Elvis fan." She glanced at Grace. "You know who Elvis was, don't you?"

"Yes, the singer. His daughter's name is Lisa," replied Grace, tempted to add that she was surprised Dr. Leakey knew who he was.

Dr. Leakey brushed an ant from her trouser leg. "I didn't know that until I asked for an explanation from the man at the research center this morning."

Grace wondered why it mattered. The air was dusty and hot, with a trace of sweat and tobacco. She tipped her head back against the tree, imagining she might somehow draw cool relief from it. Something sharp poked her flesh behind her knee where her shorts ended. She wished she could move and that Dr. Leakey would go. It wasn't so much that she wanted to be alone but rather that it seemed Dr. Leakey didn't trust her to carry out the simple tasks of watching for the cat and letting her know when she appeared. She didn't care about an Elvis fan in Africa or why it was of any consequence that he should name a cheetah Lisa. Dr. Leakey might've read her thoughts.

"I asked because names can tell you a great deal. Not about the one who is named—unless they name themselves—but about whoever named them. In paleoanthropology, archaeology, like everything else, giving something a name doesn't necessarily mean you understand, but it can help identify and classify it. There are clues in names. Knowing how Lisa's name came about could shed some light on who found her and how they treated her, which in turn will affect what she thinks of us and how she might behave when we approach her," she said.

That naming someone or something could say so much had never occurred to Grace. She couldn't help but be intrigued. "So, she's called Lisa because the person who found her likes Elvis music. What can we expect from her, then?"

Dr. Leakey looked at her, a hint of a smile on her lips. "I've never felt that interpretation was my job. I uncover things, find the treasures, take them out as carefully as possible, and present them to others to interpret. Mostly, I like to find fossils, stone tools, ancient footprints, but today's find is Lisa's name. What do you make of it?" she asked.

Grace had heard her father discussing Mary Leakey with a colleague. The other man had warned George that she was "a woman of few words" and that she could be "a terse communicator." Yet here she was, chatting about Elvis and why a stranger named the cheetah Lisa.

The girl stared at the bucket and willed the cat to appear. Then it came to her. "It's possible Lisa's rescuer gave her the name because, like Elvis's daughter when he died, the cub had lost a parent. He might be an Elvis fan, but he's probably also kind. I mean, he didn't save her because of Elvis. He saved her because he cared," she said, gazing into the distance.

Dr. Leakey didn't respond. Grace turned and looked at her. "And anyway," she added, "Lisa wouldn't have come to the camp if she didn't trust humans."

"No, but she's desperate. She has no choice."

"I suppose we're just going to have to wait and find out," said Grace.

"You mean, *you're* going to have to wait. I've got work to do," said Dr. Leakey. She rolled onto her side and, using the tree for support, slowly got to her feet.

As Grace watched her walk away, she bent her leg and swept a hand over her flesh, brushing off the tiny stones embedded there. She glanced at the spot vacated by Dr. Leakey, where the ground seemed smoother and the shade denser. As she raised herself to move, her stomach emitted a tiny rumble. It wasn't quite lunchtime yet, but she was hungry. Did Dr. Leakey expect her to keep watch all day without a break? Surely not. She'd need to eat and drink. But the woman's moods were unpredictable, and Grace dared not assume anything.

She fixed her eyes on the bucket. Perhaps if she concentrated hard enough, the powers of her mind would draw Lisa out from wherever she was to the water. Grace remembered watching a television show with her mother, during which a woman had explained how it was possible to communicate with animals telepathically.

"Acknowledge what you see. Trust your imagination. The images there will come from both you and the animal," the woman had said.

Her mother had scoffed and labeled her "flaky," but now Grace pictured the cheetah approaching the bucket. If anything, it helped take her mind off her hunger, and the nagging feeling that she'd been taken advantage of—again.

A pair of white-necked ravens swooped into view and landed several yards from the bucket. Turning his head left and right, the larger of the two swaggered toward the water. His self-assured stride reminded Grace of Dr. Leakey's assertive pace. She and the ravens knew they belonged at Olduvai.

The bird hopped onto the side of the bucket, giving Grace a clear view of his glossy black feathers and heavy bill. He cocked his head and peered into the water before emitting a triumphant "krrraw." His mate approached with the same scapula-swinging strut and sprang onto the opposite ledge. As one kept watch, the other tipped forward to drink. They took turns until they'd had their fill, when they launched themselves into the sky and glided away. How lovely to have someone to watch out for you like that, thought Grace.

She wasn't sure when she'd realized her parents were unhappy. It might've been shortly after her twelfth birthday, when her mother first showed signs of being unwell. Or perhaps that was the final crack that brought the facade crashing down.

Grace was accustomed to George being away from home for weeks—months, even. She couldn't remember a time in her young life that he hadn't traveled to work at various digs in distant places. He'd also undertaken teaching jobs in other towns, which meant he was only home for weekends. In his absence, life went on as usual in Cambridge for Eleanor and Grace. The girl went to school, and her mother did whatever her job at the publishing company required of her. Some fathers were always home, but Grace's was not.

That's just how it was. She'd believed her mother accepted it as normal too. That's why it came as a shock to her when, arriving home from school one afternoon, she stepped into the hallway and heard her mother say loudly from the kitchen, "I don't want to go over it again. We've tried. You can't let it go. Why are you making such a scene? You're never with us anyway!"

She'd placed her bag on the floor and crouched to pet Watson. Grace assumed, given where her mother was and the volume at which she was speaking, that she was on the telephone. The girl didn't know her father was home until she stepped into the kitchen and saw him sitting at the table, his head in his hands. He'd leaped to his feet when he saw her.

"Hey! You're home early," he said, wrapping her in his arms.

Grace stiffened. She'd always loved having her father home. The house was different, enlivened, from the moment he appeared. He'd absent-mindedly push aside his wife's embroidered doilies and delicate ornaments to make room for his piles of papers, books, and other dusty paraphernalia. Even when it was gray and wet outside, he had a way of breezing in and warming the place, as if bringing with him invisible sunshine. But this time was different. His chirpy greeting didn't ring true, and his hug seemed desperate. Grace looked over his shoulder at her mother. She was leaning against a cupboard, her arms folded across her chest and her expression cold.

Although her parents tried to pretend otherwise when Grace was within earshot, she knew that the tension between them intensified during the days that followed. They spoke in low, urgent voices behind closed doors, and several times when she and her mother were in a room together and her father appeared, Eleanor left the room. Now and then, Grace almost demanded to know what was going on. But if they told her and it was as serious as she feared, there'd be no going back. If she didn't know the details, she could imagine the problem might disappear. It didn't.

When she returned from school a week or two later, her mother said her father had gone and wouldn't be returning to live with them. They'd sell the house and move to a place called Tewkesbury.

"Tewkesbury. Where's that?" said Grace.

"It's in Gloucestershire. I've found a flat for us there," said her mother, not looking at her.

Grace was surprised by how quickly her tears came and how plentiful they were. She didn't remember sinking to the floor, but there she found herself, arms around the corgi.

"A flat! But we must have a garden for Watson," she'd wailed.

The thought of not being able to play outside with the dog whenever she wanted was unbearable. She had no idea how bad things were to become.

Had her mother tried to console her? She couldn't remember but realized now that it was unlikely. She'd learned later that Eleanor already knew how ill she was and had a good idea of what was to come. Her mother hadn't cared about Watson. Or Grace. She'd had other, more serious things to worry about. Nor was her father concerned about her. He'd left without trying to explain why. And here she was, she thought, pulling her legs out of the sun; still alone.

"No sign of her, then," came a voice.

Grace looked up. It was Dr. Leakey. She held out a tin mug and plate.

"It's lunch," she added. "I thought Jackson would prepare a sandwich for you, but he insists you need a proper meal."

The girl realized she was staring at the food as if unfamiliar with the concept. "Thank you," she said, taking the items.

"I realize it's early, but I have to meet your father and some others for a discussion during lunch, so," she said with a shrug.

"A pair of ravens drank from the bucket," said Grace, contemplating the chicken, rice, and tinned peas on her plate.

"Of course they did," said Dr. Leakey. She took a knife and fork wrapped in a paper napkin from her trouser pocket and handed it to the girl. "They don't miss a thing. Don't be surprised if they come back with their friends for another drink."

"I thought it was a good sign," said Grace, though she hadn't considered it until now. "If Lisa was watching the birds, she'd see that it's safe to approach the bucket."

"If Lisa is thirsty enough, she'll drink."

"But what if she's run away? Found water elsewhere?"

"Oh, she's here, all right. I think she's been staking us out for a while."

"But what about the dogs? Will you let them out now?" asked Grace.

"Yes. That's what we agreed. They'll stay with me while I work. We'll only lock them up when necessary, when the cat appears. They believe this is their territory, and the dogs take precedence as far as I'm concerned."

Grace took a long drink of water and looked at the plate again, eager to begin eating but also unexpectedly pleased to have Dr. Leakey with her again. "I wonder what'll ultimately persuade Lisa to risk approaching the camp once more?"

"Thirst. Hunger. Two things impossible to ignore. A desperate need to survive that is deeply ingrained in her, as it is for all living things," said Dr. Leakey, who stood, hands on hips, staring into the distance.

She was once again looking at the volcano, which seemed more distant and pastel than it had earlier. Even the great Lemagrut was browbeaten by the midday sun.

Dr. Leakey continued. "What compels us to take risks? I don't know. Do you?" She glanced at Grace but didn't wait for her to respond. "I can't explain why I took the greatest risk of my life, made an enormous decision that would change everything for me forever, even though it was fifty years ago, and I've had time and cause to contemplate the wisdom of it. All I know is that if I hadn't, I wouldn't be here, and that would be a pity." She gave Grace a tiny nod. "I must get back. Enjoy your lunch."

CHAPTER 8

1933
Leicester, England

DID MARY HAVE AN INKLING OF WHAT SHE MIGHT BE GETTING INTO THAT summer when, while working on Louis Leakey's drawings, they exchanged an endless stream of letters? Certainly it soon occurred to her that his letters were more frequent than the work demanded. It might also have been telling that she replied immediately. However, the content was innocuous and gave no hint of what was to follow.

They discussed particulars about the drawings, which presented Mary with something of a challenge at first. The African hand axes Louis had brought from East Africa were shaped from volcanic rocks and not flint like the tools she'd previously sketched. The stones' unusual surfaces and textures meant Mary had to master a new technique. Before finalizing it, she sent several separate samples of drawings to him. Louis responded to each individually. While they soon agreed on a suitable method, the pace of their letters never abated. If anything, it increased. In addition, each successive missive contained a few more friendly snippets of news unrelated to the illustrations.

"Did you read about the find at Falkirk?"

"What are your thoughts about the misidentification of the Grace Dieu?"

"I'm hoping to visit Tintagel Castle when excavations commence. What about you?"

The tone was pleasant and warm but, as Mary might've contended if challenged, nothing more. Had anyone—her mother, even—read any of the letters, to or from, Mary was certain they'd see no indication that she and Louis were anything more than colleagues. After all, that is what they were. However, it didn't explain why, having not met up since their introduction, Mary immediately registered to attend the conference organized by the British Association for the Advancement of Science in Leicester in September when Louis wrote that, given the number of relevant archaeology and geology sessions on the program, he'd be there.

She saw him as she trailed the many men and few women out of the De Montfort Hall after the conference's opening address. Who could miss him, as Louis stood, as conspicuous as a statue in a town square, on the manicured lawn between two pink-and-white flower beds directly in front of the main doors? Their eyes met over the heads of the crowd. Louis smiled widely, raised his arm, and waved in the manner of someone accustomed to drawing attention. Mary's pulse quickened. Two men ahead of her intercepted Louis's greeting and turned to look at her. She felt their eyes on her and chastised herself for the nudge of shame she experienced. She had nothing to be ashamed of. Why shouldn't a thirty-year-old anthropologist be pleased to see the twenty-year-old illustrator who was working on his book?

Mary lifted her chin and glared at the men. "Excuse me," she said as she jostled past them and strode toward Louis.

He placed his hands on the small of his back to expand his shoulders and chest, tilted his head, and looked at her, his eyes crinkling. He had the tall, lean, and broad-shouldered physique of a sportsman. She wondered how it was possible that, despite having been in Cambridge for months, his skin had retained the glow of the sun. Was that what happened when you were born and raised in Africa?

"There you are," he said. "Splendid."

"Yes," she replied, suddenly aware that she was trembling. She felt it in her breathing and heard it in her voice. She glanced down, afraid that he might detect her quivering and of what he might see in her eyes. Mary didn't recognize the sensation or understand it, but he, she realized, probably would.

"Come," said Louis, his hand on her elbow. "You look like you need a cup of tea, and I know where to get one."

Later, Mary told herself that she and Louis were more-or-less inseparable during the conference from the moment she responded to his wave because they were working together on his book and shared an insatiable interest in the study of human origins. Of course, it wasn't strictly true.

While in his letters, Louis had remained largely within the bounds of matters pertaining to their work and field, he seemed eager—impatient, even—for Mary to get to know him personally when they were together at the conference.

"You mentioned in one of your letters how extraordinary it is that I've already undertaken so many expeditions in Africa," he said as he placed a cup of tea on the table in front of her that first morning. "Did you know I had an injury to thank for that?"

She didn't, she said, noticing what large hands and long fingers he had.

Louis explained how, after having grown up and undergone most of his early education in Kenya, he'd attended a private school in Weymouth in Dorset.

"I found it difficult, being at school in Britain," he said. "My parents intended sending me earlier, but the war got in the way. Although I was educated by my father and various tutors in Kenya, I hadn't experienced the traditions and rules of formal schooling. I missed the freedom of Africa and, for a while, couldn't think of anything but getting back there."

Mary thought fleetingly of her school days and believed she understood how he might've felt—not that she would speak freely of her experience of school. Louis continued, saying that he eventually accepted that it was important to complete his education in Britain and, after Weymouth, he'd enrolled at St. John's, his father's old college at Cambridge.

"I thought I'd become a missionary like my father but decided to study anthropology. It was going well until, in my second year, I took a thumping in a game of rugby."

Ah, rugby, thought Mary. That explained his athletic physique.

Louis went on. "The headaches were so bad that I couldn't concentrate. The doctor advised a year away from my studies. The problem was, I was twenty and not ill enough to want to stay still. Also, I itched to get back to Africa. I'd begun collecting stone tools in Kenya when I was a boy. I think I was thirteen when I decided I had to learn about the Stone Age men who'd lived there. Everyone's obsessed with finding out about our forebears everywhere else, but I believe we originated in Africa. When I heard that the British Museum of Natural History was planning a fossil-hunting expedition to Tanganyika, I met the director, hoping to persuade him to agree that I should go along. It was fortuitous that no one else on the tour had ever been to Africa, and I was asked to lead the expedition."

Mary recalled how she'd sat at her desk in her bedroom on Fulham Road and rallied the nerve to apply to work with Dorothy Liddell at the age of seventeen. Even if her resourcefulness had only got her as far as Devon, it was comparable. She might mention it if he asked, she thought. He didn't, and as Louis described how, after the expedition with the British Museum, he'd returned to Cambridge to complete his degree with the realization that he'd not preach the Bible but rather direct his energy to studying man's origins in Africa, Mary forgot the thought. He told her how, after his graduation, he organized his first exploration of East African to Nakuru, Kenya.

"Sounds impressive, wouldn't you say?" he asked, smiling. "Actually, there were just two of us. A fellow graduate and I—but goodness gracious, it was great fun."

She knew, because of the illustrations she'd done for him, how he'd excavated in Kenya again two years later and found the Later Stone Age bones and artifacts that provided the materials for his book. Mary also knew, having listened to him in London, how he'd gone to Olduvai Gorge with Professor Reck. What she didn't know, and what Louis didn't tell her, was when and where he'd met his wife. The only reference to him being married that she had at that point was Gertrude's veiled caution after she'd orchestrated their meeting. But it didn't matter that he didn't speak of his family, Mary told herself. They were simply colleagues getting to know each other at a conference.

Above all, she was fascinated by Louis's argument that it was

Africa—not Europe or Asia, as other scientists insisted—that was the birth-place of humankind.

"You know, I'm sure, about the fragments of human skulls I found in Kenya, near Kanjera and Kanam last year?" he asked.

She nodded. Gertrude had told her how Louis had dated the Kanam find to the Early Pleistocene and hastily and confidently claimed it belonged to a true ancestor of modern man. She'd also mentioned how he'd found a fossilized jaw at Kanam, which he dated even earlier.

"Then you also know about the skeptics," said Louis, his attitude somber for the first time since they'd met.

Mary gave another nod, small enough to imply she wasn't swayed by their views. She knew that both of Louis's claims had been met with misgivings, with some saying he was too hasty in his proclamations and calling for further geological evidence. She hadn't given it a great deal of thought previously but was now eager for Louis to be correct.

"Tell me more about your childhood in Kenya," she said.

Louis rested his arms on the table and leaned forward. He'd removed his jacket and rolled up his shirtsleeves. Mary glanced at his forearms, where a sprinkling of sun-bleached hairs bristled against his tanned skin. He cleared his throat quietly. She looked up to see him watching her, his head tipped to one side as if amused.

"Well?" she said, hoping her demanding tone might disguise how self-conscious she felt.

The sparkle that had dimmed when he referred to "the skeptics" was restored as Louis described how he was born and raised at Kabete Mission near Nairobi. Although he had two older sisters and a younger brother, Louis spent more time playing with Kikuyu children than with his siblings. He learned to hunt and how to speak Kikuyu from his friends. When he was thirteen, he was initiated as a member of the Kikuyu community.

"What did that entail?" asked Mary.

He narrowed his eyes and replied, "I was sworn to secrecy. I'll take you there one day, Mary, and perhaps you'll see what it means to be a Kikuyu."

Her neck and face grew warm. She lifted her cup, only to discover it empty.

"Shall I get you some more?" asked Louis, his eyes on hers.

"No. Thank you," she replied, angry at herself for being flustered. "You spoke about lions during your lecture. What other large cats have you encountered?"

To her surprise, Mary's relative inexperience did not discourage Louis. In fact, it may have done the opposite. Perhaps, she thought, he recognized himself in her. Her readiness for travel and adventure, and her curiosity and eagerness to work and discover were obvious. However, as fascinated as she was by Louis's knowledge and confidence and the rich, varied life he led, she wasn't afraid to challenge his opinions. He was impressed by her arguments.

"I'm beginning to believe you're the first twenty-year-old intellectual I've ever met," he teased, after conceding a particularly strenuous debate.

"Intellectual? Me?" said Mary. "What do you mean by that?"

"Well, you know how one defines an intellectual, don't you?" asked Louis. She didn't.

"An intellectual is a person who always thinks they're right but is difficult to prove wrong," he said.

Mary wasn't amused. "I don't always think I'm right. I simply want to be sure of the facts," she said.

Louis threw back his head and roared with laughter. She didn't understand why he found her comment so funny, but his glee was like sunshine on her face after a stretch of rainy days.

They spent every day of the conference together, attending talks and discussing them afterward over countless cups of tea, at luncheons, dinners, and other social rendezvous. However, every night they returned to their separate lodgings without, as Mary's mother might say, "contravening any improprieties." While Louis occasionally placed his hand lightly and briefly on Mary's elbow as they walked, he didn't touch her otherwise. However, it didn't matter that their relationship was physically chaste; Mary knew and believed Louis did, too, that it was only a matter of time before that would change.

When the event ended, they agreed Mary would draw more for Louis. The illustrations for *Adam's Ancestors* were complete, but Louis had begun work on another book, *The Stone Age Races of Kenya*. The materials for this were at the British Museum in London, where they'd meet the following week. Without saying as much, it was as if arranging to meet again settled the matter: they would be lovers.

Mary thought of little else as she boarded the train in Leicester to return to London. As was her custom, she chose a place alongside a window. Once seated, she opened her notebook, meaning to make sense of what she'd written during the conference, but her mind was on Louis. She closed the book and glanced around the carriage, wondering if it was possible others recognized how she'd changed. Of course, they were strangers, but wasn't it obvious to all how being with Louis had altered her?

She pictured Louis—hands on his hips, head tilted, and eyes sparkling. The way he'd stood as she'd approached him in the gardens. She'd never forget the image of him waiting there for her and how she'd felt when their eyes met. No one had ever looked at her like that. She sighed. What had happened to her?

Mary recalled how, a few weeks previously, she'd scoffed when her mother described a woman she knew as having "fallen for" a man. She'd been "swept off her feet," Cecilia insisted. What a fainthearted namby-pamby to be so thoroughly beguiled by another person, Mary had thought at the time. Now she wondered if that was what had happened to her. Had she fallen for Louis? Been swept off her feet by him? No. It wasn't like that. What they felt—whatever it was—was mutual. They recognized what they wanted in each other. Their ambitions, interests, and desires were mirror images. There was no sweeping or falling involved. It wasn't possible, she thought; they were scientists, not idealists. She and Louis were meant to be together. It was a calming thought, which made her a little sleepy. Then she heard the cry.

She hadn't noticed a baby in the carriage earlier. In fact, Mary rarely noticed babies until they demanded attention by bellowing. This one sounded as if he'd been startled awake by news to the effect that he'd never be fed again. The noise began as a desperate combination of loud gasps and cries and settled into an eardrum-piercing wail. Mary, alert now, looked across the carriage. A short woman with uncombed hair and a misbuttoned cardigan paced a few steps up and down the aisle, jiggling the keening infant against her shoulder. The woman's head was bowed as if in shame. She was making shushing sounds, which the baby ignored. Mary wished the mother would try something else and was wondering how she might suggest as much when she noticed a little boy perched on the edge of his seat nearby. He was glaring at Mary, and when their eyes met, he stuck out his tongue. Mary was shocked. The boy, it appeared, also belonged to the woman with the bawling baby. He'd recognized Mary's disapproval of his mother and sibling. She looked away, thinking for the first time about Louis's wife and child.

He and Mary had been together at the conference for almost five days, during which their conversation never lulled. Yet Louis hadn't mentioned his family. She'd been grateful. What was there to say? However, as they'd made their way into a lecture room one morning, Mary had overheard a man ask Louis how Frida and "the little one" were. He'd responded that they were well, but Mary quickly moved away to avoid hearing any further details. She didn't want to think about Louis's family. She'd rather pretend he didn't have a wife and child. Now, though, the little boy in the train, with his pink tongue and accusing look, had forced her to face the truth.

Mary turned to the window once more. She couldn't stop herself from imagining how she might've felt if her father had left her and her mother. The thought made her angry. *He* wouldn't have done that. They were a happy family. It was different for Louis. He wouldn't risk his marriage if he was content. It wasn't her fault or his that they'd met after he was married and had a child. They shouldn't have to sacrifice their happiness because he'd made a mistake. Would he risk what he had for her, she wondered? What would she be risking? Whatever it was, it was worth it. It had been only a week, but she couldn't imagine life without Louis. She'd risk whatever necessary to be with him. Would he do the same for her?

The wailing intensified again. Mary pressed her ear against the window. She wanted to put her hand over her other ear but didn't, for fear of what the little boy might think if he noticed. In that instant, she knew she had to talk to Louis about his wife and child when they next met. She had to be sure he knew what he wanted.

The four days that followed seemed interminable to Mary. She took Fussy and Bungey on extra-long walks twice a day and, in between, tried to be civil to her mother, who, noting her daughter's gloomy mood, concluded the conference was to blame.

"You should've cut it short if it was such a miserable affair," said Cecilia. "Why didn't you come home earlier?"

Mary shrugged and went to her room, saying she needed to work on some illustrations. In fact, she lay on her bed and stared at the ceiling, her thoughts consumed by Louis and what she'd say to him when they met in Bloomsbury. Mostly she thought about how he might respond. What if he'd changed his mind about her? Perhaps he'd experienced a similar prick of conscience to what she had when they parted. Or maybe when he arrived home, he realized he wasn't as unhappy in his marriage as he'd thought. She ignored the fact that Louis hadn't suggested to her that he was dissatisfied with Frida. But he must be. Otherwise, why would he have looked at Mary the way he did, paid her the kind of attention he had every day for five days, and made it clear he wanted to be with her? She wished she could see him immediately and stop torturing herself with her thoughts.

Finally, the day arrived. Mary was at the museum more than an hour early. She'd look around to pass the time, she thought. However, nothing could hold her attention, and she made her way through several of the long, dark corridors and up a flight of stairs to the Department of British and Mediaeval Antiquities workroom Louis shared with two archaeologists, with more than forty minutes to go. The door to the room was closed, and there was no sign of anyone anywhere. Mary sat on a bench in the passageway. It was a cool morning, and the polished wood was hard and cold against her legs. As always, she carried a book in her handbag, but she knew it would be useless to try to read. If the days had dragged since leaving Leicester, the minutes seemed to have stopped altogether now.

She hadn't been there long when Mary heard footsteps on the stairs. Could Louis also be early? Perhaps he was as impatient as she was. She caught her breath. However, as they reached the top of the stairs and stepped onto the wooden floor, she recognized that the footsteps were those of someone wearing heels. Mary leaned against the wall and watched as the figure drew closer.

There was something familiar about the slight frame, brisk walk, and the tan two-piece outfit with its pleated skirt and single-breasted jacket.

"Gertrude!"

"Mary?"

Gertrude had been traveling for several weeks. Mary hadn't realized she'd returned and certainly didn't expect to see her in the museum. They spoke simultaneously.

"What are you—"

"You're back. I didn't—"

Mary smiled and gestured that Gertrude should continue. Her friend told her she'd returned a few days earlier and that she was there to meet a colleague.

"You have a meeting too?" she asked Mary.

"Yes," she replied, glancing at the door. "I'm a little early."

Gertrude looked at the door and then at Mary, her brow wrinkled. She seemed to anticipate Mary would explain whom she was to meet. She should have. There was nothing wrong with her saying that she was meeting Louis to discuss more illustrations. Instead, she felt herself redden and looked down.

"Well," said Gertrude. "I'd better get on. I'll see you next week."

The next set of footsteps, which came only a few minutes after Gertrude left, were Louis's. When he saw Mary, he broke into a trot. Even in the dim light of the museum, he seemed to glow. She stood, her heart pounding. As he approached, Louis opened his arms. Mary looked up and down the passageway, shaking her head.

"Of course," he said, his smile wide.

He fumbled in his pocket, drew out a key, and unlocked and opened the door. Mary stood, frozen in place. If she went inside where they'd be alone, she'd be able to say all the things she'd been rehearsing for days. She'd insist they talk about what was happening. But if she went inside, she wasn't sure she'd have the strength to insist upon anything.

"Come," he said, holding open the door.

She went into the room. Louis turned the lock and followed. She faced him. He stood and looked at her, his eyes sweeping the full length of her body.

"I've thought of nothing but you for days," he said, his voice catching.

Mary's mouth was dry. She swallowed. There was nothing to say. She didn't know what might be in store for either of them. She couldn't imagine what they might lose by being together, but she knew that whatever the risks were, they were worth taking. She placed her handbag on the table, stepped into his arms, and felt his lips on hers.

CHAPTER 9

1983
Olduvai Gorge, Tanzania

THOUGH SHE'D WATCHED UNTIL SUNSET, GRACE DIDN'T SEE LISA THE FIRST day. However, when they inspected the bucket early the next morning, she and Dr. Leakey agreed that it was low enough to suggest that someone with a greater thirst than the ravens had dipped into it. They examined the ground around the container, but it was dry and hard, and there were no tracks to be seen.

"If we spread some sand around the bucket, we'd see her prints, but what will it help if she only comes to drink at night and we can't approach her?" said Grace, who'd surprised Dr. Leakey by joining her for breakfast that morning before anyone else besides Mr. Jackson had risen.

Dr. Leakey took several steps beyond the bucket. Grace thought she was going to pay homage to Lemagrut again. The morning haze was dense and low, and the volcano was a faint, ghostly shape on the edge of the savanna, suggesting it, too, wasn't an early riser. But Dr. Leakey didn't contemplate the mountain. Instead, she looked down, left, and right, as if she might spot the cheetah behind a bush or in a sandy "korongo," which she'd told Grace was Swahili for gully.

"She's watching us, probably from nearby, and now that she knows we come here without Matt and Brown Dog, she'll appear," she said. "She was hand reared. She'll come asking for food."

"So I should watch again today?" asked Grace.

"Of course. You didn't think it would happen in a day, did you?"

Grace shrugged. "I might've hoped," she said quietly.

"You must learn patience. Come, bring the bucket. Let's refill it," said Dr. Leakey. Grace lifted the container and followed her down the hill. "I learned patience quickly on my first dig in England. The director—I was her assistant—told me that the earth takes thousands upon thousands of years to conceal and protect history, and if we're to learn anything from what it has hidden, we must be patient. It's the only way. Impatience can be disastrous. I thought I understood that, but Africa showed me what Dorothy Liddell really meant."

"Because the ground here is harder?" asked Grace.

Dr. Leakey stopped and turned to face her, her eyes narrow and glittering behind her wide spectacles. Today, they were a cold light blue. For a moment, Grace thought that she was going to chastise her. Had she said something stupid?

"You've never been to an excavation?" asked Dr. Leakey, as if taking a trowel to her thoughts.

Grace shook her head.

"Of course, your mother was a secretary. She wouldn't have been in the field. But surely your father—"

The girl stared at her. "You knew my mother?"

"I met her briefly. Once. At the publisher's office when I was back in England in the mid-sixties for a short time. She worked on one of Louis's books."

Eleanor and George had also met at the Cambridge publishing company. Grace knew the story about how, after he'd first noticed Eleanor, her father had invented a series of desperate reasons to go to her office before he finally plucked up the courage to invite her out. At one point, when Grace was very young, they'd repeated the account of it as if it was the most original storyline of any romance novel.

"So, your father never took you to a dig?" said Dr. Leakey.

"No. I, um, I lived with my mother when they split up, and there was never an opportunity."

"Well, there is now! Come. We'll leave the bucket at the kitchen and take the water later. Let's get the dogs, and I'll show you some of the excavations before the others get there."

Matt expressed his delight at being released from Dr. Leakey's rooms by tackling Brown Dog to the ground several times before he galloped ahead. Brown Dog shook the sand from his coat and took up a position between Dr. Leakey and Grace as they made their way through the camp. They edged through a small gap between the thorny, entangled branches of the boma that encircled the buildings and followed a well-worn road Grace hadn't noticed before.

Dr. Leakey set the pace and, after only a few yards, stepped off the track and onto a narrow footpath winding its way up a steep hill like a shiny sand snake.

"Shortcut," she said over her shoulder.

The ground rose swiftly but didn't deter Dr. Leakey. Grace was soon slightly breathless and hung back. It wasn't only that she couldn't keep up but also because she didn't want to reveal her panting. The way was rough, with loose sand and sharp outcroppings of compacted earth and rocks. She leaned forward, using her hands to steady herself where necessary.

"Careful. Thorns," said Dr. Leakey, tilting her head at a stubby green bush, which, with its wiry, knotted branches, looked like an angry little boy spoiling for a fight.

Grace grunted quietly. There are thorns *everywhere*, she thought. She glanced up. Even Brown Dog had abandoned her. She saw him ahead, nosing about beneath a low tree with Matt. Dr. Leakey continued climbing, her pace constant. Grace hoped the excavations were close by.

At the top, Dr. Leakey and the dogs waited for her. Grace stopped alongside them, her breathing steadying. The morning haze had lifted, and the view across the savanna was clear and expansive. For once, Lemagrut didn't dominate the scene. Instead, the distant horizon was defined by a low-slung range of blue mountains, with several knolls rising, rugged and broken, between the far hills and the gorge. Grace recalled how dry and bleak the landscape had seemed on her first morning at Olduvai. Today, though, the earth shimmered in the sunlight; it was softer. The vegetation was denser and greener. The acacia trees, with their dark branches and tabletop canopies, were taller and more abundant. In a shallow valley to the right, the hue of the grass hinted at fresh growth. It didn't seem likely that more rain would fall on one side of the camp than on the other. The distance that separated them was not significant. It was the same gorge. Yet the landscape seemed changed.

"You'd think you'd tire of it, but I never have," said Dr. Leakey, reaching out to rest a hand on Brown Dog's head. At her touch, he stood statue-still, barely breathing, as if to move might destabilize her. Grace and Dr. Leakey exchanged glances, smiling.

"I believe he comes from a gracious lineage of martyrs," said Dr. Leakey. "If only he could tell us his story."

"Where did you get him?" asked Grace.

"He got me. He arrived in camp out of the blue about a year ago and adopted me, enduring weeks of being terrorized by Matt. He's an enigma. He likes you too. I haven't had to share him until now. Perhaps he was raised by women."

The warmth of her tone surprised Grace. She'd understood Matt to be Dr. Leakey's favorite and Brown Dog barely tolerated. "Is that what you think will happen with the cheetah? She'll endure and stay?" she asked.

"There's no telling with animals, particularly wild ones." Dr. Leakey pointed into the gorge. "Anyway, nearly there. Let's go down."

Grace didn't move immediately. Instead, she looked to where Dr. Leakey had motioned and saw that they were overlooking a large excavation site.

Spread out below, patches of naked earth—some large, some smaller—glared lighter and brighter in the sunlight than anywhere else in the gorge. In some places, great quantities of soil had been removed, leaving deep rectangular pits with sheer walls. Grace could make out several sets of stairs, which had been cut into the earth, either to expose its layers or allow access to the depths, she supposed. In other places, strips of soil seemed to have been scraped off the surface rather than dug, leaving shallow indentations. Tracks, paths, and roads crisscrossed the quarry-like space, bearing testimony to the many feet and wheels that had tramped and rolled upon it over the years. Now, though, without anyone there, the place seemed desiccated and barren. A cemetery of empty graves. Grace lifted her eyes to scan the landscape beyond the scarred section. There, on the plains, was life—wild and yet peaceful. She looked down again. Dr. Leakey and the dogs were some distance ahead. As Grace followed, she wondered if the sterile wounds created by excavating were part of the view that Dr. Leakey never tired of.

They didn't speak as they made their way down. Dr. Leakey, Grace noted with relief, was less fleet footed on the descent. Loose sand and rocks made walking difficult, and they both slipped and slid at times. On the flat, Dr. Leakey led the way to the largest part that had been excavated.

"It might seem random, but almost every bit exposed here was surveyed and recorded before a single trowel, spade, or pickax touched the earth. Everything took time, much more time than you can imagine. Much more time than we imagined would exist for us when we first arrived," she said. "You know why we came to Olduvai, of course—and why I've stayed so long, don't you?"

"Um, I think so."

Dr. Leakey ignored her, going on to describe the history and geology of the gorge in even greater detail than George had.

"When I first arrived forty-eight years ago, I saw it as a place of incredible beauty and intrigue; a place where nearly every exposure produced archaeological or geographical excitement," she said, having finally exhausted her general description of the place and its history. "After all these years, I'm still amazed by how remarkable it is."

She pointed to the layers and explained how they represented different eras and explained what might have happened during each period. Grace imagined how the layers might be chapters of a book, with each one adding to the plot as the story progressed.

Dr. Leakey described how countless men and a few women, in addition to herself, had spent months and years there, their backs and limbs numb from digging though the layers, and their knees forever scarred from kneeling on the rock-hard earth. She told Grace how the glare of the sun could seem blinding, so much so that when she closed her eyes at night, the brightness remained, as if forever branded in her vision. She explained how, when they first came, they'd always carried rifles with them because of the risks posed by buffaloes, lions, and rhinoceroses, and how heatstroke had turned her husband's hair from brown to white overnight.

"And yet, who'd want to be anywhere else?" she said.

They walked from bed to bed as Dr. Leakey described how the work had changed over the decades. She explained how surface surveys were conducted and how complicated it was to decide where to excavate. She spoke about how the site, its units, and beds were prioritized; how layers of soil were tested and assessed; how excavators were trained; how difficult it was to raise enough money to keep digging; and, at last, how materials were recovered, recorded, and stored.

"And then, of course, there's the interpretation, which, as I mentioned to you before, I've never believed to be my job," she said. "So, you see, this work demands patience. In life, a great deal can be achieved with patience."

Grace had barely spoken since they'd arrived at the bottom of the hill. Her thoughts swam in multiple directions at once. She saw how difficult it was to work in such a remote location. Inevitably, things would take longer here than they would on an excavation site in England. She was awed by how many different things were involved and how long Dr. Leakey had worked under such tough conditions. What a highly educated, clever woman she was. Did that mean her father was similarly intelligent? She hadn't realized that his job involved so much. How satisfying it must be to be so excited by your work, as Dr. Leakey clearly was. How sad she must be to have to leave Olduvai after all this time.

"Did your family ever visit you here?" asked Grace, imagining how impressed Dr. Leakey's parents must've been by her work.

"Family? Well, of course, my husband worked here with me, and our sons have all been here at various times," she replied.

"What about your parents? You must've been young when you first arrived. Did they ever visit you here? They must've been so proud."

"Proud? Ha! Well, my father died when I was a girl, and my mother, no, she never visited me here," she said, gazing into the distance for a moment before clapping her hands. "We should go. You need to watch for the cheetah, and I need to get back to work."

CHAPTER 10

1933
Bedford Square, London

IT WAS NOT MARY'S MOTHER BUT GERTRUDE WHO FIRST LEARNED ABOUT HER and Louis. How she found out, Mary didn't know. It seemed unlikely that her friend would've cottoned on the day their paths crossed at the museum. Mary could've been meeting any number of people there. On the other hand, it wasn't long after that that Gertrude confronted her, which made Mary wonder if her friend knew *exactly* who made use of the room. Or perhaps there'd been talk after she and Louis spent so much time together in Leicester. How she came to know the truth was a mystery, but there was nothing cryptic about Gertrude's opinion on the matter.

She briefly rested her gloved fingers on Mary's forearm as they rose at the end of another lecture at the institute in Bedford Square.

"A quick word," said Gertrude, before briskly leading the way out of the auditorium.

Mary followed to a quiet alcove in the hallway. Gertrude didn't waste her breath on a preamble.

"You're not stupid, Mary. I hope that this infatuation with Louis Leakey is simply a momentary lapse of good judgment," she said, her voice low and even.

"I introduced you because of your talent and because I held you in high regard. I regret it already. Don't make it worse by making a total fool of yourself."

Her words delivered a cold, disorienting slap of shock. It hadn't occurred to Mary that anyone might suspect anything. Their kiss at the museum was behind closed doors. The tension between them was intense, but they'd withheld it in company. Until now, Mary believed that only she and Louis had any bearing on their relationship. So giddy with bliss and desire was she after the kiss that she hadn't paused to contemplate the consequences. The niggle of conscience she'd suffered on the train had vanished, dissolved by the hot thrill of Louis's mouth and body against hers. It didn't occur to her that anything or anyone else mattered.

She tried to reason. "It's not—"

Gertrude held up a hand. "I don't want you to try and explain what it is or what you *think* it is. I don't care for the detail. It's appalling in any form, and you must stop it. Immediately. Not only is Louis married, but also his wife, Frida, is a friend. They're practically my neighbors in Cambridge. She's also pregnant with Louis's second child. Second child, Mary!"

Mary knew Frida was pregnant. Louis had told her it was his wife's final, desperate effort to rescue their relationship.

"Their marriage is a failure," said Mary, unable to look Gertrude in the eye.

The other woman sighed. "From his lips. He has your head spinning. Be sensible. Think what this might do to his wife and children—and to you and both your careers. And how you've betrayed *our* friendship, Mary. I'm not sure I can forgive myself for introducing you to Louis. But that's my disappointment. I can deal with it. Give it up before Frida learns of it. Do the right thing—for everyone."

Gertrude's bluntness was a blow. Mary admired her friend's intelligence, ambition, and professionalism. Gertrude had been kind and encouraging from the moment they'd met, treating Mary like an equal whose opinion and knowledge she valued. Their bond was immediate and, Mary had believed, secure. The thought of not only losing her friend but also that Gertrude should feel responsible was humiliating. Mary shivered and wrapped her arms around herself.

"You're blameless," she said. "Louis and I, our friendship, it would've—"

"But it happened because *I* introduced you. Don't try and rationalize it. There's only one way of making this less awful: you must turn back and give it up. There's no more to be said." Gertrude took a deep breath. "Now, I need a cup of tea."

Mary almost followed as the other woman walked away. She even took two steps in Gertrude's direction, but then, instead of heading to the tearoom, she swung right and left the building.

Although she'd miss Gertrude and was sorry for having disappointed her, Mary was not swayed by her appeal. Her fascination with Louis was more powerful than anything she'd experienced. She went to the museum every day, where she spent hours scrutinizing and illustrating the stone tools for his book. Louis stopped by regularly, and it wasn't long before Mary noticed the other two men who used the rooms sharing glances that made it clear that they suspected the nature of Mary and Louis's relationship. Had one of them said something to Gertrude? It was possible Louis recognized the exchanges too.

"You should come to Cambridge next week," he said one afternoon, after they'd reviewed her most recent drawings. "We'll go through the rest of the Africa collection there and decide how to present the other material and where."

Mary stared at him, uncertain how to respond and conscious of being within earshot of the other men.

"You can stay at The Close for a week," continued Louis, not bothering to lower his voice. "We have plenty of space, and it'll give us time to finalize things."

Finalize things. What did he mean, Mary wondered? They'd discussed several different projects, many of which would take more than a week to finalize. And stay at The Close? That was his and Frida's house. Would Frida be there? Mary had had no doubt up to that point that she and Louis wanted the same thing, but perhaps she was wrong. He'd hardly introduce a woman he hoped to one day replace his wife to his current spouse, would he?

She might've tried to clarify matters if they were alone. Instead, she said, "All right."

Two days later, Louis arrived at Fulham Road to drive Mary to Cambridge. She'd explained the arrangement to her mother, who'd accepted it without question. It seemed natural that Louis's young colleague, whose income wouldn't easily stretch to cover accommodation in a hotel, should stay at his home with his family. However, when Mary introduced her to Louis, after his knocking set Fussy and Bungey a-barking, Cecilia gave her daughter a wary, sideways look. Mary suspected Louis's enthusiastic greeting made her mother suspicious. Cecilia likely mistook his eagerness as exclusive to her daughter. In fact, Louis acknowledged everyone he met with the same fervor. He said he'd learned his warmth from the Kikuyu and didn't care to adopt the cool English manner of making and receiving an introduction. Mary ignored her mother's look and wasted no time in urging Louis out the door, following him down the stairs and into his claret-colored Austin 7 car.

They'd barely driven a mile when Louis reached across the gearshift and placed his hand on Mary's knee. She looked at his long fingers, aware of her breathing quickening at the warmth of his touch.

"Is Frida expecting me?" she managed.

"Of course. She's looking forward to meeting you," he said, his eyes on the road.

Mary glanced at him. He seemed happy, relaxed. On the other hand, the tension between them was so intense that the air in the car seemed to sizzle. It occurred to her, not for the first time, that she'd signed up for a mysterious game without reading the rules. Exactly what her role might be was unclear. The only thing that was certain was that she couldn't get out of it; neither did she want to.

Set in a large garden, abutting several green fields with may and bramble hedges on one side and the village church on the other, The Close was an old house, which Mary later discovered had been purchased using Frida's inheritance. It was conveniently located in the village of Girton, about three miles from Cambridge, where Louis had a suite of rooms in his capacity as a research fellow at St. John's College. Only the maid was there when they arrived. Louis requested tea, and as the woman disappeared toward the kitchen, he led Mary inside and up the stairs. She looked away as she caught sight of a double bed in what she took to be the main bedroom and stood at the door as Louis went into the guest room and placed her suitcase on a chair.

"I trust it's to your liking," he said, smiling at her. "The bathroom is the second door down."

"Thank you," replied Mary, glancing around the neat, pretty room, with its matching floral green curtains and comforter.

They were in the study when Frida appeared. She'd been for a walk with their daughter and her nanny, she said, perching on the edge of an armchair opposite Mary. Even seated, Frida was tall. She leaned forward and smoothed her dark hair, which was cropped in a fashionable soft, wavy style. Wearing an elegant pale-green skirt that flared at the ankles and a floaty cream-colored blouse that fell gracefully around her pregnant frame, Frida was a vibrant, poised woman. She looked younger than Louis, although she was a year older than him. Mary smoothed her gray wool skirt over her knees.

"So, it's your turn," said Frida with a generous smile, her brown eyes sparkling.

Mary felt herself color. "My turn?"

"To illustrate for Louis," said the other woman. "I've done my bit, but understand you are infinitely more talented."

Louis had shown Mary some of the drawings Frida had done of stone tools, many of which were included in his volume *The Stone Age Cultures of Kenya Colony*. They were neat and accurate. Although Louis hadn't said as much, Mary had assumed motherhood demanded too much of Frida's time to allow her to continue working with him. The notion was upheld by the fact that she detected no displeasure in Frida's tone.

"It's fascinating work," said Mary, eager to remain on neutral ground.

"We'll be out of your way and working in the rooms in St. John's during the day for most of the week," added Louis, his eyes on Frida.

"Of course," she said. "Do as you must. I'll expect you when I see you—as ever." She got to her feet, and Mary saw the full extent of her pregnancy in silhouette. She looked away.

"Supper will be in an hour," said Frida.

Louis caught Mary's eye as his wife closed the study door behind her. He shrugged, as if to say, "You see? We're indifferent to each other. Our marriage is a failure." Mary wished he'd verbalized it.

The following day seemed like something of a bewildering dream to Mary. Whether it was good or bad was uncertain. She awoke to Louis's voice as he chatted playfully to his daughter, Priscilla. On her way to the bathroom, Mary spotted the little girl toddling down the passage toward her father. She was bringing him toys, which she described at great length and in words Mary couldn't decipher. Louis's unrestrained laughter and protracted replies confirmed what he'd told Mary: although he was not that charmed by her initially, Priscilla increasingly delighted him as she learned to talk and totter about independently. Mary told herself it didn't mean anything. A loving father wasn't the same as a loving husband.

Served by the maid, breakfast was brief and muted. Mary was an unexceptional guest in the home of a typical academic Cambridge family. She and Louis left The Close for Cambridge without Mary catching sight of Frida. Once out of the house and in the Austin, she felt her anxiety unravel like a tightly wound ball of string suddenly untied. The sense that she was looking in at her life from the outside disappeared. She felt her muscles expand and relaxed against the leather of the seat as she watched the countryside whip by.

Things changed when Mary and Louis arrived at his rooms at college. He held open the door for her to enter. As she wandered in and looked around—taking in the office, with its desk and chairs; second room, with a large table covered by stone tools and other work material; and small "gyp room," with its few kitchen appliances, table, and narrow bed—Mary felt a heightened sense of anticipation. Louis hadn't touched her since placing his hand on her knee in the car when they left London, but now the atmosphere was taut. Mary longed for him to pull her into his arms and kiss her the way they had in the museum. She glanced at him. His eyes were on her, bright and steady. He felt it too. Mary took a step toward him. He sighed and walked to a window.

"Trinity and King's colleges," he said, pointing out.

Mary stood next to him and looked over the gardens and lawns to the buildings with their spires, turrets, and ivy-lined walls burning red. He moved to another window.

"The wilderness, I call it," he said. "You should see it in spring."

She joined him and looked out and through a small congregation of oak and elm trees glowing in autumn shades of yellow and orange, which lay between them and the college sports fields. A patch of garden had been left unattended. The plants were tall and unruly, as if rebelling against the order of their surroundings.

"Only fellows of St. John's have the key to the gate to go there. It's nothing like the bush in Africa, but the birds, animals, and plants bring me peace," he said.

Mary wanted to go there with him. She turned to say so, but he'd moved away again.

"Let's get to work, shall we?" he said.

On their way out of the rooms that afternoon, their hands touched as they reached for the doorknob. Louis leaned forward, as if to kiss her, but drew back the moment she felt his warm breath on her skin.

The atmosphere was similarly charged the following day when, shortly after lunch, Louis snatched his jacket from the back of the chair and headed for the door.

"I'm off to London," he said. "To the Royal College of Surgeons to take a look at some material."

Mary looked at him, taken aback. He glanced away.

"Take the bus to Girton this afternoon," he said. "I'll probably only return tomorrow."

He gave her a curt nod and left the room before she could properly gather her thoughts. She stared at the closed door. Why the change of plans? The urgency?

Later, as she boarded the bus with students who resided in Girton, Mary thought how, given her age, she might be mistaken for one of them. What would they think if they knew her circumstances and that it was impossible for her to enroll at university? Would they ridicule her? Snub her? She watched as they climbed the stairs ahead of her and settled on the benches, chatting easily and laughing often. Their collegial ease made her feel odd and isolated, and she felt a fresh flush of frustration at Louis. Being with him had legitimized her presence on campus. What was he thinking, leaving her to return to The Close alone?

That evening, Frida showed no surprise to see Louis's place at the table unoccupied. She smiled at Mary and took her seat.

"I hope you like onion soup. It's our cook's specialty. We have it happily and often," she said, taking up her spoon. Mary flinched at the thought of Frida and Louis contentedly sharing a pot of soup. Aside from Louis and Priscilla playing, she'd seen no signs of contentment.

Despite their efforts, conversation didn't flow between the two women. Even when they spoke about archaeology and anthropology—matters about which they both knew a great deal—their talk was stilted. Frida was an attentive hostess, topping off Mary's water glass, offering her more to eat, and regularly inquiring that everything was to her satisfaction. It didn't help.

Mary couldn't help resenting Frida's calm disposition. She seemed to know exactly what was going on, while Mary was perplexed. Had she misunderstood Louis's desire for her? She'd imagined he'd brought her to The Close to show her how indifferent he and Frida were to each other. She also hoped he'd invited her because he wanted her with him. That didn't seem to be the case. Instead, she'd seen how attached he was to his daughter. Moreover, he'd rushed back to London, leaving Mary to work alone in his rooms at St. John's and, in the evening, to assume the role of dining companion to his wife. Frida appeared unperturbed by his erratic behavior, but Mary was disturbed, deeply so.

The following afternoon, as Mary hunched over the illustration of a hand ax in the St. John's room, the door flew open, sending papers flying off the desk. Louis froze in the doorway, staring at her. His hair was tousled and clumpy and his face unshaven. The dark half-moons below his eyes added to his haggard look. Eventually, shoulders bowed, he shuffled toward her, his steps scuffing the floor like those of someone old or wounded. Mary stood up.

"Are you all right? Were you in an accident?" she asked, making her way around the desk.

Louis shook his head, reached out with both arms, and grasped her elbows. For a moment, she thought he needed to hold on to her to steady himself, but he drew a breath, straightened his back, and lifted his shoulders.

"I can't go on," he said, his voice almost a whisper.

"What do you mean?" said Mary.

Her heart was racing—whether in excitement or terror, she didn't know. What she was certain of was an overpowering urge to thrust her body against his.

Louis's grip on her arms tightened, and he gave a low groan before releasing her and taking a step backward. Mary teetered. *He'd* been holding her up.

"There's no denying it," he said, keeping his distance. "It's the only thing I am certain of. My marriage is a failure. I want to end it and marry you."

She stared at him. How had it come to this so quickly? She couldn't deny her desire and fascination, but that such a decision should be made in such haste and without more consideration was astonishing. Louis came to her, his arms at his side this time. She felt the warmth of his body and inhaled his scent, the one that made her think of sun, soil, and adventure.

"Do you want me?" he asked, in a tone that suggested he knew the answer.

Mary whimpered as he took her in his arms and placed his mouth on hers. The kiss was long, deep, and desperately overdue.

Finally, when they drew apart, Louis asked, "Was that a 'yes'?"

"Yes," she gasped, pulling him toward her.

In the days that followed, they spent almost as much time on the narrow bed in the St. John's rooms as they did at the desk and table. At The Close in the evenings, Mary was determined to go straight to her room after she'd eaten. She was so smitten by Louis and sated by their lovemaking that she couldn't imagine keeping her elation hidden from Frida. However, most evenings, Louis's wife left the dining room first, pleading exhaustion. Louis shrugged and urged Mary to stay on a while longer so that he could teach her how to make string figures, a hobby that fascinated him. She obliged, relishing the idea of spending a few more hours with Louis, even if they were chaste ones.

They agreed Louis would wait until the baby was born to tell Frida. The only practical means to get a divorce was through adultery. However, while his infidelity was ongoing and he was certain that he wanted to end the marriage to Frida, Louis was not without compassion for his wife.

"I wish there was a way of doing this that didn't involve hurting Frida," he said, as he drove Mary back to London at the end of the week.

Mary said nothing. She knew that, if there was such a person, she was the lucky one in the triangle. Even if Frida didn't love Louis, as he insisted was the case, the betrayal, rejection, breakup of the family, and scandal would injure and anger her. Mary, on the other hand, had only her reputation to think of and the loss of her friendship with Gertrude. She didn't reckon on her mother's outrage—and certainly not so soon.

Cecilia must've been watching for Louis's car from the window of the Fulham flat. She'd opened the door by the time Mary lugged her suitcase upstairs and was standing there, flanked by the waggling dogs, with her hands on her hips.

"Unbelievable!" she snarled. "Have you no shame?"

"Hello, Mother," said Mary, trying to disguise her surprise as she stopped to pat Fussy and Bungey. "It's lovely to see you too. What are you on about?"

"He's a married man, Mary! What *are* you thinking? I am *so* ashamed of you."

Denial was futile. She and Louis were together. She'd agreed to marry him. While Mary wasn't prepared to talk to her mother about him yet, she suspected she'd never truly be ready. She wondered how Cecilia had found out. Had she spoken to Gertrude? They were acquainted through Mary. But, she reasoned, that didn't matter either.

"He's going to get a divorce," she said. "I've agreed to marry him."

Cecilia thrust her arm out, placing her hand against the wall as if she might fall. "No! Be sensible. You can't marry him!"

"Why not? Because he's a decade older than me? You forget Father was that much older than you, Mother," said Mary, stepping inside and closing the front door.

Clearly her mother was terribly upset. She was typically careful not to have conversations in the hallway with the door open, for fear of the neighbors hearing.

"I don't care about his age. I care about the fact that he is a dishonest, adulterous cad," said Cecilia, following her daughter into the drawing room.

Mary leaned her suitcase against the wall and turned to face her mother.

"He's a man in an unhappy marriage. Like all of us, he wants to be happy. He believes he can be with me. I feel the same. What's wrong with wanting to be happy? Will you deny us that?"

Cecilia collapsed into a chair. "Please, Mary, don't do this to yourself. He's not to be trusted. If he's unfaithful to his wife now, he'll be unfaithful to you. You'll rue the day you—"

"Is it too much to ask that you get to know him before arriving at such a damning conclusion?" said Mary. "I know you wanted to choose a charming, distinguished, and wealthy husband for me yourself. It's infuriating for you that I should take matters into my own hands, but I have. Louis is charming. He's intelligent and greatly admired. Most importantly, he's who *I* want."

She watched as Cecilia covered her face with her hands.

"Get to know him, Mother. Give us a chance. Don't fight me on this," she said, before taking her suitcase to her bedroom.

CHAPTER 11

1983
Olduvai Gorge, Tanzania

IT WAS ALMOST LUNCHTIME WHEN, BUTTRESSED BY THE TREE AT THE LOOKout after her tour of the dig, Grace saw the cheetah. For a moment she thought boredom, despondency, or a bit of both were playing tricks on her. The dark shape moved so imperceivably slowly, it might've been the shadow of a nearby bush. It was only when Lisa emerged far enough into the open for Grace to make out her small head and round ears that she accepted it was the cat.

She stilled her breathing as if, despite the yards between them, Lisa might catch a whiff of air expelled by her foreign lungs. The cheetah slid farther into the sunlight, stopped, and turned to look, her ears rotating in Grace's direction. She caught sight of the girl and froze. The golden intensity of her large high-set eyes seemed to pin Grace against the tree. They were encircled by thick black rims, which extended like two dark streams of tears from the inner corner of each eye to the outer edges of her mouth. Lisa could've been crying.

"Oh my!" gasped Grace.

A rush of questions flooded her thoughts. What was she meant to do? They'd agreed she'd call Dr. Leakey when the cat appeared. However, if Grace moved, she'd surely frighten her, and Lisa might flee. The idea was to feed her, but how was Grace to fetch the meat without alarming the cat?

Then she remembered Dr. Leakey's words: "In life, a great deal can be achieved with patience."

Grace exhaled, willing herself to breathe normally. The cat's ears flicked, but rather than appearing fearful, she strolled to the bucket. Grace saw the collar around her neck. She'd imagined it to be something like a dog collar, but the band Lisa wore was broad and heavy-looking, with a boxlike attachment at her throat. The equipment seemed out of place at Olduvai, where Grace hadn't even seen the radio Dr. Leakey had spoken of.

"It's okay," she whispered. "We'll sort it out."

Hoping the cat would sense her intention, she thought about the woman on television who'd claimed to communicate with animals telepathically. As if on cue, Grace's stomach gurgled like water draining from a sink. She was also hungry. In case animals could also interpret involuntary bodily sounds, she added, "Excuse me."

Lisa glanced around before crouching to drink. Grace slumped against the tree and watched, noting the hollowness of the cheetah's abdomen and the sharp jutting of her bones. She lapped for a few minutes before raising her head from the bucket.

"Don't go," said Grace.

Obligingly, Lisa took a few languid steps and lay down, her head and shoulders raised and her long, muscular tail, with its paddle-like end, curled around her back legs. Grace waited several minutes before slowly getting to her feet. Lisa watched without obvious concern.

"I'm going to fetch Dr. Leakey and your lunch," said the girl, picturing the plate of stew and rice she'd eaten the previous day. Wasn't that what she was supposed to do to communicate? But what would Lisa make of a serving of meat and grain? Should Grace imagine a cut of beef? Or a gazelle? She deliberately imagined each option, and as she backed away, she was pleased to see that Lisa didn't move. They had, it seemed, reached an agreement.

Grace wanted to shout with joy. The cheetah had returned and was waiting! Instead, she said quietly, "Stay, Lisa. I'll be back in a minute."

As soon as she was certain the cat could no longer see her, Grace spun around and sprinted to the camp. She zigzagged around huts, trees, and tents, narrowly missing three men making their way to the dining room. As she skidded around the final corner to Dr. Leakey's workroom, she heard her father call from behind.

"Grace! What's going on?"

She lifted her hand dismissively and kept running, stopping only when she entered the workroom. It was empty. Dr. Leakey had already left for lunch. Grace turned and raced in the other direction. Within a few yards, she encountered George again.

"What on earth are you up to? Are you all right?" he asked.

They stood for a moment, both puffing.

"Have you seen Dr. Leakey?" she asked.

George took off his hat and scratched his head. "She's probably in the dining room. What's the urgency?"

"I'll tell you later," said Grace, pushing past him.

He turned and tried to keep up with her, words interspersed with wheezing as he ran. "Good. Later. I want to talk. Let's have coffee. After supper. Okay?"

"Okay. See you later," she said, leaving him to recover his breath.

Dr. Leakey pushed her almost empty plate aside and got to her feet the moment she saw Grace. She didn't have to ask what was going on.

"I'll take the dogs to my hut. You get the beef from the kitchen. I'll meet you back here," she said, before taking off with Matt at her heels. Brown Dog hesitated, looking at Grace. Dr. Leakey whistled, and he followed.

Grace stared at the kitchen. The meat was no doubt there, but where, exactly? How would she recognize it? She went to the entrance, expecting to have to explain herself. Instead, Mr. Jackson met her at the door and handed her another aluminum bucket. She stared at him. How did he know?

"Beef," he said with a small nod. "For the cheetah."

She glanced at the large raw shank in the pail. "Thank you."

Grace turned to go, but he called her back. His assistant, an extraordinarily tall, lean young man with an expression that suggested he was about to tell a joke or do something mischievous, hurried toward them.

"Asante, Gatimu," said Mr. Jackson, taking a rectangular paper package and a tea flask from him and handing them to Grace. "Your lunch. Don't forget to bring the thermos back."

"Thank you, Mr. Jackson," she replied, putting the bucket down briefly to wedge the package beneath her arm so that she could carry everything.

He watched, and for a moment Grace thought he was going to say something more, but instead he nodded and went back into the kitchen.

She didn't walk far before Dr. Leakey appeared.

"What did you see?" she asked, taking the bucket.

Grace explained how Lisa had appeared, seen her, drunk, and lay down. She didn't mention how she'd talked to the cat and pictured the food and how it seemed Lisa understood. However, as they approached the lookout and Grace saw the cheetah lying exactly as she'd left her, she thought, *It worked!*

They stopped at the tree. Dr. Leakey's smile was broader than any Grace had seen as she looked at Lisa. They stood side by side, silently, watching the cat watch them.

"What now?" asked Grace eventually.

Dr. Leakey kept her eyes ahead. "We shouldn't approach her together initially. Too overwhelming. Of course, you'd like to go, but that won't do. Wait here."

"But—"

"No. Imagine your father's reaction. You'll meet her soon enough."

Grace felt a prick of shame at her relief. As fascinated as she was by Lisa, she was also frightened. She hadn't been about to object. Rather, she'd thought to ask if it wouldn't be wise to call someone else—who and to do what, she wasn't sure—in case Lisa became aggressive. The cheetah might've been hand reared, but she was a wild animal. A hungry, desperate wild animal.

She watched uneasily as Dr. Leakey walked slowly up the hill. Sure, she had lived in Africa for decades and knew a great deal about animals, but was this wise? The flask slipped in Grace's sweaty hand. She kept watching as she bent her knees and placed it on the ground. At the same time, the cat stood up, her eyes on Dr. Leakey. Grace's pulse raced. What was Lisa thinking?

"It's okay. She's got your lunch," whispered Grace.

She expected Dr. Leakey to stop when the cat stood, but she didn't. Grace wanted to call out. Tell her not to go closer. Why didn't she put the meat down and come back? Let Lisa fetch it. Why was it necessary to get so close? Grace estimated they were only a few feet apart. She heard murmuring. Dr. Leakey was talking to the cat. Lisa's ears twitched, but she was otherwise still. Finally, Dr. Leakey stopped, slowly reached into the bucket, and took out the meat. Grace held her breath. Did she expect the cat to take it from her hand? She was relieved when Dr. Leakey bent, placed the meat on the ground, and took a couple of steps back. There was a pause before Lisa slowly but decisively crept forward, crouched, sniffed the bone, took it, and slid out of sight behind the bushes. There was no rushing or panicking. Dr. Leakey turned to look at Grace. She was smiling again. Grace exhaled.

"Do you think we'll see her again today?" asked Grace when Dr. Leakey returned to the tree.

"I suspect she'll lay low for a bit when she's eaten. She won't go far, though. She knows she's in the right place."

"Will we leave more meat for her tomorrow?"

Dr. Leakey shook her head. "We'll bring it to her when she shows herself. If we're going to be able to remove the collar, she needs to trust us enough to let us touch her."

That was why Dr. Leakey went so close to the cat, thought Grace. "So I'll have to watch for her tomorrow and call you again?" she asked.

"Yes, but you can come back to camp this afternoon and do some work."

Grace forgot she'd agreed to meet her father that night. After the early-morning tour of the excavations with Dr. Leakey, excitement of seeing Lisa, and long afternoon of writing labels and notes, she was weary and eager to get to bed. Also, Dr. Leakey had offered to take her to the Ngorongoro Crater the next day.

"You can't return to England without visiting the place," she'd insisted. "It's a natural paradise for animals created millennia ago when a volcano collapsed inward."

They'd leave before sunrise. Grace should rest. However, George intercepted her as she left the dining room after supper.

"Shall we take our coffee somewhere?" he asked.

She was momentarily baffled. "What? Oh, I'm sorry. I'm so tired. Can we talk another time?"

George blinked, mouth twitching.

"Okay, okay," she sighed. "Where do you want to go?"

"I believe you've been watching the cheetah. Perhaps we could go and see whether it's around. I hear you fed it earlier," he said.

"Dr. Leakey fed *her*," she said.

Not only was Grace annoyed by him referring to Lisa as "it," but she was also reluctant to show him the lookout. She felt territorial about the spot, as if it were somehow hallowed ground where only she and Dr. Leakey were permitted. Grace also felt proprietorial about Lisa.

"It's not a good idea for anyone else to go near. We're trying to get her to trust us," she said.

George sighed. "All right. I'll get coffee, and we can sit over there," he said, indicating a table on the far side of the deserted dining room where the light of the paraffin lamps barely reached.

It was a warm evening. Although the moon had shown itself, half-bathed in milky light, it was dark enough for a full choir of crickets to have begun their nighttime chorus. Grace sat, looking out. Earlier, one of her father's colleagues had described the bush baby he'd spotted on the branch of a tree on his way to dinner.

"His eyes almost filled his entire face," the man had said. "And after we'd taken a good look at each other, he leapt several feet onto another branch. So tiny, yet so agile!"

Grace longed to see one of the little primates. Although she'd heard the eerie whooping of what she was told was a hyena and the wailing call of jackals, aside from Lisa, she'd still not spotted any wildlife at Olduvai.

"Imagine what your mother would've said if she was served these," said George as he placed two cups on the table and sat opposite her.

Grace glanced at the thick glass teacups. He was right. Eleanor would've been appalled. She'd preferred fine bone china cups and insisted that the prettiness of a tea set was crucial to the quality of the tea.

"She would never have come here," said Grace.

"No. She wouldn't have."

"Did you know Dr. Leakey knew Mum?"

Her father stared at her, blinking rapidly. "No. I mean, yes. Well, she, um, what did she tell you?"

He seemed strangely unsettled. "What's wrong?" asked Grace.

George took a sip of coffee, swallowed, and looked down. "Nothing, nothing. I'd forgotten, that's all. What did she say? About your mum?"

"Just that she'd met her once. When Mum's company published one of her husband's books in the sixties."

He nodded. "Yes. I remember."

Grace expected him to go on. To explain how the meeting had taken place. Or something. But he didn't. Instead, he quietly drank his coffee, looking anywhere but at her. She lifted her cup. As soon as it was empty, she'd go to bed, but George broke the silence.

"What did you think of the dig?" he asked.

She peered at him over her cup. Did he know her every move?

"It's an adult sandpit," she said.

It hadn't occurred to her before to be disparaging about the excavation site. She'd enjoyed being there with Dr. Leakey. Her father elicited scorn she didn't know she possessed. It was as automatic as it was mean. She no longer thought about *why* it was necessary to hurt him. It was habit. Or perhaps she'd become the cruel daughter she thought he deserved.

"Ha! So, you're not thinking of becoming an archaeologist, then?" said George.

She shrugged.

"That's what I wanted to talk to you about," he continued. "Your education."

Grace drained her cup and put it down. "Here we go again," she said through gritted teeth.

George ignored her. "You need to go back to school, Grace. You'll regret it if you don't."

"It's too late," she said.

"No, it's not. You're seventeen. There are plenty of scholars your age at secondary school. Of course there's time."

"Do you know how much I'd need to catch up?" she sneered. "No, of course you don't. You weren't there to see how soon it started. You left. You could've made a difference then, but you didn't. Now it's too late."

She stood up and reached for her cup, intending to take it to the kitchen. George caught her hand, holding it firmly in his. "I didn't know what was going on. I should've, but I didn't know. But I do now, and I want to help you get back on track. Please, Grace. Don't throw away your life like this."

Grace wrestled her hand away, glaring at him. "Throw away my life? Can't you see? *You* threw away my life! The moment you left me to take care of Mum, you discarded me. I was a girl. I needed you, and you deserted me. Now you feel lumped with me, remorseful because you don't know what to do with me. Well, don't worry. When we get home, I'll be off your hands. You can stop worrying about me again—the way you did years ago."

George stood. "What will it take to get you to listen to me? To believe me?" he pleaded.

"I listen to you. You plead. Beg me to go back to school. Bring me to this place. But I don't hear you say sorry," she said, her voice thick with emotion.

His voice was hoarse. "Sorry? But, Grace, of course I'm sorry. If that's what you want to hear, I'll—"

But Grace had already walked into the darkness.

CHAPTER 12

———◊———

1934
The Close, Girton, Cambridgeshire, England

Louis's remorse was sincere. Mary believed it, but it didn't matter how sorry he was; Frida was no less shocked, wounded, or merciless. After Mary's stay at The Close, Louis had remained largely at his St. John's rooms, day and night. Although they'd agreed he'd say nothing to Frida about their relationship until after the baby was born, and Louis claimed to be staying at the college because his work demanded it, Mary believed that Frida understood he had no intention of returning to the family home. He'd been unequivocal to Mary about the irredeemable state of his marriage. Frida had to know *something* was amiss. Mary was stunned by how wrong she was. Frida apparently had no inkling that her marriage was in trouble.

"I've told her," said Louis in an uncharacteristically staccato tone when he telephoned Mary at the museum one rainy morning late in January.

"Oh," she replied, grateful to have the room to herself and uncertain whether the tremor in her hands was due to euphoria or trepidation. She'd been hoping for the news for some time. The baby was more than a month old.

"She's livid and insists on seeing us together. At The Close. Now," he continued.

"Together? Why would she want to see me?"

"She insists."

"Now? Well, I'm in the middle of—"

"Mary, please. Let's get this over and done with," said Louis.

He sounded desperate. It was incomprehensible to Mary that Frida wanted to see her. Did she want to confirm that her husband was telling the truth about their affair? What had Louis said that made his wife want to talk to them together? However, he needed her with him, and that's what mattered.

They agreed she'd take the next train from London and he'd fetch her from the station. Mary admonished herself for wishing she'd worn the smart green suit with the Eton-type jacket she'd recently bought. She wasn't going for an interview or out for a stylish lunch. Still, it would've bolstered her spirits if she'd felt she looked her best.

Louis huddled beneath the shelter, smoking, as he waited for her on the platform. He was damp and irritable.

"Are you all right?" she asked, after he'd extinguished his cigarette and they'd climbed into the car.

"What do you think?" he replied, without looking at her.

The baby was crying when they arrived at The Close. They sat, silent, in the study for more than half an hour before the noise stopped and Frida came downstairs. Mary restrained herself from also standing when Louis jumped to his feet as his wife entered the room.

"Everything okay with Colin?" he asked.

Frida glared at him. "What do you care?"

He opened his mouth to respond, but she whipped her head around to face Mary, who straightened her back, bracing herself.

"Unbelievable," said Frida, her nostrils flaring. "You come to my home, eat my food, sleep in my guest room, and seduce my husband. I'm astounded that anyone could be so brazenly wicked."

"It wasn't like that, Frida," argued Louis. "I told you—"

Frida flashed him a look. "Oh, pardon me! I forgot. You're in love. You've suddenly discovered what you've been missing all these years. Your intellectual equal! What should I say? Congratulations?"

Louis tried again. "I've said it before. I'll say it again. I'm sorry, Frida. I hate hurting you. I hate breaking up our family. I'm sorry it's so upsetting for you. You've got to believe that I—"

"No, I don't have to believe anything that comes out of your mouth," said Frida, her voice remarkably steady now. "You want me to believe you're sorry, but I don't think you mean it. You want me to acknowledge it, to accept your alleged apology because it'll make things easier for you. Appease your conscience. What am I meant to think? 'Oh, it's not so bad; Louis is sorry.' Ha! Keep your apologies. They're meaningless and change nothing."

Louis ran his fingers through his hair and sat down. He looked defeated and ready to succumb to whatever Frida dished out. Mary wished he'd chosen the place alongside her on the couch instead of a chair so far away. Frida's attention was back on her.

"You're a hussy, Mary Nicol. I don't give a damn about how clever and talented you apparently are as an archaeologist and illustrator. It doesn't mean a thing. You're nothing more than a hussy who lacks any sense of moral decency."

It was the first time Mary had heard herself referred to as an archaeologist. She'd always been called an assistant or an illustrator. She wanted to object but also wished it were possible to somehow appreciate the moment. However, Frida was still talking.

"I'd like to think that you're young and naive and too inexperienced to understand what you're doing, but that's not the case," she said.

Mary looked at her hands, splayed on her lap. Her fingernails were short and clean. That's what happened out of season when you worked in a museum.

Frida took a step toward her, and Mary looked up. "You're not stupid," said Louis's wife. "Quite the contrary. You're smart; you know what you want and how to get it."

She couldn't help but be impressed by Frida's clarity. There was no doubt that she was incensed, but she remained very much in control. Mary couldn't see any point in responding to any of her accusations. Frida was fully entitled to be outraged. Mary would feel the same in her place. It didn't matter that she was wrong about Mary having seduced Louis. Perhaps it was easier for her to believe that her husband was the victim of a temptress ten years his junior than him playing an equal role. Not that Frida saw Louis as blameless.

"And you," she said, looking at her husband who sat, elbows on knees and head in hands, "with no thoughts or consideration for your children. You're a traitor. A cad. You've betrayed me. You've betrayed them. Don't think I'll make it easy for you. For either of you. Remember where you are. Your ambitions. What you need and what others will think of you. Your circle is my circle. It won't be easy, and you'll have yourselves to blame. Now, get out of my house and don't come back."

Neither Louis nor Mary moved until they'd heard Frida climb the stairs and a door slam on the first landing. Louis came to her, took her hands, and pulled her to her feet.

"Well, there we are. It's done," he said, wrapping his arms around her.

Mary sighed against his shoulder. It was unreasonable, she thought, to wish he sounded more enthusiastic. It was infinitely harder for him than for her to endure the wrath of Frida. They had history—and two children.

It wasn't only easier for Mary because she wasn't the married one with the family. It also helped that she was based in London, where she returned immediately after the meeting with Frida. Louis, on the other hand, had to face the music in Cambridge—and it was clamorous.

The news spread quickly. Louis and Frida's friends soon became Frida's friends. There was no sympathy for him. Why would there be? He was the unfaithful rake who'd deceived his wife while she was carrying their second child, a heartless scoundrel who'd deserted his family for a seductress who was not yet twenty-one years old.

Gertrude was not only Frida's friend but also had a fellowship at Newnham College in Cambridge, where she lived. As such, she was among the first people Frida told. Gertrude wasted no time telephoning Mary at Fulham Road to reiterate how appalled she was.

"I pleaded with you not to continue with this madness, but you ignored me. I have never been so ashamed in my life. Oh, that you should repay my friendship this way!" said Gertrude, her voice hoarse.

Mary's head spun. She'd felt numb and inert while Frida had castigated her and Louis at The Close. However, Gertrude's ongoing misery shocked her afresh. She leaned against the wall, pressing the telephone to her ear.

Gertrude took a sharp breath and continued, the quiver in her voice carrying down the line. "Have you any idea of the ramifications of this? Not only have you wrecked a marriage and a family, but you've dug a professional hole for yourself and Louis, which I doubt you will ever escape. I'm asking you again, Mary, please give it up. Give him up. If not for yourself and his family, for me," she pleaded.

The line hummed.

"Mary? Are you there? Please, Mary. For me."

"I'm sorry," whispered Mary.

She couldn't remember the last time she'd shed a tear, but as she placed the phone in its cradle, her cheeks were wet. Her sorrow had nothing to do with Frida or the children. She hardly knew them and was sure that Louis would've ended his marriage regardless of her involvement. Mary was remorseful because of how she'd enraged and disappointed Gertrude. She'd lost a friend. But it didn't matter how sorry she was. She wouldn't give up Louis, and Gertrude wouldn't forgive her. She continued leaning against the wall, uncertain that her legs would hold her.

"It can't go on," came a voice from the doorway. "Even you know that."

It was her mother. Mary wiped her eyes and moved away from the wall. Cecilia remained in the doorway.

"If you're serious about your career, you'll stop this madness," she said.

Mary looked at her, realizing how little her mother understood. "I am serious about my career, which is why it makes perfect sense," she said. "Not only do I want to be with Louis because of how I feel about him, but also because I know no one will understand, support, and help me with my career like he will. You have no idea how much I have learned from him and how much I know I will learn in the future."

"Oh, so this is for the sake of your career?" said Cecilia, her brows raised.

"If you want to think of it that way, be my guest," said Mary, pushing past her to leave the room. "I'm taking the dogs out."

As she pulled on her coat and called Fussy and Bungey, she thought about what she'd told her mother. It was true: working with Louis had opened her eyes to what might be possible for them together. More than anything, she wanted to go to Africa with him, for the work, adventure, and animals, and to experience what he'd seen so that she might understand why he was driven to prove humans evolved there. She was sorry to have upset Gertrude. She wished it wasn't so, but her regret made no difference to her decision. She'd miss her friend greatly. However, the way she felt about Louis and what might come from being with him would, she assured herself, more than compensate for the loss.

CHAPTER 13

1983
Olduvai Gorge, Tanzania

It was still dark when Grace awoke to light knocking on the door. She acknowledged it with a groan, recognizing Mr. Jackson's deep, low response that breakfast was ready. She dressed and followed the track, barely lit by the waning half-moon, to the dining room. The nighttime cricket crescendo had subsided and was interspersed by the sporadic chirp of a bird that Grace couldn't identify beyond it belonging to an early-rising variety.

"Dr. Leakey said she'll meet you at the cheetah lookout," said Mr. Jackson, placing her tea and porridge on the table as she approached. "When you've eaten."

"The lookout?" echoed Grace.

"Yes."

They'd agreed they'd drive to the Ngorongoro Crater immediately after breakfast and spend an hour or two there before returning so that Grace could continue watching Lisa and Dr. Leakey could work. Why the change in plans?

Grace lifted a spoonful of porridge and blew on it. The tea was hot too. She reached for the tiny glass jug of milk alongside her plate, tipped half into her bowl and the remainder into her cup, stirred, and bolted the lot. It was cloyingly creamy and cold but consumed.

"Thank you!" she called toward the flickering light of the kitchen as she rushed off.

There was no sign of anyone at the tree. Grace wondered if Mr. Jackson had misunderstood the instruction. She stopped, straining to see where Dr. Leakey might be. A faint, low glow indicated east in the distance, but everything before her was dark. She walked slowly toward what she'd come to think of as "Lisa's hill." With every step, she scuffed her feet. She didn't want to take anyone by surprise. A twig cracked somewhere ahead, and she stopped.

"Up here," came Dr. Leakey's voice.

Grace looked up, scanning left and right, but could see nothing but indistinct shapes, which she knew from staring at the spot for hours previously were bushes, mounds of earth, boulders, and sandy outcrops. But something moved, and gradually the solid shape of Dr. Leakey appeared against the lighter sky.

"What are you doing?" asked Grace, trying to keep her voice steady.

"Saying good morning to Lisa."

That's when she realized that Dr. Leakey wasn't alone. The dark form alongside her wasn't a bush. The cat was standing within inches of Dr. Leakey, her head level with the woman's waist. She was *much* taller than Grace expected.

"Oh," she said, aware of her own heartbeat, a loud pounding in her ears.

"It's okay. Keep coming. She's fine. Happy to see me and presumably you too."

Eleanor had claimed that, as a small child, Grace hadn't been afraid of anything. It would be to her detriment, she'd complained, warning the girl repeatedly that she shouldn't pet strange dogs. Her mother was wrong. Or maybe she'd grown fearful, because Grace was afraid now. It didn't matter that Dr. Leakey was standing as peacefully alongside the cheetah as she would with Matt and Brown Dog. Lisa was a wild animal. A tall, powerful predator with fangs and claws that could kill a wildebeest.

Grace shifted her weight as if preparing to approach. "I thought we were going to feed her later," she said.

"It occurred to me last night that we should come and see her before we left. She's relaxed and was looking for us. She came to me almost immediately," said Dr. Leakey.

Grace still hadn't moved. "She came to you?"

Dr. Leakey turned to look at the cat. "She hasn't purred yet, but it won't be long."

"Really?"

"Yes. We'll hear it soon enough."

Grace could only nod, staring at Lisa. It was still too dark to be sure, but she sensed the cat was watching her. What was she thinking? Did she trust Grace? They hadn't met yet, and it was Dr. Leakey who'd fed her the previous day. Dr. Leakey might've been reading her mind.

"Go and ask Jackson for some meat. A smaller portion than yesterday. Let's feed her and then get going."

Grateful not to be urged again to approach, Grace walked backward slowly, thinking about how Watson had only chased cats when they turned their backs on him and fled or appeared to be fleeing. Lisa might mistake her for prey if she looked away or retreated too quickly. Once she'd passed the tree, she spun around and sped back to camp.

When she returned with the meat a short while later, Dr. Leakey was leaning against a sandy outcrop and Lisa was sitting nearby. As before, they were perfectly at ease. Still, Grace hesitated as she neared the top of the hill. What if the cat smelled the meat and rushed at her?

"Don't come closer. Put it down over there. You don't have to hand it to her, but I want it to be clear that *you* brought the meat, not me," said Dr. Leakey.

Grace was relieved she understood that she was afraid of Lisa. She tipped the meat out of the bucket and moved away. Lisa lifted her head and sniffed at the air. Without urgency, she stood and slowly approached. She crouched and, her eyes on Grace, took it in her mouth and walked unhurriedly a few paces back. This time, she didn't disappear. She lay down in the spot she'd sat previously and began eating, eager but calm.

"Right," said Dr. Leakey. "Let's get going, then. Matt and Brown Dog are already waiting for us in the Land Rover."

Grace stared at her. "They'll come with us to see the animals? Surely—"

Dr. Leakey interrupted her. "They're trained to remain calm and still in the car—even when there's wildlife nearby. My life would be hell otherwise, given how much driving I do with them."

Glancing at Lisa, Grace tried to imagine Matt being passive when he sensed other animals around; it wasn't easy.

"Does she have enough water?" she asked, suddenly reluctant to go.

"Yes, but you should clean the bucket and refill it when we return."

"Bye, Lisa," called Grace as they walked away.

They walked side by side without speaking for a while. Then Grace asked, "Weren't you afraid, going to her in the dark like that?"

Dr. Leakey didn't respond immediately. The question, it seemed, required some thought.

"No. She's hand reared. We watered and fed her. Above all, she came to us for help. She's a little unsettled because she's alone and uncertain about what she's meant to do—particularly with that awful collar—but she's not dangerous," she eventually replied.

"Good," said Grace.

Dr. Leakey was still pensive, her voice low. "I've never heard of a cheetah attacking a human. Of course, if you threaten or corner them, it's another story. That'd be your own fault."

For the first bit of the drive, Dr. Leakey said nothing. She drove the old Land Rover like she did everything: with purpose and as if it was a job to be done immediately and well. It bore no resemblance to Grace's memory of her mother driving. Eleanor had perched on the edge of her seat, stiff-backed and chest inches from the steering wheel. She clutched the top of the wheel, her hands white knuckled and her expression strained. She always drove as if pursued by wolves. Dr. Leakey sat back, one hand on the wheel and the other available to smoke and change gear.

Brown Dog lay on the back seat behind Grace. Matt sat alert and panting, with his head between the front seats. The combination of Dr. Leakey's smoking and the dog's steamy breath was overpowering. Grace struggled to open the window. It was unclear whether the winding mechanism was faulty or if years of dust had congested the system.

"Don't wind it all the way," said Dr. Leakey. "It's a little cool."

Grace wrestled the handle the other way, leaving the window only partially open. As the vehicle bounced over the track, rattling and squeaking, the lights shone up and down, skimming the sandy road and the bushes alongside it.

"Polecat," said Dr. Leakey.

"Where?" asked Grace, looking left and right.

"Long gone now. You need to look far ahead. For eyes reflecting the lights."

She leaned forward and stared, but Grace saw nothing for miles until the light seeped across the savanna, lifting a curtain on the view beyond the roadside. They passed a huddle of small houses with thatched roofs. A few chickens scratched about in the soil in a determined way. They scattered as a woman carrying a hoe approached. A mile or so farther, they drove by another similar homestead with a pair of goats tethered to a small tree.

Grace pictured the busy streets of Tewkesbury and remembered the throngs of strangers she'd seen when she'd gone to the supermarket, chemist's, or library. Sometimes she'd come home the long way through the park to watch dogs being walked.

"It must be lonely living here," she said.

Dr. Leakey continued looking ahead. "Why would you think that?"

Grace shrugged. "It looks it."

"Because it's not populated? Is it less lonely where you come from?"

Grace thought about the incessant swooshing of cars on the busy roads near the flat, the days her mother hadn't spoken a word or even opened her eyes, and the evenings Grace read in solitude or stared at the television without caring what was on but not wanting it off, because sometimes box voices were better than no voices at all. Now she looked out at the endless veld to where the faraway mountains were tinged pink and orange in the early light. Three guinea fowl sped across the road.

"Not really," she said.

Dr. Leakey slowed and drew up ahead of a large metal gate set beneath a gable roof that spanned the entire road. Painted above the gate were the words "Welcome to the Ngorongoro Conservation Area." She switched off the engine, and Grace was surprised by the silence. After a moment, a tall, lean man in a khaki uniform approached from one of several buildings flanking the entrance. Dr. Leakey opened her window.

"Good morning, Simon," she said.

"Ah, Dr. Leakey, hello," he replied, ducking his head to look at Grace. "Another visitor?"

"Yes. This is Grace. She was beginning to believe there are no animals in Tanzania, so I thought I'd better prove otherwise. We don't have much time. I hope they're awake."

Simon smiled. "Dogs to stay in at all times, right?"

"Of course," she replied, turning to the back. "Down, Matt." The dalmatian lay down. "And stay."

"And the cheetah, Dr. Leakey. How are things with her?" asked Simon.

"She's eating, drinking. We're taking it day by day."

He nodded. "Enjoy your visit," he called to Grace, before turning and opening the gate.

Dr. Leakey started the car and drove through.

"How does he know about Lisa?" asked Grace, exchanging a wave with Simon.

"The distances might seem great, but important news travels fast. Sometimes even unimportant news. In this case, it's helped by the fact that Simon is Jackson's younger brother," she said.

Grace twisted in her seat to get a better view, but Simon was walking away. "He doesn't look anything like Mr. Jackson."

"Rono," said Dr. Leakey.

"Pardon?"

"Mr. Rono. His name's Jackson Rono. And that's Simon Rono."

Grace felt herself color. She'd addressed the cook as "Mr. Jackson" ever since she arrived at Olduvai. Why hadn't he, Dr. Leakey, or her father corrected her earlier? Grace's mother had stressed how important it was to call people by their proper names.

"Our names are the most personal and important things to each of us. It's disrespectful not to get every one right. If anyone addresses you by the wrong name, correct them immediately. Don't embarrass yourself or others by delaying," she'd insisted.

Had the adults ignored Grace's repeated error because she was an awkward outsider, a teenager to be pitied? She swallowed, trying to quell her humiliation, and was immediately ashamed for feeling that *she'd* somehow been wronged. Once again, Grace thought about how out of place she was here, in Tewkesbury, everywhere.

As if decreed by the gate, the surroundings changed almost immediately. The bushes clustered closer together, the trees were taller, and the grass greener. Whereas previously the road was powdery, red, and largely flat and straight, there was little dust as they drove along the hillside and followed the windier route into the caldera. Dr. Leakey drove significantly slower. Lulled by the smoother ride, Matt stretched out, his eyes closed. Brown Dog hadn't moved since they'd left the camp.

Grace lifted her nose to the gap in the window and breathed in the morning air. It was sweet with the scent of grass and the lingering coolness of the night. The road wound gently between a thicket of tall flat-topped trees, which created a dense canopy. Dr. Leakey pulled over, stopped, and switched off the engine. Grace looked at her, but she was staring out her side window, which was slightly ajar.

"There's usually someone here," she said quietly.

Dare Grace ask who or what Dr. Leakey was referring to? Should she look in the trees, the grass, or lower on the ground? Was it a bird or an animal? A person? She opened her mouth to ask but was distracted by an unfamiliar smell. It was a strong, musky scent with an oiliness to it. Grace glanced at the seat behind. Matt raised his head slowly, his nose twitching. He gave a small sigh as he lay back again. Grace sniffed closer to the window. Yes, the smell was coming from outside. She turned and there, in the grass, within a few yards of the car, stood a large broad-chested antelope with long, heavy, banded horns that formed a perfect U shape above his head. He stared at her intently, his dark eyes still, as if to say, "That took you a while."

"Oh!" she managed.

Dr. Leakey shifted in her seat. "Ah, waterbuck," she said. "I was expecting baboons."

"He's enormous," said Grace, whose previous experience of anything similar was spotting a fallow deer in the distance while she was driven somewhere by her mother. The waterbuck looked nothing like the dainty doe she remembered disappearing into the trees. His gray-brown coat was lengthy and coarse, and, as if a playful makeup artist had taken white paint to his face, his eyes were highlighted by an exaggerated pair of white eyebrows. The same paint had been used to draw a heart around his nose and a white band from his throat to the base of each ear. Not even his odor detracted from his magnificence.

"It's a bachelor herd. Young buck hoping to come across receptive does," said Dr. Leakey, turning to look out the back window.

Grace followed her gaze. Sure enough, there were three—no, four—more waterbuck standing in the grass, contemplating the Land Rover.

"They're not afraid," she said.

"The animals don't associate cars with hunters here. They're curious and, eventually, bored."

As if to prove the point, the buck closest to Grace strolled alongside the vehicle and onto the road ahead of them, offering a view of the broad white ring encircling his rump and long tail that ended in a black tuft. One by one, the others followed. Grace counted five before she was distracted by movement on the other side of the road. A baboon, much taller and broader than Matt, sauntered out of the grass and crossed the road behind the waterbuck. Dr. Leakey had already spotted him.

"That's who I expected," she said.

As he swaggered ahead of the vehicle, the baboon glanced over his powerful, shaggy shoulder, briefly considering Grace with his close-set brown eyes. He reminded her of Alfie, a boy she'd encountered when she began school. When Alfie had appeared on the playground, the other children fell quiet, retreating as he made his way to the jungle gym with his don't-mess-with-me gait. What had happened to Alfie, she wondered? Was he still terrifying others?

Followed by two slightly smaller baboons, the alpha male disappeared into the grass, which signaled the others to show themselves. The troop traipsed across the road. There were several other large males, but most were smaller females and juveniles of various ages. A baby clung to his mother's chest, while a slightly older infant rode on his mother's back. Although they didn't rush, the baboons moved purposefully—except for a trio of little ones who remained on the other side of the road.

The youngsters had discovered that an old log with a jagged, broken branch jutting out at a ninety-degree angle created an excellent climbing frame and were taking turns to clamber to the top. Once one was seated on the highest point, another would scamper up and wrestle him out of position. The rules were clear: when someone sat, he must urgently be dethroned. They leaped onto one another, hanging upside down, brawling and swinging.

"Do you think they're brothers?" asked Grace, after she and Dr. Leakey had laughed at their antics for several minutes.

"I don't think so. Brothers are more inclined to fight than to play. That's my experience, anyway."

"You had brothers?"

"No. Sons."

"No daughters?"

Dr. Leakey took the stump of the cigar she'd smoked earlier from the center console and examined it as if it might regenerate. The car was silent but for the rhythmic breathing of the sleeping dogs. Eventually, she put down the stub.

"Our dau... No, no daughters," she said, turning to watch the tussling baboons again.

Grace swallowed, aware that something had shifted in the mood. She looked in the other direction, to where the rest of the troop had disappeared into the grass. Suddenly, two of the youngsters playing on the log realized they'd been left behind and raced across the road. The third, the smallest of the trio, was oblivious as he hung upside down, tugging at a piece of the rotting branch. After a while, he pulled himself onto the top and sat in the prized position, a look of expectancy in his eyes. Nothing happened. Neither of his friends tackled him from the spot because they were gone. Everyone was gone. He twisted his neck, looking behind and up into the trees, wide-eyed.

"The other way," whispered Grace.

The baboon hopped off the log and disappeared into the grass on the wrong side of the road.

"He's lost," she said, louder now.

"They'll find him," said Dr. Leakey.

"But he's still so little. What if a lion or leopard—"

"Look."

As if sent with an older cousin by their mothers, the lost baboon's two playmates and another slightly larger companion appeared and loped across the road to where the little one had gone. Within seconds, all four reemerged, cantered ahead of the vehicle, and vanished into the bush after the troop.

Grace wanted to applaud. "Amazing," she said.

"Animals never cease to amaze," said Dr. Leakey with a tiny smile.

The discomfort was gone. She turned the key, and they drove down the steep, winding road for about a mile before Dr. Leakey pulled off and stopped in a clearing.

"We can get out here," she said. "Just be sure that the dogs stay behind."

"Really?" said Grace, looking around nervously.

Matt and Brown Dog scrambled to their feet when they heard Dr. Leakey take her binoculars from the floor and open her door. She climbed out and closed it behind her. The dogs sat, disappointed. It took Grace a moment to gather the courage to leave the vehicle. She walked briskly to where Dr. Leakey stood at a wooden rail, peering through the binoculars.

Located about halfway down the rim of the caldera, the viewpoint was perched above a dense forest. It disappeared directly below before stretching out into a flat expanse of savanna that seemed to go on forever. Although the sun hadn't risen, its light cast a gentle glow on the land, bringing color to everything it touched. Behind and below, the bush lay thick and still, and yet Grace was acutely aware of the life within it. She'd seen how quickly and quietly the baboons and waterbuck had disappeared from the road. It thrilled and terrified her. Here, she was removed from the world she'd known—from Cambridge, Tewkesbury, her mother and father—by more than distance. She could've been living another life.

"You can see them from here, the animals," said Dr. Leakey.

Indeed, Grace saw sprinklings and clusters of dark dots on the savanna. Several gathered around a shallow basin of water to the left, and she could make out a line of dots walking along a path.

Dr. Leakey handed her the binoculars. "The lake is pink with flamingos in the breeding season. You're about three months too early for that. There's a rhino to the left of the water."

Grace held the glasses to her face. The view was blurry, but she wasn't sure how to adjust the vision. She saw a larger dark blotch that could've been a mound of earth.

"What do you think?" asked Dr. Leakey.

"I'd like to get a little closer," said Grace.

Dr. Leakey looked at her, her eyes seeming to dance behind her spectacles. "Those might've been the *very* words I used the first time I stood here," she said.

CHAPTER 14

1935
Moshi, Tanganyika

It was a particularly *rainy* rainy season, Mary was told by several other travelers as she pushed her way through the crowds at the airport at Moshi. The compact one-room building was steamy, with earthy whiffs of damp fabric, warm bodies, and muddy shoes as people—coming, going, collecting, and meeting—pushed past one another. As if to corroborate the claim, the rain clattered loudly on the low roof, gutters overflowed, and water seeped in under the doors.

Mary found a spot out of the way near a wall close to the main entrance, placed her suitcase on the floor, and scanned the crowd for Louis. She'd expected to see him the moment she arrived at the airport, as eager to be with her as she was to be with him. After talking about it for almost two years, they were finally going to be in Africa together. There was no sign of him.

A small, wiry man in a rumpled tan-colored suit caught her eye as he stepped aside to allow a porter balancing a box on his head to pass. She recognized him from the plane. He stood alongside her, peering through the crowds as if also hoping to spot a familiar face.

"Your first time?" he asked.

"Yes."

"The roads are bad, worse when the rains are in progress," he said, glancing at a nearby window. The view was obscured by a milky sheet of water. "If you were expecting someone from anywhere but Moshi, you'd be wise to go to the hotel and wait there. It could take hours—days, even."

Mary longed for a cup of tea and a cigarette. "Hotel? Is there only one?" she asked.

"No, but I'd recommend the German one. It's closest and the first port of call for most people looking for anyone off a plane. Ah…" He dropped his briefcase and waved at someone beyond Mary. "My driver made it. We're heading to Arusha but could give you a lift to the hotel on the way."

So it was that Mary came to be deposited at the front door of Gasthof Moshi in the center of town. She stood on the stairs under cover for a moment and looked around. It wasn't what she'd hoped for her introduction to Tanganyika. Not only did she long to be with Louis, but she'd also understood it would be possible to see Mount Kilimanjaro from the town. The deluge allowed little more than a view of the street, empty but for the occasional car and a few pedestrians scurrying about.

The reception was airless and dark. After some uncertainty about whether the hotel could accommodate her, Mary was shown to a room on the first floor by a woman whose gray hair was so tightly braided and pinned to her head, it looked unbearable, which might've explained her pained expression.

"Supper is six thirty," she said, opening the door to Mary's room. "Bathroom two doors down."

Mary wanted to ask if it would be possible to order a pot of tea, but by the time she'd walked into the room and turned around, the woman was gone, having closed the door behind her. Mary dropped her luggage and sat on the bed. She looked at her suitcase. Was it only two months ago that the Union-Castle liner sticker was fixed to her baggage in Tilbury?

Despite its dramatic and disconcerting start, 1934 had evolved into a good year for Mary. With Louis banished by Frida from The Close and his children— and essentially from Cambridge by his former colleagues and friends—and despite Cecilia's animosity toward him, he and Mary spent a great deal of time together. For Mary, the gratification was twofold. Although Louis and Frida were not yet divorced, the news was out and soon old, which meant he and Mary didn't have to be as furtive about their relationship as before. It wasn't just that she was in love with him. More time with Louis meant Mary had greater access to his immeasurable knowledge and experience. As much as she'd learned from working with Miss Liddell and Gertrude, Mary felt that her archaeological know-how and skills accelerated at an unprecedented rate alongside Louis. She'd never known anyone as energetic and ambitious.

Although, during the early part of 1934, he'd worked primarily on the Kanam and Kanjera fossils and artifacts he'd collected during his expeditions to Olduvai Gorge two years before, Louis also completed two books. He was busy and determined but, importantly, ever garrulous, eager to share his enthusiasm and thoughts with Mary and to solicit her opinion. There wasn't a breath of tedium between them. It seemed he'd met his match amorously and intellectually, and she hers.

At a time when it was widely considered sacrilegious, Louis's theory that early humans existed during the Middle Pleistocene epoch intrigued Mary. Of course, many—most of whom were believed to know a great deal more than Louis—dismissed it outright. Who was this man, raised in Africa and barely in his thirties, to espouse such heady notions, they asked? Why not, thought Mary? Isn't it the job of thinking men and women to challenge and test old beliefs?

It wasn't only that Louis was passionate and intelligent but also that he wasn't afraid to be controversial that pleased Mary. She also shared his fascination with living wild animals, particularly those he'd encountered in Africa. When Louis described the thrill of stalking wildlife as a boy, Mary couldn't help thinking about how, when her father was dying in France, she'd distracted herself by learning to go undetected to get as close to wild animals as possible. However, she never mentioned it to Louis. He'd tracked lions, buffaloes, leopards, elephants, and rhinos across African savannas. Hiding behind trees and grassy knolls to watch foxes, deer, and wild boars in the woodlands and meadows alongside a French village was tame by comparison.

Memories of tracking animals in France wasn't the only time Mary thought about her father when she was with Louis. She realized with something of a jolt one afternoon, after they'd sat shoulder to shoulder for hours discussing proofs for his book *Adam's Ancestors*, that she couldn't remember feeling as excited by anything since she and her father had examined the horse sculptures in the caves at Cap Blanc and hunted through the spoils at Laugerie Haute. In France, she'd felt that she'd been introduced to a new world. She felt it again with Louis and his promise of Africa.

They hadn't spent all of 1934 together. In the spring, Mary's fieldwork took her back to Hembury for her final training excavation. When that was over, she hurried to join Louis at his dig in Swanscombe, intent on gaining as much experience and information as possible from him for her next project, which involved directing her own dig for the first time at Jaywick. Although her team was small, she relished taking charge of the dig. Her work at Jaywick resulted in her first publication: a technical report written together with Kenneth Oakley, who was with the British Geological Survey at the time. The account was published in the *Proceedings of the Prehistoric Society*. But it was her uncovering of Britain's largest elephant tooth at Jaywick that caught the attention of most. As director, Mary was ashamed to have been unable to immediately identify the tooth, despite it being intact and in good condition. She was grateful that Louis had arrived soon after the discovery. He immediately recognized it and helped her lift and encase it in plaster of Paris. By way of consolation, he reminded her that he'd grown up among elephants. She'd tried to find comfort in his words, but mostly it intensified her desire to go to Africa.

She'd yearned for travel and adventure before she met Louis. Now her longing had a definite destination. It never burned more fiercely than on the occasions she and Louis went camping over the weekends. As they set up camp and she watched him light the fire and prepare a meal, Mary pictured them together at Olduvai Gorge, which had come alive for her through him.

"Let's go together," she'd said one night as she lay in his arms in the tent, listening to the rain on the canvas. He'd complained how regularly the weather ruined camping trips in England, adding that, by contrast, the storms of Africa enhanced them.

"You know how hard I'll work and that I'm prepared," she added.

Louis pulled her close and kissed her forehead. She knew he wanted her with him.

Her work at Hembury, Swanscombe, and Jaywick meant that, despite her youth and lack of formal education, Mary had archaeology experience across a range of periods of prehistory, from the early Paleolithic to post-Roman times. Also, working alongside many leading archaeologists, she'd been exposed to a variety of techniques of excavation.

When autumn loomed and the season at Jaywick came to an end, Louis had told Mary he'd raised enough money to return to East Africa. He'd leave in October. Mary's heart gave a dull thump, as if something holding it in place had given way. Her airways seemed to constrict.

Stop! I don't want to hear more, screamed her brain.

But Louis wasn't finished. If she could arrange to get there, he'd meet her in Tanganyika in April the following year, he'd said. Having by then completed the first part of his expedition, he'd take her to Olduvai.

Mary felt a drumming in her chest—whether the result of relief or elation, she wasn't sure. She clenched her fists and clapped them together.

"Yes, of course I can arrange it," she'd said, without hesitating to consider the details or logistics.

She knew her mother would rally against the idea. In fact, Cecilia would do everything in her power to prevent Mary and Louis from being together. However, Mary's resolve was stronger. She worried only about Bungey and Fussy, whom she'd managed to either have with her or see regularly while working in England. But not even having to leave the dogs would prevent her from joining Louis in Africa. So enthused and excited was she by the prospect that she barely registered Louis's confession that, while he'd not spared his parents the news of his broken marriage, he *still* hadn't told them about Mary's existence. She didn't care. She and Louis would be together in Africa.

Mary waited until Louis left for Africa one gray October morning before telling her mother that she'd join him in seven months. Cecilia hadn't tried to disguise her relief when Mary said Louis was leaving. With him out of the way, she might succeed in convincing her daughter what an unsuitable match he was. Mary had left Cecilia to revel in her delusion until she'd seen Louis off, reasoning it would be easier to contain her mother's ire with him already gone.

"He got off as planned, then?" asked Cecilia magnanimously when Mary returned to the flat after having bade Louis farewell.

Mary had hung her coat and scarf on the rack. "Yes, he did."

Her mother stared at her, her brow furrowed like someone had run a plow across it. "What's going on?" She stepped forward as if to smell the truth. "Why do you seem pleased?"

"I'm going to meet him in Tanganyika in April. He's going to take me to Olduvai Gorge," said Mary, unable to suppress a smile.

Although she'd anticipated her mother's wrath, Mary had underestimated the extent to which Cecilia would go in her efforts to induce her to give Louis up. Still, Mary was firm.

"I *am* going to Africa," she repeated whenever her mother brought up the subject.

Finally, Cecilia gave an inch. Or rather, she took another tack. "If it's Africa you want, let's go," she'd said at breakfast one morning a few weeks after Louis had left.

Mary looked at her over the rim of her teacup, an eyebrow raised.

"Let's go soon. Why wait?" asked her mother, before setting out her proposal.

They'd give up the flat on Fulham Road, find a temporary home for Fussy and Bungey, and, in January, board a Union-Castle liner at Tilbury bound for Cape Town. Once there, they'd visit excavations in South Africa and Rhodesia and do some sightseeing.

Cecilia was biding her time. She hoped that by accompanying Mary to the southern African countries, she'd quench her daughter's desire to see the continent and find an opportunity to deflect her from her plans to travel on and meet Louis in East Africa. Perhaps Mary would meet a more suitable chap while they were at sea. If the lives of movie stars were anything to go by, ocean liners were the epitome of romance and sophistication. Cecilia mentioned none of this to her daughter, of course. She didn't have to. Mary understood her mother and guessed what she was hoping for, but she also knew that nothing and no one would change her mind about Louis.

The trip was a grand success on all fronts for Mary. She was enthralled, particularly by Cape Town's spectacular mountains and beaches, the opportunity to dig at excavations at Oakhurst rock shelter in the southern Cape with John Goodwin, the empty expanse of the Karoo, and the magnitude of Victoria Falls in Rhodesia. The experience made her want to see more of the continent, and she was ever more impatient to get to Tanganyika, where not only would she be reunited with Louis, but the savanna and its wild inhabitants beckoned. Indeed, the trip was a success for Mary and, it thus followed, a failure for Cecilia. In April, she'd said a teary goodbye to her daughter in Johannesburg and caught the train to Cape Town, where she'd board a ship back to England while Mary flew to Moshi.

Mary went to bed still simmering at Louis for not having been at the airport. She shook the pillow vigorously, trying to revive its clumpy innards and resentful about spending her first night in Tanganyika alone in a shabby hotel. The drip, drip, drip of large drops of water falling from a gutter into a puddle outside the window finally put her to sleep.

Despite her sulk and the lumpy pillow, Mary slept deeply and awoke with her spirits much improved, along with the weather. The rain was gone, and the sun shone. It might be possible to see Kilimanjaro from somewhere on the street, she thought. She'd take a walk after breakfast. She was buttering her toast when she heard her name and looked up to see Louis striding between the tables and chairs toward her. She caught her breath and froze, knife stilled midway between butter dish and plate.

Louis's hair folded onto his forehead like a shiny wave breaking on a beach. It was longer, his skin was browner and frame leaner. Mary had forgotten how handsome he was. She knew from his few letters that he'd had a difficult time. One of the imperatives of the tour was for Louis to provide geographical and photographical evidence to support his claims about the early ages of the Kanam and Kanjera finds. He'd been dismayed to find that every one of the iron pegs he'd set out to mark the spot at which he'd excavated the Kanam jaw in 1932 had been removed. The absence of the iron pegs—Louis supposed they'd been transformed into spearheads and harpoons for fishing—was aggravated by extensive erosion in the region, which made it impossible to relocate the exact spot the jaw had been found. Although Louis and his colleagues had fixed the site within reasonable limits and undertaken new excavations, no further fossil hominid remains were found to corroborate the 1932 finds. However, there was no evidence of any frustration on the face of the man Mary watched sailing toward her. His smile was wide and his eyes bright as he opened his arms. She glanced around the room before dropping the knife, standing, and walking into his embrace.

"You're here," he whispered into her ear. "At last."

Mary felt something shoot through her, something she wouldn't have recognized before she knew Louis. She stepped back, aware of others in the breakfast room. She was about to say how she'd arrived yesterday, as planned, and tell him how unhappy she was not to have found him waiting for her, but Louis spoke first.

"It's been hell. The roads have turned into rivers of bottomless black clay. I lost count of how many times the car got stuck in the quagmire near the Ngong Hills. My back barely held up. Thank goodness I sent Heselon ahead in the big truck with Ndekei. We'll meet them and the others at the top of the Ngorongoro," he said, pulling out a chair and sitting.

Louis had often spoken of his Kenyan friend Heselon Mukiri. They'd been initiated into the same Kikuyu group when they were thirteen and shared a fascination with archaeological work. Heselon was a natural, said Louis, with talent for both finding and excavating fossils. He and Louis had been taught by the Kikuyu elders that if they believed something to be somewhere but didn't find it, they shouldn't resolve that it wasn't there, but rather that their powers of observation were faulty, and they should keep trying. As such, Heselon joined Louis's field expeditions whenever possible. Ndekei was the truck driver. He, too, had worked with Louis during earlier expeditions.

The "others" Louis referred to were zoologist Peter Bell, surveyor Sam White, and geologist Peter Kent. In addition to working alongside Louis, Peter Bell was to gather mammals and birds for the British Museum of Natural History. Sam White would create maps, while Peter Kent would undertake a geological survey of Olduvai.

Mary watched as Louis summoned a waiter and ordered a fresh pot of tea.

"Are you hungry?" she asked, gesturing to the pile of toast on the table.

Louis shook his head. "No, tea will be fine. We need to get going. With any luck, the weather will hold, and we'll make it to the Oldeani turnoff before dark." He leaned back in his chair, his eyes on her. "It's wonderful to see you." His voice was a low murmur. Mary felt herself blush.

"How far is the Oldeani turnoff from here?" she stammered, looking into her teacup.

Louis chuckled quietly.

At first, it seemed the weather would hold. Louis and Mary bundled into his sturdy Rugby pickup truck, and as they departed Moshi, she saw Kilimanjaro rising above a girdle of clouds, its snowcapped dome magnificent, and yet inconsistent with the tropical vegetation on the roadside. They drove through avenues of tall trees, passing modest farmlands and stretches of bushveld where the trees were shorter and the grass more abundant. After about forty-five miles, they arrived in Arusha, where they collected Louis's friend, Sam Howard. On leave from his job at the Shell Company in Dar es Salaam, Sam wanted to experience the wilderness. With Mary wedged between the two men, they continued west. By midafternoon, the sun was barricaded by a bank of clouds. The sky grew darker and lower with every mile.

Louis groaned. "I hoped we'd navigate the new road before the rain arrived, but it looks unlikely."

He'd told them earlier—when they stopped briefly to eat their lunch of flatbread, chicken, and fruit—that he expected they'd reach the district officer's headquarters on the rim of the Ngorongoro Crater that evening and that he'd packed food accordingly. He'd sent the large truck carrying supplies for their stay at Olduvai Gorge ahead because it would travel slower. They'd meet it at the district officer's place, where the plan was to spend the night before undertaking the final part of the journey to the gorge the next day. Louis added that the last sixteen miles from the base of the Ngorongoro range to their night stop would follow a route that had only recently been cut through the forest.

"It shortens the distance significantly," he said.

They'd barely turned off the older, better-worn road onto the narrow, new route when the first raindrops spattered across the windshield. The gradient was steep, and the trees on either side grew thick and close. While clearly hacking through the forest and excavating a pathway had required huge effort, the track was as uneven and earthy as a freshly plowed field. Mary glanced at Louis. He smiled without turning his head. Mary sat back. If Louis wasn't worried, she'd relax too.

Her calm was short lived. Within a mile, the rain fell with such intensity that Louis hunched over the steering wheel, his nose almost pressed against the windscreen. No one spoke until, in a particularly rutted spot and with the rain creating a murky curtain, the vehicle lurched violently and swerved to the left. There was a shout as Sam's head thumped against the side window. Louis had missed a corner and driven off the trail. He wrestled the wheel and righted the car, flinging Mary against Sam, who placed his hand against the side of his face where it had collided with the glass.

"Impossible. We'll have to wait it out," said Louis, stopping and switching off the engine. His face was gray and taut. He glanced at Sam. "Are you okay?"

The other man nodded, massaging his cheek.

They sat in the car, quiet with their thoughts. The rain intensified, settling into a deluge. They waited but it showed no sign of abating, and, as evening approached, threatening to take the last of the light, Louis said they'd set up camp and continue in the morning.

Sharing a tent with the two men on the side of the road during a rainstorm wasn't how Mary had pictured her first night back with Louis. She thought about how they'd lain together in the tent and listened to the rain in England. She also recalled how annoyed she'd felt when Louis hadn't been at the airport and felt a little silly. It wasn't like England, where if you missed a train, you could have a cup of tea and wait for another. She looked at Sam, who sat back, arms folded across his chest and head down.

"Well, let's get to it," she said, nudging him with her elbow.

"Will it clear overnight, Louis?" asked Sam a while later, after they'd set up and settled in the tent.

He was sitting on an upturned wooden box. Mary was perched on another, a gas lamp flickering between them. The rain drummed steadily on the canvas, but despite the dampness of her clothes, Mary wasn't cold. Louis turned to face his friend from where he'd been peering out through the opening into the night. He shrugged and removed the small towel he'd used to dry his hair earlier from his shoulders.

"It's hard to say. Even if it does, the damage to the road is done." He looked at Mary. "What I can say is that it's impossible to count on travel to run to schedule in this country, regardless of how short and simple a trip might seem. Expect people to arrive when you see them. Man has built roads, created lines of communication, and written books about the place, but we're in the wild and always at the mercy of nature."

She wondered now why, if one couldn't count on a journey to run on schedule in this place Louis knew so well, he hadn't packed more food. She might've asked if Sam hadn't been there.

The sound of the rain was replaced by birdsong the following morning. Mary was the last to leave the tent, and as she walked to a clearing a short distance away in the sunlight, she was aware of the stillness and the extent of the space around her. Of course, she'd seen the countryside the previous day before the rain had created a blurry gray barrier. She'd observed the changing vegetation— dense and tropical in places and more expansive grasslands in others. She'd peered out the windows, longing to see the animals Louis had spoken about. She was thrilled to catch sight of monkeys, gazelles, and a mongoose on the roadside, but she was eager to see more. Although she'd wished she was alone with Louis in the car, she'd experienced a sense of liberation and heightened adventure that she'd never known in Europe as they drove. The vast, unpeopled stretches of land—with their rugged and ever-changing vegetation, geography, textures, and colors—stirred unfamiliar excitement, and now, outside the confines of the vehicle and without Louis and Sam on either side of her, the feeling intensified. It was a strange land, and yet she didn't feel out of place. She was acutely aware of the birds in the trees; the rich, earthy smell of the mud; and the sparkle of moisture on the leaves. She looked up and watched a large bird wheel across the sky.

"Augur buzzard." Louis walked toward her. "Easy to identify because of its light underside, black back, and orange-red tail," he said.

Mary watched, repeating the name to herself. *Augur buzzard.*

"I wouldn't wander too far from the car around here," said Louis. "Sam and I spotted fresh lion tracks a little way up the road."

Of course you did, she thought, feeling inexplicably happy.

"We could also make out a few tire marks from the truck. It'll be waiting for us at the top. We should get going," he said.

Packing didn't take them long. However, plowing through the quagmire to get to the summit of the Ngorongoro did. In fact, it took two and a half days to cover the less-than-sixteen miles of newly made track. The Rugby regularly sank so deep in the dark mud that its passengers were compelled to climb out, unload it, carry the luggage ahead out of the worst of the mud, and then return to extract the vehicle and drive on. Sometimes, Louis drove on and walked back to assist Mary and Sam as they carried their belongings. It didn't help that the rain returned, forcing them to set up camp and endure further cold, hungry nights. It wasn't long before they ran out of dry clothing.

Finally, after days of manhandling the vehicle and luggage and growing increasingly short tempered with one another, they reached the top. Covered in black mud from head to foot, Louis called Mary to where he stood several feet away from the road. She glanced down as she made her way to his side. She was just as filthy.

"At last," he said, pointing.

They were on the rim of the Ngorongoro Crater. She looked down into the caldera. Two thousand feet below, the enormous circular area spread across twelve miles of verdant grassland with a shallow soda lake, fringed pink with flamingos, in the distance. She could make out dark dots in the grass, some of which were moving. She could discern a herd of elephants, some buffaloes, and two rhinos lying side by side.

"What do you think?" asked Louis, after a moment.

"I think I'd like to get closer," said Mary.

CHAPTER 15

1983
Ngorongoro, Tanzania

AFTER SHE'D SHOWN GRACE THE VIEW FROM THE RIM, DR. LEAKEY DROVE down the steep, forested road that spilled onto the floor of the caldera. The grassland was unlike any other Grace had seen during her short time in Tanzania. It was as dense and lush as the pastures of a dairy farm.

"It's a sunken Eden," said Dr. Leakey. "When the volcano collapsed in on itself about two million years ago, the fertile material—a combination of ash and soil—was contained, creating a rich bed for vegetation and, it follows, for animals. That water puddles in the depression helps, too, of course."

The wheels of the Land Rover had barely rolled onto the flat when Grace spotted a series of bold black and white stripes, distinct against the pale grass. As one of the animals lifted her head, Grace recognized the horselike shape of a zebra.

"Stop!" she shouted.

Matt and Brown Dog scrambled to their feet, barking. Three zebras closest to the vehicle raised their heads and stared. Dr. Leakey swiftly scolded the dogs, who quickly quietened and lay down again.

"Sorry," said Grace.

"It'll be hell in here if you call out every time you see an animal. They know to lie still, but if you yell, they'll forget," said Dr. Leakey.

"Sorry," she repeated, glancing at the dogs as if apologizing to them too.

She turned to watch the zebras from her window, curious about the way their stripey manes grew perpendicular rather than folding onto their necks the way horses' manes did. It was a style that might've inspired the upscale mohawk haircut favored by punks. Grace remembered her mother saying that however they were worn, stripes were unflattering. It was true: the bands of white and black did nothing to detract from the zebras' barrel-shaped bellies. Rather, they seemed to stretch to accommodate the bulging. The effect was beautiful.

"Ah, there you are. I wondered," said Dr. Leakey quietly.

Grace turned to look at the other side of the road, where a trio of wildebeests made their way toward the zebras in an unhurried, stiff-legged way. She covered her mouth to suppress an involuntary guffaw. What comical creatures they were, with their boxy heads, broad snouts, curved horns, thick necks, robust shoulders, spindly legs, and narrow hindquarters.

"It's rare to see zebras without wildebeests and vice versa," said Dr. Leakey. "They're grazing and traveling partners. Zebras see better than wildebeests, while wildebeests have superior hearing and an excellent sense of smell. They warn one another about predators. They like the same grasses, but their mouths and teeth are different. Zebras graze on the longer bits of grass, and wildebeests clean up the shorter growth. They're interdependent."

They watched the wildebeests tread languidly across the road, where they and the zebras were joined by several more. The animals grazed as quietly as a herd of cattle and horses might, not even lifting their heads when Dr. Leakey drove on.

They hadn't gone far when they spotted a hippopotamus making her way toward a muddy pool.

"Something's following her," said Grace, noting a smaller animal behind the enormous rotund creature, with her smooth, naked skin; short legs; and broad, muzzled head.

Dr. Leakey stopped the car and put her binoculars to her face. "You're right. It's a calf," she said, handing the glasses to Grace.

The baby hippo—not a newborn, but pinker around the ears and neck than his mother and his snout undeveloped—trotted to keep up. As Grace followed them, she caught sight of something else slinking through the grass.

"Is that a cheetah?" she asked, pointing and handing the binoculars back.

It didn't take Dr. Leakey long. "A serval cat," she said. "Hunting for breakfast."

Bang on time, the lithe, long-legged cat reared and pounced. For a moment, it disappeared into the long grass, and then there it was, trotting away with something dangling from its mouth.

"Has others to feed, I suspect," said Dr. Leakey.

From there on, they spent almost two hours driving, spotting, stopping, and watching animals. Grace said little but took in everything as Dr. Leakey seemed to magically summon animals and birds every few minutes as they crisscrossed the grassy plains, which were steadily flooded by sunshine. At one point, she pulled up alongside a small herd of buffaloes, explaining that the animals were known to be "erratically cantankerous." Grace nodded, her mouth agape at their massive proportions and heavy horns curling up on each side of their heads. She gasped when, having previously only spotted them in the distance, a herd of elephants emerged from the grass and strolled along the verge. Dr. Leakey kept driving. Grace swallowed.

"Is it safe to approach them?" she whispered.

Dr. Leakey pursed her lips. Grace felt her heart speed up as one of the elephants stopped and turned to face them, trunk raised and ears flapping. Dr. Leakey braked, coming to a gradual stop. The elephant stared and flapped his ears once more before turning and walking away with the others.

"It's never safe among wild animals, but mostly they issue a warning," said Dr. Leakey.

They didn't move until the elephants took a right turn and made their way across the grasslands. A little later, Grace giggled when five bristly-bodied warthogs scarpered at great speed across the road, tails held aloft like antennae. The hogs had barely vanished into the grass when a black-backed jackal emerged from where they'd come. The jackal sniffed the road and trotted slowly after them.

"Is he chasing the warthogs?" asked Grace.

"I doubt it. They're far too fast and fierce for a jackal. They just happen to be going in the same direction."

After a while, Grace stopped noticing the zebras and wildebeests. Once Dr. Leakey had pointed out the difference between Thomson and Grant gazelles—the Grant gazelle had masklike markings, with a thick black stripe running from its nose and across its eye to the base of its horn, while on the Thomson gazelle, the stripe ended at its eye—she lost interest in them too. There were so many in the caldera. They spotted a rhinoceros in the distance and watched it through the binoculars for a while. They also saw hyenas and several gray-crowned cranes and Kori bustards.

Eventually, having arrived at a sandy intersection, Dr. Leakey glanced at her watch. "We're going to have to head back," she said, taking a right turn.

Grace stared across the plain, which seemed to shimmer in the sunlight. Another herd of zebras and wildebeests grazed in the distance, where she could just make out the sparkle of the lake. Out here, it was possible to imagine that Tewkesbury didn't exist and that it didn't matter how uncertain her future was and how much she hated her life. If only there was a way to contain the way she felt in that moment and take it back to England. She was certain she could do anything if she felt as unencumbered as she did here.

The two hours they spent in the Ngorongoro caldera had been unlike anything she'd experienced before, and yet Grace felt a twinge of disappointment. Aside from the serval, they hadn't seen any cats. She thought about Lisa.

"Is it possible Lisa came from here?" she asked.

"It's unlikely. The cheetah population in the caldera is small, probably because of how many lions, leopards, and hyenas live here. However, there are plenty of cheetahs in other places nearby," said Dr. Leakey.

They'd barely driven a mile when Dr. Leakey slowed and pointed to the road ahead. Grace looked and saw large swirls in the dust. "What is it?" she asked.

"Something large took a tumble," said Dr. Leakey, driving closer. "It seems to have been dragged up this way. Oh! Here we are!"

Grace held her hand over her mouth to stifle a cry. There, in the grass to the side of the road, lay three young lionesses with their breakfast. They stopped eating for a moment to look at the vehicle. Their muzzles were caked with blood, and their tails flicked in annoyance. They'd killed a zebra, which they'd disemboweled and partially consumed. Grace took a deep breath, uncertain whether she felt shaky from awe or horror. The lionesses resumed eating. They placed their paws—the size of porridge bowls—on the carcass, sank their fangs into its flesh, and tugged large chunks of meat from it. Grace was grateful that she was unable to see the zebra's head. It made it easier to think of the prey as lion food rather than one of the beautiful animals she'd admired earlier. A pair of vultures watched from the branch of a dead tree nearby.

"These are the youngsters," said Dr. Leakey. "The others have already eaten."

"Others?"

"Near the tree. To the left."

A large male lion, with a massively bouffant dark mane, stared at the car, his amber eyes narrow. Two lionesses stretched out in the sunshine nearby. They didn't move. Grace shifted her gaze back to the male just in time to watch him lift his head and open his cavernous mouth to yawn, exposing a set of massive yellow fangs.

"Incredible," said Grace. "I had no idea they were so big."

"Neither did I—until I practically walked into one."

"What? How?"

Dr. Leakey chuckled quietly. "I was in Tanzania for the first time. We'd been at Olduvai for several weeks when Louis decided we should have a look at another site in the region called Laetoli. Your father might've mentioned the hominid footprints my team and I found there?" Grace nodded and Dr. Leakey continued. "Well, Louis and I were exploring alone one morning when I almost stepped on a sleeping lioness. I'm not sure who got the biggest fright— her or me. We fled in opposite directions. I do recall Louis wasn't sympathetic. Said something about how meeting a lioness on foot wasn't as disastrous as it could've been if she had her cubs with her."

Grace didn't take her eyes off the lions. She remembered how nervous she was about being near Lisa and couldn't imagine how terrified she'd be if she came face-to-face with a lion.

"There aren't any lions at Olduvai now, are there?" she asked.

Dr. Leakey turned to her. "There are. Particularly when the game is abundant. This country isn't a zoo. Wild animals go wherever they want. How do you think Lisa got to us?"

"She came because she knows humans. She was reared by people. Isn't that what you said?"

"Yes, that was her motivation. It doesn't mean that animals with other reasons don't live there or pass through. They are plentiful in the rainy season, but there at other times too."

Grace thought about how she'd headed off into the bush alone the first morning. Her father's concern was justified. Then she thought about how she and Dr. Leakey had walked the dogs and how they'd hiked to the excavations.

"Aren't you afraid when you walk the dogs or go to the dig like we did?" she asked.

"I always keep a lookout. Check for tracks, scan ahead. We always carried rifles with us when we first came. But I like to think we have an understanding, me and the animals of Olduvai. I don't wander around too far from the camp, and never in the dark. I don't bother the animals, and they don't bother me," said Dr. Leakey.

Grace wasn't convinced.

Simon Rono was no longer on duty when they left the conservation area. Grace looked for him while Dr. Leakey exchanged a few words with the similarly uniformed man who opened the gate, but she didn't spot Jackson Rono's brother.

As they drove away, Grace tugged her sweater off, rolled it up, leaned it against the window, and rested her head on it, closing her eyes. She didn't mean to sleep but wanted to think about what they'd seen in the caldera so that the images wouldn't fade. If only she'd borrowed her father's camera—but she hadn't even told him they were going.

Despite her intention, Grace nodded off shortly after they left the gate to Ngorongoro. She was roused by the sense of the vehicle stopping, opened her eyes, and sat upright. Were they back at camp already? She looked around. No. They were on the side of the road with nothing but grass and bush on either side.

"The dogs need a stop," said Dr. Leakey as she climbed out and opened the back door.

Matt and Brown Dog hopped out and sniffed around. Grace, stiff from sitting, got out, too, taking a few steps before raising her arms and stretching. The sun was warm on her face and the air cool. It was silent but for the snuffling of the dogs.

"Do you drive?" asked Dr. Leakey from the other side of the car.

Grace hesitated. What a ridiculous notion, she thought. When would she have had occasion to drive?

"No."

"Would you like to?"

No one had ever asked Grace the question. Although it hadn't occurred to her before, she realized how unusual it was for someone her age not to drive. At seventeen, she could've had her driver's license, and yet she had no idea how to operate a car. Her mother had become too ill to drive two years before she died. Or had she sold her car because they'd needed the money? Grace wasn't sure. She'd been in a car with her father so seldom that it hadn't crossed her mind that she might learn from him. Anyway, she wouldn't have wanted him to teach her. But would she like to drive?

"Yes," she replied.

"Okay. Come on, then." Dr. Leakey pointed at the steering wheel. "Matt! Brown Dog! Time to go."

Grace stared across the hood. "What? Now?"

The dogs leaped onto the back seat; Dr. Leakey closed the door behind them and walked around the car. "What's wrong with now?" she asked, pushing Grace's sweater aside and settling in the passenger seat.

Grace felt her heart race. She swallowed but didn't move. "I have no idea. I don't even know where to begin."

Dr. Leakey peered at her. "That's not unusual…before one learns how to do something."

There was a long silence. Grace looked at her feet.

"You want to learn to drive, but you're frightened," said Dr. Leakey.

Grace nodded.

Dr. Leakey persisted. "Are you afraid of driving off the road? Having an accident?"

The girl shrugged.

"We'll start slowly. It won't be dangerous. The dogs and I don't want to be involved in an accident, either, do we, boys?" said Dr. Leakey glancing at Matt, who panted in her direction as if worried about why *she* wasn't behind the wheel. Brown Dog was lying down, ever obedient. "Or are you afraid of failing?"

Grace exhaled. "I don't know," she said. "I've never had the chance."

"The chance to drive or to fail?"

"Neither."

Dr. Leakey looked at her as if she didn't understand. Why would she? Grace tried to think of something that she might be able to do that the older woman couldn't. Would Dr. Leakey know how to use a Walkman? Why would she want to? Anyway, she operated a radio at Olduvai, so she could probably work it out. Nothing else came to mind. Grace wished she hadn't admitted that she wanted to learn how to drive.

"You've probably never failed at anything," she muttered.

Dr. Leakey blinked three times in quick succession.

Grace swallowed, realizing how disrespectful her comment was. "I'm sorry. I didn't—"

"At one stage of my life, I failed so often that, quite frankly, it was shocking when I didn't," said Dr. Leakey.

CHAPTER 16

1935
Ngorongoro, Tanganyika

IT WAS WITH A TINY WRENCH OF RELUCTANCE THAT MARY SLID ACROSS THE SEAT of the Rugby to allow space for Sam as they prepared to leave the district officer's camp for the final leg of their journey to Olduvai. Once again, assuring everyone that the road would be easier from here on, Louis had sent the truck ahead.

"Look, not a cloud in the sky. This'll be a smooth ride." He smiled, winking when Sam caught his eye.

Mary intercepted the look and frowned.

"Honestly, Mary, we'll follow the route I took in '31—through the trees, down the shoulder of the volcanic highlands, and onto the Serengeti. It'll be easier. The topography, vegetation, weather...everything is different on this side," he said, serious now.

It wasn't just the route that she was concerned about. She'd longed to visit Olduvai from the moment she'd heard Louis talk about it. His descriptions of the gorge and its fossils fascinated her. It was the kind of place she'd fantasized about when she'd imagined working beyond England. On the other hand, she'd known very little about the Ngorongoro Crater and had barely given it any thought until, two days earlier, they'd peered down into the caldera after their taxing drive from Arusha. Mary had been unprepared for it. Even from high above it, she realized it was an extraordinary place. If she hadn't been weak with hunger and caked in mud, she might've insisted they make the descent immediately. Instead, Louis had said they'd go into the caldera when they were refreshed the following day, and they'd driven on to the district officer's camp. There, they'd found the truck with their supplies parked alongside a large fig tree.

The two Peters—Kent and Bell—and Sam White had gathered around the car as Louis made the introductions. He was telling the men about their difficult journey when he caught sight of someone behind them.

"Heselon, hello!" he called. "Come and meet Miss Nicol and Sam Howard."

A tall, muscular man with round features, close-cropped black hair, and wary dark-brown eyes approached and shook Mary's hand quickly, murmuring a greeting. His khaki shirt and trousers were spotless and might still have been warm from the iron. Mary was once more conscious of how filthy and disheveled she was. After he and Louis had exchanged a few words, Heselon stepped away from the group. She felt his eyes on her and couldn't help wondering what he was thinking. Having known Frida, was Heselon suspicious of her? Or did his guarded attitude have something to do with his kinship with Louis?

The next day—bathed, fed, and rested—Mary, Louis, and Sam had squeezed back into the vehicle to navigate the sticky descent into the caldera. The clouds had lifted, the sun shone, and the surroundings were lively, but Mary and Sam were mute in amazement. They gaped as Louis pointed out lions, leopards, rhinoceroses, hyenas, jackals, hippopotamuses, and baboons. They were stunned by the sights of immense herds of buffaloes, elephants, gazelles, wildebeests, and zebras; and varieties of birds they didn't know existed. It was extraordinary.

As they'd circled the caldera, encountering breathtaking scenes of more and more animals, Mary tried to comprehend why being among them moved her so deeply. She envied their freedom and marveled at their diversity. Aside from Louis and a few colleagues who'd traveled to Africa, Mary didn't know anyone who might've laid eyes on such sights. Was she stirred because seeing so many wild animals gave her a sense of a connection to the natural world she hadn't felt before? The interludes with wild animals in France couldn't compare. The size and strength she recognized—particularly that of the lions, elephants, buffaloes, rhinoceroses, and hippopotamuses—were evidence that human dominance wasn't inevitable. Besides, the presence of so many different living animals heightened her excitement about what they might find a little over thirty miles away at Olduvai. She'd been unprepared for the animals and beauty of the Ngorongoro Crater. Something had shifted in her; this experience had changed Mary Nicol.

Now, two days later, back in the Rugby with Louis and Sam on the final part of their journey, Mary wondered if anything could rival what she'd felt in the caldera.

They'd barely left the district officer's camp when, as he slowed to maneuver the vehicle around a large boulder, Louis said, "I'm going to try and get back into the caldera in a week or so."

Mary stared at him. "What for?"

"Apparently lions killed a hippo a few days ago. I've asked someone to secure the bones once the animals have finished with them so that I can examine them."

"Oh?"

"Given its isolation, it's possible that the Ngorongoro hippo population has survived an uncommonly long time. So long, in fact, that I have a hunch it might still show evidence that it descends from *Hippopotamus gorgops*." He leaned forward and looked at Sam. "That's the Pleistocene form we found at Olduvai when I was there with Professor Reck. This is a great opportunity to examine it, see if they are related and what other clues to the past it might reveal."

Something pinged inside Mary. Was it pride? Louis's hunches were unexpected. She was intrigued by the connections he saw between living creatures and their ancestors and how he interpreted what they might mean. But no, it wasn't pride she felt this time. She leaned back in her seat, remembering why she'd come to Africa. It wasn't for Olduvai Gorge, the Ngorongoro Crater, or even Louis Leakey. She'd come to discover and learn. She'd come to appease the curiosity ignited by her visit to the caves in France with her father, a curiosity that had burned fiercely ever since. It was why she'd felt so alive among the animals in the caldera and why she was eager to get to the gorge. She felt buoyed by anticipation.

Louis was right about the weather. The rain had sluiced deep gullies across and alongside the steep, twisty track that took them down the flank of the highlands. However, the sky was cloudless and the sun warm. On the other hand, despite Louis's assurances, the journey wasn't easy. Whereas, in 1931, he'd traveled in the dry season and only had to clear away a few boulders and trees to pass, the recent rain meant the grass was long and dense. It was difficult to spot the rocks and tree stumps, and progress was slow. The upside was that the passengers could admire their surroundings at leisure, including sightings of large herds of zebras, gazelles, and wildebeests.

"I hadn't expected it to be so green and pretty," said Mary, scanning the grass and sprinkling of wildflowers.

"That's the advantage of coming at the end of the rainy season. It'll change quickly during the next few weeks," said Louis.

He leaned out of the window. "Hmm, the sweet smell of the acacia blooms."

Mary breathed in but smelled only earth and the musky scent of one—or both—of the men alongside her.

They were nearing the end of the descent when, having emerged from a lightly forested section and rounded a corner, they saw the Serengeti Plains suddenly stretched out before them.

"It's like a lake," said Sam. "A vast green lake."

He was right, thought Mary, looking across the savanna as it flooded their view before softening into gentle hues of blue and gray in the distance.

"As it once was," she said.

Louis took over, telling Sam how, millions of years ago, the region comprised a lake that supported life as varied and abundant as that of the Ngorongoro caldera. Over time, faults and volcanic action drained it. Later still, water and wind eroded and incised the land, exposing a well-defined sequence of strata across what was once the shore of the lake. Protecting fossils, bones, and stone tools, the layers kept records of the ages. It was here, Louis believed, that he'd find material evidence that human forebears originated in Africa.

Mary glanced at Sam. She knew he'd heard Louis's tale before, but he nodded amicably as he gazed out the window. Who could be bored in such a beautiful place?

As they drove on, Louis pointed to the right, indicating Precambrian outcrops in a landscape Mary imagined might resemble the surface of the moon.

"And that's the extinct volcano, Lemagrut," he said, shifting his gaze to the left, where a mountain formed the background to a fragmented, jagged smattering of volcanic rocks and acacias.

"Can we stop? I'd like to get out and look," said Mary.

Louis obliged, pulling up and turning off the engine. She climbed out and walked a few paces beyond the vehicle. The surroundings were rugged and desolate. It was so different from the caldera that they could've driven hundreds of miles rather than just over twenty. The breeze was light, carrying with it a honey-like scent, which she realized came from the acacia blooms Louis had mentioned. The delicate smell seemed out of place in such a rough setting. She gazed across the plains to several small hills on the horizon. The distance was so great that it was difficult to gauge their sizes. She heard the crunch of Louis's boots.

"You have some admirers," he said.

Mary glanced at him, confused. He pointed to the left, where she turned to see a pair of giraffes looking at them over a small clump of trees.

"Oh! Hello," she laughed.

That giraffes were the world's tallest mammals, Mary knew. However, she hadn't realized just how lofty they were. The animals gazed down at them, their ears occasionally flicking on either side of their short hair-covered horns.

"Are they males, given the horns?" she asked.

"Ossicones," said Louis. "That's what the horns are called. No, both males and females have them."

He'd explained, while they were in the caldera, that there were no giraffes there because of the steep descent. That this pair had obliged Mary with an early appearance on the plains seemed especially accommodating. Their long, thick eyelashes reminded her how her mother had insisted she apply cake mascara before one of the dances Cecilia had forced her to attend.

"It'll enhance your eyes," her mother had said, handing her the miniature brush.

Mary had loathed it, complaining that she might just as well cover her eyes in boot polish. Elaborate eyelashes, she now concluded, were best worn by giraffes.

"There," said Louis, pointing directly ahead. "You can just see the gorge. There's the main ravine." He moved his hand to trace a narrow line that Mary could make out in the distance and then lifted his arm slightly to run his finger up at an angle. "And that's the smaller side gorge."

Before they left, Mary gave the giraffes a final look. They'd lost interest. The taller of the two walked away while the other wrapped her long tongue around the leaves of the tree and pulled them into her mouth. As Mary climbed back in the vehicle, she wondered if they might find the remains of a forebear of the giraffe at Olduvai.

"It'd be helpful if you learned to drive," mumbled Louis as he lay down alongside her on the air mattress that night. He was annoyed and exhausted because the pump hadn't worked, and he'd had to blow it up himself.

Mary wondered how his frustration with the bed might've triggered thoughts of her needing to drive.

"If anything happened to me, you'd want to be self-sufficient," he added.

"Yes, of course."

"We'll start tomorrow."

"Tomorrow? But we've just arrived, and I thought we'd—"

"We need to use as little petrol as possible. So I'll only teach you when it's absolutely necessary to use the vehicle, whenever opportunity arises," he said.

She nodded without speaking. Louis had told her how Frida had driven almost two thousand miles from Johannesburg to Nairobi when he'd developed a leg ulcer on their return from a conference in South Africa. Mary wanted to learn to drive, not only because it might one day be crucial but also because she liked the independence that it would allow. She couldn't deny that it also niggled that there was something Frida could do that she hadn't yet mastered. However, they'd just arrived at Olduvai, and there were many more exciting things to do than learn to drive, as they'd discussed during supper earlier—before the lions made their presence known.

When Louis visited the gorge four years earlier, he'd set up camp on the open plain. However, this time he wanted to explore the part southwest of where the main and side gorges met and decided to camp nearby. Moreover, the previous site was exposed, with the wind constantly sweeping layers of fine dust over and into everything. As such, Louis and Heselon established camp on a level spot in a natural clearing between two patches of wild sisal. Louis was pleased with the position and even more so by the fact that there were pools of water in the gorge. A scarcity of water had bedeviled the 1931 expedition, when they'd had to travel great distances to get to it.

They'd set up camp, eaten supper, and, with darkness having long settled, were about to go to bed when they heard a series of deep grunts from somewhere above the campsite. Mary felt the hair on the back of her neck prickle and looked at Louis. The others were also staring at him. The sound increased in volume, culminating in an extended groan.

"Lion," said Louis calmly.

"Close by?" whispered Peter Kent.

Before Louis could reply, the sound came again. This time the grunting continued, increasing in volume and frequency, and building to a crescendo before it changed into a deep, throaty growl and ended in another series of grunts.

"What do we do?" asked Mary, her voice high.

Louis took his rifle, which he'd leaned against his chair earlier. "He's telling us we're in his territory."

As if concurring, the lion boomed again, so loud and near that Mary felt the sound vibrate through her. It seemed that they should run, but where? When the roar was joined by another deep-throated snarl, Peter grabbed Louis's arm.

"A warning shot! Fire a warning shot!" he gasped.

Louis shook his head. "Go to your tent. Close it. Get into bed and sleep."

"Sleep?" said Peter, incredulous.

"Yes. Good night," said Louis, walking toward his and Mary's tent. "Are you coming, Mary?"

She'd trailed him closely. The other men, wide-eyed and silent, had scurried off in the other direction. The lions' roars, grunts, and moans followed them into their tents.

"You're sure they won't…do anything?" asked Mary, securing the opening behind her.

Louis shrugged. "It's unlikely. I didn't want to say anything while the others were around, but last time we found lion prints inside one of the tents one morning. The inhabitants had left it open when they went to bed."

She swallowed. "I'm not sure you should've told *me* that," she said, turning to check that she'd fastened the tent properly.

Louis had laughed and taken her into his arms. "You'll get used to it."

Despite her apprehension about the proximity of the lions and their possible intentions, Mary had relaxed against Louis. She'd been in Tanganyika for almost a week, and finally, they'd be alone together overnight. It was at that point that Louis had noticed the deflated mattress. He'd muttered, released her, and set about blowing it up. Now, as she lay by his side in the gentle light of a small lantern, Mary tried to work out why he felt it was pressing that she learn to drive.

"Are you worried about the lions?" she asked.

He turned to look at her. "What lions? They're quiet. They wanted us to go to bed."

Mary listened. He was right. The night was once again still but for the chirruping of the cicadas.

"Why do you ask?" said Louis.

"The sudden urgency that I should learn to drive."

"It's not sudden. I just hadn't mentioned it yet. Why are you worried? It's hardly as if you're likely to fail at it," he said, switching off the lantern and turning to her.

She wondered what Louis would say if she told him how often she *had* failed in her life. How she'd failed to make and retain friends of her own age. How she'd never passed a test or examination. How she hadn't fit in as a scholar and had disappointed her mother on multiple fronts and occasions. How it was only when she realized how her ability as an illustrator coupled with her insatiable curiosity might make her useful as an archaeologist that she'd felt a glimmer of hope that she wouldn't always be a failure. But, as Louis's hand glided over the curve of her hip, Mary stopped thinking and sank against him.

CHAPTER 17

1983
Olduvai Gorge, Tanzania

ALTHOUGH, FOR THE MOST PART, GRACE KEPT HER EYES FIRMLY ON THE ROAD
ahead, she recognized the short hill where the dogs had first chased Lisa. It was
within a mile of the camp, and she was *still* driving. She'd expected Dr. Leakey
to instruct her to pull over so that she could take back the wheel long before,
but she hadn't. After a little stuttering and twice stalling the engine, Grace
had—to her astonishment—mastered the clutch, gearshift, and brake pedal in
an adequately coordinated manner. It wasn't long before she also grasped the
gear pattern. Eventually, she was driving so smoothly that even Matt settled
and slept, and Dr. Leakey leaned back in her seat.

"You can go a little faster," she'd said at one point.

Grace had taken a deep breath and applied pressure to the accelerator.

"That's better. No! Too fast. Slower. Okay. Yes, that's it. You're doing well."

They'd driven on without talking beyond Dr. Leakey's occasional
instructions to "change up," "change down," and "turn the wheel more
gradually; it's a curve, not a ninety-degree angle." After a while, almost
breathing normally, Grace recognized the noises of the engine and was
beginning to judge for herself when to adjust the gears. She pictured herself

driving across the Serengeti alone. Where she'd go and why, she didn't know, but the idea and their silent camaraderie made her thoughts dance as if set free. It was only now, when the camp was almost in view, that Dr. Leakey spoke at any length.

"I'd like to think that you learned faster than I did because modern vehicles are much easier to drive than Louis's old Rugby," she said, her tone pensive. "But it's probably not true."

Grace didn't respond. She lengthened her spine to peer over the steering wheel and hood, determined to keep the wheels on the track as it turned down the hill.

"Actually, he wasn't a good instructor. Too nervous and impatient. Hated being in the car when I was driving. It was bad enough trying to teach me out here, but when we returned to England and there were other cars around, he couldn't bear it. Even so, I guess it wasn't his fault that I failed my driving test several times," said Dr. Leakey.

Grace thought again how unlikely it was that Dr. Leakey hadn't achieved exactly what she set out to do in all instances. She seemed unwaveringly confident and competent. She'd lived in wildest, remotest Africa for most her life and was fearless. No one else would be brave enough to approach a cheetah in the dark. And what about her career? Dr. Leakey was, as George had repeatedly told Grace, famous. What did it matter that she hadn't passed her driver's test decades ago? She'd lived such a long, interesting life and achieved so much. What did she have to regret? Grace could tell her about regret. She remembered how she'd tried to console her mother when she'd raged against the world and the injustice of her prognosis. Eleanor had wailed, saying that she hadn't done any of the things she'd dreamed of as a girl. Even when pain knocked the fury from her, she'd whimpered for more time. Eventually, her moaning ceased, and Eleanor was silent—so quiet that Grace had difficulty detecting her breathing. That was failure. George had failed Eleanor. The doctors had failed her. And what about how Grace had failed? She was only seventeen and she'd already failed monstrously at life. What was Dr. Leakey on about? What right did she have to claim that she'd failed?

"You're going a little too fast to park," said Dr. Leakey.

Startled to see that they were already in the camp, Grace lifted her foot from the accelerator without changing gear. The Land Rover jerked, shuddered, and before she could rectify her mistake and push in the clutch, the engine died and the vehicle stalled.

They'd stopped outside the kitchen. Jackson Rono stepped into the doorway, a white cloth slung over his shoulder and a hand shielding the sun from his eyes as he peered at them. Matt and Brown Dog clambered to their feet and stood, heads straining over the front seats and tails wagging.

Dr. Leakey looked at Grace, her extraordinarily variable eyes narrow and dark. "What happened?" she asked.

"I wasn't concentrating," mumbled Grace, hot with embarrassment.

"Hmm. Come on, then. Start it up. Park where it belongs," said Dr. Leakey, inclining her head toward her hut.

Grace's hands slid from the steering wheel onto her lap. "I'd rather not," she said, eyes down.

"What?"

"I'd rather not drive anymore."

"Because you stalled? You're ready to give up because you made a small mistake? That's ridiculous."

"No. It's just—" She glanced at Mr. Rono, who was still squinting into the sun.

"You're nervous about driving while Jackson's watching?"

Grace didn't reply. Instead, she wrenched open the door, jumped out, and walked away, shoulders hunched and head down.

Mr. Rono stepped out of the doorway and came toward her. She kept her eyes low, pretending she hadn't seen him, hoping he'd let her go, but he caught up and walked alongside her.

"The cheetah has been waiting for you, Miss Grace. She's been lying under your tree since breakfast," he said.

She stopped and stared at him.

"Some of the men are afraid of her. Your father..." Mr. Rono tried to hide a smile. "I told them they should leave her alone, that you and Dr. Leakey will take care of her."

"Why are you telling me? Tell Dr. Leakey," said Grace.

He frowned. "Dr. Leakey told me that you are responsible for the animal."

They stood in silence for a moment. Mr. Rono looked at Grace while Grace looked at her shoes.

Eventually, she spoke. "She's been lying under the tree? Where I was watching from?"

He nodded.

Grace smiled. She couldn't help it. The idea of Lisa leaving the security of the hillside and coming to the tree made her happy. It was possible the cheetah chose the spot because of the shade. Maybe it was more sheltered and comfortable there, but maybe she'd gone there to look for Grace.

"The problem is, I don't know what to do next," she said, as much to herself as to him. She raised her head and met his gaze. "What do you think I should do, Mr. Rono?"

He blinked as if surprised. She felt her cheeks color. Of course, he was accustomed to her addressing him as "Mr. Jackson." Should she explain how she'd met his brother, discovered her error, and apologize?

"You should ask Dr. Leakey," he said, looking over his shoulder to where she was climbing into the driver's seat. "She'll know what to do."

Grace swallowed and contemplated her feet again as the Land Rover started up and rattled past them.

"She'll park near her house. Go quickly. She won't want to be disturbed when she starts working," said Mr. Rono, his voice warm.

Dr. Leakey didn't seem surprised to see Grace waiting for her moments later. The girl had taken a shortcut between the other huts to arrive first. As she'd run, she'd thought about what she'd say. She should apologize for her rudeness. Apologies were due all around today, it seemed. Perhaps she could issue a blanket one, get it over with once and for all, even though Mr. Rono had given no indication that he'd been offended by her having gotten his name wrong.

She approached as Dr. Leakey opened the door for Matt and Brown Dog. "I'm sorry about—"

Dr. Leakey cut her off. "Take the dogs for a quick walk before you do anything else. Fifteen minutes or so will suffice. I need to get to work."

"Yes, but Mr. Jack—I mean, Mr. Rono said Lisa's come down."

"Down? She's in the camp?"

"Under the tree. At the lookout. He said she's been there since breakfast." Grace looked at the dogs, who stood, wagging their tails in anticipation. "Do you think the dogs—"

Dr. Leakey adjusted her spectacles. "No. Take them for a run in the other direction and then to Jackson. Ask him to keep them with him. Meet me back here. I need to radio someone."

Grace wanted to ask who. Was she going to ask for advice about Lisa?

"Go on," said Dr. Leakey.

Brown Dog followed her immediately, but Matt was uncertain. It was only when Dr. Leakey pointed at Grace and commanded that he should also "Go on" that the dalmatian joined her.

With a dog on either side, she set off at a trot. It was a mild day, but Grace was soon hot and out of breath. Once she'd turned the corner, she slowed to a walk. She was eager to get back, but Dr. Leakey had been clear that the dogs needed a fifteen-minute outing. She zigzagged her way around the camp, between the huts and back again, avoiding Dr. Leakey's hut and the space near Lisa.

On the second lap, Matt trotted into a raggedy patch of sisal, tail up and nose down. Brown Dog followed half-heartedly. Grace sat on a low sand-bank. She'd give them a chance to explore and then head back. She looked at Lemagrut. Today, the mountain rested beneath a blue haze, as if reflecting the sky. There was something comforting about its simplicity and solid presence.

Brown Dog picked his way out of the spiky plants and sat alongside her. Grace wound an arm around him and pressed her face against his warm neck. It was an absent-minded act but felt good. The dog turned slightly, acknowledging her embrace, and flapped his tail sheepishly. Grace loved him. It was as if the moment they'd met, he'd understood her. He demanded nothing of her. Brown Dog had chosen to be her friend. She'd reciprocated, and that was it. It seemed impossible that they'd only known each other for a few days.

With the sun on her back, Grace couldn't remember feeling as calm. It was midmorning. Everyone else was at the dig or elsewhere. Grace's enjoyment of the stillness was unexpected. She hadn't experienced such quiet before arriving at Olduvai. It wasn't just that the surroundings were peaceful; the stillness had permeated her mind. Even her concerns about having been rude to Dr. Leakey and Mr. Rono disappeared. It was more than that, though. Something had shifted. Her friendship with the dog, the hours watching the animals in the caldera, Dr. Leakey showing her the dig and teaching her to drive, and meeting Lisa—all these things separated the girl she was when she left England from who she was now. Everything felt different.

She leaned a little more heavily against Brown Dog. He glanced at her. She didn't want to think about leaving or how she might feel when she did. On one hand, she wanted to absorb everything around her. The peace. The solid presence of the dog. The warmth of the sun. The faint scent of dust. On the other hand, she wanted to shut down her senses so she could guard her thoughts against thinking about being back in Tewkesbury. Taking care of Lisa would help distract her.

"We should go," she said, getting to her feet.

She called Matt, and he and Brown Dog trailed her to the kitchen, where Mr. Rono met them at the door. He ushered in the dogs without question after she'd explained Dr. Leakey's instructions and, with a nod and small smile, closed the door. Turning to leave, she was startled to see her father standing on the path.

"Gosh! You have a weird way of popping up unexpectedly," she muttered.

He smiled. Had he always looked so shy?

"Dr. Leakey's waiting for you," he said.

Grace squinted at him, wondering why he wasn't working and what Dr. Leakey had told him. "I'm on my way," she said.

George fell into step with her. "You went to the crater."

"It was amazing."

He looked at her as if she might elaborate. She didn't. Although Grace hadn't thought of telling her father about her morning among the animals, she was inexplicably disappointed that he'd heard about it from someone else. Had Dr. Leakey also told him about her driving? They walked without talking until they reached the path George would take to the excavations.

"Grace," he said, stopping.

She paused and looked at him.

"About the cheetah." He held her gaze. "I'd rather you didn't."

"Didn't?" she asked.

He dropped his eyes. "Didn't handle it. The cheetah."

"Her. Lisa. The cheetah's name is Lisa."

"All right. I don't want you near her. Near *Lisa*." He said her name as if it embarrassed him.

Grace felt her scalp prickle. "Why not? Do you think that Dr. Leakey would allow it if she was dangerous?"

"She doesn't know. I asked her. She said she can't guarantee what might happen with a wild animal—even a tame one."

Grace blinked. "You asked her for a *guarantee*?"

"No, but I wanted to be sure you'd—"

"I have to go," she snapped, walking away.

Lisa turned toward them as they approached but didn't get up. She was lying on her chest, alert, with her head raised, as if expecting them. Grace slowed and, for a moment, walked slightly behind Dr. Leakey.

No, I mustn't be afraid, she thought, speeding up to keep pace once more.

"Hello, Lisa," said Dr. Leakey.

At the sound of her voice, the cheetah stood, unfurling her lean, tawny form, with its black spots and long legs. Her amber eyes, large and unblinking, were fixed on them. Grace bit her lip. Less than three feet separated them. Lisa was even bigger close up. Grace felt a hand on her arm.

"Give her a moment," said Dr. Leakey as they stopped.

Although her gaze was intense and steady, Lisa seemed calm. Her ears and long tail were still. If she was anything like her domestic cousins, she'd flick her tail and flatten her ears back against her head if she felt threatened, wouldn't she? The girl's heart was racing, and yet this time, she didn't want to run away. She wanted to be there, with the cat and Dr. Leakey. They hadn't spoken about George's concerns. In fact, they hadn't mentioned him.

"Did you touch her this morning?" asked Grace.

Dr. Leakey nodded. "Put your hand out. Let her come to you."

Grace lifted her arm, her hand flat, palm down, and her fingers straight. She was pleased to see that she wasn't shaking. Lisa glanced at the outstretched limb before taking a few smooth steps forward and dipping her head so that the top of her skull glided across Grace's palm.

"Oh my God!" said Grace, her voice quivering.

"Go on. She's given you permission."

The girl slowly ran her hand over Lisa's head, stroked her ears, and gently scratched the side of her face. Her fur was not as silky as it looked—not as coarse as Brown Dog's coat but nowhere as soft as that of a domestic cat. Lisa nudged Grace's hand with her head, urging her to continue caressing her. The collar encircled her neck, a dirty dark band made of stiff plastic material Grace didn't recognize.

Dr. Leakey stroked the cat's back. "I think it's safe to say that she was very lovingly raised," she said.

Grace thought about Brown Dog, how they'd leaned against each other and the peace she'd felt as they'd waited for Matt. She looked up to the hill, where the ravens were once more taking turns drinking from Lisa's bucket.

"Do you think since she's so tame, we might be able to introduce her to the dogs? That they might be okay together in camp?" she asked.

"I was on the radio earlier, trying again to get in touch with the people who raised her and the man who collared her. No one was available."

"Did you want to ask whether she'd get on with the dogs?"

"Any information might be useful. I'm concerned about her health." Dr. Leakey ran her hand down Lisa's spine. "She's far too thin and, I noticed earlier, has bad diarrhea."

Grace grimaced.

Dr. Leakey looked at her. "Why the urgency about the dogs?" she asked.

"If they get on, it'll be easier for all of us. We can't keep locking Matt and Brown Dog up, and now—" Grace glanced at Lisa, who stood between them, her tail swaying gently from side to side. "Now that we know how much she likes us, we need to work out how to keep her safe."

Dr. Leakey sighed and looked toward the camp. "She can't stay here. You'll be gone in a few days, and I'll leave shortly after. There won't be anyone here to take care of her."

"What? Then why are we doing this?" Grace's head spun. "What'll happen to her? You said yourself she can't hunt with this stupid collar. She won't survive."

The older woman didn't reply immediately. Instead, she tucked her fingers beneath the collar and slowly rotated it around Lisa's neck until the metal studs that fastened it were visible.

"Hmm. They've made sure this thing isn't easy to remove," she said. "We'd need bolt cutters."

"Do you have one?" asked Grace, uncertain what such a thing might look like.

"Unlikely. This is a dig, not a metal workshop."

"What are we going to do?"

"Get a bucket of fresh water and take it and her back up the hill. She needs to stay there. Jackson and Gatimu are on their way to leave the gazelle in the shade at the top."

"Gazelle?"

Dr. Leakey nodded. "She'll do better on the kind of meat she'd eat in the wild, and there's not enough beef to satisfy her."

"But—"

"I know. I don't like hunting, either, but until she can do it herself, there's no other way."

There was a long silence.

"What are we going to do in the long run, though?" asked Grace. "I mean, over the next few days?"

"I don't know, but I do know that there are almost always ways of achieving things that at first seem impossible—unexpected, different ways." Dr. Leakey paused. "I've spent a lifetime proving that."

CHAPTER 18

1935
Olduvai Gorge, Tanganyika

IT TOOK JUST ONE ATTEMPT AND A FEW MINUTES FOR LOUIS TO ABANDON THE idea of teaching Mary to drive after their first full day at Olduvai. The lesson was motivated by needing to move the Rugby away from the firepit shortly before supper. When she stalled the engine for the third time, he told her to stop.

"We're wasting petrol," he muttered. "We'll try again somewhere else, another time."

Mary looked at him, her eyebrows raised. "What about—"

"The others drive."

She didn't respond but was pleased to be able to focus on exploring the gorge. That's why she'd come. She *would* learn to drive. There'd be another time and way, and she'd do it—not because of what Louis wanted, but because it would allow her to undertake the kind of expeditions she dreamed about. It wasn't that she disliked the idea of being useful to Louis, but rather that she loved the idea of being independent.

As Mary turned to open the car door, Louis placed his hand on her arm. "Another thing," he said. "You need to be more circumspect with the water you use."

She stared at him. "Of course, but—"

Louis glanced away. "Heselon noticed you filling a bucket this morning. As I told everyone yesterday, the rains are over. We have to conserve every drop."

"Why didn't Heselon speak directly to me?" she asked.

There was a long silence.

She tried again. "Am I missing something?"

Louis scratched his head, still unable to meet her eye. "It's difficult for him. He and Frida got on, and he, well, he's unsettled by the, erm, nature of our relationship."

Mary sighed. "Of course. Why would it be any different in Africa?"

"He'll come around."

She opened the door and climbed out.

Along with the rest of the party, they'd risen before dawn that morning, as they did every day from there on. When they'd eaten breakfast—by which time, the birdsong had amplified and the sun created a bar of yellow above the horizon—they left the camp on foot. Carrying food, water, notebooks, pencils, brushes, dental picks, and trowels, they descended the gorge, dodging precipitous overhangs, strips of loose earth, and thorny clumps of vegetation. Louis's objective was that the party would explore the lesser reconnoitered side gorge and its gullies, locate exposed stone tools and fossils, map their locations, and make notes about them for future excavations. This was not the time, he said, to collect. However, if they spotted something of interest that was exposed on the surface, putting it at risk of being damaged by animals and the weather, they should remove it and take it to camp.

Louis had shown them a map, pointing out the parts previously explored. He'd named places after those who'd discovered them, using their initials, followed by a K for korongo. For example, FLK was the abbreviation for the Frida Leakey Korongo, which lay on the right bank of the main gorge where, in 1931, the excavation team, including Frida, had discovered stone tools. There was also a site designated with Frida's full name, Henrietta Wilfrida Korongo (HWK). North of FLK, Hopwood's Korongo—or HK—was named for Arthur Hopwood, who was also part of the previous expedition. Mary had studied the map carefully, deciding that her favorite name for a site thus far was Elephant Korongo (EK), where, four years earlier, Louis had found the fossilized remains of an ancestor of the elephant and stone tools he believed could be as old as six hundred thousand years.

Given the region Louis wanted to examine, it was a massive task. By the end of the four months that they planned to be there, he hoped to have explored one hundred and eighty miles of exposures in Olduvai Gorge, including those surveyed in 1931. As such, he was determined to stick strictly to an exploratory approach without undertaking any major digging.

"As you know, patience doesn't come easy for me, but it's absolutely essential in this case," he insisted. "If we don't work to a plan, we risk wasting time on less important sites while significant ones remain unstudied—all because we ran out of time to locate them."

It occurred to Mary more than once, as they crawled over the rough terrain on their hands and knees, that Louis's resolve to "work to a plan" frequently tested, rather than rewarded, his resolve to be patient.

"Time to move on," he'd say, when he felt anyone was spending too much time in one place.

Mary understood his reasons and the goal of the expedition. He wanted to survey as much of the gorge as possible so that when he—they, she hoped—one day returned to undertake a detailed excavation, work could begin on the most interesting sites. However, she also knew the importance of diligence, even when the objective was exploratory rather than to excavate. How could they be certain they'd prioritized the most interesting sites if they didn't examine each one minutely and take the time to accurately document what they saw? Mary had learned at Dorothy Liddell's side to pay attention to the tiniest of details. Her work as an illustrator had sharpened her meticulousness. She shared Louis's goal but believed there was more than one way of achieving it.

"Not yet," she'd typically respond to his calls to hurry from where she knelt on the ground, her hands busy with a pick or brush.

"We're *not* collecting," Louis would say through clenched jaws.

She'd ignore him and work on—scrutinizing the earth, brushing sand away from finds, and recording the details of what she saw in her notebook—until she was satisfied.

One afternoon, as the sun softened and shadows grew longer, Mary heard the crunch of boots climbing the ravine toward her. She rose from her hands and knees, arching and stretching her back. She'd been working in an eroded spot where two different beds intersected about a mile from where the main and side gorges met. The earth had been severed in such a way that numerous irregular exposures cut through several of the layers. Here, Mary had found various small flake tools and choppers in one bed, some fossilized animal bones, and, at the junction of two other beds, a clutch of fossilized mussel shells, most of which were still intact.

As she'd anticipated, the footfall belonged to Louis on his afternoon rounds to check the team's progress. She showed him what she'd found.

"Extraordinary! I knew we'd be onto something here, but didn't imagine this," he said.

Some of the tools, Louis agreed, resembled those identified as Acheulean hand axes, which were once thought to exist only in Europe. Finding such tools at Olduvai supported his theory that man originated in Africa. The fossilized bones appeared to have been those of some sort of antelope and pigs.

He held up one of the shells. "Freshwater mollusks," he said. "They're still around in some of the larger rivers and streams in the region."

Louis took her book and read Mary's notes, nodding his head as if in agreement.

"You've done a great job," he said, handing her the notebook. "I don't think I've ever read such detailed field notes. You might consider writing less during the day and adding the detail in the evening."

She frowned.

"It makes sense to use the daylight to explore," he added, as if she might've missed his point.

Mary looked beyond Louis to where a small flock of guinea fowl scratched in the sand between the bushes, clucking and clattering like gossiping villagers on market day. They'd been in the vicinity for several hours, and she'd grown accustomed to their chatter. It had been the kind of day Mary had dreamed about when she first imagined working on a dig in a foreign land. The space between earth and the sky had never seemed vaster. Although the sun burned brightly all day, the temperature was moderate. The knees of her trousers were stained by the gray-brown soil, which was also deeply embedded beneath her fingernails. Mary hadn't only spent the day doing work she loved, she'd also uncovered some remarkable fossils and stone tools. She felt a twinge of resentment that Louis had spoiled it by criticizing her methods.

He stood. "Well, I guess we've got a name for the site, then," he said. "Mary Nicol Korongo. MNK." He smiled at her. "What do you think of that?"

"I wouldn't expect anything else," said Mary, pretending indifference.

"Good. Will you come with me to see whether Sam's come up with anything?"

"No. I want to keep at it here. The light will be good for another hour."

"I think we've ascertained that this is an interesting site. There's no need to stay."

"I'll see you later," she said.

"Mary, we're not going to *have* to have this discussion again, are we?"

She took a deep breath, willing herself to stay calm. "No, we're not. You're going to leave me to do things my way. My notes will be detailed, and I'll write them as and when I like. I'll explore a site for as long as I think it's necessary. I won't let you down, Louis. I might do things differently, but the results will be those you require. No, in fact, they'll exceed your expectations. You'll see."

Louis stood without speaking for a moment. The guinea fowl grew quiet. Mary turned to continue working. Finally, she heard Louis walk away.

The birds had resumed their chatter when—having expanded her exploration a few feet northwest from where she'd found the shells—Mary saw the dull-white fragment of what looked like bone partially exposed in a small dry gully. She crawled forward and leaned in for closer scrutiny. Weathered and discolored, it was bone. Although dry now, the narrow channel had been cut recently. If left in place, the bone might be dislodged by the next rains. She'd need to extract it.

Mary took her notebook and a pencil from her canvas bag, marked the location on the map she'd sketched earlier, and made further notes. She examined the area around the bone and jotted down a few more lines. Louis hadn't exaggerated, she thought. Her notes were copious. She'd have to write smaller to avoid running out of pages.

With the soil dry and the fragment already well exposed, it was easy for

Mary to pick and brush the soil away and gently dislodge it. As with every ancient item she'd encountered since she and her father had dug about in the heap in France, she thought about who it might've belonged to and how it came to this place. Her initial instinct was that it was a cranial fragment of a large animal. However, when she held it, Mary's heart gave a thump, as if caught napping. The curvature of the bone was more pronounced than that of most animals. She blew away the granules of sand attached to it and lifted it to examine from the side. The layers of compact bone or cortex on the outer parts of the bone and the spongy diploe between them were more distinct than usually seen in animals. It was what one might expect of a human cranial fragment.

"Could it be?" she gasped.

Mary swallowed. She gently placed the bone on her notebook and fished about in her bag for her water canister. She needed to slow down. It wouldn't do to get excited and jump to conclusions. She might not have the training others had, but this was science, and she'd be scientific at every step. She opened the container and tipped it to her lips, thinking briefly about Heselon's comment to Louis about her use of water. Some of the pools they'd found when they arrived had already dried up. They'd discovered that the largest remaining one was the favored watering hole of a resident rhinoceros. It wouldn't have been a problem—animals took precedent when it came to sharing water—if only the ungulate hadn't incessantly urinated in the pool after drinking.

Mary took a sip, keeping the water in her mouth for a moment before swallowing. It calmed her, and when she lifted the bone to scrutinize it again, noting its smooth surface and distinct venous groove markings, she decided with clarity that she had enough clues to accept that it belonged to a human and not an animal.

The sun was low. Within an hour, the shadows would make work difficult, and it wouldn't be safe in the gorge. They regularly saw lions in the distance during the day, and at night their roars reminded them that they were in the big cats' territory. Mary didn't want to linger long. However, she did want to sit for a moment and think about what her discovery might mean.

Louis insisted that, from the moment he found stone tools at Olduvai Gorge on his first visit in 1931, the earth would present evidence of who made them. Here, in Mary's hand, was what he hoped for. Surely, despite his insistence that this time their work should be of an exploratory nature only, he'd want her to examine the area more closely.

Mary was so deep in thought, she didn't hear Louis approach until he spoke. "A drink before dinner?" he asked, his tone playful.

She stood and held out her hand to him, the fragment resting in her palm. "A celebratory drink, perhaps."

He stepped forward and peered at it for a moment before looking at her, his eyes narrow.

"Take it," she said. "Look closely."

Louis was quiet as he examined the fragment. Eventually, he looked at her. "Human skull," he said. "The second hominid from Olduvai after Reck's 1913 find."

Mary nodded. "I said I wouldn't let you down," she said quietly.

CHAPTER 19

1983
Olduvai Gorge, Tanzania

IT SEEMED INCONCEIVABLE TO GRACE THAT IN ONE DAY SHE'D SEEN MORE animals live in the wild than she'd encountered in photographs and on screens in seventeen years, learned to drive, and had a cheetah rub against her as she petted her. Not that the day was over. They'd led Lisa up the hill, Grace carrying a bucket of fresh water. She'd averted her eyes when the cheetah spotted the hooves of the gazelle and trotted eagerly toward them. They'd left the cat eating and fetched the dogs from the kitchen. By then, it was lunchtime. Surprised by how hungry she was, Grace had eaten a second helping before they returned to the workroom to continue sorting and packing.

Dr. Leakey had instructed Grace to check the labels and documentation of a box of fossils she'd set aside for the museum at Olduvai. With her half cigar extinguished but poised at the ready in an ashtray nearby, she sat at the table opposite, writing. Brown Dog and Matt lay at the entrance, where they'd been commanded to stay, along with an instruction to Grace to "keep an eye on them."

They worked quietly. Grace was determined to focus on the task at hand and not think about Lisa. They'd agreed to wait another day before considering options. Dr. Leakey hoped that at least one of the parties she'd radioed would get back to her. Would that mean someone would come to Olduvai to remove the collar or take Lisa away, Grace wondered? Dr. Leakey said she needed to learn patience. So she dared not ask.

"Well, what do you think? Live animals or fossilized ones?" said Dr. Leakey, picking up her cigar and a lighter.

Grace squinted at her. "What do you mean?"

Dr. Leakey propped the cigar in the corner of her mouth. "A career. For you. Animals or fossils?" she said, her words muffled.

Grace gave a light chuckle.

Removing the still-unlit cigar from her lips, Dr. Leakey narrowed her eyes. "What? You're not interested in either?"

"My father didn't tell you?"

"Tell me what?"

"I stopped going to school regularly four years ago. When my mother got ill," said Grace, looking down.

"So what?"

Grace watched as Dr. Leakey put the cigar back in her mouth, lit it, and took a few short puffs, before slowly inhaling and eventually allowing the smoke to escape her lips in a fine plume.

"You missed out on a few years of school," she said. "I barely attended school. I didn't let it stop me." She looked at Grace, who stared at her, slack jawed. "My father was an artist. We traveled. I had a governess once or twice. Didn't work out. When my father died—I was barely thirteen—my mother thought a convent school might work for me. It didn't. Neither the first nor the second one."

"Really. What happened?"

"I realized soon, at the first one—it was a very large school—that I didn't want to be there. The classwork bore no resemblance to the realities of life as I knew it, and I had nothing in common with the other girls. I wasn't used to people my own age. Within a year, my hiding place in the boiler room was discovered. I went there to avoid having to read poetry aloud. It was decided that I should be punished by having to recite a poem before the entire school. Ha! Of course, I refused and was told to leave."

Grace pictured a small version of Dr. Leakey, covered in soot, being sent home. She chortled.

Dr. Leakey leaned back in her chair. "It gets worse," she said. "My mother found another convent school for me, this one run by Ursuline nuns. I think I lasted a little longer than I did at the previous school. Perhaps almost a year. But it wasn't any better, and I can't say I learned anything useful. This time I was expelled for deliberately creating an explosion in chemistry class."

"Oh!" exclaimed Grace.

"Indeed. It wasn't a big explosion. Barely caused any damage. Really, the only real surprise was that I'd paid enough attention in class to detonate anything. Anyway, after the second expulsion, my mother gave up."

"But how—"

"No, I didn't attend university either. Or college. They wouldn't have me without a school certificate. I've never passed an examination in my life. I was your age on my first dig. I learned from watching others, listening, questioning, reading, and attending as many courses as I could. Not attending school didn't stop me."

Grace was stunned. Dr. Leakey's voice was as impassive as if she was talking about the weather.

"But your mother just gave up?" she asked, wondering if she could learn anything that might help her change her father's mind.

"After the second failure, she was too embarrassed to risk sending me to another school. She tried a few private tutors for a while, but they didn't really work out."

"Do you regret it? Not going to school?"

Dr. Leakey took another drag from her cigar, eventually blowing a thin stream of smoke from her lips.

"I think school and I were simply an impossible combination," she said at last. "And the governess and tutors? It seemed to me that formal education was, well, unnecessary."

"How did you come to this, then?" Grace gestured to the table, strewn with papers, books, fossils, and stone tools.

"My father taught me to draw when I was very young. I kept it up. After the schooling debacles, my mother suggested I turn it into a career. Become an artist. But I was also interested in archaeology—also encouraged by my father. I told her I'd rather train in that." She hesitated for a moment. "To her credit, my mother recognized that I was serious. She sold our house, and we moved to Central London, where I'd be closer to talks and lectures occasionally available to the public at museums and institutes."

"And yet she never came to see what you achieved here?" said Grace.

Dr. Leakey laughed quietly. "No, she didn't, but that had nothing to do with whether she approved of archaeology or not."

Grace looked at the ledger in front of her. She'd forgotten where she was on the page. She was thinking about what Dr. Leakey had told her. Grace's father was adamant that she should return to school and start again, however far back that might be. He argued she'd have no future without formal education. Without his university degree, he'd be nothing, he said. However, George was in Dr. Leakey's thrall. He might even be her biggest admirer. It wasn't just her work at Olduvai he admired, but also that she'd discovered footprints at Laetoli that proved man's ancestors walked upright much earlier than previously believed. Did George know that Dr. Leakey didn't have a formal education? That she'd attended school for less than two years and hadn't gone to university? It seemed impossible that he didn't. Dr. Leakey had spoken openly about it to Grace. Why would she have kept it hidden from others?

"You asked about regret," said Dr. Leakey, staring at what was left of her cigar. "I do regret something."

"Oh?" said Grace, with a nudge of disappointment.

"I regret that I wasn't more confident about my abilities as a scientist when I was young. For years, although I'd accepted that school hadn't been for me and that that ruled out university, I worried that I might never know quite as much or be as competent as those who had been through academia. I regret being insecure, uncertain during the early years."

"What changed it for you? I mean, made you certain?"

"I always thought I'd just do my best. After all, what more can a person do? One day, having worked with and alongside many highly educated, clever, and capable people, I realized the work I did wasn't just *my* best; it was excellent by anyone's standards. I saw that my work was important. It didn't matter how I'd got them; it mattered that I had the skills, knowledge, and veracity to do really important work in my field." She dropped the remains of her cigar in an ashtray. "Of course, you might argue that I was insecure before because I didn't yet have the experience. But that wasn't the reason for my uncertainty. I was unsure because I did things differently to others. Being different and taking a different route isn't a good reason to doubt yourself." She shrugged. "My life has been far from ordinary, but it worked out well. I regret taking so long to realize that."

They were silent for a moment, Dr. Leakey's eyes on Matt and Grace staring at the jumbled words on the page in front of her.

"Animals," said the girl eventually. "I'd like to work with live animals."

Dr. Leakey nodded, still looking at Matt. "I thought as much. Have you narrowed it down at all?"

Grace stared at her. How could she have narrowed it down when she'd only just decided upon it? No. That wasn't true. Of course she'd thought about it, when she worked at the animal rescue center. But it was a long time ago, before caring for her mother had taken over her life, and when Eleanor died, she'd transferred her energy to hating her father.

She shook her head. "No, I haven't. I've been too busy—"

There was a scuffle at the entrance. Both Matt and Brown Dog were on their feet, their attention straining down the path leading away from the workroom. Matt gave a long, deep growl, lowered his head, and shifted his weight forward onto his front legs as if preparing to attack. Brown Dog quivered alongside him, his hackles raised along his back in a bristly bar and his ears flat against his head. Matt growled again, this time baring his teeth and twitching his nose in a distinctly more menacing manner. Brown Dog glanced at Dr. Leakey and gave a loud bark, as if confirming that his friend meant business. Grace hadn't heard him bark before. She and Dr. Leakey stood simultaneously, Dr. Leakey's chair tipping to the ground. As they approached the dogs, Matt hurtled ahead, snarling and baying. Brown Dog followed in a dust storm of scrambling paws and furry limbs.

"What is it?" called Grace, hurrying to keep up with Dr. Leakey as she marched after the dogs.

"I don't know. They've clearly seen something. It's as if—" She stopped an arm's length ahead of Grace. "Oh God! It's the cat!"

Initially, Grace saw only Matt and Brown Dog. Their cacophony of growling, howling, and barking boomed across the camp as they charged forward and then retreated. Back and forth the dogs went, as if jousting with something to the left of a wall of a nearby hut. Then, as Matt rushed closer to the structure, the tall, tawny form of Lisa reared above him, fangs bared as she struck at him with a large paw, claws curved inward to create an intimidating hook. Matt cowered and recoiled. Lisa delivered another smack, narrowly missing his head.

"She'll kill him!" shouted Grace.

"He doesn't know that. He expects her to run."

Dr. Leakey put her fingers to her mouth and emitted a piercing whistle. Grace covered her ears, but the dogs showed no sign of hearing it. Dr. Leakey shouted their names until her lungs objected and she began coughing. Grace took over, cupping her hands around her mouth and calling for them. Neither dog acknowledged hearing anything.

They watched as Matt advanced and began circling Lisa, who'd indicated her willingness to fight by prowling into the open. She crouched, small head low, neck extended, and lips drawn wide in a threatening snarl. Matt, though significantly shorter than the cat, took up a similar pose. Like wrestlers in a ring, they skulked around each other, looking for a sign or the perfect time to attack. Several yards behind Matt, Brown Dog barked incessantly.

"Let's get Brown Dog away," said Grace. "I'll catch him and drag him off. Without him there as backup, Matt might retreat."

Dr. Leakey, having recovered from her coughing fit, nodded, her eyes on the animals. "That might help. Then I'll try and get hold of Matt. As long as they don't interpret our arrival on the scene as joining the fight." She looked around. "We need a rifle first."

Grace spun to face her. "What? Why?"

"We don't know what she'll do."

"But—"

"Jackson! Thank God."

As if Dr. Leakey had conjured him, Mr. Rono walked toward them, a rifle in his hands. Gatimu followed closely.

"We'll get them, Dr. Leakey," said Mr. Rono.

"Wait!" shouted Grace.

They stared at her. "Lisa doesn't know you. She knows us. You should stay here. Please." She looked at Dr. Leakey, willing her to agree, before turning to Mr. Rono. "Let us catch the dogs and bring them to you. Then we can go to her, get her away."

Mr. Rono glanced at Dr. Leakey. An ear-piercing yelp drew their attention back to the animals. It was Matt. A patch of crimson appeared behind his ear. Lisa's claws had found their mark.

"I'm going," said Grace.

"Slowly," cautioned Dr. Leakey. "We'll all get a bit closer, and then I'll hold back while you get Brown Dog. Once you have him, I'll go for Matt. Jackson, Gatimu, you stay back. Keep the rifle on the cat."

Grace wanted to object, but she knew it wouldn't help. Dr. Leakey was right: they didn't know what Lisa might do.

She looked at the rifle. "Please, Mr. Rono, don't—"

"Only if I have to, Miss Grace," he said, his face impassive.

They approached gradually, Dr. Leakey gesturing to the men to stop when they'd reached about halfway across the yard. As she and Grace continued, she called the dogs again. This time, they registered her presence by glancing at her. Still, they didn't come. Dense globules of blood plopped from Matt's neck onto the sand. He ignored the wound. Instead, his growling intensified and was interspersed with yowls, which sounded angry rather than aggrieved. When they were about three yards from Brown Dog, Grace placed a hand on Dr. Leakey's arm.

"I'll go now," she said.

Dr. Leakey stopped. Grace glanced behind and saw Mr. Rono lift the rifle. She shuddered, looked ahead, and walked slowly. She was about to reach out and grab Brown Dog's collar when Lisa saw her. The cheetah, who was panting heavily, lifted her head quickly, as if surprised. Their eyes met, and Grace imagined she recognized disappointment in Lisa's. Did she think the girl had come to the dogs' aid? As if to correct her, Grace snatched Brown Dog's collar. He swung around in shock.

"Come!" said Grace sharply, pulling him backward.

Whether triggered by Lisa being distracted or something else, Matt chose that moment to launch his attack. He flung himself at the cheetah, twisting his head to aim his teeth at her throat.

"Matt! No!" roared Dr. Leakey.

She might've taken her eye off the dog for a moment, but Lisa was too quick for Matt. She sprang out of his reach and, in a fluid movement and with the agility of a cat with resolve, landed on top of the dog, biting and kicking. Matt yowled in pain.

"Shoot her!" screamed Dr. Leakey.

"No!" yelled Grace.

She dragged Brown Dog to the other woman, grabbed Dr. Leakey's hand, and wrapped it around his collar before running toward where the dalmatian and cheetah were entangled in a dusty ball of fur, fangs, limbs, and claws. She didn't think what she'd do when she reached the animals. All she knew was that she had to break up the fight.

Dr. Leakey's shout rang out. "Don't be an idiot!"

Before Grace could take another step, a loud blast shattered the air. She flung herself to the ground, stomach down. Had Mr. Rono taken a shot at Lisa with her in the line of fire? As the sound reverberated across the gorge and faded into an echo, she dared to look up from where she lay. Lisa sped away, leaving Matt stretched motionless in the dirt. Dr. Leakey raced to the dalmatian. Grace sat. Brown Dog came to her, his tail wagging slowly.

She stood and stumbled forward. "Is he—"

"Lots of bleeding," said Dr. Leakey, from where she knelt alongside the bloodied black-and-white form of Matt.

The men approached. Mr. Rono handed Gatimu the rifle and crouched alongside Dr. Leakey.

"What did you do that for?" asked Grace, glowering at Mr. Rono.

He and Dr. Leakey shared a glance. Gatimu looked at Grace. She hadn't seen him frown before.

"What did *you* do that for?" said Dr. Leakey, her tone inexplicably calm.

Grace opened her mouth to object but was silenced by the sight of Matt raising his head. He was panting hard but was very much alive.

"Jackson shot in the air," said Dr. Leakey.

"Oh! I—" She wheezed. It could've been a sob, but Grace didn't cry. She took a deep breath and exhaled. The world stopped spinning. "Thank you. I'm sorry, Mr. Rono, Dr. Leakey."

Mr. Rono nodded.

Dr. Leakey ignored her, running her hands over Matt. "Stupid dog. He's exhausted. Some rather deep scores. The claws, I think. Most of the blood came from this ear," she said. "We'll need to clean and disinfect the cuts. The bleeding has almost stopped."

"No stitches?" asked Mr. Rono.

"I don't think so." Dr. Leakey looked at Grace. "You can give him a thorough check when you've cleaned the wounds."

"But what about Lisa?" she asked, kneeling to take a closer look at Matt.

"Lisa's fine. Did you see how she ran?"

"But she's gone. Will she come back?"

Dr. Leakey got to her feet. Matt stood, too, wagging his tail weakly. Mr. Rono and Gatimu walked away.

"I don't think she'll go far," said Dr. Leakey. "The shot might put her off for a while, but she's not going to be scared off by Matt. The fact that she came looking for us here despite us feeding her on the hill indicates that she's comfortable with us. Don't you agree?"

Grace thought about the way the cat had looked at her when she'd seen her approaching Brown Dog. She'd seemed shocked, as if she'd been betrayed. Grace wasn't certain Lisa would come back. If she didn't, where would she go? How would she survive with the collar still firmly holding her back from being able to hunt with ease?

"I'll go and look for her as soon I've cleaned Matt," said Grace.

"From the lookout," added Dr. Leakey.

They turned to make their way back along the path. The dogs followed slowly.

"You're not to go beyond the lookout on your own," said Dr. Leakey, her voice firm.

"We'll have to keep Matt and Brown Dog inside—now that we know just how much they hate one another," replied Grace.

"Yes. If anything, the fight will make things worse. Matt won't let the beating discourage him."

"If…when we find her, what are we going to do with Lisa?" asked Grace, as if the last half hour had changed things and they hadn't agreed to wait in the hope that someone would radio with a solution.

"If we don't hear from anyone who can help by this time tomorrow, we'll come up with something else. We'll come up with a plan. It's what we've always done out here."

CHAPTER 20

1935
Olduvai Gorge, Tanganyika

MARY, LOUIS, AND SAM HOWARD SPENT ANOTHER FULL DAY SEARCHING MNK where she'd found the fragment of hominid skull the previous day. The sun was directly above when Mary drew the tips of her fingers around a small section of flat bone and gently lifted it from its sandy bed. She examined it for several minutes before filling a page of her book with notes. Only then did she show it to Louis. His response was immediate.

"Yes!" he declared, loudly enough to startle Sam several yards away. "Another piece of the puzzle."

The trio discussed it for a while before resuming their hunt. If only they could find more bits of the skull and piece together a clearer picture. However, by sunset, MNK revealed nothing more other than two hand axes. That evening, Mary reluctantly agreed with Louis that while the gully should take priority during future expeditions, it was time to move on to unexplored places.

It wasn't easy. The next morning, Mary turned her head away, concerned that if she saw MNK, she'd return, as if lured by mythical sirens. The pull to go back was powerful, but she resisted, picking her way down the gorge and way beyond her namesake gully.

A dazzle of barrel-bellied zebras took off in a flurry of black and white from alongside the shrinking puddle. Although, with the water diminishing, there were fewer animals around every day, it wasn't unusual to come across the equines as well as shaggy-necked wildebeests and spindly-legged gazelles in the gorge. Mary had also grown accustomed to seeing the lofty silhouettes of giraffes and to being warned about sightings of lions, buffaloes, rhinoceroses, and hyenas. She'd even stopped shuddering when she saw snakes and scorpions. The creatures almost always retreated. Where they didn't, Mary did. It was an easy arrangement.

It amused Mary to hear her colleagues refer to their surroundings as "the wilderness." Yes, the area was wild, in that it was untamed and in its natural state. Animals roamed where they would. Trees and plants grew where they could. However, whereas once the word "wilderness" might've conjured images of disorder and fear, it was the most peaceful place Mary had ever known—and so different from anywhere else.

It wasn't just the prevalence of sunshine and wildlife, or the isolation, lack of water, and geology that distinguished Olduvai Gorge and the Serengeti from places Mary had known. It was largely unpeopled, and the ground was harder, drier, and more rugged than any she'd taken a trowel to. The chronological scope spanned a much longer period than excavations she'd encountered in Europe.

Indeed, the list of characteristics that distinguished Olduvai from Mary's old world was long. However, what struck her most was how infinite her surroundings were. The only thing grander than the boundless savanna was the inestimable sky. Their combined magnitude made her feel at once insignificant *and* mighty. The Mary Nicol who'd hidden in a boiler room, unaware of where her proficiency with a pencil and her perpetual curiosity might take her, had found her spot in the sun. She might only be a speck on the earth, but she had a place and purpose.

As the dust churned by the galloping zebras settled, Mary thought about how, even at the base of the gorge, the scale and remoteness of Olduvai prevailed. Although, most days, she could see and hear the others as they worked, they were always far enough away not to intrude. The peace allowed her to concentrate on what lay before her. Louis no longer harried her, and Mary moved at her own pace, taking her time to examine, sketch, and make notes. Being alone allowed her to think and examine her thoughts carefully, calmly, and critically. Was that why her father had painted alone? Because of the satisfaction that came with introspection?

She took off her hat and tilted her face to the morning sun for a moment. There was no place she'd rather be.

Mary might've enjoyed working alone, but sometimes her work demanded extra hands. One morning at breakfast, having discovered the skull of a giant extinct pig in a particularly fragile condition the previous day, she asked Louis if he'd accompany her to help encase it in plaster of Paris so that it could be lifted and stored safely.

Louis looked at her over the rim of his mug. "Heselon's the man for the job," he said.

"Oh? He's done it before?" she asked with a bump of regret. It wasn't just that if she had to work with anyone, she'd like it to be Louis, but also that there were no signs that Heselon's misgivings about her had changed.

"No, but you have, and I know he'd like to learn. I'll tell him," said Louis, getting up.

Heselon appeared shortly thereafter. He offered, gesturing silently and unsmiling, to carry her equipment, but Mary declined. She'd resolved on her first day on-site at Hembury to *always* transport her own things and, while excavating, carry her own dirt. There was no reason anyone else should do it for her. He shrugged with a look that might've said, "I wouldn't want you to touch my things either," and turned to walk to the site. Mary followed, moving as quickly as she could. Heselon strode on several yards ahead, never glancing back.

By the time Mary arrived, he'd hung his bag in the shade of a tree and was crouched alongside the skull, examining it from various angles. Mary had dug around and slightly underneath the find the previous day, leaving it sitting on something of a pedestal of earth. She arranged her equipment close by. The skull wouldn't survive in place much longer and was too crumbly to risk moving without encasing it. She explained to Heselon that they'd use a technique Louis had taught her in England, applying plaster of Paris to reinforce the find so that they could safely carry it to camp.

"I've done as much as I can alone," she said. "I need you to support it while I do the final cleaning. Then we'll place this cotton padding around it to avoid the plaster touching the fossil, wet the plaster to create a paste, paint it over the cotton, and layer these strips of fabric on the paste. Once it's dry and hard, it'll be ready to move."

Mary noticed how, as she spoke, Heselon's expression changed. His eyes widened before he frowned ever so slightly. The technique was new to him, but maybe what most surprised him was that Mary was the one teaching it to him. She was twenty-two, a decade younger than him and Louis, little more than a girl who'd worked only in England until now. It wasn't unreasonable that he might doubt her experience.

Heselon nodded, and for a moment, Mary thought he was going to speak, but he didn't. It didn't matter, she told herself. She liked the quiet. They'd work with minimal discussion. If he understood and did as she asked, there was no need for conversation.

It was a finicky job. Not only was the fossil desiccated and flimsy, but it was also difficult to brush off all the sand without applying too much force.

"We need a softer, finer brush," said Mary, thinking aloud.

Heselon got to his feet with an agility that belied his size and, without a word, disappeared between the bushes. He returned minutes later and handed her the exact brush she required.

"Thank you," she said.

He nodded and sat down to continue working.

The job took several hours. When the skull was clean, Mary took her time examining it once more.

"Hmm, I thought we'd manage without it, but we're going to have to use a bit of mud," she said.

Heselon stared at her. "Mud?"

"Yes, it'll mean using more water than I thought we'd need, I'm afraid."

"But we've just removed the dirt," he said, scowling.

She understood his confusion. Mary explained how refilling certain cracks and gaps with mud would temporarily reinforce the skull. He sighed, apparently unconvinced, but followed her instructions.

Finally, Mary pressed the last strips of fabric into the paste and sat back on her heels.

Heselon straightened and looked at her. "Now we leave it to dry?" he asked.

"Yes. Then we turn it over and do the same on the other side."

He leaned forward and gently touched a strip of fabric where the white paste seeped to the surface. "So, it becomes hard, like a shell, does it?"

"Yes."

"Then later, when we want to continue studying it, how do we remove the plaster?"

"We cut it. The fabric makes that possible."

They knelt in silence for a moment, looking at the parcel between them, which was unnaturally white against the muted-brown earth.

Heselon chuckled. Mary stared at him. She hadn't heard him laugh before. "What is it?" she asked.

"I was thinking about how carefully we cleaned it. And then you added mud," he said, laughing again.

"But I—"

"No, no, I understand now why you did it, Miss Mary," he said, trying to contain his smile. "It's just that it seemed absurd. It's the first time I've spent so long cleaning something only to add dirt to it afterward." He held her gaze, serious now. "I've learned something today. It was interesting."

Mary smiled. It had been a good day. Not only had she and Heselon done an excellent job with the pig skull, but he'd let his guard down, laughed, and talked. Perhaps he might now think of her as a worthy member of the team.

Despite Louis's directive that they were exploring and not excavating, they accumulated a considerable number of fossil bones and stone tools. In addition to Mary and Heselon's pig skull, the team had reinforced the skull of an extinct hippopotamus. They'd also discovered a pair of horns belonging to a defunct species of enormous wild cattle. The horns were six and a half feet long and required a bar of iron *and* plaster of Paris for fortification. Geologist Peter Kent had gathered numerous rock samples while Peter Bell's boxes of zoological material for the museum mounted by the day.

Mary's sense of belonging deepened, and with each find, her curiosity grew. The more she learned about the gorge and its inhabitants—past and present—the more she realized how little she knew and the stronger her desire to stay.

In 1931, Louis had set up a clinic at Olduvai. He'd treated wounds, malaria, eye infections, headaches, tapeworms, and a multitude of other problems suffered by some of the Maasai people who lived nearby or traveled through the region. They returned the favor by providing milk. The exchange worked well, and he did the same in 1935.

Most days, Louis returned to the camp late in the afternoon to run the clinic. A few of Louis's patients exhibited interest in fossil hunting and told him about old bones and curious-looking stones they'd seen in other places. One such conversation, with a man called Sanimu, gave Louis reason to contemplate closing the Olduvai camp for a few weeks to drive beyond Lemagrut and explore a place called Laetoli.

Mary was dubious about the sudden change of plans.

"But you were *so* determined to stick to the schedule," she said, when Louis explained his thoughts to her and the others at dinner one night.

"Yes, I know, but Sanimu insists that we'll find a great deal more there. I asked him to fetch samples. He'll be back in a week or so," said Louis. "He says he'll show us a spring on the west end of the gorge and others near Naibadad Hill on the way. How does that sound?"

The idea of finding fresh water *was* compelling. The stagnant pool in the gorge was small. With every passing day the ratio of water to rhinoceros's urine approached equal. One afternoon, they'd been delighted to see an unexpected bank of dark clouds gather on the horizon. A late storm ensued, and they dashed around the camp with containers, collecting as much water from where it lay in pools in the hollows of their canvas tents as possible. It was only hours later, when they were all laid low in excruciating pain and with upset stomachs, that they realized that they'd poisoned themselves. The canvas tents were treated with insecticide against mosquitoes, which had leached into the rainwater for which they'd been so grateful. It was an agonizing lesson, which would've served them well—had any further late storms occurred. Alas, there was no more rain, which was why Sanimu's promise of freshwater springs was so appealing.

So it was that when Sanimu returned days later with a little leather bag containing fossilized pig and antelope teeth embedded in hard rock, Louis decided they'd all leave for Laetoli for a few weeks. They loaded the truck, to be driven by Ndekei, as lightly as possible and followed it in the Rugby. Sanimu walked ahead as the vehicles bumped over the trackless terrain, zigzagging through mazes of thorn bushes and straining up steep, rocky ascents and across plains of wavy, tall grass. The three- to four-feet-high swards not only concealed rocks, tree stumps, and gullies but their seeds also blocked the radiators and the engines overheated. Mercifully, Sanimu's springs were flowing. The abundance of wildlife also compensated for the uncomfortable journey.

Finally, they arrived in the Laetoli valley, where they camped beneath a cluster of large fever trees near a sparkling stream. It was beautiful, said the others. Mary wasn't sure. Certainly, the stream was prized, and there were many animals and birds of great variety. Lions were also plentiful but, said the local farmers, not to be feared. There was too much wildlife for the cats to threaten humans. Within the undulating green landscape, they came across exposed expanses of gray sediment and gullies in which they found fossil bones and teeth. Even so, for Mary, Laetoli lacked the allure of Olduvai. It didn't help that she was the subject of intense scrutiny by the farmers who regularly gathered around the camp.

"What do you think it is, Heselon?" she asked as yet another group of men congregated nearby, pointing at her while deep in discussion. "What makes me so fascinating?"

Heselon didn't miss a beat. "It's your trousers," he said.

Mary glanced down. "My trousers?"

"They're not sure whether you are a man or a woman."

She laughed. "Oh? Well, if that's *all* they're concerned about, I'll stop worrying. Shall we get going?"

Heselon chortled and they strolled to where the others waited to head out for the day. Mary thought how accustomed she'd become to Heselon's laughter since they'd worked on the pig skull—and how much she enjoyed it.

The party had walked together for about a mile when, with the others having headed off in different directions, Louis and Mary found themselves alone in a sandy ravine. They walked side by side in companionable silence for several moments, looking at the eroded earth where knobs of sand and oddly shaped rocks dotted the surface. Louis stopped, examining a sandy patch. Mary walked on.

"Lion," he said, his voice low and composed. "They're fresh. Don't wander too far."

Mary heard but didn't react. She'd keenly studied animal tracks at Olduvai when they'd first arrived, learning what animals they belonged to and how recently the prints might've been made. At first, the sight of any paw or hoof print had excited her. But gradually, familiarity took the edge off the thrill. The sound of lions roaring in the dark was no longer cause for alarm. Heselon's description about how he was charged by a rhinoceros in the gorge amused rather than scared Mary. She learned that unless she saw the animals from a distance and could engage the stalking techniques that she'd taught herself in France, they'd flee long before she was close enough to fear them. Their senses were infinitely sharper than hers, and they didn't hang around to see whether she was friend or foe. As such, Louis's warning about the lion prints didn't concern her.

Louis followed Mary into the ravine, walking on when she paused to inspect the layers of volcanic ash in a nearby bank. She glanced up at a low mound of fossiliferous deposits several yards away and wondered what might lie behind it. She contemplated how unusual the geology was. The group had discussed earlier how the deposits at Laetoli seemed to have been laid down in dry conditions, whereas the beds at Olduvai were alluvial. The previous day, they'd found fossilized remains of tortoises and their eggs, which supported the notion of very different ecological settings and perhaps even distinctive geographical ages. The remains at Laetoli were older than those they'd found at Olduvai. This alone suggested that the site would be worth excavating in the future. These were the matters that occupied Mary's thoughts as she ambled around the mound.

It wasn't the color or even the shape of the cat that registered for Mary, but the texture of her fur. The lioness was sunning herself behind the embankment. Mary gasped, her legs threatening to give way. The animal sprang to her feet in a split second, her large sandy-colored eyes, with their perfectly round black pupils, fixed on Mary. Mary held her breath, taking in the massive proportions of the animal. She'd seen several lions but never as close. The lioness's head was long and broad and her legs solid. She opened her mouth and snarled, revealing two sets of magnificent canines. Her hiss turned into a low growl that seemed to come from her belly. Mary gave a piercing shriek, turned, and ran. The lioness, apparently shocked by the high-pitched cry, spun around and sped in the other direction. Louis rushed toward the sounds. Mary flew around the mound into his arms as the lioness disappeared over a grassy slope. Mary struggled. She was still fleeing. He held her.

"It's okay," he said. "She's gone."

Mary leaned against him, breathing heavily. She closed her eyes and thought for a moment how safe she felt in his arms. She didn't often need his protection but liked feeling she could count on it. Louis stepped back, held her elbows, and looked into her eyes.

"I warned you," he said. "You're lucky she didn't have cubs with her."

She held his gaze. "I'll pay more attention next time."

Predictably, Louis regaled the others with an account of Mary and the lioness that evening. The men roared with laughter, and, noting Mary's reticence, Louis draped his arm around her shoulders in a rare public display of affection.

"I'd rescue you from a whole pride of lions if I had to," he said.

They all laughed again. Mary shook her head, smiling.

Their lovemaking was particularly tender that night, and she wondered briefly as she lay on his shoulder if Louis wanted to *have* to protect her, subconsciously or otherwise. She'd believed since her father died that she must take care of herself. Her mother maintained she and Mary should never become anyone else's burden. Among Cecilia's primary parental objectives was to raise her daughter to be an asset and not an encumbrance to anyone in any circumstances. However, it was possible that Louis *liked* protecting her. She fell asleep, amused by the notion.

"We'll be back," said Louis as they settled into the Rugby to leave Laetoli a few days later.

"I hope so," said Mary, who'd grown so fascinated by the place that she'd stopped comparing it to Olduvai. The sites were just thirty to forty miles apart, but the differences were immense. Most compelling was that Laetoli was home to older fossilized material than Olduvai.

They would've explored longer if it wasn't that Peter Bell, Sam White, and Peter Kent were due to return to England via Olduvai and Nairobi. It was decided that Ndekei would drive the truck, with its larger wheels and high ground clearance, over a more direct route to the gorge, while in the Rugby, Louis, Mary, and Sam Howard would follow the route they'd taken to Laetoli. They hadn't driven far when Louis expressed doubt about the plan.

"Look at the grass," he said, gesticulating ahead. "It's still flat, as if we drove across it yesterday. This route is going to be much easier to follow. I shouldn't have agreed that Ndekei go the other way."

"But you said that the route is much shorter," replied Mary.

"Only if they're able to follow it as planned."

Louis was right to be concerned. He, Mary, and Sam waited at Olduvai a full day before the truck rumbled into camp. They'd gotten lost and driven much farther than anticipated. This presented two challenges: they'd be hard pressed to get the Englishmen to Nairobi in time for their flight, and because they'd used additional fuel, they'd have to follow a shorter but infinitely more difficult route. Nor was there time to overhaul the truck; they had to take their chances and get going quickly.

As if that wasn't enough to worry about, in their absence, the water situation at Olduvai had become critical, and, along with the lack of fuel, food supplies were also low. Most of the animals had moved on, leaving only the rhinoceros, who wallowed and urinated in the already putrid puddle twice a day. The water tasted foul, but it was all that was available. Louis instructed Ndekei to deliver the Englishmen to the airport, get the necessary repairs done to the truck, and then return with food and water, and enough fuel for them all to undertake the return trip in the truck and the Rugby.

There was little game to hunt, and only a few tins of vegetables and sardines; small portions of tea, flour, and maize meal; and a handful of potatoes remained. After they'd given half to the traveling party, Louis estimated that, in camp, they'd have enough to eat for about ten days. Once they'd bade the Englishmen farewell, Louis assured Mary that ten days was more than enough time for Ndekei to get to Nairobi, service the truck, and return with supplies.

"It's the water I'm worried about," she said.

"Yes. I was there earlier. It's very low," he replied.

"It's not just that. It's rancid. Unpalatable. It's only a matter of time before it'll make us ill."

Louis shrugged. "Let's hope not. There's nothing we can do about it."

Was there really nothing they could do? The closest other water was one of Sanimu's springs. It was too far away to go without using the Rugby, which was impossible, given the scarcity of fuel.

"What will the rhino do when the pool dries up?" Mary asked Louis the following morning after she'd forced herself to drink a cup of tea. With the fruit juice long since finished, tea was the only way to try to disguise the dreadful flavor of the water. It barely helped.

"He'll do what the other animals have done: go."

"What if we barricade the puddle? Prevent him from getting there? So that he goes sooner?"

Louis raised an eyebrow, gazing at her over the rim of his mug. "How do you propose doing that?"

"Acacia branches," she said, thinking about the bomas the Maasai built to protect their animals from predators at night.

"He's a rhino, Mary, not a dairy cow." Louis leaned back and folded his arms. "Thorny branches won't keep him from his water." His shoulders shook as he gave way to laughter.

Mary felt herself redden. It *was* a silly suggestion. She was embarrassed but also annoyed. At least she was trying to solve their problem. Louis didn't seem to grasp the seriousness of the situation. Boiling the water might've helped get rid of some of the contaminants, but it wasn't enough and certainly didn't improve the taste. Every day the puddle smelled and tasted fouler.

That night, Mary awoke to Louis's groans. He clutched his belly and begged for a bucket.

"Could be anything," he moaned, catching Mary's eye.

She didn't respond. His illness *could've* been caused by anything. A spoiled sardine, stomach flu, or another bug carried in something other than the water. However, it was likely caused by the water, and she had to do something.

Louis didn't leave the tent the next day. Although his cramps and nausea abated, he was feverish, dehydrated, and weak.

Mary asked Heselon to accompany her to the water hole. They should take spades, she said, uncertain what they'd do with them. The smell—a combination of ammonia and decay—reached them as they rounded the corner. The spring was less of a pool and more of a mishmash of messy, circular puddles stomped into the mud by the rhinoceros. On the one side, the mire had been pushed up to create a dense, tubelike wall where the animal had sloshed about. The surface of the small opaque pockets of water glistened with an oily sheen, broken here and there by floating objects of various shapes and sizes.

"Why do rhinos urinate in water?" asked Mary, wrinkling her nose.

Heselon shook his head. "I don't think they mean to. They spend a lot of time at water holes. Mostly in the afternoon and evening. They lie about, drink. Then they need to urinate, and so they do."

"Louis seems to think it's their way of keeping puddles liquid so that they can prolong their wallowing."

"Yes, but it's just his theory; there's no science behind it," said Heselon.

They stood without speaking for a moment. Mary lifted the spade she was leaning on.

"Science," she said. "That's what we need."

She thought about how Louis had laughed at her idea about keeping the rhino from the water. A barricade might not work, but what if they channeled some of the water away from the pool so that the animal didn't contaminate it more? Or perhaps they could siphon some of the polluted water through a natural filter, let it settle, and collect it away from the main water hole. That way, by the time they got it back to camp to boil, it would already have been clarified to some degree.

"We should use charcoal," said Heselon, after Mary explained what she was thinking.

"Charcoal?"

"To filter it."

It took them most of the morning and a couple of hikes back and forth between the water and camp to devise and implement the plan. By lunch, Mary and Heselon had dug a trench at an angle to divert a portion of the water away from the rhinoceros's pool. They directed the new watercourse into a short metal pipe, which they'd found at camp and packed with charcoal to create a filter. The water trickled through it into a deep, narrow well, into which it was possible to sink a bucket. They'd taken care not to encroach on the path that the rhinoceros used, ensuring that their modification to his puddle was as unobtrusive as possible. Mary watched Heselon arrange an old acacia branch over the pipe that they'd buried in a shallow furrow.

"Just in case the rhino thinks about changing his route," he said as Mary watched him. She smiled, nodded, and wished Louis was there.

That afternoon, back at camp, Mary created an additional filter using more charcoal and the oldest of her blouses, through which they'd strain the water for a final time.

Early the next morning, she and Heselon boiled and tested the filtered water. It was nowhere nearly as muddy, and while the charcoal added something of a smokiness and the tang of ammonia was still discernible, it was more palatable.

Heselon raised his mug to Mary. "It's much better," he said.

She swallowed. "Not the purest, but greatly improved."

"You've adapted well," said Heselon.

"Adapted?"

"To Africa, where we always come up with a plan."

CHAPTER 21

———————◆———————

1983
Olduvai Gorge, Tanzania

THERE WAS STILL NO SIGN OF LISA WHEN GRACE AND DR. LEAKEY CLIMBED the hill after breakfast the next morning. The water level in the bucket was the same. Dr. Leakey said it was possible, given how much of the gazelle Lisa had eaten, that she'd taken refuge somewhere to "rest and digest," but Grace wasn't convinced. The cheetah had come into the camp *after* she'd eaten when she and Matt had brawled. She was lonely, and now she was gone. Equally worrying was the fact that no one had radioed.

"I'll give it until this afternoon. Then I'll try again," said Dr. Leakey.

"But we agreed that if we hadn't heard—"

"A few more hours won't make a difference."

Grace wanted to argue. She understood that things took much longer to happen here than they might elsewhere, but they were running out of time. What if Lisa didn't come back? They'd need to go and look for her. But then what? What would they do with her when they found her? Grace and George were due to leave in five days, and Dr. Leakey was busy.

"Stay here," said Dr. Leakey, gesturing to the lookout spot. "If she appears, stay with her. I'll come back at teatime."

"Will you—"

"Yes. I'll make sure the dogs stay with me and lock them up before I return."

Despite a ragged right ear and some long pink scars from Lisa's claws along his neck and shoulders, Matt had given no indication that he recalled his fight with the cheetah when Grace had seen him at breakfast with Dr. Leakey. On the other hand, Brown Dog had lowered his head and wagged his tail slowly as he approached her, as if repentant. Grace had patted him, silently reassuring him that he was forgiven and that she blamed Matt for initiating the attack. A little later, when Dr. Leakey asked Mr. Rono to keep the dogs while they went to look for Lisa, Grace had felt Brown Dog's eyes on her once more. Not for the first time, she'd wondered whether it might be possible to train Brown Dog not to chase Lisa if Matt wasn't around. Dr. Leakey had taught the dogs to be still in the Land Rover—even within feet of wild animals. Surely it would be possible to train Brown Dog to accept Lisa.

"Waiting and watching again, I see."

It was George. As he ducked beneath a branch and approached, Grace thought how healthy he looked. His skin no longer appeared translucent. He'd rolled up his sleeves to reveal lightly tanned, muscular forearms. His eyes seemed brighter and his movements brisker, as if he was much more alive than when they'd left England.

"Yes. We haven't seen her since yesterday. Since the fight," she said.

"We heard the gunshot from the gorge and were relieved that it wasn't something more serious when we returned."

"It *was* serious," said Grace.

"Of course. Yes. But, well, you know what I mean." George sat alongside her, which surprised her. Didn't he have to get to work? The team working on the excavation typically left together immediately after breakfast. "Jackson told me what happened." Grace braced herself for his reproach about her recklessness. He'd no doubt insist again that she stay away from Lisa. Instead, he added, "He says you have 'a way' with animals."

Grace stared at him. "Mr. Rono said that?"

"Yes. He said Dr. Leakey pointed it out to him initially. Then he saw how her dog, the brown one, responded to you. Apparently, he didn't let anyone other than Dr. Leakey touch him before you arrived."

"Well, yes, Brown Dog has a mysterious past."

"That's why Dr. Leakey wanted you to help take care of the cheetah."

Grace looked across to where the bucket glinted in the sun. Not even the ravens were interested in it today.

"Did you know that Dr. Leakey didn't go to school?" she asked. She heard George shift in the sand. "Well, she went, but only for about two years. In total. She was expelled from two convents. Then her mother stopped forcing her to go."

"She must've—"

"She didn't go to university or college either. Just attended some talks and went to work on digs."

"Did she tell you this?"

"Yes." Grace turned to look at her father. He was staring at her, his eyes wide. "I'm surprised you didn't know. I mean, you know everything else about her."

"I didn't. I don't. I know about her work, but I don't know everything about her. Nobody knows everything about anyone else," he said.

"That's true."

They were silent for a moment, looking beyond Lisa's hill, over the plains toward Lemagrut.

"Have you noticed how the view of the mountain changes every day?" she asked.

"Yes. Sometimes it's blue, other times brown. Some days clear, others hazy," said George. "It's beautiful, though, the view, every day, don't you think?"

Grace nodded.

They were silent for a while.

Eventually, he asked, "Why did Dr. Leakey tell you that she didn't go to school?"

"Because I told her I hadn't."

"But you did, Grace. You went to school every day until four years ago. I don't know what happened to Dr. Leakey and why she didn't go to school. Did she have a tutor? A governess? That must've been it."

Grace shook her head.

"It doesn't matter," said her father. "Her situation wasn't anything like

yours. You went to school and were doing perfectly well until your mother...
Until she got too ill and—"

He raised his hands as if in surrender.

She spoke quietly. "Mum didn't tell me to stop going to school. I've told
you that. I stopped because I had to. There was no one to take care of her. You
left us. I didn't have a choice."

Grace hadn't cried in her father's presence since he'd left her and Eleanor.
Now, she couldn't stem her tears.

"No," said George, his voice muted too. It sounded as if it was coming
from far, far away. "You didn't have a choice. You were thirteen. You shouldn't
have been alone with her. You shouldn't have had to make *any* decisions on
your own."

"But you left."

He sniffed. He, too, might be crying, she thought. She didn't look. She
didn't want to see it.

"I did," he said, sniffing again. "She told me to go, and I went. I shouldn't
have. I should have stayed and watched everything that happened. I should've
kept an eye on you. I shouldn't have left the country and returned to find you
gone with no idea where she'd taken you."

Grace felt cold. She turned toward him. He held a hand over his mouth,
tears trickled onto his fingers.

"What?" she asked.

He looked at her. His eyes were red, pleading. "I didn't want to tell you.
It makes me seem even more pathetic than I am."

"Tell me," she said, angry now.

George swallowed. "When your mother told me to leave, I went to work
in Greece. We'd agreed she'd sell the house in my absence, and I'd signed
the papers to allow her to do so. So, when I returned to find it sold, I wasn't
surprised. She'd left some documents for me with the person who handled the
sale. Even that didn't alarm me. What shocked me was that she'd disappeared,
taking you with her. No one knew where you'd gone. At least, no one would
tell me."

Grace thought about how quickly her mother had sold the house, found a
home for Watson, and had their belongings moved to Tewkesbury. She'd been

so caught up in the misery of saying goodbye to the corgi and the life she'd known in Cambridge that Grace hadn't realized at the time how flustered and hasty Eleanor had been. It was, in retrospect, more like they were taking flight than moving away. What was her mother running from?

She stared at George. "That doesn't make sense. Why would she do that? It's not what she told me. She said *you* disappeared. You're lying again, Dad. She can't defend herself against your lies, so you just keep on telling them."

Her father shook his head, his eyes down. How depleted he seemed now as he sat beneath the tree, his knees drawn up and his head in his hands. She didn't want to believe him, but why would he lie to her? He'd left them. He didn't deny it. There was no need to fabricate another story. He wasn't cruel. No matter how often Grace had tried to convince herself otherwise, she knew that her father was kind. She didn't want to forgive him for leaving—he shouldn't have left her—but she knew, even if she tried to tell herself otherwise, it wasn't because he didn't care about her.

"Why would Mum not let you know where we were?" she asked.

George shrugged, still not looking at her.

"Others knew. You could've asked," said Grace, though she recalled how her mother had quickly cut them off from almost everyone they'd known. After Grace's grandmother's death, Eleanor had no interaction with anyone from her family. It had seemed to the girl that her mother's friends disappeared along with George, which was strange since Eleanor was the more sociable of the two. Now she wondered what had really happened.

George took his hat off and smoothed his hair. "I did. I asked everyone we knew. Most had no idea she'd gone, let alone where she'd taken you. I even hunted down several of your mother's old colleagues and friends I hadn't known. One, a woman she'd worked with, said Eleanor had warned her that I'd come looking for her. Said she shouldn't tell her anything. That I was...that I was a threat or something, and she and you were hiding from me."

"What? Dad, are you—are you sure that's what she said? She was lying. The woman, I mean. Mum would never say that!"

"I didn't believe it either," he said, although his tone indicated otherwise.

"Why didn't you tell me this before?"

George looked away.

"Why?" she repeated.

"I didn't want to believe it. I didn't, at first. But then, when I couldn't find you and realized what lengths she'd gone to to disappear, I had to. I didn't want to believe Eleanor would keep you and I apart. It didn't matter that she didn't want me but to…I didn't imagine she would be so…so cruel. That's why I didn't tell you. I knew you wouldn't believe it. You wouldn't want to. You loved her."

Grace sniffed. "And now? Why tell me now?"

This time he looked directly at her, his eyes on hers. "Because I don't know what else to do to rescue you. I found you, but it seems you're still lost to me. I'm desperate."

She looked down to where a trickle of ants scurried toward their hole. What were they running from or to? She watched, mesmerized by their speed and purpose. Was it easy being an ant, she wondered? Or did ants also wonder whether their lives would ever make sense?

"It doesn't change anything," she said, not looking up. "I'm not going back to school."

"Will you think about it, at least? A different school. Perhaps in Cambridge." George spoke quietly now. "Anywhere you want, really."

Grace watched the ants. If only she could quickly vanish the way they did when they reached their hole. "If I say I'll think about it, can we stop talking about it for the rest of our time here?" she asked.

Her father got to his feet. "Of course," he said, reaching to briefly rest his hand on her shoulder. "I have to get back to work."

CHAPTER 22

1935
Olduvai Gorge, Tanganyika

WITH LOUIS HAVING RECOVERED AND THE WATER LESS TOXIC AND MARGINALLY more appetizing—though the puddle continued to shrink every day—the party at Olduvai resumed the exploratory schedule they'd abandoned when they went to Laetoli. Mary took the opportunity to spend several hours at MNK, hoping to find more fragments of skull but coming away with none. However, she was distracted and wondered if the others were also counting the days since the truck's departure. On day nine, she began surreptitiously scanning the horizon for dust that might signal its return. That evening, she noticed Louis walking between the tents, searching the ground.

"Lost something?" she asked.

He didn't look up. "We're down to the last of the cigarettes."

"Hmm, yes," she replied. They'd been rationing themselves to two smokes a day for more than a week.

"I thought we could salvage tobacco from old stubs and roll it in toilet paper to make new cigarettes," he said.

"But Ndekei will bring more. Tomorrow's day ten."

Louis added another dusty, crumpled stump to the small pile of grubby relics in his hand and squinted at her. "I know but just in case it takes him longer."

It *did* take longer. By day twelve, Mary was grateful for Louis's foresight as they eked out the cigarettes made from cast-off tobacco. They were all irritable and hungry. On day fourteen, it was decided categorically that something must've happened to the truck. They speculated how it could've broken down, been involved in an accident, or met some other fate on the way to Nairobi or on its return. There was no way of knowing what exactly had happened. What was clear was that they couldn't wait indefinitely.

"If Ndekei was within walking distance of the administrative post at Loliondo, someone would've found a way of getting the news to us," said Louis.

"If they're able to get news to us, then surely we can get to Loliondo," said Mary.

It was midmorning. Too hungry and worried to hunt for fossils, they lingered at camp, uncertain exactly what to do but aware that they couldn't risk waiting any longer.

"I don't know. We have so little fuel." Louis looked across the gorge. "We could drive, I guess. Get as close as possible and, if necessary, walk the rest of the way. Then borrow fuel from the district commissioner, go back to the vehicle, and go on looking for the truck."

"Do you know the distance?" asked Mary.

"More or less. As you know, there's no road. We engineered some crossings over the deeper gullies in '31. Ideally, we'll find them."

"Is it the same route as Ndekei would've taken?"

Louis nodded. "Yes, unless he got lost, we could probably follow his tracks."

"Then we should go," said Mary.

They packed the Rugby, taking the remaining petrol and some rancid water, bid the others farewell, and left before sunrise the next morning. As Louis hoped, the grass was still flat where the truck had crushed it fifteen days earlier. The tracks led them to the crossings Louis had spoken of, some of which appeared to have been repaired by Ndekei. The route wasn't only much smoother and faster than anticipated but the Rugby was more fuel efficient too.

"Well, I certainly didn't expect this," said Mary as they glided down the smooth track toward the district commissioner's home and offices at Loliondo late that afternoon, having bumped their way out of the wilderness about two miles earlier.

Neither did she expect the greeting they received when they pulled up in the yard surrounded by tall fever trees. Mary opened the car door but was prevented from exiting by a couple of excited red setters who shoved their snouts into her lap.

"Hello to you too," she said, ruffling their ears and thinking about Bungey and Fussy with a pang of longing.

"Red! Rosie! Come away!"

Mary looked up to see a woman with glossy blond hair styled in tidy waves walking toward them. She wore an immaculate white dress with a blue trim and, with a pair of shears in one hand and a small bouquet of flowers in the other, could've stepped out of one of the women's journals Cecilia read. Louis hurried across the driveway to introduce himself. Mary watched, amused by the reappearance of his version of an obsequious English gentleman, a personality who'd been absent since they'd been in Africa. The woman laid her shears and flowers on a nearby wall, accepted Louis's handshake with a dainty hand and wide smile, and introduced herself as Mrs. Rowe, the district commissioner's wife.

"Delighted to meet you," said Louis, taking a step back and bowing his head. "And if I may say so, what a picture you and your magnificent hounds make beneath these beautiful trees."

Mrs. Rowe blushed and giggled. Mary was reminded of how charismatic Louis was, particularly around women. Cecilia had once complained, "He fancies himself a Lothario." Mary had replied that Louis simply liked women the way others like flowers and that they responded to his attention likewise.

"My goodness," said Mrs. Rowe, glancing at Mary as she stood up and gently pushed Red and Rosie out of her way. "You're the first woman I've seen in months!"

Mary was acutely aware of her khaki trousers—stained by the earth and torn at the knees from crawling around the gorge—and cotton blouse, which was badly in need of a wash. At twenty-two, she was younger than the other woman, but she felt timeworn and dowdy by comparison. Louis might've been thinking the same.

"Forgive the state of us," he said, having hastily introduced Mary. "We've had to do with very little water of late."

They stood in the yard while Louis explained where they'd come from and the purpose of their journey. Mrs. Rowe knew nothing about the truck, but they should come to the house, she said, where she'd call for tea and send word for Mr. Rowe. She led them onto a wide veranda festooned with potted plants and invited them to sit on wicker chairs with floral cushions.

When he joined them, Mr. Rowe—a large, cheerful man with a bright head of orange curls and beard to match—confirmed that the truck had indeed passed through on its way north but, alas, hadn't returned. The conversation was interrupted by the arrival of tea, accompanied by plates of sandwiches and scones. Mrs. Rowe poured. Mary caught Louis's eye as she took a long drink of tea. It was delicious. He took a sip and winked. However, when, a little later, their host offered him another cup, he declined.

"Could I trouble you for a glass of water instead?" he asked with a smile.

Mrs. Rowe scowled. "Is there something wrong? With the tea, I mean."

Louis chuckled. "It's like nectar, particularly after the stuff we've been drinking. It's just that I'd like to taste the water unadorned to see if it's as good as I suspect."

A jug of water arrived. Mr. and Mrs. Rowe were amused by the pleasure drinking it gave their visitors. Mary wondered if their hosts might invite them to take a bath. She would've accepted. Indeed, the district commissioner and his wife were eager to entertain Louis and Mary for the night. Mary's heart sank a little when Louis declined, insisting they should leave soon to continue searching for the truck. However, he did accept the offer of fuel, a few tins of meat, and some fresh fruit and vegetables for their journey. Most of all, Mary and Louis were grateful to be able to discard the water they'd brought and refill their containers with fresh water from the spring at Loliondo.

The sun was low by the time they crossed the border into Kenya and approached the dusty huddle of small houses and shelters that formed a trading center near the water hole at Pussumuru. Louis had mentioned earlier that they'd stop there to ask the traders whether they'd seen the truck. He braked in a sandy patch alongside the largest of the buildings as two men hurried to the car. Their turbaned heads filled his window, and they began talking excitedly when he switched off the engine.

"Just a minute," said Louis, holding up a hand as he opened the door.

Mary climbed out the other side, relieved to stretch her legs. She tried to make sense of the hurried conversation, but the men were talking over each other, and she caught nothing more than a few words, including "uprising," "warriors," "protection," and "no, no truck."

Louis's voice was low and composed by comparison. She could hear by his tone he was asking questions, but exactly what, she couldn't tell. Then he shook his head. "No, we can't stay. I'm sorry. We're looking for our truck. Anyway, we'd not be able to protect you."

The men were joined by two others, who added their voices to the appeal. One held up a large bolt of white cloth, telling Louis he could have it if they stayed. Louis shook his head again. Finally, the men fell quiet, and Louis gestured to Mary to get back in the car.

"What was that about?" she asked as they drove on.

Louis glanced in the rearview mirror, as if the men might pursue them. "They said the commissioner at Narok was killed. There was a confrontation with a party of Maasai warriors."

"Good grief. Do you—"

"They're panicking, concerned that the violence will spread. They wanted us to stay so that we could help protect one another."

Mary stared at him. "You don't think it might be a good idea?" she asked, although clearly he didn't.

"I wonder if that might explain the truck's delay?" he said, his tone pensive. "Political trouble."

"So, you don't think it's just a rumor, then?"

He kept his eyes on the track, driving fast. "I'm not worried about what the warriors might do to us. The story is that the murdered commissioner ordered them to work on a road. That incensed them."

"But—"

"Maasai warriors do not undertake manual labor. Demanding that they do so *will* lead to trouble," he said, as if she wanted to debate the issue.

Mary said nothing. She felt a little nauseous—whether from the news or because of how fast Louis was driving, she was unsure. It had been a long, bumpy day.

"There's nothing to worry about," said Louis. "We'll be fine. We're in Kenya now. I know the people. As long as Ndekei and the truck are okay, all will be well."

But all was not well. They'd had a much easier drive than they'd anticipated when they left Olduvai more than twelve hours earlier, but their luck was about to change.

It was dusk, and Louis was no doubt as tired as Mary was—though he'd never admit as much—when, aware of her silence, he turned to her. Mary had closed her eyes to try to quell her queasiness. Louis took his hand from the wheel and reached toward her knee.

"Are you all—"

Mary felt the car sink beneath her with a jolt. She opened her eyes to see Louis suddenly rise above her. He wrestled with the wheel, trying to right the vehicle, as she was thrust away from him against the door. Slowly, as if fighting the fall and apologetic about failing, the Rugby toppled onto its side, coming to a standstill with a solid thump. The engine cut out with a shudder. Mary groaned under the weight of Louis, who'd slid onto her, pinning her in the corner. There was some brief rattling and knocking as the boxes in the back of the vehicle came to rest.

They were silent and still for a moment. Finally, Louis reached for the steering wheel and slowly eased his weight from Mary.

"Are you all right?" he asked.

"What happened?"

"I don't know. I'll get out and let you know if it's safe to move."

Louis pulled himself up through the cab, opened the driver's door, heaved himself out, and disappeared.

After a moment, he peered in. "It's safe. Come. She won't budge at this point," he said, reaching down to take her hand and help her out.

There was just enough light to see what had happened. Louis had driven too close to the edge of a deep ditch that ran parallel to the road. The side had crumbled, and the car had tumbled into the gully, where it lay, the wheels on the left side resting on the bed of the ravine and right wheels almost level with the road. The hood was neatly jammed into the side of the trench.

Mary sniffed twice. "Petrol," she said.

Louis nodded. "Must be from the carburetor. Fortunately, the opening for the tank is facing upward. We'll have to be careful, though. No lighting lamps."

They stood side by side, staring into the ditch. The night was warm and quiet. A cicada gave a tentative chirrup, and before long, several others joined in.

The night they spent in the ditch alongside the Rugby on the road from Pussumuru made Mary think about the first time she and Louis camped together in England. Being alone together outdoors, without anything more to do than eat and sleep, reminded her why she'd fallen in love with him. Louis was so at home in the wild that she couldn't help but relax alongside him. He identified the night sounds and described the creatures who made them. He told her stories he'd heard from the Kikuyu and recalled other nights he'd unexpectedly spent in the Kenyan wilderness. Louis was a raconteur, regardless of whether he had an audience of one or a hundred.

The moon provided enough light for them to get by and the fresh water and tinned fruit from Loliondo were deeply satisfying after so many weeks of rice, sardines, and rhino-flavored liquids. Mary laughed when Louis mimicked Mrs. Rowe's horror when he'd turned down her offer of more tea in favor of water.

"I thought about suggesting she try some of the Olduvai water to prove that I wasn't being rude about her tea," he said.

"She was so taken by you, I suspect she would've tried it just to impress you," said Mary.

Louis chortled.

They fell asleep in each other's arms, certain that daylight would reveal that freeing the car from the ditch was easier than it seemed in the dark.

Alas, morning shed no light on how they might get the car back on the road.

"There's nothing we can do," said Louis, his hands on his head. "We'll just have to wait and hope that help arrives."

Mary was shocked. "Wait and do nothing?"

"What do you propose, Mary?" he asked. "Other than digging with our bare hands, there's nothing to be done. We have no tools, remember?"

"There must be a way," she said, going to the pile of their belongings alongside the car.

She returned with a sheath knife, two table knives, and a pair of enamel dinner plates.

"You're joking," said Louis.

"We can't just sit here hoping to be rescued. You of all people know how unlikely it is that help will miraculously arrive. Even if it does, we can get started."

He didn't reply.

Mary pointed to the edge of the ditch nearest the road. "We'll start by digging this away."

"We'd have to create a slope to somehow get it on an even keel," said Louis.

"Then dig out the bank in front to turn it so we can pull and push it out," she added.

He took the large knife from her. "It won't be easy."

"No, but it's something of a plan, at least," she said.

It was a massive job. Using the knives, they chopped and gouged the dense, dry earth before shoveling it with the dinner plates. It was soon clear that the digging alone was going to take more than a day.

They'd been working for several hours when Mary heard voices. She glanced at Louis. He stopped digging and stood. Mary saw the tip of a spear before four young Maasai warriors peered down at them. She lifted a hand to acknowledge them and continued digging. Louis greeted them, and they exchanged a few words and some easy laughter. The men sat, their legs hanging over the ditch, and, chatting quietly to one another, watched Mary and Louis work for about half an hour. When they stood to leave, one of the men called to Louis, who laughed and waved as they walked away.

"What did he say?" asked Mary.

"That they'd return later to help push."

She was surprised. "They'll help? I thought that was below the dignity of warriors?"

"Digging is. I offered them a reward if they helped but they refused. However, it seems that pushing the car is different."

"You didn't think suggesting they help might be dangerous?"

"Asking for help isn't the same as demanding it, particularly if you offer a reward," he replied.

The warriors returned twice that afternoon, but, noting that there was still plenty of digging required, left again without assisting.

By evening, most of the digging was done. Mary and Louis sat, drinking water. They'd stop for the day and, in the morning, move the earth in front of the car and start pulling it.

"Do you think the men will return?" asked Mary.

"I hope so. It'll be difficult for the two of us."

"Perhaps you could ask them if there are any oxen that are trained to pull plows nearby. Or donkeys."

Louis nodded. "Yes, I could ask." He cupped his hand behind his ear. "Do you hear that?"

Mary listened and heard a distant rumbling. It could've been thunder, but the sky was clear, and anyway, it was continuous. "A vehicle?"

"I think so," said Louis. "It sounds like a big one. Maybe they have a tow rope. That might do the trick!"

They walked to the road and stood, looking north toward the sound. Mary glanced at her hands. That her fingernails were filthy was something she was accustomed to. Now, though, her palms were calloused from gouging the earth with a knife and her arms were covered with a film of dirt that looked like it might be under her skin. It was unlikely that whoever was in the vehicle was another woman with glossy hair and wearing a fashionable frock. Even so, Mary dusted off her trousers and straightened her blouse.

Louis looked at her. "Expecting the king?"

"I don't care who it is as long as he has a tow rope."

It wasn't royalty but, more incredibly still, Louis's truck with Ndekei at the wheel! The driver stopped, leaped out, and greeted Mary and Louis with equal surprise. He'd arrived in Nairobi in good time, he said. The Englishmen were delivered to the airport, and the truck was taken for repairs and even ready for collection earlier than anticipated. However, less than five miles from Nairobi, the clutch gave out, and Ndekei had to return the vehicle to the mechanic. This time, the repairs took much longer. However, all this was in the past. The truck had arrived, and not only was it equipped with picks, shovels, and a tow rope, but they were also able to get the Rugby back on the road that night by lighting the ditch with the big vehicle's headlights and getting it free with Ndekei's help.

As they left to return to Olduvai at first light the next morning, Louis chuckled. "I wonder what the warriors will think when they find us gone?"

Mary shrugged. "That we made a meal out of the ditch with our knives and plates."

CHAPTER 23

———◦———

1983
Olduvai Gorge, Tanzania

GRACE WAS SO DEEP IN THOUGHT, SHE DIDN'T SEE WHEN LISA REAPPEARED ON
the hillside. Although ostensibly watching the ants skitter across the dry earth
in an endless, spasmodic black stream before they disappeared into a tiny hole
below a lumpy root, her mind was on her mother.

For years, Grace had steered her thoughts away from the move to
Tewkesbury. She had loathed the idea of leaving Cambridge. It was the
only home she'd known. Eleanor cut short her protests, saying she'd chosen
Tewkesbury because of its proximity to the oncology center. They were
unpacking when Grace asked when she'd see her father again.

"I don't know. Perhaps never. He's finally free to do what he loves. Don't
expect anything from him. Don't expect anything from any man," Eleanor
had responded.

The girl was stunned. *Free to do what he loves.* Didn't he love being with
her? She'd never doubted it before. Grace knew her father's work meant he
was often away, sometimes for months. After the initial shock of her parents'
separation had worn off, she'd even accepted that he wouldn't live with them
again. But she'd never imagined she wouldn't see him. She briefly argued with

Eleanor, insisting she was wrong. Her father would visit her. Eleanor shrugged and turned away.

As Eleanor grew weaker and ever more needy, Grace frequently stayed home to take care of her. Eventually, frustrated by missing so many school days and always worried about leaving Eleanor alone, she recalled the note her mother had written to her old school advising them of the move. Grace re-created it, addressing it to the new school. There was no response. It was possible she hadn't been there long enough for anyone to notice her absence. Or perhaps no one cared. Grace stayed at home, her world shrinking to fit between the walls of the two-bedroom flat.

Now, as the ants scurried before her, Grace thought about how quickly she'd accepted her mother's allegations about George. Why wouldn't she? She was young and Eleanor was her mother—her sick, helpless mother. Grace had to take care of her, not argue with her. Also, she'd trusted Eleanor, which, by default, meant mistrusting her father. It wasn't hard to do when he didn't show up to prove her mother wrong—until it was too late. She hadn't doubted her mother while she was alive. And now? How could she betray Eleanor by doubting her in death?

It was the sharp cry of a raven that made Grace look up. Two birds swooped into the sky above the hillside. Below, stretched out in the sunshine, was Lisa.

Grace scrambled to her feet, walked quickly to the foot of the hill, and ascended slowly, repeating Lisa's name as she approached. The cheetah watched her, amber eyes steady and her tail slowly furling and flattening. She seemed relaxed, but Grace was wary. Who knew what she might be thinking, given the events of the previous day?

"I'll stay here," said Grace, stopping about two yards away as she recalled Dr. Leakey's method. "You come to me when you're ready."

Lisa didn't hesitate. She stood and sauntered to her, dropping her head to be stroked as she reached Grace. There was no ambiguity in her greeting. Grace gently stroked her forehead, gradually moving her hand over her back. When she rubbed her chin, Lisa pushed into the stroke. Without thinking, Grace crouched and put her arms around the cheetah's neck. Lisa tilted her head and pressed the side of her face against the girl's ear.

At first it sounded like a low hum. Then, for a moment, Grace thought the cheetah was growling. However, as the volume increased and she felt the vibrations, she realized Lisa was purring. Dr. Leakey was right: cheetahs purred, and it was wonderful.

"Oh, you beautiful girl. You're whirring as loudly as a little tractor," said Grace, running her hands over the top of the cat's head and down her spine.

Lisa purred and bumped her head against Grace until, a little stiff from crouching, Grace eventually stood. It was then that she noticed the raw spot on the right side of Lisa's neck. The collar had rubbed off the fur and top layers of skin, leaving a patch of flesh exposed, glistening pink and yellow where it wasn't caked with dirt. It was infected and, with the hard plastic shifting against the spot with every movement Lisa made, continually aggravated.

"We have to get this off," said Grace, running her fingers beneath the band as if she might miraculously find a way of removing it. "Even if there's nothing else we can do, this *has* to go."

She looked toward camp. There was no sign of Dr. Leakey. Was it safe for Grace to leave Lisa to go and look for her? The fact that Lisa hadn't come to her when she was at the lookout suggested the cat realized she should stay on the hill. Perhaps, after the commotion of meeting Matt and Brown Dog and the noise of the rifle, she'd stay away from camp.

Grace fetched the bucket, placing it in front of Lisa. The cat sniffed it, took a few unhurried laps, glanced at Grace, and lay down, stretching out on the same sunny spot she'd chosen earlier.

"Good girl," said Grace, bending to stroke her once more. "You stay here. I'll be back soon."

Lisa emitted a short, sharp call, part meow and part chirrup. She might've said, "All right" or "Hurry."

Glancing back several times before she reached the bottom, Grace hurried down the hill. Lisa watched for a while, her head raised, but by the time Grace passed the lookout, the cat was lying flat, apparently content to snooze in the sun.

There was no sign of anyone as she ran toward Dr. Leakey's workroom. However, as she drew closer, she heard Dr. Leakey's voice. Someone responded in a deeper tone. It was her father. Grace slowed to a walk. What was he doing there? Hadn't he said he had to work? Grace had assumed that meant he would go to the dig. She was a few steps from the entrance when she heard her name.

"It didn't occur to me when Grace was born. I didn't suspect anything," said her father. "Eleanor told me later."

"She told you outright?" said Dr. Leakey. Her voice was quiet, distracted, as if she was only mildly interested.

"Yes." His voice cracked.

There was a long pause. Grace waited, out of sight, holding her breath.

Eventually, Dr. Leakey sighed. Or perhaps she was smoking. Then she spoke. "No. It wasn't possible. Anyway, what does it matter, George? After all this time. I don't understand why we're discussing it—why you think I need to know and why you're letting it worry you. They're both gone."

George didn't respond. Grace imagined him blushing and shaking his head. She couldn't make sense of what they were talking about beyond understanding that it concerned her and her mother.

Dr. Leakey spoke again. "Is that why you brought her here? Without telling me her mother had died?"

"No," said George, his tone suddenly firm. "You know it isn't. I didn't tell you about Eleanor because it was difficult enough to get you to agree to Grace coming with me. If you'd known she'd just lost her mother—well, you know." He sighed loudly. "I brought her because I hoped we'd reconnect, find a way to move ahead. Instead, the only ones she's formed relationships with are the animals and you. So I guess I'm looking to you for answers."

"Ha! What do I know about teenage girls?" Dr. Leakey gave a dry laugh. Then she added, so quietly Grace barely heard it, "What do I know about having a daughter?"

The girl didn't want to hear more. It didn't matter. All she understood was that she was a problem that no one knew what to do about. In fact, her father was so desperate, he'd turned to someone who barely knew them for help. If only everyone would leave her alone. It's what she'd wanted all along. What she'd asked for when her father had reappeared after Eleanor died. She glanced around at the camp, with its small sandblasted buildings, dusty tracks, and smatterings of trees and bush. She didn't want to be here. She should go. If it wasn't for Lisa, she'd head off across the Serengeti.

Grace was startled from her thoughts by a nudge on her hand. It was Brown Dog. He'd found her hiding behind the wall. She patted his head, once, twice, thinking about what her mother had repeated shortly before she died. At the time, Grace had thought her unhappy ruminations were a result of the powerful painkillers Eleanor required. Now she realized her mother was right.

"Ultimately, you're alone. It doesn't matter how much you care about others or them about you. You're responsible for yourself. At the end, there's only you," she'd said.

She turned from the workroom and ran back the way she'd come. However, at the end of the track, instead of turning right to where Lisa lay, she went left. Brown Dog trotted alongside her as she headed to the kitchen.

CHAPTER 24

1936
Ware, Hertfordshire, England

WITH FRIDA HAVING FINALLY GRANTED LOUIS A DIVORCE AND HIS PARENTS
reluctantly accepting it, he and Mary were married in the registry office of the
little town of Ware in Hertfordshire on Christmas eve in 1936.

Although she attended the wedding as one of just three witnesses cum
guests (the others being Mary's aunt and one of Louis's Kenyan friends who
happened to be in England), Cecilia hadn't softened toward Louis. Convinced
her daughter was making a mistake of massive proportions, she endured the
nuptials stony faced, her arms folded over her stomach in a protective huddle.
While Mary had returned from Africa the previous year a changed woman, it
hadn't been, as Cecilia had hoped, because she'd fallen out of love with Louis,
but rather because she'd *also* fallen in love with Africa.

Water fouled with rhino urine, a close encounter with a lioness, the desperate search for a missing truck, and the unearthing of a car from a ditch with
eating utensils notwithstanding, the continent had cast a spell on Mary Nicol.
Even if it wasn't as Mary Leakey, she knew before she left that she'd return.
For Louis, East Africa was home. For Mary, the untamed Serengeti, with its
tremendous wildlife, ancient beds of Olduvai Gorge, and warm embrace of the

sun, evoked a primal connection to the world she'd never known. Even when she was alone there—perhaps *mostly* when she was alone—she experienced an unprecedented sense of composure and peace.

It wasn't just the place; Mary also fell in love with freedom. She'd had a taste of it in France with her father. In England, after his death, she'd been cloistered by four walls until she worked at Hembury. Even there, though, the shell of convention, academia, and propriety was restrictive, sometimes repressive. At Olduvai, with its view across the plains to Lemagrut, she'd felt she might soar like an augur buzzard. She was no longer anxious about the future and her place in it. The disquiet, which had lurked at the base of her stomach like a jackal nosing for scraps, disappeared. Moreover, Africa promised to feed her curiosity. If she and Louis were patient, persistent, and meticulous, the African earth would reward them with answers.

They'd returned to England in 1935 into something of a vacuum. Louis remained an outcast, and their resources were limited. The means to return to Africa came about unexpectedly months later, when the Rhodes Trust asked Louis to study the Kikuyu in Kenya. The offer would cover his salary and expenses for two years. With the project due to start in 1937, they had just enough time to get married and pack.

"What will you do in Nairobi while he works with the Kikuyu?" asked Cecilia when Mary had told her the news.

"I don't know yet," she'd replied. "But Louis and I agree that it's less important to work out everything in minute detail than it is to accept opportunities and overcome obstacles as they present themselves."

Her mother had rolled her eyes and left the room. However, by the time the couple left for Nairobi three weeks after the wedding, Cecilia had agreed to keep Fussy. Bungey was taken in by another devotee of dalmatians, who had a large garden.

Work kept Mary and Louis in Kenya for the most part during the years that followed. After he'd completed the Rhodes Trust study, Louis was appointed curator of Nairobi's Coryndon Museum. Money was tight, and he also took on police work, wrote radio broadcasts, and analyzed handwriting.

For Mary, it was a time of metamorphosis. From the wide-eyed apprentice who'd climbed into the Rugby alongside Louis in Arusha in 1935, she transformed into an assured, determined archaeologist who directed excavations and made a complete survey of a rocky ridge called Hyrax Hill outside Nairobi. Here, she found a Neolithic settlement with a cemetery.

Mary also managed a team at another Neolithic site on the Mau Escarpment at Njoro River Cave, which was on the farm of the Honorable Mrs. Nellie Grant, who welcomed Mary to Kenya and became a firm friend. At Njoro River Cave, Mary discovered the burial place of more than eighty individuals, who'd been wrapped in skins, adorned with jewelry, and laid to rest with their drinking vessels.

So absorbed was she by her work that when, in 1940, Mary gave birth to the couple's first child, Jonathan, she barely paused to consider what motherhood might mean. By enlisting the help of a nanny, life went on more or less as before for Mary—as it did when their second son, Richard, was born in 1944. However, when, after the war had ended in 1945, she received word that her mother was gravely ill, Mary stopped working long enough to endure an uncomfortable sea voyage to visit Cecilia and introduce her to her grandsons.

Having neither been to England nor seen her mother for nine years, Mary was shocked by the severity of the English winter but even more so by how diminished Cecilia was. Although she lived in Kensington with her sister, who was a kind, capable caretaker, Mary's mother was frail and rarely awake. So Mary was surprised when, a few days into the visit, Cecilia grasped her hand one morning and spoke with vigor.

"Stay with me today," she said, her eyes brighter than Mary had seen them. "Let your aunt take the boys. I want to know about your life."

Mary made the necessary arrangements and pulled up a chair alongside her mother's bed.

"What do you want to know?" she asked, trying to keep her tone light.

"Everything."

Cecilia listened, nodding and smiling, as Mary spoke about her work, saying how she'd overheard one of Louis's colleagues refer to her as "a foremost expert on the stone-tool culture of early humans in East Africa." Whereas days before Cecilia's eyes had closed within minutes of a visit, today she was alert and interested.

Mary told her about Hyrax Hill and Njoro River Cave, including how, while she was excavating a fossilized skull surrounded by ornaments in the cave, she'd felt a hard smack on her shoulder.

"I was infuriated that anyone would do anything as idiotic as to slap me while I was engaged in so delicate an operation. I didn't look up immediately but said, 'Go away, for God's sake!' When I did stop to see who it was, there was no one anywhere near me. I asked but everyone said they hadn't come close."

"What are you saying?" asked Cecilia from her pillow.

"I can't explain it. The Kikuyu men working with me insisted it was a warning from the spirits not to disturb the skull. They said I should cover it up and leave it alone."

"But you're a scientist. You know that doesn't make sense," said her mother.

"That's what I told them. I explained that it wasn't rational. That scientists believe in the tangible, the facts. Things that can be understood and proven," said Mary. "But it happened, the hard thump on my shoulder. I felt it just as I feel your hand beneath my fingers now."

They were silent for a moment.

"Tell me about your home," said Cecilia eventually. "Someone who claimed to have visited Mrs. Grant said she told him that you 'live on the smell of an oil rag.'"

Mary chuckled. It was true, she said, they had very little money and lived modestly. She described the house she and Louis had rented while the museum curator's bungalow was being renovated. It was on the edge of a forest in the Nairobi suburb of Karen—named for Danish author Karen Blixen, who'd lived there—and had black ceilings. As odd as the place was, her four dalmatians loved the wild surroundings, said Mary.

"Four? How on earth do you cope with four?" asked her mother.

"It's nothing like having dogs in London," said Mary, thinking about Fussy and Bungey, who'd died in England several years before. "In Africa, the dogs essentially run free, and when they're with me on a dig, they warn me when there's any wildlife about."

"But they don't warn you about spirits," said Cecilia with a wink.

Mary was stunned. She'd never seen her mother wink. Cecilia recognized her surprise and laughed. It was quick and quiet, a light laugh, but the pleasure it brought Mary was considerable, and she responded with a giggle. They laughed together before Cecilia resumed her questioning.

"Who takes care of the boys while you work?"

"What do you do in Nairobi on weekends?"

"Do you entertain?"

It was unusual for Mary to talk about herself. She couldn't recall ever having told anyone so much about her life. Neither could she remember sustaining so long a conversation with her mother without one or both growing angry. It was comforting, and as the hours passed, she found it easier to talk. Cecilia didn't interrupt, but when Mary concluded her response to a question, she always had another. Finally, after covering the boys' well-being, household issues, Mary's hopes for future projects, and various other matters, she asked about Louis.

"And your marriage, Mary. Is Louis the man you believed him to be?"

She should've anticipated it. There was no reason for her mother to have grown fond of Louis. But Mary was surprised all the same. She'd been lulled into imagining that, for once, she and her mother would *not* disagree. Cecilia's long-held disappointment in her daughter had, up until that moment, looked to have disappeared. It had seemed possible that they'd smooth over their difficult past with understanding and love. They knew Cecilia didn't have much longer. Didn't she also want peace?

Mary stood and walked to the window. For once, it wasn't raining. Even so, the clouds were low and dark. She hadn't noticed them earlier while she'd talked about Africa, her work, the dogs, the boys, and their home. Now, though, with thoughts of Louis, she saw the gloom. She turned to Cecilia to find her mother watching her. Instead of the cold and accusing expression Mary expected, Cecilia's eyes glistened, and her chin quivered. It was an expression of concern but also hopefulness. Mary understood.

She returned to the bedside, sat down, and took her mother's hand in hers. "My marriage and Louis are *more* than I hoped for," she said.

Later, while Cecilia slept, Mary bundled Jonathan and Richard into their coats, scarves, hats, and gloves, which—having no need for such garments in

Kenya—they found novel. As she led them along the gray streets to Kensington Gardens—with the boys peering through windows and into front yards as though at a zoo—she tried not to think about how she'd lied to her mother. How sad it was that when Cecilia opened her heart to her, Mary had been compelled to hide the truth.

If she'd been honest, she would have admitted how, even before she'd married Louis, Mary had noticed how his eyes softened and gleamed when he looked at other women. She'd tried to deny it initially, but Mary realized when Mrs. Rowe had floated across the district commissioner's yard at Loliondo that Louis couldn't contain the pleasure he got from charming women. Their response seemed to validate something in him that Mary alone didn't, and he was blind to how it wounded her.

Had Mary been truthful, she would've told her mother how often she scolded herself as weak and needy for the sickening jealousy that washed over her when Louis lowered his voice for other women. She would've described how excruciating it was when he reproduced for others the slow smile that she'd believed was hers, the same smile that had reeled her in across the lawn outside De Montfort Hall twelve years earlier. But Mary told her mother none of this, not only because she was ashamed but also because she knew Cecilia wanted to believe that all was well—and so it was for Cecilia, when she died a few days later.

While the visit to England might've compelled Mary to acknowledge, if only to herself, how deeply she resented Louis's fascination with other women, it also reminded her how much she loved him and their life in Africa. Soon after Cecilia's funeral, she and her sons said farewell to her aunt and the wintery island and returned to Louis and the sunshine of Kenya.

The three years that followed were busy and included expanding the museum and organizing and holding the first Pan-African Congress of Prehistory and Paleontology in 1947. Whenever time and money allowed, Mary and Louis packed their belongings, dogs, and sons and left Nairobi to visit various East African sites to hunt fossils. However, until 1948, hominid remains eluded them.

That season, sustained by funding they'd received after the congress,

Mary and Louis undertook an expedition to Rusinga Island in Lake Victoria, Kenya, where they'd previously searched for Miocene fossils. One morning, while Louis was excavating the remains of a large extinct creature related to the crocodile, Mary sought fossil apes. She hadn't walked far when she came across the fragment of a bone with a tooth attached. It had a hominoid look.

It took several days for the team to excavate the remains, with Heselon painstakingly sieving each grain of sediment to remove every tiny fragment. Finally, with about thirty pieces in hand, Mary fitted the half cranium, upper and lower jaws, and a full set of teeth together. She'd found the sixteen-million-year-old skull of a tiny Miocene ape, or Proconsul. It was an extraordinary find that promised to provide vital clues about the evolutionary split of monkeys and apes. Moreover, it underpinned Louis's theories about mankind's East African roots.

Louis wanted the skull delivered to Professor Wilfrid Le Gros Clark's laboratory in Oxford urgently. Not only was Le Gros Clark the leading authority in primate evolution, but he also supported Mary and Louis's Miocene research.

Mary wasn't surprised by Louis's eagerness to get it to England. What was unexpected was his suggestion that *she* should present it to the professor. After all, it was Louis who loved talking about their work. He was a natural story-teller. It's what drew her to him at the Royal Anthropological Institute. His appeal was universal. It didn't matter who the audience was, Louis inevitably captured their attention when he opened his mouth. He was a fast-talking raconteur with a talent for winning people over. Mary, who preferred to do almost anything rather than talk to groups of people, was amazed by the pleasure Louis got from it. That he would suggest she travel to England with the Proconsul skull was remarkable.

"Really?" she responded.

Louis looked at her with a close-lipped smile. "Well, you found it, Mary."

She had. She'd found *and* reassembled it. It was the first truly important fossil she'd discovered. Louis was a consummate speaker, a magician of the spoken word, but Mary was a meticulous technician. She was a determined, thorough scientist, whose approach was systematic and organized and who was always eager to listen and learn from others. Yes, she had found and reconstructed the Proconsul skull. She *should* take it to England.

"All right," she said.

Louis's eyes widened. "What?"

"I'll go."

He stared at her for a moment, expecting more. She didn't add anything.

"Good, good," he said. "I'll make the plans."

A few days after they'd returned to Nairobi from Rusinga Island, Louis told Mary what he'd negotiated with the East Africa manager of the British Overseas Airways Corporation. The airline, he said, would give her a return flight to England in exchange for the significant publicity it would get.

"Publicity?" she echoed. "I thought I'd deliver it to Oxford, discuss it with Le Gros, and come home."

"Of course not. We need to generate as much interest in it as possible. The airline has called in its public relations people. You'll talk to reporters. There'll be photographers. Television," said Louis. "It's exactly what we need if we're to attract the kind of funding we're after."

It was true. They needed benefactors if they were to undertake the work they dreamed of. It was the ideal opportunity. Already, news had broken with international newspapers printing headlines such as "First-Ever Miocene Hominid Skull" and the inaccurate "The Leakeys Find Important Fossil-Man Ancestor." There was no better time to apply for grants and seek other funding. Even so, the idea of facing the press filled Mary with cold dread. It would've been easy for her to back out. Louis would've accepted her change of heart with a laugh, possibly without disguising his relief. But she didn't back out; she would go.

Mary left Nairobi in a converted Royal Air Force York bomber with the skull in a box on her knee. It was a long, bumpy flight, and she was distracted from her anxiety about facing journalists and cameras by worrying whether the skull would be damaged during the journey.

At Heathrow, she was met by an embankment of reporters, photographers, and cameramen, who thrust microphones and cameras at her. For a while, after a pair of policemen had escorted Mary to the special room in which she'd present the skull, she was paralyzed by fear. Could she even utter a sound, let alone form lucid words? Why, she wondered, when she'd hidden in a boiler room to avoid reading poetry as a girl, did she think she could face a room full of strangers? She thought about how Louis would've loved the attention and berated herself for coming.

Mary unpacked the skull and placed it on a small table in front of the room. When she glanced up, she saw that all eyes were on the bones. The audience wasn't interested in her. Their attention was focused on the Proconsul. She took a deep breath and felt the weight of apprehension rise from her shoulders as if she'd shrugged off a heavy mantle.

"Are you ready, Mrs. Leakey?" asked a man nearby.

She nodded, the room went quiet, and Mary spoke. Like everyone else, she kept her gaze firmly on the skull.

When she watched a newsclip of the presentation on television later, she cringed at the sound of her voice. It was tiny, girlish, and Mary imagined people might've wondered why Louis had sent his timid young wife cum assistant to present such an important find. On the other hand, she'd done it. She'd spoken—though more nervously than she might've liked—with knowledgeable certainty, without exaggeration or fanfare. She'd described the skull like a scientist. Her presence instead of Louis and her scientific competency might've surprised many—particularly since most were unaccustomed to women in the profession—but she'd broken through.

"She is an archaeologist in her own right, and this is not her first important find," reported one newspaper.

After the presentation, Mary had taken the skull to Professor Le Gros Clark in Oxford, where she'd spent a few days working in his laboratory while he studied it before making his findings known.

One morning, as she sat alone in the laboratory, examining some indeterminate fragments of skull Louis had found near the Proconsul site, Mary heard a tap on the open door. She looked up and was startled to see Gertrude in the doorway. She was grayer around the temples and smaller than Mary recalled, but wore her signature matching skirt and jacket and a gentle, familiar smile. Mary caught her breath. Although her old friend attended the Pan-African Congress in Nairobi the previous year and Louis and Gertrude had had professional interactions in recent years, Mary hadn't had an opportunity to find out whether she'd been forgiven. She got to her feet.

"No," said Gertrude. "Stay there. I don't want to interrupt but was in town and wanted to congratulate you."

"Thank you," said Mary, rooted to the spot. "This is a lovely surprise." There was a pause. "Do you have time for a cup of tea?"

Gertrude glanced at her watch. "Well, yes, but only if you're sure you do."

Mary took her coat from the back of a chair. "We're in England. There's always time for tea."

They went to the nearest cafeteria, where, over two pots of strong tea, they discussed the Proconsul skull. There was no mention of the angry words or disappointment that had passed between them thirteen years before. Neither was there any awkwardness when Louis's name came up. For a moment Mary wondered if she should say something, rid the room of the elephant. But then she realized the elephant had left of its own accord.

Eventually, as the lunch crowd trickled into the cafeteria, Gertrude tapped the table with the palm of her hand. "I have to get going. It was wonderful to catch up. I'm so glad we did this."

They stood together. "Yes, me too. We'll stay in touch," said Mary.

"We most certainly will," said Gertrude.

Mary returned to Nairobi a few days later with a sense of great accomplishment. She'd overcome her fear of public speaking. It didn't change the fact that she preferred being alone, working outdoors in East Africa. But she was encouraged to know that if her back was against the wall and she had to, she could hold her own with an audience. It helped, too, that the Proconsul skull had earned them a grant from the Royal Society. What pleased her most, though, was that she'd renewed her friendship with Gertrude.

CHAPTER 25

1983
Olduvai Gorge, Tanzania

GRACE PUSHED OPEN THE KITCHEN DOOR AND PEERED IN. GATIMU LOOKED up from where he was peeling potatoes on the far side of the room. He was alone.

"Is Mr. Rono around?" she asked.

She heard her tone. It was anxious and abrupt. Rude.

"Sorry. Good morning, Gatimu," she added, trying to smile. "It's just that I, um, need his help."

"It's his day off. He's at his house," said the young man, tossing a potato into a bowl of water.

The plop of the potato could've been Grace's heart. Now what? Mr. Rono was her lifeline. The only way to block out the conversation she'd overheard between Dr. Leakey and her father was to focus on something else, something more important than her feelings. She'd learned how to do that while taking care of her mother. Every time she'd missed her father or felt sorry for herself, Grace had shoved the emotions out of sight, the way one might thrust a blouse that's lost a button to the back corner of a cupboard. To be dealt with another day. Or never. Her feelings weren't important. What was critical then was taking care of her mother. Eleanor needed her. Her father didn't. Her own happiness didn't matter as long she helped her mother manage her pain. Now Lisa needed her. She couldn't wait for Dr. Leakey to speak to some or other man who'd left the cheetah to take care of herself with a collar that not only hindered her hunting but had also created an infection. Dr. Leakey might've insisted that life at Olduvai required patience, but the days were ticking by. She had to do something now.

"Is he at his house here in the camp or has he gone somewhere else?" she asked.

"No, he's here," said Gatimu.

"Thank you," she called, backing out so quickly that she almost fell over Brown Dog. Grace had forgotten he'd followed her from the workroom. She patted him and apologized before running the short distance from the kitchen to where Mr. Rono's lodgings were. Again, the dog followed.

Mr. Rono was sitting on a chair in the shade of his house reading. He looked up at the sound of her footsteps, got to his feet, and closed the book and placed it on the chair.

"What's wrong?" he asked, walking toward her.

It was only then that Grace realized how rash she'd been. Mr. Rono's typically unruffled expression was gone. His brow creased and his eyes narrowed. He thought something terrible had happened. She swallowed, embarrassed to have disrupted him on his day off without consideration. But what else was she to do? Her back was against the wall. There was no one else to turn to.

"No, nothing's wrong," she began. "I mean, it is, but it's not serious. Well, it is serious, but it's, well, it's the cheetah. She's got, I…"

Grace let the sentence trail off. Mr. Rono didn't look comforted. He closed his mouth, lips flattened. Was he angry? Did he despise her? He had every right to. She'd addressed him as "Mr. Jackson" for days initially and essentially accused him of shooting at her when Matt and Lisa were fighting. She still hadn't apologized properly. He must think her an idiot *and* a pest.

"Did Dr. Leakey send you?" he asked.

Grace curled her fingers around Brown Dog's ear, grateful for his presence at her knee. "I need your help, Mr. Rono. Please."

He tilted his head.

"Lisa, the cheetah, has an infection on her neck, where the collar's rubbing. She's already sick and it's going to make her worse. We must get it off. The tracking collar." She spoke quickly, her words tumbling over one another. "She can't hunt with it. The man who put it on doesn't care where she is or how she is. Can you please help me get it off?"

His expression softened just a little. "What does Dr. Leakey say about this?"

"She agrees it must come off," said Grace.

It was true, she assured herself. Dr. Leakey did say it should come off. It didn't matter that she hadn't said it *that* day.

"She said we need bolt cutters for the job," she added, pleased with herself for remembering the name of the tool; it surely added weight to Dr. Leakey's agreeing that the collar be removed.

"You want to take bolt cutters to a cheetah's neck?"

Grace nodded, though she was suddenly unsure. What exactly were bolt cutters?

Mr. Rono rubbed his chin.

"Do you have them?" she asked. Perhaps if she saw them, she'd understand his hesitancy. "Bolt cutters, I mean."

"No, but I believe my brother does. You should ask him. He'd know if they'll work for the cheetah."

"Your brother, Simon? The one who works at the Ngorongoro reserve?"

He nodded, not surprised that she knew who his brother was. Perhaps, thought Grace, they'd spoken about how she and Dr. Leakey had visited the caldera. She remembered Simon Rono's interest in Lisa. Of course! He was a ranger, who'd know what to do and how to help her. It hadn't occurred to her when she'd rushed to elicit Mr. Rono's help. She'd gone because she didn't know what else to do or where to go to get away from Dr. Leakey's workroom. Now, however, it seemed she'd subconsciously known he'd have a solution.

"Can we go to him? Now?" she asked.

He sighed and glanced at the book on the chair. Grace shuffled her feet and felt for Brown Dog's ear. She shouldn't have come. She should leave. But then what? She'd have to face Dr. Leakey and her father. She *had* to get away from the camp—if only for a while. She had to help Lisa. That was more important than anything else now. Grace looked away, ashamed but uncertain of what to do next. The hood of Mr. Rono's truck protruded from the far side of his hut.

"I could drive your car," she said, recognizing as she spoke what a ridiculous notion it was. She plowed on. "Dr. Leakey taught me."

He blinked—once, twice, three times—took a long, chest-expanding breath, and laughed. It began as a low rumble from beneath his chest before erupting into a roar. Grace had never heard him laugh before. Though she didn't know why he was amused, so wholehearted an expression demanded company. She gave a short chortle. It was small alongside Mr. Rono's robust reverberations, as small and insignificant as the warthog she and Dr. Leakey had watched trotting alongside an elephant in the Ngorongoro Crater. The memory made her giggle and soon Grace was laughing as vigorously and freely as he was. Brown Dog moved to stand between the girl and man, glancing quizzically at her, then at Mr. Rono and back again, as if watching a game of tennis. They looked at the dog and laughed louder and longer.

Eventually, they stopped. Grace was exhausted, as if she'd run a mile but she also felt lighter.

"I'm sorry I got your name wrong when I first arrived, Mr. Rono," she said.

He wiped his eyes and shrugged.

"I also apologize for thinking that you would fire a shot at Lisa when I was trying to get Matt away from her."

"It didn't cross my mind to shoot her, even when you were *not* in the way."

"Oh."

They were silent for a moment.

"All right," he said eventually, nodding at the car.

Grace swallowed. "Do you mean—"

"I'll come with you. You can drive my car to see Simon to ask about the bolt cutters and the cheetah."

CHAPTER 26

1959
Olduvai Gorge, Tanganyika

DESPITE HAVING EXPLORED SEVERAL OTHER ARCHAEOLOGICAL SITES IN EAST Africa, Mary and Louis seldom missed an opportunity to visit Olduvai Gorge. Mary's love for the rugged canyon and expansive Serengeti Plains prevailed and she and Louis remained certain that the gorge held key clues to mankind's origins.

When time and money allowed, they assembled small teams and made the bone-jarring, dusty three-hundred-and-fifty-mile journey from Nairobi to set up camp and work as intensively and systematically as they could. The dalmatians and Jonathan, Richard, and their third son, Philip, born in 1949, always accompanied them.

Over the years, Mary and Louis collected thousands of artifacts at Olduvai, chiefly stone tools classified as choppers, scrapers, and pounders. Their excavations also revealed the fossil remains of many extinct mammals, including whole skulls and skeletons of giant species. They discovered pigs the size of hippopotamuses and relatives of the buffalo whose horn cores were wider than Louis's Land Rover. One of the most exciting discoveries was what Mary and Louis believed to be the living floor of early hominids. The area was strewn with stone tools used to butcher, skin and dismember mammals, as well as the fossilized remains of their feasts. However, the toolmakers, hunters, and butchers were elusive. Aside from two teeth of indeterminate origin, hominoid fossils remained at large.

In 1959, twenty-four years after she'd first fallen in love with Olduvai, Mary was back in the gorge. This time, she and Louis were accompanied by Armand and Michaela Denis, who were neighbors in Langata, the Nairobi suburb in which the Leakeys had built a home in 1952. Armand was a film-maker, while Michaela had trained as a dress designer before succumbing to the glamour of the big screen. She'd been British actress Deborah Kerr's double in the film *King Solomon's Mines* before joining Armand to make documentaries in East Africa.

The Leakeys and Denises had similar backstories. Armand was eighteen years older than his wife. Their relationship had also begun as an illicit affair that set tongues a-wagging. Mary and Michaela were of a similar age. None of it mattered; the women had nothing else in common.

Although she no longer worked in fashion, Michaela was slavishly vogue. Regardless of what she was doing and how hot and dusty the circumstances, her Marilyn Monroe–inspired hair was immaculately styled, lipstick as vivid as the blossom of the flamboyant tree, penciled brows perfectly arched, and wardrobe crisply coordinated. She accessorized her looks with a vivacious personality and, thanks to her Russian mother, an exotic accent. Michaela drew looks of admiration wherever she went, including the lingering gaze of Louis.

Mary felt invisible alongside her. She fought to crush the tendrils of jealousy that coiled her heart when Louis's eyes rested approvingly upon Michaela. But they pierced her thoughts with dark insistence. Mary loathed how inadequate and feeble jealousy made her feel. She'd constantly tried—and failed—to be indifferent to Louis's duplicity.

At fifty-six, he was no longer the lithe, suntanned adventurer Mary had fallen in love with. His hair, as unruly as ever, was gray and he'd lost several teeth. In addition, his appetite for excess had caught up with him, leaving him paunchy and ponderous. However, Louis's ego and charisma were entirely intact. He was interesting and interested, with unflagging zeal for a myriad of different subjects. Never without ideas and always eager to consider new ones, Louis continued to have a magnetic effect on others, particularly women.

Louis has that powerful, if indefinable, quality of attractiveness to women that is perhaps ultimately a matter of chemistry, Mary frequently told herself. It was a force he wielded widely. He couldn't help himself. It didn't mean anything. He was drawn to other women, but he loved her. Hadn't he proved that four years earlier?

In 1955, shortly after Louis returned to Kenya from England—he'd spent several weeks studying the fossil pig collection at the British Museum of Natural History—a young English woman called Rosalie Osborn arrived in Nairobi, ostensibly to work as his secretary. Mary soon realized he and Miss Osborn had been together while he was away and were lovers. This was no mere flirtation. Mary was furious and made it known, demanding Louis cease both his (alleged) professional and personal relationships with her. He'd done so, which confirmed to Mary that his attachment to her and the boys was greater than whatever it was that induced him to philander.

Now, although she'd resolved to ignore the waves of self-doubt elicited by Louis's attention to other women, Mary had objected to the idea of Armand and Michaela accompanying them to Olduvai. However, Louis stood firm. The Denis couple would film an excavation from start to finish for their *On Safari* series, which was broadcast on British television. Mary conceded it was an exceptional opportunity for publicity, which might attract funding that would allow them to expand their work at Olduvai. So Armand and Michaela accompanied them to the gorge.

The party set up camp beneath a roundel of large acacias in the side gorge and agreed they'd film at the east end of the main gorge when the cameraman, Des Bartlett, arrived in a few days. They were still waiting when, on the seventeenth of July, Louis succumbed to a feverish dose of flu and took to his bed.

Restless and eager to be alone, Mary headed into the gorge with her dalmatians, Sally and Victoria. Away from the low-level excitement of the filmmakers and their incessant chatter, she followed the familiar path and, without much thought, headed to FLK. Perhaps if she'd quizzed herself at the time, she'd conclude she chose the site because she'd often found bones and stone artifacts on the surface there. As it was, she was thinking about how pleasing it was to be away from everyone. Of course, with the dogs trotting ahead, she wasn't truly alone. But their presence was different. They offered companionship without words or judgment. A sense of solitude prevailed but she was also comforted and safe. The dogs added to the peace by leaving her alone with her thoughts.

FLK was slightly west of the junction of the two gorges and, as she picked her way up the rocky hillside, Mary saw there was more material strewn on the eroded surface than expected after heavy rains earlier in the year. However, it was not a fragment on the surface that caught her eye. Instead, she saw a scrap of bone projecting from beneath the soil and knelt to examine it. It looked like a piece of skull, including the bony bulge below the ear. Her pulse quickened. Could it be hominid? No, surely not. It was too thick.

Accustomed to waiting while Mary worked, Sally and Victoria lay in the sun behind her. She used a brush to gently sweep away the light layer of soil that covered the bone. There was more to it than she'd imagined. In fact, it wasn't all bone. There was something else, something smoother and shinier. Mary leaned in for a better look. There they were: two teeth in place, in an upper jaw. She took a deep breath, her heart dancing. They *were* hominid. She sat back, allowing the sunlight to flood the spot as if the tiniest of shadows might mislead her. They didn't. The bone with its big molars was unchanged. Her thoughts raced. Was this what they'd been searching for all these years? How much of it remained hidden?

She scrambled backward away from the find, forcing Sally and Victoria to clamber to their feet.

"Come," she said, shepherding them away.

Louis was asleep when Mary lifted the flap of their tent. She'd gone there directly, offering Armand and Michaela a vague wave as they watched her hurry by from where they sat beneath a tree, torsos in the shade and legs stretched out in the winter sun.

Mary leaned over Louis's motionless shoulders and whispered, "I've got him. I've found our man."

He sat up in a single movement, his eyes on hers, shining and alert. If anyone else had uttered those words, Louis's response would've been a salvo of questions. Mary, however, was meticulous in everything she reported. She didn't give voice to her thoughts until she'd examined them from every angle and turned them upside down. She never exaggerated or elaborated upon the facts to provoke a response, make a point, or win an argument. Louis knew that if Mary said she'd found their man, she had. Interrogation was unwarranted.

"Pass me my trousers," he said instead.

Mary handed him one of the khaki boiler suits, which had, over the years, become his uniform on digs.

Armand got to his feet when he saw Louis following Mary, Sally and Victoria back across the camp.

"No, no," called Louis. "Don't come yet. Wait here. We'll let you know when we're ready for you."

His mind was ten paces ahead, planning the best course of action with the filmmakers on hand. There was probably no one in the world better able to exploit the opportunity than Louis, thought Mary.

As they approached the korongo, Mary became aware of an unusual sensation. Her insides were vibrating. Was she coming down with something? Louis's flu? She glanced at him, wondering if she should mention it.

"Where is it?" he asked, his tone sharp.

She led him to the spot, where Louis sank to his knees. She crouched alongside him. Sally groaned as she and Victoria lay some distance away. Louis leaned over the molars. Mary recognized the long hissing sound of his inhaling. Her stomach fluttered. He scraped at the knobby, dry earth with a thin, wooden stick before taking Mary's brush to it briefly. Finally, he turned to look at her. His eyes were glistening.

"I think it's Australopithecine," he said with a short sniff.

Mary placed her hands on the ground as a wave of lightheadedness washed over her.

Louis returned his attention to the find. "It's not an early Homo," he said eventually, his disappointment apparent, though muted. "The molars are twice the width of ours."

Mary responded with a small nod. She understood the letdown. Louis hoped they'd find Homo in the Lower Pleistocene. He believed Australopithecus was too distant a relative to have made the tools they'd found in the gorge.

He reached out and, without taking his eyes off the fossil, absent-mindedly patted her knee. "But it *is* a distant relative. Well done, Mary. This is a priceless discovery."

"There's work to be done," she said, noticing that the tremors had stopped and she was breathing normally.

"We're not going to do any work until Des arrives," said Louis. "Let's cover it."

A while later, having stacked a protective pile of stones over the bones, they made their way down the gully and along the bed of the gorge. Louis was unusually quiet. Mary wanted to believe it was because he was not feeling well. The idea that disappointment silenced him bothered her. As they approached the path that led up to the camp, he touched her arm.

"Don't say anything to the others yet. I want to give this a little more thought before Des arrives," he said.

Mary was surprised. Louis was not one to hold back. "You're not thinking of passing up the opportunity to film the excavation, are you?" she asked.

Louis snorted. "Of course not. That would be absurd. I want to plan a bit myself before they get carried away with their own ideas about how we should do it. We really need to make this work for us."

As they walked, Mary thought about how different their priorities were. They were both set on finding evidence of early hominids in East Africa. Now, however, Mary's focus was firmly on the scientific significance of the find. Louis's thoughts had leapfrogged ahead. He was thinking about what it might mean in terms of fame and finances. Mary understood they needed to raise funds. More money would allow them to continue their work and, if there was enough, enable them to increase the scale and specialization of their sites and research. Still, she wondered at the pace and scope of Louis's thinking. They'd just found the skull. Excavations hadn't begun. It was exciting, but they had no idea of the magnitude of the work that lay ahead or exactly what it might reveal. Yet already, he was contemplating how the find might be a money spinner. Both aspects mattered, she thought, which was one of the reasons their partnership worked.

"We're going to film at the table under the tree this morning," said Louis at breakfast weeks later. "You might want to change your blouse and, um, do something with your hair."

Mary set her mug on the table with a sharp rap. "Really? Is it necessary to move everything again?"

Louis scratched his ear. "Yes. It'll work well for the scene."

She stood, went to their tent, and pulled a comb through her hair. The previous day, as they filmed, Michaela had offered her a hair band.

"What for?" Mary had asked, touching her short hair.

Michaela flashed her a smile. "It's fashionable."

Mary hadn't known how to respond and so, said nothing. Perhaps now, though, since Louis had suggested she "do something" with her hair, she should ask Michaela for the band. What did he mean about her blouse though? She glanced down. There was nothing wrong with the pale-blue cotton top she was wearing. It might not be as safari modish as Michaela's matching khaki shirt and trousers, but it was clean and freshly ironed.

They'd filmed at FLK every day since Des had arrived, beginning with the extraction of the jaw and molars. Although it was always the intention to shoot an excavation from start to finish to allow the team to ostensibly work as usual, the process was inevitably disruptive and tried Mary's patience. She wanted to work systematically without interruption. The first day of filming had been particularly taxing, given how eager she was to discover what else lay around and beneath the teeth.

As Armand had directed Des with the camera and Michaela looked on, Louis had lain on his side and Mary knelt while they carefully brushed, scraped, and picked the crumbly, dry earth away from the bones. Before they'd moved anything it became clear that there was more of the skull preserved. Mary's heart had galloped. She glanced at Louis. He gave her a conspiratorial smile.

"One minute," said Des, lifting his face from the camera. "Louis, can you shift a little to the left. You're casting a shadow. Right. If you repeat the movement with the brush. No. From the other side."

So, it went on. Mary, Louis, Heselon and their team excavated, scrutinized, and deliberated. Des, Armand, and Michaela circled them like jackals around a lion kill. The filmmakers asked the excavators to move this way and that, requesting that they repeat various actions, asking questions and making notes. Mary kept her head down, hoping that her wide-brimmed straw hat would hide her exasperation. It was an exercise in restraint. She longed for the film crew to be gone so that she could dig, brush, scrape, and pick away at the earth without interference.

After the first day of excavation, Mary saw that any disappointment Louis might've harbored about the skull belonging to a side branch of the genus Homo rather than a direct line was offset by how much of the find was preserved. Over the following weeks, they excavated, not only the spot around the initial find, but also the slope below, digging, searching, sieving, and washing the soil. Although there were many—around four hundred, in fact—the fragments they recovered were in good condition. They also found a section of leg. While filming, Des had spotted a length of bone alongside a trench they'd dug. He called Mary, who excavated it. It was a hominid tibia, which Mary and Louis agreed was probably part of the same skeleton as the skull.

Finally, having carefully transported all the pieces back to camp and laid them out on a table in the largest tent, Mary had been ready to begin the painstaking task of cleaning, sorting, organizing, and reconstructing the skull. She'd work with Kamoya Kimeu, the young Kenyan who'd joined the expedition as a field-worker and soon demonstrated extraordinary levels of precision, concentration, and patience. His attention to detail was exactly what Mary needed for the task at hand. She and Kamoya were eager to begin, but, as Louis informed her that morning, the film crew wanted to include a scene of the pieces outside once more.

Whether anyone noticed the black hair band Mary tolerated while Des filmed and photographed her and Louis sorting fragments of the skull at a table beneath the acacia tree months later was unlikely. She took it off the moment the camera was packed away, handed it to Michaela and began taking the trays of fragments back to the tent so that she and Kamoya could finally begin reassembling the skull.

It was a meticulous and complex task. They worked together for days, cleaning and examining each piece, analyzing the texture, color, and shape to establish where it belonged and piecing the bits together. It was not an undertaking that could be rushed.

"Only someone as patient and skillful as Mary is up to this job," said Louis one afternoon. Mary looked up to see him standing outside with Michaela. "She has the most dexterous fingers. Mine are too large."

Michaela giggled, and Mary forced a small smile. The filmmakers would be gone soon, she thought. She could concentrate on her work without interruption. She had no inkling of what lay ahead when the find was presented to the world with the razzmatazz Louis so shrewdly orchestrated.

CHAPTER 27

───────⚬───────

1983
Olduvai Gorge, Tanzania

GRACE TRIED TO IGNORE THE PANIC THAT WHIPPED THROUGH HER WHEN MR. Rono opened the back door to allow Brown Dog to hop into his Land Rover and placed the key in her hand. As he settled in the passenger seat, she climbed behind the wheel and looked at the controls, relieved that the setup seemed identical to that of Dr. Leakey's car.

"I can go forward, right?" she asked, peering over the hood. "I don't want to reverse."

"Forward is good," said Mr. Rono, his eyes straight ahead.

She slotted the key into the ignition, listening for—and grateful to hear—Dr. Leakey's voice in her head. "Make sure you're in Neutral. Turn the key. Press down the clutch pedal. Shift the gear to first. Release the hand brake. Slowly lift your foot off the clutch. Gently accelerate."

The engine rumbled to life, and, with only one discernible shudder, she eased the vehicle away from Mr. Rono's hut and onto the track that led out of the camp. She stopped holding her breath once they'd passed the kitchen. There was no one about.

Mr. Rono sat, silent and still, even as the whine of the engine indicated she should've changed gear earlier. He paid no attention as she briefly struggled with the gearshift. He didn't suggest she slow down or speed up. Neither did he tell her which way to go when she approached the T-junction. Grace turned right, following the route she and Dr. Leakey had taken to the Ngorongoro Crater. For a while, the road was straight and flat and driving easy. Grace saw a pair of doves on the sandy track ahead and watched as they fluttered from the ground and flew away. She imagined that, driving across the plains with Mr. Rono and Brown Dog, she was as free as they were. She liked the thought and let it linger.

"Will your brother be at the gate to the caldera?" she asked eventually.

"No. He's off this week. He'll be at the staff village."

"Oh. Is that nearby?"

Mr. Rono nodded. "We'll turn soon."

So, Simon Rono was also on leave. Grace thought again about how impetuous she'd been. But she was doing it for Lisa. Didn't that vindicate her? She wondered whether Dr. Leakey had gone to the lookout and seen the cheetah there without her. Had she noticed that Brown Dog was missing? She glanced at Mr. Rono, ashamed again for having misled him into believing that Dr. Leakey had had anything to do with her coming to him to ask for the bolt cutters. Perhaps she should explain. But then what? Would he be angry and instruct her to turn around? Then nothing would change for Lisa.

"My brother will know," said Mr. Rono, as if in response to something she'd said.

Grace glanced at him. He looked ahead. "What do you mean?" she asked.

"You're worried about the cheetah. Simon will know what to do. He knows animals better than anyone."

"Why didn't Dr. Leakey ask him to help?"

She heard Mr. Rono shift in his seat. "She asked you." He paused. "Also, she had to follow the rules. She couldn't ask Simon without trying to get hold of the people who own the cheetah. There are ways of doing things, and it's important not to upset people. Next road right."

Grace didn't speak as she concentrated on changing gear, braking, and taking a sharp turn from the main road onto a narrow track. With the vehicle headed straight once more, she stared at her white knuckles on the steering wheel and took a deep breath.

"Mr. Rono, I have to tell you something."

He didn't respond.

"Dr. Leakey didn't tell me to come to you to ask for bolt cutters. I mean, we spoke about needing them, but I came myself. I decided to ask you. She doesn't know that I did," she said.

"I know," he replied.

She gave him a quick look. His face gave nothing away.

"You knew?"

He nodded. "Dr. Leakey asked me if we had any in camp days ago. I told her no."

She felt herself redden. She was angry, though she knew she had no right to be. "But you didn't say. You asked about them. Wondered if they would do the job. Why didn't you tell me that she had already asked? That you knew that she hadn't sent me?"

"Because it was important to you to help the cheetah. When something is important to someone and they ask for help, there's no need to make them feel silly. You must help them. Simon might have bolt cutters. Maybe they'll work. If they don't, Simon will have another idea about what to do. It doesn't matter what I knew or didn't know. You asked for help."

Grace groaned inwardly. However, her limbs seemed suddenly light, as if someone had released a knot somewhere at the top of her spine, releasing a tautness she wasn't aware existed.

"Thank you," she said.

Simon Rono wasn't in his room when they arrived at the cluster of barrack-style buildings but appeared within minutes after one of two young men Jackson spoke to called him. Simon walked toward them, smiling at both as if he and Grace were well acquainted and he'd anticipated their arrival. They stood alongside the Land Rover, talking, while Brown Dog watched them through an open window.

"You shouldn't need bolt cutters to remove the collar. But I'd have to see it to know exactly how to do it," said Simon, after Mr. Rono had explained why they'd come. "So, no one has claimed her, then?"

Grace looked at Mr. Rono as if he might reply. He raised his eyebrows and motioned for her to speak.

"Dr. Leakey has radioed several people, but no one has responded with anything helpful. The collar is rubbing an infected patch on her neck. It's raw, oozing, and bleeding. She already has diarrhea," she said.

"She's still eating and drinking?"

"Yes, but we can't keep waiting, because I'm going in a few days and Dr. Leakey is very busy and will be leaving soon too."

Simon sighed. "It's going to be difficult. If the person who was taking care of her isn't available to collect and care for her, I'm not sure what her future will be."

"What do you mean? The infection must be treated and the collar removed so she can hunt. Then she'll be okay," said Grace. "Won't she?"

He leaned against the Land Rover, looking into the distance. "Rewilding animals isn't simple. Particularly predators. With cheetahs, there's the additional problem that they have their own predators. Mostly lions and hyenas. If they're released in unsafe areas, they don't survive. It's a long and difficult process, releasing cheetahs back into the wild. That's why she has a collar in the first place. To keep track of her and make sure she is coping. She wasn't ready to be in the wild. That's why she came to you," he replied.

"She came because she was hungry and thirsty. Sick," said the girl, feeling increasingly desperate. "Because of the collar. No one kept track of her."

"Or because she doesn't know how to hunt yet. Or was running away from apex predators. Possibly a combination of things," said Simon.

"Does it matter why she came to us? Surely what's important is what we can do for her…don't you think?"

The men shared a glance. The yard was quiet but for the long, rough strokes of a grass broom sweeping a nearby porch.

"Your brother was so sure you could help," said Grace, only a little embarrassed by her pleading.

"It's true," said Mr. Rono, smiling.

Simon chuckled. "Of course. I just wanted you to know that it might not be as simple as removing the collar. It might take longer for the cheetah to return to the wild, and it's not something that just anyone can get right. I'll come to Olduvai. First let me see if I can get hold of the vet. He should come too."

Grace clenched her fists and jumped, both feet off the ground. She hadn't hugged anyone since her mother's funeral when it seemed obligatory for the few people there to embrace one another. She wanted to hug Mr. Rono and Simon. Instead, she turned to Brown Dog, who stood on the back seat, tail wagging and head through the window.

"Did you hear that, Brown Dog?" she said, scratching his ears. "Something useful is happening for Lisa."

George was standing near the kitchen, hands on hips and head jutting forward when Grace drove into the camp. He looked like an anxious tortoise, she thought.

"Stop here," said Mr. Rono.

"Why?"

"Because you must speak to your father."

She pulled up and turned off the engine. Mr. Rono got out, nodded at George, released Brown Dog, and walked to the driver's side. Grace hadn't moved. He opened her door.

"Simon and I listened to you. It's your turn to listen," he said, tilting his head toward her father.

She'd already thanked him for allowing her to drive his car to visit Simon. Several times. She'd also apologized for intruding on his day off. He'd accepted her gratitude and regret with a few affable nods. There was nothing more to say. She slid out and walked to her father, head down, Brown Dog at her heels. She didn't want to meet George's eyes, not only because she was afraid of what she might see, but also because she was worried about what she might say.

"Where have you been?" he asked.

"To see Mr. Rono's brother. He's a ranger who's going to help with Lisa."

"Why didn't you tell anyone where you were going?"

Grace shrugged.

"Dr. Leakey said you'd agreed to wait if the cheetah appeared until she arrived. Why didn't you listen to her?"

I did listen to her, thought Grace. *I listened to you both, which is why I went.* She shrugged again.

George sighed. "We're leaving tomorrow."

Her head jerked up. "What? No! Why? We have three more days."

"One of the geologists is going to Nairobi tomorrow. We'll get a lift with him. It's too much, Grace. I can't expect Dr. Leakey to put up with this kind of behavior. She wasn't keen to—"

"I know! She didn't want me here. She *doesn't* want me here. Nobody wants me here. Or anywhere. But I am here, and Simon is coming with the vet tomorrow so we can sort things out for Lisa."

"It's too late. You can't just—"

She wouldn't listen. "Why don't you all just leave me alone? Forget about me. Let me get on with my life. Isn't that what you want? To get rid of all the trouble I cause?"

"No, Grace! You know that's not what I want. I wanted to come here with you so that we could—"

"I don't care what you wanted. It doesn't matter. It's too late," she said, before turning and storming away. Brown Dog followed.

It was only when she saw the lookout that she remembered she couldn't go to Lisa while the dog was with her. She turned to him. He looked at her expectantly, tail wagging slowly.

"Go home!" she said.

Brown Dog flinched, lowered his head, and took two steps forward.

"Go away!" she shouted, lifting her arm. "Go to Dr. Leakey. Get away from me!"

He shrank.

She raised her arm again, approaching him with long, slow strides. "Go away, Brown Dog! Go!"

He turned slowly and slunk back toward the camp.

Lisa sat on her haunches, tall and alert, watching until Grace crested the hill, at which point, she sauntered toward her, giving a short, sharp chirp as she lowered her head to meet the girl's hands. It took only a few seconds for her to begin purring while Grace stroked and tickled her face and ears.

"Simon and the vet are coming," she said, looking back to where she'd shouted at Brown Dog.

What had she done? Would he trust her again? Brown Dog hadn't attached himself to anyone other than Dr. Leakey until Grace had arrived. Perhaps he'd just begun feeling confident with other people when she arrived and now, she'd set him back. Lisa gave her hand a nudge, urging her to keep up the petting.

"I wish you and the dogs could be friends," said Grace. "It would make everything much easier. Dr. Leakey could take care of you in the camp when I'm gone."

The thought of leaving brought with it a tightness that began in Grace's chest and traveled upward. She forced herself to swallow, but panic had taken hold. It wasn't just the notion of deserting Lisa and leaving Olduvai, but also the shame of having shouted at George and rejected Brown Dog—not to mention how unsettled she was about what she'd overheard that morning. It was all too much. She knelt, wrapped her arms around Lisa's neck, buried her face in her fur. The cat stood firm, her body pulsating as she purred loudly and continuously, impervious to the girl's tears. Eventually, Grace felt herself relax. Her breathing returned to normal, as if she'd absorbed Lisa's low rumble and vibrations and they'd soothed her. She pressed her forehead against Lisa's neck, soaking in the comfort she found there.

It was only when she felt Lisa look up that Grace realized they were no longer alone. She lifted her head and turned around. It was Dr. Leakey.

"You're back," she said.

Grace nodded, releasing the cheetah and getting to her feet. Lisa walked to Dr. Leakey, leaning against her legs and purring even louder.

"Hello, you big softy," said Dr. Leakey, running a hand down the cat's spine. "You're happy now, aren't you?"

"She has a nasty sore on her neck," said Grace, hoping that her eyes didn't reveal that she'd been crying.

"Show me."

Grace crouched alongside Lisa and gently separated the fur to reveal the spot.

"That is bad," said Dr. Leakey.

"That's why I was so eager to get her collar off."

Dr. Leakey looked at her, her brow furrowed.

"I went to Mr. Rono to ask him whether he had bolt cutters. I didn't know you'd already asked him. Then we went to see his brother, Simon. To see if he had any. If he could help."

"Ah, so that's where you were. And?"

Grace was surprised by how calm Dr. Leakey seemed. She'd imagined, from George's reaction, that she'd been angry to find Grace gone. She showed no signs of it now.

"He's coming to see her. With the vet."

Dr. Leakey seemed deep in thought as she quietly stroked the cat. Finally, she spoke. "All right." She sighed. "That's probably for the best."

Grace felt a nub of fear. "What do you mean? Why wouldn't it be for the best?"

"I didn't want to involve Simon and the authorities yet. They're sometimes obliged to make drastic decisions with these kinds of cases."

"What kind of drastic decisions?"

Dr. Leakey looked at her. Her eyes were dark, unreadable pools of blue. "There are rules about hand-reared animals. Some believe they can become dangerous."

"You mean—"

"There aren't enough facilities to take care of them."

Grace felt sick. What had she done? She thought she was helping Lisa by going to Simon. Would the vet put the cat down? Her tears began again. She turned away, looking toward Lemagrut. Perhaps if she ran now, she'd perish somewhere between Olduvai and the old volcano. The hyenas, vultures, and jackals could fight over her corpse. That way she wouldn't have to face what she'd done by asking for Simon's help and her father could stop worrying about her. She felt a hand on her shoulder.

"We're getting ahead of ourselves," said Dr. Leakey, patting her awkwardly. "Simon is a caring, reasonable man. I'm sure the vet will be reasonable too."

It didn't help. "But my father wants to leave early tomorrow, so I won't be here to plead her case. I can't help anymore. I got us into this situation and now I have to leave," said Grace.

"Leaving tomorrow? But you're here for three more days."

Grace rubbed her nose with her hand. "He says you want me gone."

"What utter nonsense. What gave him that idea?"

"Because I disappeared without telling you I was going. Because I asked Mr. Rono to help and drove his car to Simon."

"You drove? How did it go?"

Grace looked at her. She seemed sincerely interested. "Fine. Well, actually," she replied with a sniff.

Dr. Leakey smiled. "I'm clearly a good teacher."

She sat on the ground, facing Lemagrut. Lisa sat next to her. Grace was uncertain what to do. The cheetah turned her head, looking at the girl with her amber eyes. Grace sat on the other side of Lisa.

"Why didn't you come and tell me that Lisa had returned before heading off to Mr. Rono?" asked Dr. Leakey.

Grace ran her hand down Lisa's shoulder and leg. "I did. I was there. You were with my father. I came but then I, erm, I thought I'd go to Mr. Rono first. To ask about the bolt cutters."

She felt Dr. Leakey's eyes on her from the other side of the cat, where she leaned forward. "You came to my workroom while your father was there? While we were talking?"

Grace looked away, nodding.

"I see," said Dr. Leakey, exhaling for a long time. "What did you hear?"

"Nothing," snapped Grace, before adding, in a more subdued tone, "I don't know."

They were silent for a moment.

Dr. Leakey pointed. "Giraffes," she said.

Grace could just make out the animals in the distance, where they moved across the savanna, their heads and necks gliding above the trees. She counted five.

Dr. Leakey pulled up her knees and wrapped her arms around them. "I'm going to tell you something I've never told anyone else, because it wasn't their business and also it didn't matter to them," she said, looking straight ahead. "I have three sons. Everyone knows that. Few people know I had a daughter too. Her name was Deborah. She was my second born, after Jonathan. She died when she was about three months old. Of dysentery."

"I'm sorry," said Grace.

"I tried telling myself—I might've even told others—that it was for the best. Not that she died, of course, but that she died so young. Before we really knew her. Before she'd become *someone*. That bit, others might know. What I haven't admitted until now is that none of it was for the best. I might not have known her as well as I got to know the boys, but that didn't mean I didn't think about her as the years went by. Perhaps watching my sons grow, I learned that a large part of who they became existed when they were born."

She stopped. They watched as Lisa stood, went to the bucket, and lapped for a while before returning and stretching out behind them.

Dr. Leakey straightened her legs, placed her arms behind her, and leaned back on her hands. "She might've been very young when she died, but Deborah *was* someone. As I got older, I realized that I *did* know her. Without meaning to, I imagined how she might respond to things I did and said. In reality, she didn't live beyond three months, but she lived on in my thoughts whether I liked it or not."

"I'm sorry," repeated the girl, thinking about how, when she and her mother had first moved from Cambridge, she'd imagined telling her father about things she thought would interest him. That was before she'd shut him out of her thoughts.

"The reason I'm telling you this is because I've learned that if you don't talk about your feelings when you're experiencing something hard, the emotions don't magically go away. I recognized it too late. It's something I've been thinking about recently as I make notes for my memoir." Dr. Leakey took a long breath and exhaled. "When my father died, my mother sprung to action. She had to take care of affairs. Of me. There was no time to wallow, to be miserable. I felt suffocated by his death. Who knows, my mother might've too. But we didn't stop to grieve. We didn't talk about how we felt. What was important was to be strong and practical and get on with life. That's how I was raised to handle loss."

She turned to look at Grace. "I don't know how different things might've been if I'd talked about how I felt, mourned openly, but I think it would be better. Animals mourn. Did you know that? Elephants. Even giraffes." Dr. Leakey lifted a hand and gestured to where they'd seen the giraffes. "It's natural. I wish I'd known that when I was young. Like you."

They sat on the hillside without speaking for several minutes. Lisa lay behind them, her tail curling and unfurling in a calming rhythm.

"What should I do?" asked the girl.

"Talk to your father. Tell him how you feel."

Grace stared into the distance. What would she say? She didn't know how she felt. The anger that had burned so fiercely when they'd arrived in Africa had dwindled. It was as if the flames had vanished and all that remained were coals. Were they even still warm? Or had her determination to hate George smothered them? Maybe her resolve to focus her attention on Lisa had worked. Was it possible she didn't care how she felt anymore? She was unsure. Of her feelings for her father. Her mother. Herself.

"I don't know how I feel," she whispered.

Dr. Leakey didn't move as she spoke. "I know how *that* feels."

CHAPTER 28

1968
Olduvai Gorge, Tanzania

After closing the back door of the Land Rover behind Janet, Sam, Smudge, and Sophie, who'd leaped aboard in a spotty, tail-wagging mass, Mary squared her shoulders and marched to the driver's side. She was going to put the matter to rest for once and for all. She settled behind the wheel and waited while Louis, red-faced and grunting, heaved himself into the passenger seat and wedged his walking sticks between them.

"All right?" she asked as he slammed the door, discharging a cloud of dust. He nodded.

Years of living rough, crawling up and down sandy ravines, lying on the ground in awkward positions, walking mile upon mile searching for fossils, and carrying too much weight had left Louis with a severely arthritic hip. His strenuous youth, particularly the years he'd spent running through the Kenyan bush with his Kikuyu friends and, in England, over rugby fields and tennis courts hadn't helped either. Louis was sixty-five but seemed older, as he hobbled about between two sticks and faced the inevitable installation of an artificial joint. Pain meant he was unable to move about easily. It also rendered him bad tempered, irrational, and fatigued. However, his discomfort was only one of the reasons for his rare visits to Olduvai.

By then, Mary had accepted that the 1959 discovery of the hominid skull at FLK was as much an end as a beginning for her and Louis. Thanks to the presence of the film crew and Louis's foresight and showmanship, the discovery and ensuing publicity had thrust the Leakeys into the spotlight. Louis had reveled in the attention. Mary loathed it but resigned herself to how valuable it was. Fame brought the kind of funding they hadn't dared to dream about; money essential to finance archaeological research in remote places. Most notably, it attracted a sizeable sum from the National Geographic Society of the United States, which had allowed Mary to undertake a full excavation of FLK. However, it also laid bare a crack in their partnership; a fracture that would eventually become a rift.

Once Mary and Kamoya had reassembled the hundreds of fragments they'd scraped, picked, and sieved from the earth at FLK in 1959, there lay before them the skull of a hominid with an immense jaw and molars twice the width of those of modern man. Also remarkable was the thin ridge of bone, or sagittal crest—as seen in gorillas—that ran along the midline on the top of the skull. Not only was it the first substantial hominid fossil found at Olduvai, but it was also unlike any other skull found elsewhere. Louis had named the discovery *Zinjanthropus boisei*. Zinj was an old name for East Africa, anthropos was Greek for human, and Boisei honored engineer and businessman Charles Boise, who'd supported Mary and Louis financially when no one else did.

Although Mary and Louis referred to the skull as "Zinj" or "Dear Boy," others preferred "Nutcracker Man," which referenced its mighty jaws and was first used by Professor Phillip Tobias of the University of the Witwatersrand in South Africa. In fact, all the monikers worked well for the popular press and—buoyed by Des Bartlett's camera work and the rampant international media coverage that followed—the skull did a great deal more than stir the kind of scientific controversy typical of such discoveries; it also captured public attention. The timing was additionally fortuitous. Zinj came when curiosity about evolution was at its peak, both among scientists and the public. Everyone was fascinated by what the skull might reveal about human development. In its first public outing, Louis presented the skull at the British Academy of

London in October 1959. A newspaper reported the next day that so many people attended that "television stars like Sir Mortimer Wheeler had to stand against the wall."

Public fascination notwithstanding, the scientific significance of the skull was immense. It was more complete than comparable finds and, as Louis reiterated, was unearthed from a living floor that also revealed many broken bones and stone tools. While he might've originally been disappointed that Zinj was not a direct ancestor to man but part of an unsuccessful sideline, Louis was initially convinced that the skull *did* belong to the maker of the tools, and he wasted no time making his opinions known, starting with an article in *Nature* magazine.

While Louis's tour with Zinj began in England, it was in the United States where he amassed a following described as "cult-like." During the autumn of 1959, Louis gave sixty-six lectures at seventeen different universities and scientific institutions. It was the first of his marathon lecture tours, which became annual events and heralded a shift from his role of hands-on field archaeologist to internationally traveling front man, fund finder, lecturer, and arguably the world's most famous anthropologist. His presentations—where he spoke with warmth, humor, and passion, using simple words to explain complicated matters—were sold out. Basking in the adulation, he took on more and more new commitments without giving up existing ones. Louis was a master juggler of projects, but the efforts took their toll, not only on his health but also on his and Mary's private and professional partnerships.

The deterioration was as gradual as it was sure. When Mary felt detached enough to think about it, she accepted that a culmination of difficulties had chipped away at her affection and respect for Louis over the years. At times, she'd *almost* assured herself that his flirtations with other women were inconsequential to their relationship. Aside from his affair with Rosalie Osborn in 1955, she'd almost always succeeded in separating her relationship with Louis from those he formed with other women. She'd tell herself they didn't matter and guard herself against feelings of jealousy and insecurity—even when she felt she'd choke at the brazenness of his dalliances.

On one occasion, when they were in England together briefly, Mary had accompanied Louis to a meeting with his publisher in Cambridge. Afterward, he'd lingered in the offices. After waiting in the hallway for a while, Mary went back and found him with the publisher's secretary, a young woman who'd been introduced to Mary earlier as Eleanor but who'd clearly met Louis before. Louis and Eleanor were oblivious to Mary's presence in the doorway. That he'd delayed to regale an admirer—particularly an attractive young female—with a story or two or to lend an interested ear came as no surprise to her. However, when Mary recognized Louis's tone as the very one in which he'd professed his passion for her moments before they'd made love for the first time in his rooms in St. John's, she clutched her throat, struggling to breathe. Something was strangling her. She'd fled the building, hands over her ears as if they hadn't already recognized Louis's tone. Outside, Mary had closed her eyes, pictured Lemagrut against a clear sky, and breathed in deeply, once, twice, thrice.

It wasn't what Louis's behavior said about him, she'd told herself, *but rather what the way she responded to it said about her.*

However, it didn't matter what she thought or how she tried to steel herself against being hurt—Louis's liaisons inevitably changed the way she felt about him and herself. This, Mary finally accepted, months later when she was alone at Olduvai. She was sipping her morning tea—her dalmatians at her feet and Lemagrut hazy blue in the distance—when Mary realized with absolute clarity that she was happier when she and Louis were apart than when they were together. She'd never succeeded in completely suppressing her feelings of inadequacy in the face of Louis's liaisons, she finally conceded. However, when they were apart and she didn't see evidence of other women, she didn't have to deal with how his behavior made her feel. Dissociation and distance made life easier. Mary was happy.

Her withdrawal from Louis had a knock-on effect. He couldn't ignore how cold and uncaring she seemed. Mary saw how this might vindicate his seeking comfort elsewhere. She wasn't sure how she felt about that and tried not to dwell on it. If she didn't see it, she didn't have to think about it.

It wasn't only their private partnership that suffered; their professional paths also diverged. Just as—in the aftermath of Zinj and little over a year later when Mary and Jonathan found fragments of another hominid, whom Louis named *Homo habilis* and declared the de facto toolmaker—Louis had to travel extensively, Mary became professionally independent. Louis was not available to discuss matters or offer his opinion. Her confidence bloomed, and she grew accustomed to directing work at Olduvai and forging ahead without deferring to him.

Professional independence notwithstanding, Mary also felt that Louis's intellectual power and judgment were declining. His ill-health, unworkable schedule, and ever-accumulating projects inevitably contributed to this, and although she despaired at his inability to turn down appeals for appearances or involvement in new projects, Mary tried to be sympathetic. However, when Louis commenced excavations at Calico Hills in the Mojave Desert in southern California in 1963, she was appalled. She, along with others, didn't believe that the stones found there were tools made by humans. She was certain the site didn't warrant excavation and suspected that Louis felt compelled to fulfill his American fans' dream of finding evidence of early man in their country. Whether or not he was swayed by public sentiment, that Louis viewed the site as important enough to study confirmed to her that he was no longer academically competent. It was the ultimate blow to their relationship.

Now, about five years later, as Mary drove Louis and his walking sticks to the excavations on one of his infrequent visits to Olduvai, she anticipated his wrath at a decision she'd made and was determined to stand by.

"Richard said you've turned down the invitation from Johannesburg," she said without taking her eyes off the track.

Prompted by their colleague and friend Phillip Tobias, the University of Witwatersrand Vice Chancellor had written his intention to confer joint honorary degrees on Mary and Louis. The news had pleased Mary. After working in the field and illustrating and writing countless papers and books for almost four decades, she felt she'd earned a degree. She also liked that the offer came from the continent, as she'd noted in a letter to Tobias, "It is a very great honor and although I've never sought academic distinction, it gives me a nice warm feeling particularly coming from an African university instead of from overseas, where values tend to be distorted."

However, when she'd mentioned the offer to Richard, he'd replied that Louis had said he wouldn't accept it.

Louis turned to her now, a frown etched across his forehead. "Of course we're turning it down."

"*You're* turning it down," said Mary.

Louis ignored her. "Why Phillip imagined we'd accept, I can't imagine."

"I've accepted."

She felt his eyes on her. "What? You can't—"

This time, Mary ignored *him*. "As you know very well, Phillip is an anti-apartheid activist. He stands as categorically and firmly against discrimination as we do. So does his university. There are universities in South Africa I wouldn't wish to be associated with, but Witwatersrand is not one of them. I'm accepting the degree from a university, a specific university in South Africa that we admire and respect, *not* the government," she said.

"Oh, for goodness' sake, Mary, that's not how others might see it," he replied. "You *cannot* accept it. You cannot go there."

"I've made my decision, Louis. I'll not rebuff Phillip."

"Don't you care about us? About the family. The Leakey name."

Mary gripped the wheel as a hot wave surged through her. How dare Louis imply that she would besmirch their reputation? She opened her mouth to challenge him but clamped it shut without speaking her mind. She didn't want to demean herself by pointing out the obvious.

They drove on in silence until Mary pulled up as close to FLK as they could drive when Louis gave a low chuckle. "I'm sure a worthy institution will recognize you with a degree in the not-too-distant future. I know how much it means to you," he said.

She turned to glare at him. "I'm accepting this one. I've thought about it, Louis. I've made up my mind," she fumed before opening her door and walking to the back to allow the dogs out. She didn't linger to wait for Louis to struggle from the car.

CHAPTER 29

1983
Olduvai Gorge, Tanzania

FOR ONCE, IT WAS GRACE WHO SURPRISED GEORGE BY APPEARING UNEXPECTedly before him. He stopped dead at the sight of her sitting on the doorstep of his hut when he returned from the dig that evening.

"I don't want to leave early," she said, standing up. "I've spoken to Dr. Leakey. She understands."

He stared at her, his eyes bright against the dusty pallor of his skin.

"The vet's coming tomorrow with Mr. Rono's brother. I have to be here. We don't know what they'll do with her." She spoke quickly, without breathing. "I have to be here to make sure she's okay."

George sighed. "What did Dr. Leakey say?"

Grace looked at her feet. "That I should talk to you. Tell you how I feel," she said quietly.

He nodded, waiting.

"Do you want to meet her?" asked Grace.

"What? Who? The cheetah? Lisa?"

"Yes."

Grace led the way through the camp and past the lookout. They didn't speak until they reached the foot of the hill.

"She's not here," said George, looking up.

"She is," she replied without hesitating.

He was nervous, she could tell. It was understandable—she'd also been afraid of Lisa—but it made her smile. She was eager to introduce her father to the cheetah. She wanted him to experience how magnificent she was, to share her excitement.

"Wait," she said when they reached the top of the hill.

George stopped alongside her, looking around anxiously. The sun seemed to balance on the horizon where it illuminated a few wispy clouds. Somewhere in the distance, a francolin rattled its "chee-chakla, chee-chakla" warning that nightfall wasn't far away. Grace heard Lisa's purring before she appeared from the bush nearby. George grabbed his daughter's arm and pulled her back, stepping forward to stand between her and the cat. Grace wriggled free.

"It's all right, Dad. She won't do anything."

"But the growling," he said, his voice a rasp.

Grace moved past him and put her hand on Lisa's head. "She's purring." She glanced at her father. He was wringing his hands.

"Don't worry. We fed her earlier," she said, smiling now. "Hold out your hand. Let her smell it. That's it. See how she comes to you. Now pet her. Cheetahs are like domestic cats. They purr to show pleasure."

George gave Lisa a tentative pat. She pushed her head against his thigh. He emitted a nervous chuckle and patted her again.

"She loves having her ears rubbed, like this," said Grace.

He smiled and followed suit. Lisa purred louder.

They stood on the hill for several minutes while the cat wove her long, vibrating body between them, around their legs and back again, purring incessantly as they ran their hands over her head, neck and back.

"She really is like a cat," said George looking at Grace. "Just, erm, much, much bigger and louder."

She laughed. "You see. It's not a growl. She's happy. Pleased to know us."

"I see," he said with a quiet chuckle.

Grace showed him the sore on Lisa's neck and demonstrated how the collar aggravated it. She ran her hands down the cat's rib cage and repeated what Dr. Leakey had said about her being too thin. She explained what Simon had said about the difficulties of rewilding predators, and how the cheetah might not have learned how to hunt properly or evade predators like lions and hyenas before she was released.

"The problem is that there isn't a place nearby that can take care of her," she said, trying to keep the tremor from her voice. "Some believe hand-reared animals are dangerous. Especially if they don't know how to hunt. So then they…the game authorities think it's better, safer to—"

Grace couldn't go on. She couldn't bring herself to tell him that it was her fault. That by asking Simon for help, she might've signed Lisa's death warrant. Dr. Leakey had said she should talk to her father. She wanted to. Not only was she consumed with the need to confide in him how she'd failed Lisa, but she also wanted to tell him how, alone with her mother, she'd felt hollow, as if she, too, was dying. Nothing had mattered because she had no future. She'd left all hope with her friends and Watson in Cambridge when George left, and she and Eleanor moved to Tewkesbury. When her mother died, she'd stopped caring about anything. There was nothing *to* care about. No one mattered until she'd met Lisa and Dr. Leakey had told her to take care of her. Now she'd done the opposite; put her in danger.

She felt George's eyes on her. Her throat thickened, and she struggled to swallow. He didn't hesitate, stepping forward to wrap his arms around his daughter. Her shoulders shuddered as she cried on his chest, vaguely aware of the warmth of Lisa's body against her legs. George's scent was familiar and his embrace secure.

They stood like that long enough for the sun to slip away and for Lisa to grow bored and lie down some distance from them. Finally, Grace pulled away, giving a tiny smile as she glanced at her feet. They spoke simultaneously.

"Sorry—"

"We'll return—"

She looked at him. His eyes glistened. He'd been crying too.

"We'll return as planned," he said. "On Monday."

"Thank you," said Grace, letting out a huge breath. "I don't know if it'll make a difference, but I have to be here to try."

His response came a second too late. "Of course. But you must promise me you won't do anything rash. No repeat performances of this morning."

It came rushing back. She saw herself near the entrance to Dr. Leakey's workroom where she'd unintentionally overheard their conversation. What was it her mother had told George about Grace before their divorce? What did it have to do with Dr. Leakey? Who was she referring to when she said, "They're both gone"? Dr. Leakey had urged her to talk to her father. But what was there to say? It was George who was keeping secrets from her. She'd always been kept in the dark. By her father and, according to him, also by her mother. She was no longer a child, but nothing had changed. There was no way of escaping the past, no matter how recent or far.

"Sure," she said, her voice dull.

She turned away and went to stroke Lisa once more before striding ahead of him to camp.

CHAPTER 30

———⟡———

1972
Olduvai Gorge, Tanzania

Mary was alone in her workroom at Olduvai sorting through a collection of stone tools in the early afternoon of the first of October 1972, when she heard a small plane fly low over the camp. She wasn't expecting anyone, but it was possible Jonathan, Richard, or Philip had reason to visit her. She called the dogs, loaded them into the Land Rover, and drove to the airstrip.

Although the boys had long since left home and Louis traveled extensively, the family had kept the house at Langata for their sporadic visits to Nairobi. However, Mary had lived and worked largely at Olduvai Gorge since 1968. She'd been visited by numerous experts over the years, all of whom were struck not only by her dedication and hard work, but also by Mary's systematic, meticulous methods of mapping and dating each site, and her exacting records of the geologic levels, which accurately dated every find. Few had seen such immaculate field research.

In addition to the hominid and mammal fossils they'd found, Mary and her team had collected Oldowan stone tools as old as two million years. Noting how the artifacts altered over time, she'd introduced a second category of tools manufactured about five hundred thousand years ago, which she'd named Developed Oldowan.

Once she'd completed analyzing and writing up the finds from Beds I and II, Mary had moved on to Beds III and IV. She and her team had also helped set up tourism sites at the gorge, including a small museum. The 1971 publication of her book, *Olduvai Gorge: Volume 3, Excavations of Beds I and II* not only underscored her professional independence from Louis but also confirmed her place in the top ranks of prehistorians. She was the world's best known woman archaeologist and anthropologist.

The years hadn't altered how Mary felt about Olduvai. She never grew tired of the changing hues of the view across the gorge and Serengeti Plains to the volcanic highlands. Waking up, walking into the morning light with the dalmatians at her heels and greeting Lemagrut brought her satisfaction beyond her understanding of it. For a moment each morning, she'd pretend she and the dogs were alone in camp. However, Mary had long ago learned how important it was to welcome others. She worked with vast teams of experts, fossil hunters and excavators, and industrious support staff who kept them fed and the camp in operation. With scientific methods evolving all the time, Mary was pleased to work alongside people who introduced her to new information, techniques, and equipment. It wasn't just that it helped advance research at Olduvai, but also that she enjoyed learning new things.

Louis had continued to relentlessly take on new projects and pursue funding for them. He also constantly added to his lecture tour program, and—despite his deteriorating health—refused to rest. At sixty-nine, he'd finally undergone an operation on his hip. He'd also been treated for heart problems and a series of strokes. While these issues might've convinced others to slow down, they had the opposite effect on Louis. He continued his work and travels at a frenzied pace and, while they never formally separated, his and Mary's paths seldom crossed. Louis's visits to Olduvai had been rare and brief. Occasionally, they'd encounter one another at Langata, where there were a few awkward incidents when Mary arrived to find that Louis was not alone. She didn't hide her aversion to having other women in the family home and the visitors inevitably left immediately.

Mary wasn't thinking about Louis as she drove to the airstrip that warm, still October afternoon. However, when she recognized her youngest son,

Philip, climbing out of the plane, she knew. On a previous occasion, he had flown to Olduvai with news that Louis had been rushed to the hospital. She felt a heaviness in her stomach and sensed the inevitable.

"Another heart attack?" she called out as he walked toward her. "Or is he dead?"

"Dead," said Philip.

Louis had died of heart failure that morning after collapsing at his friend Vanne Goodall's flat in London.

Mary drove back to camp in stunned silence, packed a bag, and returned to the airstrip so that Philip could fly her to Nairobi to prepare for Louis's funeral.

After two memorial services—one private and the other a packed event in the All Saints Cathedral in Nairobi—and with Louis buried alongside his parents in Limuru about an hour from the city, Mary was exhausted by the events and interactions.

Gertrude phoned to offer her condolences while Mary was preparing to leave Langata for Olduvai.

"How are you?" she asked.

"I don't know," said Mary. "I've always believed that death is a very private matter. However, Louis's demise has reflected his life; it's attracted enormous attention. I can't help thinking he'd be pleased."

It was only back at Olduvai that Mary found enough peace to ponder her emotions.

One morning, as she and the dogs navigated bone-jolting corrugations of the track on her way into the gorge to work, she thought about the last time she'd seen Louis.

A week before his death, Mary was in Nairobi and had arrived at Langata to find Louis there alone. He'd been in uncommonly high spirits, having just had lunch with his and Frida's son, Colin, who was en route to London from Uganda. Richard, by now an eminent paleoanthropologist himself, arrived, too, bubbling with news of a discovery he and his team had made near Lake Turkana, Kenya.

Mary, Louis, and Richard had spent a few enjoyable hours discussing Richard's find. Whereas in the past, he and his son had disagreed on several matters, this time Louis shared Richard's and Mary's enthusiasm and excitement. It was the cheeriest Mary had seen him in years and for a while she forgot how unhappy they'd made one another. Even so, because of his health and the fact that he was about to embark on another marathon tour, Mary had thought, when she waved them goodbye as Richard drove his father to the airport that night, that she might not see Louis again.

Now, as the Land Rover bumped and rattled its way into the gorge, it seemed surreal. She might've imagined two weeks ago that it was possible he'd not survive the trip, but she hadn't believed it. She hadn't thought it through. Just as life had seemed implausible to Mary when her father died, a world without Louis was inconceivable. Good times and bad, he'd been part of her life for forty years. He was why she'd come here, discovered Olduvai Gorge, moved, and dedicated her life to researching mankind's origins in East Africa. It didn't matter that their partnership hadn't lasted; he'd given her so much. What had she given him in return?

Suddenly, the air seemed thin. Mary opened the window and breathed in the hot wind. She felt a cold nudge against her neck. It was Janet, who'd hopped over the back seat when she heard the groan of the window winder. Mary tipped her head, resting against the dog's muzzle. Janet responded by licking her ear.

It was in that moment that Mary let go of Louis. There was something about the warm air, Janet's presence, and the shaking of the Land Rover that assured her she didn't owe him anything. Her remorse was unwarranted. She'd come to Africa because she was curious, ambitious, and adventurous. That Louis had mirrored these attributes was part of their attraction. She'd fallen in love with him, and they'd worked side by side for years, ambitious and eager to learn more about human ancestry. He'd begun the search, and she'd joined him, but the quest wasn't only his. She'd taken what Louis had taught her and found her own way. Louis was the eager propagator of ideas and opinions, the broadcaster of events, and the grandstander of all undertakings. At his prime, his professional stature was unequaled, but it hadn't lasted. He'd stumbled in his eagerness to be all things to everyone and do more than was possible for one man. Mary was the methodical scientist who didn't shy away from self-scrutiny and hard work. She'd recognized the vision, plotted the way, and stayed true to the path. There was no ultimate destination in her work, but a journey fueled by curiosity and driven by science. She owed her success to no one but herself.

CHAPTER 31

1983
Olduvai Gorge, Tanzania

GRACE WAS THE FIRST TO ARRIVE AT THE DINING ROOM THE NEXT MORNING. A line of light beneath the door and the rattling from behind it indicated Mr. Rono was busy in the kitchen, but the tables were bare. She'd hoped to see Brown Dog the previous night. However, neither the dogs nor Dr. Leakey had appeared for dinner. When she awoke, Grace had told herself it was too early to expect him. Still, she felt a ping of disappointment when he wasn't outside waiting for her.

She pulled out a chair, sat down, and looked out across the camp, where the light was gradually coloring the silhouettes of the night and the collective calls and twittering of the birds were swelling. The rhythmic crunch of gravel alerted her to Dr. Leakey's arrival. Matt led the way while Brown Dog took up the rear.

Dr. Leakey pursed her lips. "It's been a while since anyone beat me to breakfast."

Grace stood and walked toward Brown Dog. He hesitated, but, as she crouched and called his name, came to her. She ran her hands over his head and patted him, whispering, "I'm sorry, Brown Dog. I'm sorry."

"What's going on?" asked Dr. Leakey, sitting down.

"I shouted at him yesterday. On my way to Lisa. He was following me, and I told him to go away. I was angry and took it out on him."

"Ah, that explains his woebegone expression yesterday. I wondered. But he forgives you. Look at that tail," said Dr. Leakey.

It wasn't only his tail. Brown Dog wiggled his entire body.

"Good grief, girl, if I was that concerned about everyone I yelled at, I wouldn't have time to think about anything else. Ask anyone who excavated the hominid footprints with me at Laetoli."

Grace pressed her face into Brown Dog's neck to hide her smile. She wasn't sure whether she was amused by the idea of Dr. Leakey not having time to do anything except apologize or whether she was simply happy to have Brown Dog in her arms again.

Greetings were exchanged when Mr. Rono appeared with a tray. Grace returned to the table. Brown Dog followed and sat close by.

"I'm told you were chauffeured to visit your brother yesterday, Jackson," said Dr. Leakey as he set out the breakfast things. "How did you find the drive?"

Mr. Rono didn't look up. "You taught her well, Dr. Leakey," he said.

Grace felt her face redden and, for the second time that morning, she was unable to suppress a smile. She glanced at Mr. Rono as he left the room and saw that he was also smiling.

"Why are you up so early? You're not leaving today, are you?" asked Dr. Leakey.

"No. George, erm, my father said we'll leave as originally planned after all. I'm up because Mr. Rono's brother and the vet are coming."

"Of course. Though I doubt they'll be here for a few hours yet."

Grace sprinkled sugar on her porridge. She'd grown to enjoy the hot, starchy grain since she'd been at Olduvai. "I don't want to miss them."

They didn't speak for several minutes as they ate.

"Did you have a chance to speak to your father yesterday?" asked Dr. Leakey, setting aside her plate, and reaching to pour the tea.

Grace kept her eyes on the small puddle in her bowl, as if guarding it from escape. "Yes. I asked him if we could leave as originally planned and not today and he agreed."

She'd walked Brown Dog and Matt, fed and watered Lisa, and packed three boxes of stone tools by the time Grace heard the low voice of Mr. Rono approaching the workroom. Dr. Leakey, who was working silently on the other side of the room, looked up and caught her eye shortly before the three men appeared in the entrance.

Where the Rono brothers were tall and angular, the veterinarian was short and stocky. He wore the same khaki uniform as Simon. However, Simon's sleeves were rolled up, and he'd left a top button open at the collar, while Dr. Rwambo's shirt was closed at the cuffs and neck. His greeting was a tight smile and a blink. It was the look of someone who was there for a purpose, and it wasn't to make small talk.

Mr. Rono led Brown Dog and Matt away while the others went to find Lisa. Grace said nothing as Dr. Leakey told the vet about the cheetah. However, when they reached the lookout and Grace saw Lisa stand swiftly at the sight of them, she couldn't restrain herself.

"We can't all go at once," she said. "We'll frighten her."

The men looked at Dr. Leakey.

"She's right. Grace, you take the doctor to Lisa. We'll wait here for a bit."

"It's not that she's dangerous," said Grace, her eyes on the vet. "Not at all. She's gentle. Calm. It's just that she might be overwhelmed by so many of us."

"Of course," said Dr. Rwambo. "Come on, then. Take me to your friend."

His tone was unexpectedly kind. It wasn't that Grace had imagined that he was uncaring, but rather that he'd seemed impatient and perhaps a little aloof. Her step felt a little lighter as they headed to the hill.

"Simon, I mean, Mr. Rono said there aren't many places nearby that take care of hand-reared cheetahs. I could look after her here. I mean, I have been, and it's been all right," she said.

"Except for the fight with the dogs," he replied.

"We're keeping them apart. Lisa knows she has to stay here. That she can't come into the camp."

Dr. Rwambo nodded. "How long will you be at Olduvai?"

Grace swallowed. "Well, I don't know. We're meant to leave in a few days but I could maybe—"

"Even if you could stay a bit longer, it can take years to rewild a cheetah. Also, it's something that requires knowledge and experience."

They were nearing the crest of the hill. Lisa, who'd kept them in her sights throughout, gave a cheerful chirp and walked to Grace.

"Please, Doctor, don't take her," said the girl as she placed her hand on the cat's head.

She's all I've got, she thought.

The vet held out his hand. Lisa gave it a cursory sniff. "You are indeed a calm one," he said, stepping to the side before walking slowly around her.

With Grace stroking her, Lisa paid little attention to Dr. Rwambo as he examined her. Even when he crouched in front of her to peer into her eyes and ears, and lift her lips to inspect her teeth, she showed no signs of mistrust or discomfort. Nor did she seem unsettled when Dr. Leakey arrived with Simon.

"You're right about her being underweight," said the vet, addressing Dr. Leakey. "That she's eating is a good thing, but it won't help if she has persistent diarrhea. That has to be treated."

"Couldn't we do it here?" asked Grace.

"We'll have to run tests. They can't be done here. The sore on the neck is simple to treat. Ideally, the collar could be removed, but it might not be essential," he said, using both hands to move Lisa's fur aside so that he could examine the infected area.

"But she can't hunt properly with it," said Grace, her voice rising.

"We need to give the researcher more time to respond. These collars are expensive, and we can't interfere without speaking to him."

Grace scowled at him. "But surely her life is the most important thing?"

The vet straightened and looked at her, his expression stern. "There are many things to think of in matters such as these. Things you know nothing about," he said.

"Researchers are not the enemy, Miss Grace," said Simon, who was gently rubbing Lisa's ears. "They help us understand animals so that we can do more for them. It's not just about this cat; it's about her species. And other wildlife."

Grace wanted to object. She didn't care about "her species" and "other wildlife." She cared about Lisa and anyway, wasn't it the vet's responsibility to care for *every* animal, case by case? She looked away, across the plains to Lemagrut. It wouldn't help to anger the men. She'd already tried their patience.

"What do you propose, Doctor?" asked Dr. Leakey.

"That we take her to our facility so that we can examine her properly and treat her accordingly. We don't have the capacity to rewild her there, but it'll allow time for the researcher to get back to us at which stage we can discuss the next step," he said.

"But what if he doesn't get back to you?" asked Grace. "Dr. Leakey has tried to reach him and he hasn't responded. What if he doesn't care about her? It already seems that way."

Simon glanced at Dr. Rwambo.

"I don't know, Miss Grace," said the vet. "But this is the best thing for the cheetah now, and you'll have to trust that I'll do the best for her in the future too."

Whether Lisa got into the large wooden crate on the back of the vet's truck willingly or not, Grace didn't know. She'd hugged the cat, whispered goodbye on the hill, and sprinted to camp before the men even discussed the logistics of loading her. Brown Dog and Matt were delighted when she fetched them from the kitchen and ran with them to the far side of the camp, where Matt disappeared into the sisal.

Dr. Leakey found her sitting on the same sandy bank she'd occupied with Brown Dog a few days earlier. Only this time, the mongrel sat to her left.

"Dr. Rwambo said you're welcome to visit Lisa before you go," said Dr. Leakey, easing herself onto the earthy shelf alongside the girl.

Grace didn't trust herself to speak. She hadn't cried. It seemed running herself breathless had drawn on the same resources required by sobbing. But she'd been still for some time now, and it occurred to her that she might've recovered enough to weep.

"You could drive there tomorrow. Or the next day."

"I don't want to see her in a cage," said Grace.

"She won't be. They apparently have a large, outdoor enclosure for her. She'll be all right."

"Why didn't you demand that they leave her here? At least for the next few days? I could've taken care of her."

Dr. Leakey sighed. "Dr. Rwambo is a good man. So is Simon. I was worried about what they might feel obliged to do before they got here. The authorities can be inflexible. But when I saw them with Lisa, I knew that they'd do their best for her. They're better equipped than we are. There's no danger that she'll be attacked by dogs with them. I know you wanted to take care of her, and you've done an excellent job, but this is the best for her."

Grace leaned forward, her elbows on her knees and head in her hands. There was no holding back her tears now. They fell on the earth between her feet in tiny, dusty plops. How was it she was crying again, she thought? She'd done more of it in two days than she'd done in a decade. She felt the cold, wet nudge of Brown Dog's nose near her ear and the warmth of a hand resting on her back.

"One of the many things I learned living here was how to let go," said Dr. Leakey quietly. "I don't mean that you should let go of how you feel about Lisa. Not at all. Neither do I expect you to stop thinking about what might happen to her. We're not machines with switches that we can flick on and off. What you might try to let go of though is the belief that only you can save her. That'll eat you up and spit you out. I discovered over many years that I couldn't control everything in life. I also saw that I could achieve a great deal more by trusting that others could do things I couldn't and that they knew things I didn't. I asked for help, for expertise. I let go of the idea that I should, that I could, do everything. And you know what? I got so much more done. It was better. And I was happier."

Grace lifted her head and turned to look at Dr. Leakey. "I thought that..." she said, sniffing.

"Thought what?"

"That I could save her. I thought if I did everything the doctors told me I could save my mother." Grace took a long, shaky breath. "Even when it was clear they didn't believe she would get better, I thought I could save her."

"I'm sorry."

Tears coursed down her cheeks again. "With Lisa, it was different. It seemed possible. I didn't think I'd fail."

"You didn't. You haven't. Don't give up on her. Just let go of the belief that it's *all* up to you and that you can't rely on others to help."

"I'll try."

Dr. Leakey gave Grace's back another pat. "Letting go of things can be very freeing. I read somewhere that it's like clearing out an old, messy drawer. Once you throw away the things you don't need, you make space for other stuff. Useful things that'll bring you happiness."

CHAPTER 32

1983
Olduvai Gorge, Tanzania

THE DAYS AFTER LISA'S DEPARTURE WERE SIMULTANEOUSLY INTERMINABLE AND finite for Grace. On one hand, it was hard to be at Olduvai with the cheetah gone. On the other hand, every hour brought Grace's day of departure closer.

She avoided the lookout when she walked the dogs and was relieved that Dr. Leakey hadn't repeated the idea of visiting Lisa. It wasn't that Grace didn't think about it herself. She'd lain restless each night, scolding herself for being cowardly. She *should* visit, not only because she cared and wanted to be sure that Lisa was all right, but also because she'd like to remind Dr. Rwambo about his promise to do his best for the cat.

Grace did eventually sleep. However, hours later, when her body decided it had had enough rest, she woke in the predawn hours at that ghastly time when her thoughts took her to the deepest, darkest corners of despair. A doctor had explained the reason for the phenomenon to her mother.

"It's because, at that time of the sleep cycle, the body is meant to be recovering physically and emotionally and our internal resources are at their lowest. If you wake up, the mind sees only problems of the worst kind and no solutions, which can lead to catastrophizing. Even when you know you're being irrational, it's hard to pull free. I've heard it referred to as 'barbed-wire thinking' because you get stuck in it," he'd said.

Indeed, at that hour, the overriding themes of Grace's thoughts were distress and disaster. She imagined various scenarios that inevitably ended with Lisa's death. Grace pictured the cheetah escaping while on the truck and being run over. In another setting, Lisa was summarily put down when they arrived at the center. There was an imagined situation in which the cat was traumatized and refused to eat or drink. Grace also visualized Lisa's wound becoming so bad that she'd died from an infection. In the dark hours, Grace's mind was a bottomless pit of dreadful imaginings.

Even when the sun had risen and she was up, eating breakfast or working alongside Dr. Leakey, and recognized how unreasonable her early-morning thoughts were, Grace couldn't convince herself to visit Lisa. The thought of saying goodbye to the cat again punched her in the hollow spot beneath her ribs. That she'd have to bid farewell to Brown Dog was bad enough.

"Do you have a large garden in Nairobi?" she asked as she and Dr. Leakey packed notebooks into a box the day before Grace's departure.

"For the dogs, you mean. Yes. It's nothing like being out here but they have plenty of space." Dr. Leakey hesitated and looked at Grace. "And of course, they'll be walked there. You don't have to worry about Brown Dog...or Matt."

"I know," said Grace reddening. "I just wondered."

She carried a box to the entrance, stacked it on top of another and returned to continue packing.

"Did you meet my father in Cambridge when you knew my mother?" she asked.

Dr. Leakey reached for some books. "No. He wrote to me years later. I didn't really *know* your mother. I met her once." She dropped the books into a box with a loud thump. "Louis knew her."

"Did he say anything to you about her?" asked Grace.

Dr. Leakey straightened and stared at her. "Why the questions?"

Grace held her gaze. "You asked the other day what I overheard when you and my father were talking. I said nothing. That wasn't true. I did hear something, but I didn't understand it. You were talking about me, my mother and someone else. You asked my father why he was worried about it. 'They're both gone,' you said. Who were you talking about? What does it have to do with me?"

Dr. Leakey went to the table and took a cigar from its pack. "We were talking about someone we both knew. He and your mother are dead," she said, her back to Grace.

"What did he have to do with me?" asked Grace.

"Nothing," replied Dr. Leakey turning to face her once more. "He had absolutely nothing to do with you." She huffed. "That's the danger of eavesdropping; you only hear bits and pieces and misunderstand what's going on. Make assumptions. Jump to conclusions."

Grace stared at her. Was Dr. Leakey lying? Although Grace hadn't heard the entire conversation, the bit that she had heard was clear. Why would she lie? She was the most forthright person Grace had ever met. If she couldn't believe Dr. Leakey, who could she trust?

"I'm sorry," she said. "I shouldn't have listened in or, um, interrogated you."

Dr. Leakey chuckled. "Well, interrogated is a strong word. Let's finish up here so that we can do something a bit more interesting after lunch."

Grace had avoided being alone with her father since she'd introduced him to Lisa and soaked his chest with her tears. The way he looked at her across the table at mealtimes had made it clear that he knew what had happened to Lisa. However, she didn't want to talk to him about it. She didn't want to discuss anything with him, particularly since she knew conversation would be unavoidable on the long, dusty drive to Nairobi and then in the plane home. And then? Would she stay with her father in England? If not, where would she go? What would she do? She didn't know and didn't want to think about it.

He caught up with her as she left the dining room that night.

"You're all packed and ready, I take it? We'll leave at daybreak tomorrow. Jackson said he'll pack breakfast for us," he asked, eyes eager and with a smile.

She nodded.

He touched her arm. "Everything all right?"

"Yes. Why wouldn't it be?" she replied, stepping back.

George waited a beat. "Well, I'm going to have a last nightcap with everyone before I go to bed. Do you want to join us? Have a soft drink or some tea?"

"Will Dr. Leakey be there?"

"She said she'd come later. She's finishing off some work."

"No. I'll see you tomorrow."

Grace expected Dr. Leakey to be up in time to say goodbye to her and her father in the morning but, although she was uncertain exactly what she'd say, she wanted to talk to her alone. As she made her way through the dark campsite toward the workroom, she recognized the low pitch of Mr. Rono's voice. He and whoever he was talking to were obscured by a nearby building. Grace stopped. She'd take the opportunity to say goodbye to Mr. Rono without George around too but didn't want to interrupt his conversation.

"When did they notice she'd gone?"

It was Dr. Leakey. Grace grew warm with shame. She was eavesdropping again. She should walk on. Wait for Dr. Leakey in her workroom. She meant to, but Mr. Rono's response came too quickly.

"Apparently Dr. Rwambo went to the enclosure with his assistant yesterday morning to dress her wound. The gate was open. Simon thinks whoever fed her the night before didn't close it properly," he said. "They spent the day searching and found some tracks, which disappeared onto a rocky hillside."

"What about the collar? They hadn't set it up again then, I guess," said Dr. Leakey.

"They took it off to treat the wound," he replied.

Dr. Leakey sighed. "Well, there's that. It might be a good thing. Perhaps she'll be a more successful hunter without it."

CHAPTER 33

———⚬———

1983
Olduvai Gorge, Tanzania

IT WAS STILL DARK WHEN, AS MARY AND THE DOGS APPROACHED, GEORGE Clark lobbed the last of his bags into the back of the Land Rover the next morning. Jackson appeared from the kitchen at the same time, lugging an old wicker picnic basket they'd used at Olduvai to carry food and drink on road trips for decades.

"I'll put it on the back seat so it's easy to reach," he said, addressing the other man. "Which side does Miss Grace like to sit?"

George looked up, his face pale and blank as it reflected the light from the kitchen. "Oh, I don't know. She sat behind the passenger seat on the way up. So perhaps that side."

"Where is she?" asked Mary.

"I haven't seen her," replied George, glancing at his watch. "Hmm. She's late. I'll—"

"I'll go," she said. "She's sure to wake up when the dogs jump on her."

Although she understood George was eager to get going, Mary didn't hurry. She wasn't feeling entirely awake. Sleep hadn't come easily. It wasn't unusual. With her time at Olduvai dwindling, Mary felt an increasing heaviness on her chest at night. Even at rest, her breathing was ragged, which made it difficult to slide into the soothing rhythm of sleep. She'd closed her eyes, determined not to think about leaving the gorge for good, but it was impossible. She'd spent the happiest, most exciting times of her life here. The dusty gorge, with its gullies, cliffs, and sandy bed, was her home. The Serengeti, with its acacias, sisal, commiphora bushes, and red oat grass, was her garden. The animals and birds that roamed and flew across the gorge and over the plains were her neighbors, her companions. And then there was the comforting, solid presence of Lemagrut that greeted her each morning, reminding her that no matter what the day might bring and where the future might lead, some things were always there, exactly where they'd always been. No painting, picture or any other view could bring her greater contentment. How was she supposed to give it up?

That night, her thoughts had also been weighed down by Grace's leaving. Mary hadn't welcomed the idea of the teenager being in camp. She'd agreed that she could accompany her father with more than one misgiving. What would a teenager do at Olduvai? What mischief would she get up to? If he wanted his daughter to experience Africa, George Clark should jolly well take her on a safari, she'd thought. But then she'd met Grace and surprised herself by liking the girl. There was something familiar about her reticence, her brooding. She'd recognized her anger and grief. Despite Mary's initial reservations, she'd almost immediately wanted to get to know her. The girl's adoration of Brown Dog and the cheetah pleased her. Their visit to the caldera was as enjoyable as Mary's first trip there in 1935. It was novel and rewarding to see the place and animals afresh through Grace's eyes. Mary was ridiculously proud of how quickly Grace had learned to drive and how serious she was about the cheetah's well-being. She didn't want to leave Olduvai. Neither did she want Grace to go.

News of Lisa's escape had added to the bedeviled state of Mary's mind when she'd sought sleep. When she'd finally drifted off, she was woken twice by Brown Dog whining to be let out. It was unusual for him to be unsettled while Matt slept. She'd admonished the mongrel to be quiet, wondering if the dalmatian's run-in with the cheetah had troubled him more than she'd realized. It didn't matter. No one was going out. Typically, when the dogs were restless at night it was because there was a wild animal in the vicinity. It was possible, Mary had thought, that Brown Dog sensed the hyenas Jackson had spotted in the gorge that evening. She hoped the carnivores weren't foraging in the camp for scraps of food and whatever other items hyenas found palatable. Although Mary and Jackson hadn't mentioned last night's sighting, they routinely warned everyone who came to Olduvai not to leave anything that might appeal to scavengers, notably their shoes, outdoors at night.

Now, arriving at Grace's hut, she saw the door was ajar. She knocked and called into the room. "Are you up? Your father's waiting."

There was no reply.

"Grace? Are you there?" she asked, pushing the door open so that Matt and Brown Dog could enter. "The dogs are on their way."

Still, there was no response. Mary went in. Matt sniffed at the girl's suitcase, which was packed, closed, and stood against the wall with her small backpack and neatly rolled-up sleeping bag alongside it. Brown Dog examined the empty camp bed. Mary found the nearby bathroom unoccupied too.

"Is she on her way?" asked George moments later when Mary returned alone to where he and Jackson waited at the car.

Mary shook her head. "Not there. She might've gone to look for me—to say goodbye," she said. "Or you, Jackson. I'll check my hut and you go to yours."

A while later, having looked in places they imagined the girl might be, Mary and George returned to the car. Although the sky was still a deep indigo, the birdsong had amplified, and others had begun making their way to the dining room. George approached the men one by one, asking if they'd seen his daughter.

Mary watched as Jackson hurried toward her. "What is it?" she asked quietly when he reached her.

"My car," he said, matching her tone. "It's gone. I left it outside the workshop yesterday after a puncture repair."

"Are you sure? Perhaps someone moved it."

"I checked. It's not in the camp," he replied. "Did you tell her about the cheetah?"

"No. If you didn't, she wouldn't know," said Mary. Then she remembered how Grace had overheard her and George talking. Was the girl within hearing distance last night when Jackson told her about Lisa's escape? "Unless—"

Jackson leaned toward her. "What?"

They were interrupted by George. "No one's seen her. Where on earth could she be? She'd packed. She was ready. What could've happened?"

He stared at Mary and then Jackson. "What's going on? Do you know something?" George's voice rose. "You don't think she's—"

Mary raised a hand, urging him to stop talking. "Jackson's Land Rover is missing."

George gasped.

She continued. "It's possible Grace has driven it to where Simon, Jackson's brother, lives."

Mary glanced at Jackson, who nodded. "Or to the Ngorongoro where Simon works. He'll be there today," he added.

"Driven? But she can't, I mean, she barely knows how. My God! In the dark. And why? Why would she go?" asked George, breathless. "She has! She's run away. Driven away. What am I—"

Mary shook her head. "She hasn't taken her things. She hasn't run away."

George lifted his hands, the whites of his eyes gleamed. "Then what? Why?"

"The cheetah escaped. Grace has gone to look for Lisa," said Mary.

She turned to Jackson. "She must've overhead us talking." He nodded again. Mary looked at George. "Come. It'll be all right. We'll go and find her."

George started, "But—"

"You get on with things, Jackson," said Mary, gesturing toward the empty kitchen. "Where's Gatimu?"

"It's his day off," replied Jackson. "But I'll get him up so we're not too behind schedule."

Mary led the way to her Land Rover, opening the back to allow Matt and Brown Dog to hop in. George climbed into the vehicle and closed the door without a word. They'd driven through the camp and turned onto the road before he spoke, his voice dull with misery.

"Whatever your theory, I think you're wrong," he said, looking at the illuminated track ahead. "She's run away because she can't bear the thought of going back to England with me."

Mary glanced at him. She wanted to object. She was sure he was wrong.

It didn't make sense for Grace to have fled. Not only would she have taken her belongings if she'd gone, but it wasn't in keeping with who she was. As unsure as Grace was about her future, she wasn't reckless. Mary felt certain that whatever Grace had done was motivated by her love for the cheetah. She thought about saying as much to George but held her tongue. His despair would mount if she implied that she knew his daughter better than he did.

"It's hopeless," he said. "Even if we find her, I've ruined our relationship. She doesn't trust me. Or respect me. It'll never come right. It's just hopeless."

"Hopeless?" echoed Mary. "In my experience, hopelessness rarely lives up to expectation. There's always something that trips it up."

George looked at her.

"What do you think of my driving?" she asked.

"What?"

"Do you feel safe with me at the wheel on this bumpy road in wildest Africa with first light barely upon us?

He frowned. "Well, yes."

Mary smiled. "Good. Then you won't be bothered by the fact that I'm totally blind in my left eye."

CHAPTER 34

1983
Olduvai Gorge, Tanzania

GEORGE TURNED IN HIS SEAT AND STARED AT MARY AS SHE EXPLAINED HOW— back at Olduvai after completing her fieldwork of the hominid trails at Laetoli in 1979—she'd finalized the footprint report, completed her study of artifacts from Olduvai's Beds III and IV, and written up her findings for a monograph.

"By November last year, I knew my time here was coming to an end. I'd begun thinking about planning my departure and writing my autobiography," she said, her eyes on the road. "It was a reflective rather than a sad time, and I felt relatively relaxed. I'd even taken to resting after lunch every day. Nothing prepared me for waking up one afternoon blind in one eye."

"What happened?" asked George.

"My sons got me to a doctor in Nairobi. He said a blood clot had settled behind my eye. Insisted I was lucky that it wasn't worse but confirmed the blindness was permanent. I thought I'd never read, write, draw, work, or drive again. Believed my life might as well be over," she said.

"But then how—"

Mary chuckled. "If you ever meet my sons, ask them how utterly depressed

I was by the whole business. I was ready to give up. Woke up every morning feeling that it was hopeless and went to bed convinced of it."

"But November…that's less than a year ago," said George.

"Exactly!" she replied. "I moped in Nairobi for a while, took my medication, and was distracted by the children over Christmas. By mid-January, I was back here, working, writing, drawing, and, here we are, driving as if I'd never stopped."

"But your eye—"

"As sightless as the afternoon it happened," she said, chortling again. "But life goes on much as before. You see, it's as I said; hopelessness is overestimated."

They drove for several minutes without talking. For an instant, Mary closed her right eye. She did it occasionally to check whether the sight hadn't miraculously returned in the left. It hadn't, but the exercise reminded her how well she coped without it.

The sky was brighter and the lights of the car barely discernible on the sandy tracks. As Mary slowed and turned onto the larger road, she saw bright blinking ahead. Another vehicle was approaching.

"Ha!" said Mary. "Who could that be?"

George leaned forward. "It looks like a Land Rover."

Mary nodded. As the vehicles drew closer, she recognized the other as Jackson's.

Thank God, she thought, straining to confirm that Grace was driving. With less than yard between them, the two cars stopped.

"It's not her," said George, his hands clasped across his forehead as if his skull might explode.

Mary switched off the engine and watched Gatimu step out slowly from behind the steering wheel of the other vehicle and walk to her window. Matt and Brown Dog stood at her shoulder, panting happily as they recognized the young man.

Gatimu raised a hand and ducked his head to look into the cab. "Good morning, Dr. Leakey, Mr. Clark," he said.

"What's going on, Gatimu? Where've you been?" said Mary.

He looked at his feet. "Visiting a friend. He's just moved here to work at Ngorongoro," he said. "It's my day off."

Mary's disappointment at not finding Grace spilled over. "But Jackson didn't give you permission to use his car," she said.

Gatimu looked at her, his eyes wide. "I meant to get back earlier. I thought it would be—"

"Did you go alone?" asked George.

"Yes," replied the young man, frowning.

"We're looking for Miss Grace," said Mary. "She wasn't in camp this morning."

Gatimu blinked, confused.

Mary sighed. "I thought she might've taken the car."

"I'm sorry, Dr. Leakey," said Gatimu.

For a moment, the only sound was the dogs' panting.

The young man shuffled his feet and scratched his head. "When I left last night—it was very late—I heard something. It sounded like sloshing water." Mary and George stared at him. "It stopped. I waited for several minutes before moving because I, um, didn't want to disturb anyone when I drove away."

"Sloshing water. As if in a bucket, perhaps?" said Mary.

Gatimu nodded, adding quietly, "I also saw two hyenas as I left camp."

"Hyenas?" said George. "In the camp? Last night?"

"Just outside the boma," said Gatimu.

George stared at Mary. His face was paler than ever. "You don't think—"

She couldn't look at him. "No, but George, you go with Gatimu. Gatimu, I'm going back to camp. You and Mr. Clark go and look for the hyena tracks. It might be useful to know where they went."

"Why? What do you mean? What are you going to do?" asked George.

"Go," she replied. "I'll see you shortly."

Jackson ran out of the kitchen as Mary sped back into camp. She stopped the vehicle and climbed out. He opened his mouth to speak but Mary beat him to it.

"We bumped into Gatimu," she said.

"In my—"

"Yes, in your car," she replied. "You can deal with him later. Mr. Clark is with him. They're looking for hyena tracks on the other side of the boma."

"You saw the hyena?"

Mary shook her head. "Gatimu did. Two. Last night. We'll go there later. He also heard water sloshing in a bucket. Fetch your rifle. I'll stow the dogs in the kitchen and meet you at the lookout tree. Be quick."

Jackson headed to his hut. Mary called Matt and Brown Dog. They followed her to the kitchen where she ordered them inside and closed the door. As she strode through the camp, Mary felt sick with regret for not searching the surroundings before heading out to look for Jackson's vehicle. She'd been so certain that Grace had taken the Land Rover that she'd all but forgotten the hyenas and the danger they might pose to an unarmed person wandering around alone at night.

Although there was no sign of Grace from the lookout, Mary knew the moment she saw the bucket of water on the top of the hill that the girl had gone there. As soon as she caught sight of Jackson striding toward her with the rifle, she set off. He caught up quickly.

"No one I spoke to has seen the hyenas this morning," he said.

"Good," said Mary. "I didn't spot any tracks in the camp either. However, Gatimu saw them close by and Brown Dog was restless last night."

"Perhaps the dog heard Miss Grace leaving the camp."

"That's possible. See the bucket?"

Jackson nodded.

"It wasn't here yesterday. We brought it back days ago after Simon and the vet took the cat."

"Ah. So, she left us a clue."

They were near the top. "The question is, how far would she have gone?" said Mary, stopping to look around. "We should've warned everyone, especially her, about the hyenas last night."

"She's a clever girl. She wouldn't go far."

Mary sighed. "If she was *really* clever, she wouldn't have left camp. We agreed that the lookout tree was as far as she would go alone."

"But we know she came up here by herself when she visited the cheetah."

"Not in the dark."

"I think you would've done the same thing under the circumstances," he said quietly.

Mary narrowed her eyes at him.

Jackson shrugged. "You and Miss Grace are much alike, Dr. Leakey."

"What nonsense, Jackson. She's—"

There was a gentle rustling of a low bush alongside a mass of large boulders. They turned toward it together. Jackson raised the rifle. For moment, the air was still and quiet. Mary placed a hand on her chest as if to quieten her lungs. As they stared at the spot, the branches shifted. Mary gasped and Jackson released the gun's safety lock.

Then they heard it; the purr of a cheetah as she slid out from between the plants.

"Lisa! You *are* here," said Mary breathing again as the cat sauntered to her, giving Jackson and his rifle little more than a passing glance.

He lowered the weapon. "She came straight back. It's incredible."

"No doubt about it," said Mary, running her hands down the animal's spine. "Got rid of the collar and returned forthwith!"

They looked at each other, shaking their heads in disbelief. Lisa purred.

"That's one missing soul found. Now where's the other?" said Mary. She crouched and held Lisa's face in her hands. "Have you seen Grace? Do you know where she is?"

Jackson went to the bushes out of which the cheetah had appeared. Using the barrel of the rifle, he pushed the branches apart and stretched his neck to investigate behind the vegetation.

"Dr. Leakey," he called, without turning around. "Over here."

Mary's heart skipped a beat. What had he found? It couldn't be good if it wasn't moving. Cold with dread, she stood and walked to where Jackson was peering into the bush. He shifted so that she could see past him. There, curled up on a bare patch of ground between the bushes, her face turned away, was Grace. A section of earth alongside her bore the indentation and marks of another. Lisa must've been lying near her.

"She's breathing," said Jackson when Mary turned to him, wide-eyed.

"Is she injured? Can you see any signs of—"

"I think she's sleeping. See how her back moves? Her breathing seems normal," he said.

Mary bent to look through the bushes. "How can we get to her? Can you crawl through there?"

"Or we could just wake her up."

Mary glared at him for a moment, leaned forward, and said loudly, "Grace! Wake up! Lisa must be fed."

The girl's shoulders twitched.

"Grace! Wake up!" shouted Mary.

She sat up slowly, shoved her hair from her eyes, and looked around, confused.

"Here!" said Mary, shaking a branch to direct Grace's vision.

"Oh! Dr. Leakey. Mr. Rono. Oh dear. Where is she? Where's Lisa?" asked Grace, looking around.

"Out here. Having a drink," said Jackson, a smile in his voice.

They stood back as Grace crawled out from under the bushes and got to her feet in front of them. Her face was caked with sand, her clothes rumpled and dusty, and her hair a tousled mess. Lisa approached and stood at her side like a furry, affable bodyguard. Mary stared at the pair; her mouth tightly clamped.

"I'm sorry," said Grace eventually. "I heard you talking last night. I couldn't sleep. I *knew* she'd come here. I wanted to be sure that she wouldn't come into camp looking for us and get into another fight with Matt. So, I got some water and came here." She pointed at the bucket as if affirming the evidence. "And she was waiting, Dr. Leakey. She was here, waiting for us. She came back. She found her way back to us. Isn't it amazing?" She placed a hand on the top of Lisa's head. The touch reignited her purring. "I tried to stay awake so that I could be back in camp before anyone else woke up, but I was so tired. I followed Lisa to her sleeping spot and, well, then I didn't wake up."

Mary sighed. "Jackson, take my car and find George."

"Of course," he said. Then he smiled at Grace. "I'm glad you're all right, Miss Grace."

"Thank you," she replied, her voice shaky.

They watched him walk down the hill.

"Is my father, well—is he all right?" asked Grace.

"He's frantic. Obviously. I'm not sure exactly what's going through his mind, but I'm certain he imagined several horrible scenarios, particularly when he heard about the hyenas."

"Hyenas?"

"A small pack was seen skulking about near FLK yesterday. I thought perhaps they'd come into the camp when Brown Dog woke me up twice last night. It could've been them. But maybe it was you getting water to bring to Lisa."

"I didn't see any hyenas," said Grace.

"Thank goodness."

"I'm sorry. I didn't mean to worry anyone, Dr. Leakey. It's just—"

"I know."

Grace took a deep breath. "Will Dr. Rwambo take her back?"

Mary shrugged. "I can't see why not."

The girl nodded. "Dr. Leakey, do you think, if my father agrees to it, could I stay here for a bit longer? Until you have to leave?"

Mary stared at her, uncertain how to respond.

"I'll help you sort your things, pack, take care of the dogs, and I could drive to Dr. Rwambo's and help take care of Lisa for a few hours every day. Maybe he and Simon could teach me how to rewild her. I'd like to learn."

They were quiet for a moment, both stroking Lisa, whose body vibrated in appreciation.

Eventually, Mary spoke. "You'd learn. You have good instincts about animals," she said. "But what about your father, Grace? He wants you to go back to school. He wants you with him."

The girl looked toward the camp. "I'll talk to him."

"Hmm," said Mary, doubtfully.

"I know. I'm sorry. I promised you I'd talk to him before, but I didn't. This time I will. I have to."

"You do. He's on his way."

Grace followed Mary's gaze to see George trotting toward the hill, his fists clenched.

"Does that mean I can stay? If he agrees?" asked Grace.

Mary nodded. "Be honest. With him. With yourself. If he leaves you here, let it be with hope."

CHAPTER 35

———◦———

1983
Olduvai Gorge, Tanzania

GRACE WATCHED AS DR. LEAKEY AND GEORGE PASSED EACH OTHER AT THE bottom of the hill. They didn't pause to talk and soon George was with her.

"Hello Lisa," he said, glancing at the cheetah who, stretched across the earth in a patch where the sun's rays had just arrived, was perfectly at home.

"I'm sorry, Dad," said Grace, determined to face matters head on. "I meant to be back before dawn. I was packed and ready to leave. I fell asleep."

George took a deep breath. His eyes, she saw, were glittering. He cleared his throat. "I can't be angry. I'm too relieved to see you unharmed."

They stared at each other without speaking for a moment. Grace was overcome by an urge to wrap her arms around him, the way she used to when she was younger. She longed to feel safe, to breathe in the dusty, salty scent she remembered and know she was forgiven. She took a step closer and placed her hand on his forearm. George blinked and put his fingers over hers.

"I've asked Dr. Leakey if I can stay." Grace paused, expecting him to object. Instead, he gave a tiny nod. "She said I could, if you agree," she added.

"For how long?"

"Until she leaves. I'll help her and hopefully spend some time with Dr.

Rwambo and Lisa." She glanced at the cheetah, lowering her voice. "She'll have to go back, but I want to learn how to rewild her."

"Will that be possible?" asked George. "I mean, for you to learn."

"Yes. Why not? It's what I want to do. Work with animals. I don't want to go back to school, Dad."

George nodded again. "Will you come back to England? Eventually?"

She swallowed, surprised. "Of course. Probably, but perhaps we can leave that decision for now. I mean, you like it in Africa, don't you? You could come—"

"You're right, we can leave that decision until later," he said. "But you've got to promise me you won't wander into bush alone again. Gatimu spotted hyenas last night. We saw their prints. They're huge."

Grace looked at her feet. She was going to stay. George had agreed. "I know. I promise," she said.

She wanted to call out to Lisa, tell her the news, but she knew there was more to say before her father left. She gave his arm a gentle squeeze.

"I'm sorry I've been so awful to you. There are so many things that I didn't understand when you left. Still don't. It's hard to accept that Mum would let me think that you'd abandoned me if you hadn't. Why would she do that?"

"I don't know," said George, closing his eyes.

"I guess we'll never know," said Grace. "But the one thing that being here has made me realize is that if I'm ever going to be happy again, I have to stop trying to work out why Mum did what she did, what happened to make her take me away. I don't want to keep going over it in my mind. It doesn't help. Except then…"

"Then what?"

Grace took her hand from his arm. "Then I heard you talking to Dr. Leakey about Mum. How she'd said something about me that upset you."

George looked at her, his face pale. He rubbed his forehead. "You heard that? No more?"

She shook her head.

He looked away again. "You're not the only one who has learned something from being here," he said, exhaling loudly.

"Tell me."

George swallowed. "Your mum was infatuated with Dr. Leakey's late husband. They met in Cambridge shortly after we were married when Eleanor's boss published one of his books. He, Louis Leakey, was a fascinating man. Warm, interesting, passionate. He knew so much. We were all in his thrall, charmed by him." He paused. "Eleanor more than most."

Grace blinked. Her mouth was dry. "Mum and Dr. Leakey's husband. You mean...did they have an—"

"No," he said. "But I thought they did. I convinced myself that that was why she'd stopped loving me. I drove her away with my accusations."

"What?"

George ran his fingers through his hair. "Your mum told me she'd been in love with Louis Leakey. It was when news of his death broke...that she told me, I mean. You were just a little girl. She'd been drinking and said it lightly, as if it didn't matter how her declaration would make me feel." He glanced down.

Grace's stomach lurched. She wanted to tell him to stop, but she'd asked for the truth.

He went on. "It was then that I realized how little she cared for me. I imagined the two things were related. She'd fallen in love with Louis Leakey and *out* of love with me. I was hurt and lashed out. I couldn't stop myself. Every time we'd argue about anything, I'd accuse her of having an affair with him." He scratched his ear. "She denied it, but it was too late. She'd been in love with him. She said it herself. There had to be a reason she didn't love me. It had to be someone else's fault. It couldn't be that she simply didn't love me. That I wasn't enough. We were happy. Then we weren't, and she said she was in love with another man."

Grace shook her head. "I never saw it. Everything seemed fine," she whispered.

George breathed out. His shoulders slumped. "It helped that I was away a lot. We never argued in front of you. It wasn't easy. My accusations made it worse. She asked me to stop. Said I needed help. If I didn't get help, she'd leave. I didn't listen. Even when she got sick, I couldn't let it go. That's why she took you and disappeared. I didn't abandon you, Grace. My God, I love you so much. I wanted us to be a family. The way we had been. I wanted her to love me, the way I loved her. But it was my fault that she left and took you, I accept that. I might as well have deserted you."

Grace's thoughts were jumbled. She felt as worn out as George looked but she'd had enough of being miserable. "You said you learned something from being here. From Dr. Leakey. Did she tell you her husband and Mum *didn't* have an affair?"

"Yes. She showed me it wasn't possible. They were almost always on different continents. It was that simple. I don't know why your mum told me she was in love with him. It was unthinking. Cruel. But I did the real damage; I let an obsession ruin my life. Your life."

"No, Dad," she said, taking his hands in hers. "It won't. We won't *let* it ruin our lives. Your mistake was loving Mum too much. You didn't want to let go. We'll never know why Mum told you that, whatever she said about Dr. Leakey's husband. It doesn't matter anymore. And it's not too late to let it go."

George gulped. His eyes filled with tears. Grace didn't look away.

"It's all right," she said. "Forgive yourself. I do. Let it go, Dad. That's another thing Dr. Leakey taught me. When you let go of things that make you unhappy, you make space for new things to happen. New things that could make you happy. Nothing's ruined forever."

A little later, having fed Lisa and asked Mr. Rono to get word to Dr. Rwambo about the cheetah's whereabouts, Grace and Dr. Leakey stood with Brown Dog and Matt between them and waved as the Land Rover carrying George to Nairobi drove from the camp.

"Do you think it would've made a difference if I'd known my parents were unhappy when I was younger? It might've freed them to get divorced. Mum wouldn't have felt we had to disappear." Grace glanced at Dr. Leakey, who showed no sign of hearing her. "Not that it matters, I guess; the past is the past," she added.

"Louis and I often discussed the value of researching the past. He believed knowing about it could help us understand and possibly control the future," said Dr. Leakey, turning to walk to the workroom.

Grace fell into step alongside her. "What do you think?" she asked.

"The future is unpredictable. We can't control what will happen to the world to any significant degree, regardless of what we know. Nature and evolution will take their course and what we do will follow an irreversible pattern."

"So the past doesn't matter?" asked Grace.

Dr. Leakey glanced at her. "Of course it matters. But what we must remember is that what we think we know about the past—whether because of what we learn from and about each other, from evidence about animals and man's activities left in the earth, or any other sources—are very small clues. We can't make assumptions. What we discover gives us a biased view of the truth because it's such a tiny sample of what happened."

Grace didn't respond.

"Have I confused you?" asked Dr. Leakey.

"No, I understand. I think. It's just that if that's what you believe, why have you worked so long and so hard to learn about the past?"

"You mean, what motivates me?"

"Yes."

"Just because I believe it's impossible to know everything doesn't mean I don't want to try. Basically, I'm impelled by curiosity. This career is perfect for me; there's no risk that my curiosity will ever be satisfied." She smiled at Grace. "Find yourself a career that serves your primary inclination, and it'll never seem like work."

Grace returned the smile and stopped outside the workroom alongside Dr. Leakey, whose eyes were once again on Lemagrut. Today, the outline of the old volcano was clear against a cloudless sky with the Serengeti stretching long, wide, and wild before it. For once, there was no dust to obscure the view.

Dr. Leakey sighed. "Find yourself a place like this, and you'll never be lost," she said.

The only thing better than being somewhere you want to be is knowing that others want you there too, thought Grace as she felt the gentle, warm nudge of Brown Dog's muzzle against her knee.

AUTHOR'S NOTE

I'm often asked why I write historical fiction about real people rather than inventing my own cast of entirely fictional characters. It's a good question. Contrary to what some might believe, I think it's easier to write pure fiction (if there is such a thing) than it is to write biographical fiction.

Writing an imagined version of a real life comes with enormous responsibility. Even when it's an author's intention to applaud their subject—as it is mine—writing biographical fiction is a delicate endeavor that requires extrapolating, interpreting, and, to fill in the gaps, speculation. The research required is immense. In fact, where knowledge and theories change all the time, as they do when the subjects are archaeology, paleoanthropology, and evolution, the research can seem insurmountable. On the other hand, it's utterly fascinating. The more I learn about my subjects and their work, the more I want to know. In addition, the pleasure I get from melding fact and fiction about extraordinary women—like Mary Leakey—makes every document scrutinized, journey undertaken, interview transcribed, and fact checked and double-checked worthwhile.

Why do I write historical fiction about real people? Because I'm drawn to stories about remarkable people who've achieved extraordinary things. Above all, I write about women from history whose lives I want to celebrate.

In this sense, *Follow Me to Africa* is like my previous books about Aleen Cust (*The Invincible Miss Cust*) and Bertha Benz (*The Woman at the Wheel*). Like Aleen and Bertha, Mary Leakey was an exceptional, utterly original woman who disregarded what was expected of her, blazed her own trail, and carried her own dirt—literally and figuratively. From a young age and without formal education, Mary was compelled to sustain her curiosity and appetite for adventure. She was a scrupulous scientist and, eventually, one of the world's most successful archaeologists and paleoanthropologists. My accounts of Mary's childhood, education, career, relationship with Louis, family, and archaeological accomplishments are factual, having been recorded in, among other places, the books I reference in the bibliography. These include Mary's autobiography. Of course, because my work is fiction, I have imagined some of the thoughts, conversations, and emotions around these facts.

Unlike my other work of historical fiction, I introduced to this story a largely fictional component, which runs alongside the biographical account of Mary's life. While Mary was indeed packing to leave Olduvai Gorge in 1983, Grace and George Clark are entirely fictional, as are the other people at the camp during their visit. However, Matt and Brown Dog, along with all Mary's other dogs mentioned, were real, as was Lisa the cheetah. I share Mary's love of animals. Her animal friends feature extensively in her autobiography, and I never turn down an opportunity to write about animals! However, in truth, Lisa's appearance at Mary's camp at Olduvai Gorge happened several years before 1983. I took the liberty of adjusting the time scheme to suit my story alongside the fictitious arrival of seventeen-year-old Grace.

The idea of introducing a troubled, seventeen-year-old girl to seventy-year-old Mary Leakey came about when, shortly after reading Mary's autobiography, *Disclosing the Past,* I watched an unrelated interview with a successful author. "What would you tell your younger self?" asked the interviewer. It made me think about Mary and how she recounts her past in her autobiography. I wondered how she might've responded to such a question? What might she, who'd experienced and overcome so much, say to a teenager who faced the same kind of difficulties and uncertainties she had at that age? Would she urge the youngster to get a standard education? What would Mary learn about herself in retrospect? I imagined how inspiring it would've been for a young woman to be at Olduvai Gorge with Dr. Leakey at a time of reflection for the older woman and how it might change things for them both. The idea proliferated.

One of the most rewarding things about writing biographical fiction is that it's an opportunity to introduce or tell readers more about incredible people. Like Aleen Cust and Bertha Benz, Mary was passionate about her work and paved the way for other women in her field. I've highlighted some of her most significant accomplishments in my story, but there are many more, including her work on the hominid footprints at Laetoli. When Mary died at the age of eighty-three in 1996, she'd won numerous prestigious awards and had been awarded four honorary doctorate degrees, including one from Oxford University. What would Professor Sollas and her mother have had to say about that, I wonder?

In one of the last interviews Mary gave (she spoke to Marguerite Holloway of *Scientific American*), she admitted that, while she'd never had the patience for formal education, she was pleased with the honorary degrees bestowed upon her. "Well, I have worked for them by digging in the sun," she said.

I understand the value of formal education, but I'm among those who enjoy discovering stories about people who've succeeded without it because of their passion, determination, curiosity, and unequivocal hard work. Take a bow, Mary Leakey, and thank you for inspiring me to create a version of your story.

READING GROUP GUIDE

1. Mary's love of archaeology developed at a very young age because of her father's love and interest in the subject. Did your parents' or caregivers' profession or interests influence your own?

2. Both Mary and Grace lost a parent at a young age. How did this affect them and shape their paths in life?

3. Mary says to Grace: "We all want to be worth something, do our bit, matter somehow. Work it out, girl, for yourself—before someone else does it for you and you find yourself stuck in a life you don't want." Have you ever felt as though you were pushed or encouraged to follow one path that wasn't necessarily the path you wanted to be on? Did you then divert from that path later on or wish you did?

4. Both Mary's and Grace's fathers were interested in archaeology, and Mary's father was an artist. While Mary followed in her father's footsteps in that she became an illustrator, Grace had no interest in doing so. Why do you think each of the women had such different reactions to their father's pursuits?

5. Mary had a couple female role models and mentors that helped her along her path to becoming an archaeologist, including Dorothy Liddell and Gertrude Canton-Thompson. Have you ever had a mentor to guide you? In what ways did they shape you and your life's journey?

6. Even though Mary and Louis's romance did not last as long as their marriage, their relationship no doubt still benefited Mary's aspirations and her career. Do you think the heartache at the end of their marriage was "worth it" to Mary?

7. When Grace is learning how to drive on their way back to camp from the Ngorongoro crater, she is surprised to learn that it had taken Dr. Leakey a while to master driving, and Grace assumed that Dr. Leakey had never failed at anything in her life, despite Dr. Leakey saying that she had failed many times. What does this say about how we as humans judge ourselves and what we believe about others?

8. After having only been in Africa for a few days, Grace already felt changed, wondering how she would ever revert to her old self when she returned to England. Have you ever felt that way after traveling somewhere? What place that you've traveled to has had the most profound effect on you and why?

9. Mary never graduated from school or went to college, yet she became one of the most successful archaeologists in the world. What role did education play in your life? Do you believe it's possible to be successful without a formal education?

10. At one point, Mary tells Cecilia: "It's less important to work out everything in minute detail than it is to accept opportunities and overcome obstacles as they present themselves." Do you agree with this statement? Or do you think a plan should be 100 percent settled and all contingencies planned for before an opportunity is accepted?

11. Mary had to work hard to earn the respect of her colleagues, especially because she had no formal education and because of how her and Louis's relationship began. Do you feel that she was treated

unfairly? Had the roles been reversed, do you think Louis would have had to work as hard to earn people's trust and respect?

12. When Mary returned home after her mother fell ill, why do you think Mary wasn't honest with Cecilia about her marriage to Louis?

13. Dr. Leakey taught Grace many valuable life lessons during their time together. Which lesson do you think had the most impact on Grace? Have you ever learned a lesson from someone that had a profound impact on you or changed how you viewed yourself or the world around you?

A CONVERSATION
WITH THE AUTHOR

What drew you to Mary Leakey's story?

I'm fascinated by people who recognize and follow their passions regardless of the obstacles, particularly women who overcome patriarchy and perceptions to succeed. When I first encountered Mary Leakey, I immediately related to her love of Africa, the outdoors, and animals, and to how she enjoyed being alone in the wild. I admired her independent spirit and curiosity and her dedication to her work. When I discovered that she hadn't received a typical education and was largely self-taught, I was utterly intrigued. Although I accept that standard forms of education are effective, I'm excited by stories of people who find other ways of amassing the knowledge and skills they need to pursue their dreams. In addition, I was inspired by the way Mary quietly but determinedly extricated herself from Louis Leakey's shadow.

What is the most surprising thing you learned about Mary through your research?

In addition to the fact that she only attended school for about two years in total and had no other formal tertiary education, I was surprised by how young Mary was when her interest in archaeology began. She was a young girl when her father took her to the prehistoric caves in France and they rummaged through the spoils of an excavation. She was hooked from there on. Despite her father's death when she was barely a teenager, Mary never lost her fascination with the subject. It made me realize how powerful childhood influences and experiences can be.

This is your third historical novel. The first two, *The Invincible Miss Cust*

and *The Woman at the Wheel,* were told through a singular points-of-view and one chronological timeline. Talk about your choice to tell Mary's story through both Mary's and Grace's perspectives and in a dual-timeline narrative.

I decided not to write Mary's story using a singular, first-person point-of-view because, unlike Aleen Cust and Bertha Benz, Mary Leakey authored several books. Her voice is already established in literature, and I didn't want to try to emulate it. I wrote the story from both Mary's and Grace's perspectives using a dual-timeline narrative because, in addition to telling Mary's story, I wanted to impart something of what she'd might've learned to someone younger. I liked the idea of Mary looking back and imagining what she might say to her seventeen-year-old self if she had the opportunity. Grace provided that role. I was also drawn to the notion of a young woman learning, not only professional advice but life lessons, from Mary. She lived a fascinating life, overcoming challenges and blazing a trail for others to follow. How wonderful it would be to learn from and be inspired by her, I thought. So, I began writing.

When writing biographical historical fiction based on the lives of real people, how do you balance fact and fiction?

I enjoy writing and reading biographical fiction because it brings historical characters to life, conjuring names from the past into vital, multifaceted individuals with emotions, motives, virtues, and flaws. In some cases, it introduces readers to exciting characters they might otherwise never have encountered. Perhaps the most compelling reason to write and read biographical historical fiction is because history contains enthralling stories, some so astounding they're almost unbelievable. One of the challenges is to do all the research necessary to establish all the facts as they are publicly known. The next endeavor is to sift through those facts and select those that are most intriguing and suitable for the story. Then, where there are gaps in what is on record, one can imagine what might've happened and how characters might've responded. Every story is different. Some invite more fiction than others. The key, I believe, is to remember that readers want to be entertained above all else. I love how interested readers are in how much of historical biographical fiction is fact versus fiction. Perhaps a way of ascertaining whether the fact-fiction balance works is to see whether readers are inspired to do their own research to separate the two once they've read the book.

The three women featured in your historical novels—Aleen Cust, Bertha Benz, and Mary Leakey—were similar in their ambitions to break the mold of what it meant to be a woman in their times. Do you think if the three women had lived at the same time and place, they would have been friends?

Absolutely! In fact, I fantasize about inviting them all to dinner and watching them interact. It's possible, I imagine, that they might be a little shy initially, perhaps recognizing themselves in one another. However, within minutes—probably once they discover their shared love of dogs—they'd be chatting, laughing, and sharing experiences. They'd exchange stories about how they won over those who stood in their way, simply by continuing to do what they loved and did best. I'd sit back and watch, glowing with joy and admiration. Indeed, Aleen, Bertha, and Mary would be a formidable trio of friends.

Each of your books has celebrated animals and pets in some way or another. Tell us about your pets! Both those still with us and those from your past.

I could write forever about animals I've known and loved. They include dogs, horses, cattle, and cats. I was raised on a farm with animals and loved them all. One of my early childhood dog friends was Bingo, an indistinct, medium-sized, brindle combination of countless breeds with an undershot jaw and tombstone teeth. She had a curious beauty and was one of the happiest and most loyal creatures I've met. However, Bingo had an incurable addiction: she loved hunting African porcupines, who often live in underground burrows. One day, she pursued one of the rodents, disappearing after it down its hole in the earth. We called and dug for her for two days to no avail. Bingo was gone. Eventually, certain she'd been smothered to death, we mourned her. Imagine our surprise when, more than a week later, she happily reappeared at home. She'd dug her way out with only her worn claws and muddy fur to attest to her adventure. For sure, I've known many wonderful dogs. More recently, my first Scottish terrier, Mary, and I were inseparable for ten years. I loved her confident independence and her "don't call me, I'll call you" attitude. We understood each other perfectly. These days, I joyfully share my life with the massive, gentle boerboel, Lily; cheerful, friendly Labrador-cross-allsorts, Molly; and playful, energetic Scottie, Sophie. They bring me great happiness and ensure I have plenty of exercise by encouraging me to take long walks before I sit down to write every day.

BIBLIOGRAPHY

Cole, Sonia. *Leakey's Luck.* New York: Doubleday, 1975.

Leakey, L.S.B. *Adam's Ancestors.* London: Methuen, 1934.

Leakey, L.S.B. *By the Evidence.* London: Methuen, 1974.

Leakey, L.S.B. *Olduvai Gorge.* Cambridge: Cambridge University Press, 1951.

Leakey, L.S.B. *White African.* New York: Charles Scribner's Sons, 1937.

Leakey, L.S.B. and Vanne Morris Goodall. *Unveiling Man's Origins.* London: Watts & Co., 1969.

Leakey, Mary. *Disclosing the Past.* London: Weidenfeld and Nicolson, 1984.

Leakey, Richard. *The Search for Mankind.* New York: Harper & Row, 1973.

Morell, Virginia. *Ancestral Passions.* New York: Simon & Schuster, 1995.

ACKNOWLEDGMENTS

My parents knew I dreamed of becoming an author from an early age. For as long as I can recall, my mother told anyone who'd listen, "Penny loves making up stories." She didn't *always* imply that it was a positive characteristic. However, my father—who, despite the long hours and grueling nature of dairy farming, always had a book on the go alongside *Farmers' Weekly*—never made light of my dream. He had an idea for a novel, which he was determined I should one day write. We spoke about it for years. It involved a brain transplant, and while I could see why he thought it might make fascinating reading, it never completely gripped me. Sorry, Dad.

My father died several years before my first book was published. My mother has dementia and no longer even recognizes my name on my books. I wish it wasn't so. My father loved history and would've been interested while my mother would surely have nodded, smiled, and said, "Penny loves making up stories." In their absence, I thank my parents for raising me to be a reader and a dreamer and for allowing me to believe that it was possible to be an author. Thank you, Mom and Dad.

A big thanks, too, to archaeologist Amy Hatton for agreeing to read the manuscript of *Follow Me to Africa* to help ensure that I was technically on track—despite the enormous demands of her own research. Your knowledge, time, and generosity were invaluable and are much appreciated. Thank you, Amy.

One of the things I've realized in recent years is what a burden friendship with an author can be. We're largely a demanding, insecure bunch. When we're not antisocially hunched over our keyboards, we're talking endlessly about our books, hoping our friends will listen and read them. I am so lucky and grateful to have Katie Allen, Rina Cronwright, Sue Dods, Gail Gilbride, Lee Kingma, Marianne Marsh, Paul Morris, Sue Reynolds, Nancy Richards, Anne Schlebusch, Joelle Searle, Karen Stark, Karina Szczurek, and Christy Weyer among my cheerleaders. Thank you for your kindness, interest, support, and great humor.

Another thing I've learned is how fortunate I am to have a fabulous publisher. Literary journeys are littered with uncertainty, but one thing I am sure of—this is my third books with the imprint—is that Sourcebooks Landmark is exceptional. It is not only that I have the best editors I could wish for in Erin McClary and Liv Turner but also that everyone who I've interacted with at Sourcebooks has been unfalteringly professional, kind, and supportive. It comes from the top. Once, during an author seminar with the company, I posed a general question regarding international distribution. CEO Dominique Raccah responded immediately, and the issue was resolved without delay. Authors are important to Sourcebooks, and it shows. Thank you, everyone at Sourcebooks, for your expertise, care, energy, and diligence, all of which make me so proud to be among your authors.

Thanks, as ever, to Jill Marsal of Marsal Lyon Literary Agency for being in my corner. I couldn't wish for a calmer or more experienced, responsive, and supportive agent.

Last but never least, I thank my family for their support and encouragement. Thank you, Jan-Lucas, Sebastiaan, Claudia, Inga, and Ulf for being my most enduring champions—and for never complaining when I insist that we celebrate another writing milestone with a bottle of bubbly.

ABOUT THE AUTHOR

Photo credit: J-L de Vos

Penny Haw worked as a journalist and columnist for more than three decades, writing for many leading South African newspapers and magazines before yielding to a lifelong yearning to create fiction. Her stories feature remarkable women, illustrate her love for nature and animals, and explore the interconnectedness of all living things, including *The Invincible Miss Cust* and *The Woman at the Wheel*. She is the recipient of the 2024 Philida Literary Award and lives near Cape Town with her husband and three dogs, all of whom are well walked.